## ANNE STUART

loves Japanese rock and roll, wearable art, Spike, her two kids, Clairefontaine paper, quilting, her delicious husband of thirty-four years, fellow writers, her three cats, telling stories and living in Vermont. She's not too crazy about politics and diets and a winter that never ends, but then, life's always a trade-off.

Visit her at www.Anne-Stuart.com.

## CATHY GILLEN THACKER

is married and a mother of three. She and her husband spent eighteen years in Texas and now reside in North Carolina. Her mysteries, romantic comedies and heartwarming family stories have made numerous appearances on bestseller lists, but her best reward, she says, is knowing one of her books made someone's day a little brighter. A popular Harlequin Books author for many years, she loves telling passionate stories with happy endings, and thinks nothing beats a good romance and a hot cup of tea! You can visit Cathy's website at www.cathygillenthacker.com for more information on her upcoming and previously published books, recipes and a list of her favorite things.

BESTSELLING AUTHOR COLLECTION

*New York Times* Bestselling Author

# ANNE STUART

*Glass Houses*

HARLEQUIN®

entertain, enrich, inspire™

Recycling programs
for this product may
not exist in your area.

ISBN-13: 978-0-373-18063-9

GLASS HOUSES
Copyright © 2012 by Harlequin Books S.A.

The publisher acknowledges the copyright holders of the individual works as follows:

GLASS HOUSES
Copyright © 1989 by Anne Kristine Stuart Ohlrogge

HER SECRET VALENTINE
Copyright © 2005 by Cathy Gillen Thacker

www.Harlequin.com

**Printed in U.S.A.**

Dear Reader,

*Glass Houses* has long been one of my favorite series romances, with a peculiar genesis. Years ago Harlequin gave a very strange party in a San Francisco warehouse, with various models hired to portray iconic heroes. One of them was Frank, exquisitely gorgeous, dressed like a sheik. Being a demure young lady, I ogled him from a distance but decided I needed to immortalize him in a book, and he ended up being a secondary hero in *Glass Houses* (no, not as a sheik, as a model).

And the primary hero is even hotter.

Good old Frank is probably middle-aged, married and paunchy, but man, was he pretty back in the day! I'm glad he gets to live forever.

Cheers,

Anne

# CONTENTS

GLASS HOUSES                                    7
Anne Stuart

HER SECRET VALENTINE                          267
Cathy Gillen Thacker

# GLASS HOUSES

*New York Times* Bestselling Author

## Anne Stuart

# Chapter 1

Laura de Kelsey Winston stepped into the bronze and smoked glass elevator, leaned her narrow back against the rear wall, and shut her eyes, waiting to be carried aloft to the twelfth floor of the Glass House, the famous New York landmark built by her great-grandfather, St. Clair de Kelsey, in the early part of the century. The building contained only two of its original three elevators—the third now resided in the Museum of Modern Art, having been donated by Laura's grandmother to the museum, which had always enjoyed her patronage—and in its place stood a modern, silent, soulless pale gray Otis. Laura never rode it, even if she was in a hurry, even if the other two elevators were in one of their constant funks. She'd race up or down twelve flights, rather than endure the modern travesty of an elevator that had invaded her building, her legacy, the only thing in this world that she cared about unconditionally. The Glass House was the only thing that had never turned on her. It just sat there in all its 1920's glory; solid, incontrovertible proof that Laura de Kelsey Winston was loved; even if it was only by her widowed grandmother, it was proof that she was worth something. Even if the elevators were more effective as works of art than as pieces of machinery.

Today the old elevator ran smoothly, carrying Laura, up, up, away from the blazing heat of late-September pavement, away from the noise and bustle and elegant haste of East Sixty-sixth Street in New York City. As she felt the familiar peace settle around her, the sense of ownership that was to her the most important thing in the world, a smile curved her brightly painted mouth. It wasn't a huge, amiable grin; it wasn't even the dangerous little upturning of her lips that her assistant, Susan Richards, and half the people who worked with her knew to beware of. It was the smile of a woman who was taking what pleasure she could in a world that had once more gone awry and shifted on its axis.

The doors slid open with a graceful, elegant whoosh, and the sparse, perfectly appointed reception room of Glass Faces appeared, the small, exclusive, up-and-coming modeling agency, run out of the famous Glass House by Laura de Kelsey Winston herself. Laura made a moue as she stepped off the elevator onto the kilim she'd filched from her mother's apartment, her spiked heels sinking into the thick wool. Through the heavy glass doors she could see Susan deep in conversation with Emelia Millhouse. Susan's curved, deep-bosomed figure was an odd contrast to Emelia's racehorse leanness. Emelia was gesturing, her long slim hands flying through the air, as Susan simply shook her head and looked calm.

Susan was good at that, Laura thought, for once not moving with her characteristic haste. Good at calming aging models who were overwrought, good at soothing advertising executives who didn't know what the hell they wanted, good at convincing Laura that things weren't quite as desperate as they appeared to be.

Susan would need to be at the top of her form today, Laura thought with a grim smile. Things were desperate indeed, and even her assistant's well-known serenity might take a few knocks.

She wasn't going to walk into her office looking like a whipped dog, Laura reminded herself, tugging just slightly at the bright red leather micromini that had come directly from Kamali. She didn't need to check her hair—she paid a fortune to Gregorio to make sure that the midnight-black sheaf was razor-cut into a perfect shingle around her narrow face, that its bangs framed the rims over her metallic glasses with a military precision, and that no matter how she flung her head about in rage, humor, or the sheer zest of living, it would always fall back where it belonged. A cut like that was worth every penny she paid for it, she mused for a moment. And if she just had the sense most people had, she'd give up the one thing that mattered to her—and never have to worry about how she was going to pay for her haircuts and her red leather miniskirts.

But she wasn't going to do that, she reminded herself. She wasn't going to let them win. And she certainly wasn't going to let Emelia Millhouse see her sweat. Emelia was at the end of her modeling career. At thirty, the lines were starting to show, desperation was shadowing the famous violet eyes, and the generous, sensuous mouth, which had sold more lipstick than any other mouth in the western hemisphere, was beginning to tighten with panic. Emelia didn't need to see that the invincible Laura could show panic, too.

If Susan's warm brown eyes showed relief as Laura breezed through the doorway, her face was, as usual, impassive. She stood by, saying nothing as Laura enveloped Emelia in a scented embrace. As usual Laura was unable to dismiss the chronic sense that she was a young girl hugging her mother. It was hell to be five foot one and a half in a world of six-foot-tall models.

"There you are, Emelia," Laura greeted the model, her low, slightly husky voice vibrant with an enthusiasm she could almost believe herself. "I was hoping you'd still be here. I'm sorry I'm late—you know what a pain mothers can be. One would think mine would be an improvement, but I suppose that was too much to hope for. How are the acting classes coming?"

If Susan could calm Emelia, Laura could charm her, and the tall model preened like the thoroughbred she was. "Well enough. Gene Frankel said I had a very unusual quality."

"Anyone can see that, darling," Laura said, craning her neck to look up into the famous eyes. "What about the Spielberg screen test? Any news?"

"Everyone in New York City is trying for that one." Emelia frowned, and tiny lines marred her perfect face. "That's why I'm here. You know everyone who is everyone. Can you pull a few strings?"

"I've called everyone I know."

Emelia's face fell. "Everyone?"

"That doesn't mean I can't call them again." Laura soothed almost as well as Susan. "Go home, go shopping, get your mind off things. We've had to wait for good things to happen before, haven't we? And they've always come through. We should be used to waiting by this time."

"But before, I wasn't getting older by the minute."

"Emelia, I'm two years older than you are," Laura pointed out with just a hint of wryness.

"But in your case it doesn't matter!" Emelia wailed.

The twelfth-floor offices of Glass Faces were lined with mirrors, and there was nowhere Laura could look without seeing her reflection. Next to Emelia's perfection stood a short, brightly dressed gamine, her coal-black hair hanging around her piquant face, her boyish body radiating energy—and none of Emelia's languid grace.

"I suppose not," Laura said with a twinge of regret. "But the more you whine, the more it will show on your face."

Emelia's petulant expression immediately vanished, leaving a cool, unruffled exterior, only her famous eyes showing the terror that still haunted her. "Call someone, Laura. For God's sake, do something!"

"Everything I can, darling. Everything I can."

Susan waited until the glass and gilt elevator doors closed behind Emelia's figure. "You need coffee," she said, a statement, not a question.

"I need a drink."

"It's not even noon."

"It feels like midnight. The witching hour, and I'm about to turn into a pumpkin."

"What does that make me?" Susan responded with her usual cheerfulness.

"Chief rat. We're in deep trouble. No, we're beyond that. We're mired in disaster up to our elbows."

"So what else is new?" She handed Laura a cup of coffee, taking one for herself. Laura barely repressed the shudder that ran through her as she took a tentative sip. Susan made the worst coffee in the world, always had, and probably always would.

"My family."

"That's nothing new. What have they come up with now?" Susan moved over to the spotless steel and glass table that served as her desk and sank into the vintage Breuer chair, the real thing, also filched from Laura's mother.

"They haven't come up with anything this time. Someone's come up with them."

"Someone?"

"Michael Dubrovnik."

"The Whirlwind? Good God," Susan said faintly.

"How about good grief?" Laura countered, running a thin, beringed hand through her straight black hair. "That man has never lost anything he's wanted in the last fifteen years. And he wants the Glass House."

"For heaven's sake, why? It's not general knowledge, but you and I both know that the building, gorgeous as it is, is on the verge of being dangerously unstable. It would cost a fortune to renovate it, repair it, a fortune even you don't have. Why would Dubrovnik want to involve himself in something like that?"

"Why? You ask why? This is a prime piece of real estate, Susan. You can't get much better than this."

"I suppose not. And he has enough money to renovate half a dozen Glass Houses and never notice the cost."

"Are you suggesting I sell to him?" Laura demanded icily, setting down the oily coffee with a clatter.

Susan was the one person she couldn't cow with her temper. "Hardly. You wouldn't give up the Glass House if you were down to your last nickel. I just think it's curious that he wants to fix this place up. I'd never heard that he was interested in historic landmarks."

"He's not," Laura said flatly, throwing herself onto the Italian leather sofa. The crushed pink clashed with her bright red skirt, but she was beyond caring. "He's bought up everything surrounding us. He wants to tear us down and put up some awful plaza. Some road-show skyscraper, and I'll be damned if I'll let him do it."

"I don't see what you're getting so worked up about," Susan said mildly. "Other people have wanted to buy the Glass House over the last few years and you've always refused."

"Other people haven't had my mother on their side," Laura said morosely, her leather skirt sticking to the sofa as she thrashed about, longing for the cigarettes she'd given up three years ago. "Other people weren't known as the Whirlwind. He knocks down everything that stands in his way."

"Yes," said Susan. "But he hasn't come across you yet. I'd back you against a dozen whirlwinds, your mother included."

Laura lay facedown on the sofa, thinking about the latest engineers' reports, thinking about her financial adviser's long, gloomy face, thinking about a million things that she wasn't ready to face. "I only hope you're right," she muttered, her face against the pale pink leather.

Michael Dubrovnik, Michael to his women, the Whirlwind to his competitors, Mischa to a very select few, stared out at the New York skyline in the direction of the Glass House. He couldn't see it, of course; its twelve meager stories were dwarfed by the towering skyscrapers around it. But he knew it was there.

Michael sighed, dropping his pen onto the teak desk and leaning back in the curved leather chair that had been designed and built specifically for him, a chair that fitted his lean, wiry body to such perfection that he seldom even noticed its existence. This whole mess had gone on too long, and for the first time in his life he was being stymied by one lone, stubborn female. Every time he thought of Laura de Kelsey Winston he wanted to kill.

He wasn't used to thinking of women as the enemy. He'd been in business long enough to know he should never underestimate anyone, but Laura Winston had done what no one had been able to do in more than a dozen years—stop the Whirlwind cold.

He considered calling in his assistant and dictating a scathing letter to the Winston female, but thought better of it. His intelligent, ambitious assistant had made the major mistake of falling in love with him, and he didn't want to look into her soulful blue eyes a moment longer than he had to. The smart ones, he thought, the ambitious ones were always the worst. Appealing as they were, sooner or later their brains went out the window, and they grew more annoying than the most mindless debutante, the most vapid model. Why women couldn't maintain their intellect while conducting an affair was a mystery to him. He'd never lost control, of his emotions, of his ambition, and least of all of his razor-sharp intelligence. He'd learned long ago to start with someone who was little more than ornamental. That way he wouldn't be bored and disappointed and dragged down by useless expectations.

Women, the women he chose nowadays, knew exactly what to expect from him: loyalty and monogamy, for as long as the relationship lasted. Generosity, both during the affair and at its inevitable conclusion. A voracious sexuality that combined a deep, seldom filled hunger with the experience of a man approaching forty. And no emotional involvement whatsoever. No broken hearts, no broken promises, no broken lives.

Occasionally he wondered whether he was even capable of falling in love anymore. He'd been in love when he was twenty, that mindless, boy's love that was so intense he'd thought he might die from it. But it was the love that had died, not Michael. She'd married someone else, someone richer, and right now he couldn't even remember what she'd looked like.

He'd been in love when he was thirty, or at least, he'd supposed he was. Why else would he have married Ilsa, with her perfect body, her glorious face, her wicked smile and her marvelously inventive ways? The fact that she'd been called the face of the decade hadn't been instrumental, though he'd liked the sense of possessing, of owning the world's most beautiful woman. But when she'd left, when she'd finally grown as bored with him as he was of her, he'd felt nothing more than faint regret and an overwhelming relief.

He should have learned his lesson by now. And indeed he had. He knew perfectly well that that kind of breathless, aching love was the province of adolescence. He also knew that he wanted children. As he approached forty he felt the need, the hunger for them in a way he'd never imagined. For the first time he could understand his father's insistence on family above all things. He'd always dismissed it as old-country gibberish, not belonging to the brave new world to which Feodor Dubrovnik had emigrated. Now he knew his father had been right all along.

He wondered whether men could feel a biological time clock running out, just as women could. Of course, men could father children well into their seventies and beyond. Nevertheless, the need to experience fatherhood was becoming overwhelming. What was required in his situation, he thought, was the face of this decade. An undemanding ornament to decorate his life and bring him children, and not to interfere with his headlong rush toward immortality. He'd already made and lost several fortunes, and he had no doubt that he'd make and lose several more. He was among the top fifty of the wealthiest men in America. By his fortieth birthday he planned on making it to the top ten.

But first things first. Dubrovnik Plaza was the next on his agenda, just about ready to go. He had the architects' model in the boardroom, a shiny glass and steel structure that would replace half a city block. As soon as he could wrest that architectural anachronism from its stubborn owner and start razing it, then he could begin to think of the future. For now he had to spend a few moments in his busy day defeating a stubborn young woman who'd been ignoring his offers for well over two years, though he doubted she'd known those offers had all come from him.

Enough was enough. Everything was ready to proceed, except for the obstacle of the Glass House. Once he'd finished with that minor detail, Dubrovnik Plaza could start to become a reality. He'd waited long enough.

He pressed a button on the keyboard of the console that looked more like the instrument panel on a space shuttle than a telephone. Zach's smooth voice answered.

"Give Laura Winston one last offer," Michael said. "Make it generous—I want to get through with this as quickly as possible."

"When she refuses?"

"When, not if?"

"You haven't talked to the lady, Mischa. The word is when," Zach said flatly.

"When she says no, start blasting at the Rinkman building site."

"What for? We can't accomplish anything until the rest of the area is razed."

"Just start blasting. As close to the Glass House as you

can get away with. Suggest that the contractor make a mistake or two. He knows he'll be taken care of."

"You're a rat, Mischa. You know that." Zach's faintly southern voice was approving.

"I know it. And Zach. Get me a new assistant. This one's fallen in love with me. Do it now."

"She's gone."

Michael Dubrovnik stared out his window, out over the vast New York skyline. He owned two apartments in the highest tower in this area, and his view was spectacular. But soon, he promised himself, that view would be obstructed—by the graceful, spearlike towers of Dubrovnik Plaza. And no one, no one on this earth was going to stop him.


"Don't you think you're overreacting?" Susan questioned. "So the man's made an offer. So he's flirting with your mother. Maybe he's just pretending to be interested in the Glass House as a way of getting to Jilly."

"Jilly is twelve years older than he is."

"So what?"

"Dubrovnik has bought up everything around me. Every building, Susan. He's not going to take no for an answer."

"Then give up. Sell him the place, cut your losses and get away."

"I'd rather die."

"Then don't just lie there," Susan recommended. "Be ready to fight."

"You're the only one who can see me," Laura grumbled. "You're allowed to know I'm not Superwoman."

"Surprise, surprise. But I'm not the only one who can see you. Someone just got off the elevator."

Laura's response was short, succinct and obscene. She

rolled off the couch, landing on her spiked heels, and tossed back her head. The shiny black hair fell into place, the leather mini settled around her narrow hips, and her mouth curved in a cool smile. "Bring on the lions," she muttered. "I'm ready for the games to begin."

Susan looked up at her. "For heaven's sake, show some mercy."

"Mercy?" Laura echoed. "What's that?" And lifting her head, she met the mild eyes of Zach Armstrong as he walked through her beveled glass doors.

Mary Ellen Murphy stumbled off the bus at the Port Authority building in the heart of New York City and stared around her in numbed surprise. She'd been traveling nonstop for the last fourteen hours, and she was amazed that her long, slender legs still held her upright. The narrow, tile-lined hallway stank of diesel oil and stale sweat, and no one even spared her a glance as they rushed past her. This was the New York she'd always heard about, but it still surprised her. Mary Ellen Murphy wasn't used to being ignored. Six feet tall, with rippling blond hair hanging to her tiny waist and eyes as big and blue as a Montana sky, she was used to stopping traffic, to fending off ardent admirers, to receiving homage and admiration as her just reward for having been born to be an extraordinary beauty.

For once no one noticed. Her mother had warned her of all the criminals who flocked to meet buses in the heart of wicked New York. If her mother was to be believed, several dozen pimps and white slavers would be there, just to run off with Mary Ellen Murphy.

Her mother was a stupid fool. Mary Ellen had always known that. And Jeff wasn't much better. She was heartily glad she'd left them behind. Of course she'd call them.

She'd make sweet, reassuring phone calls to tell them she was fine, that everything was all right, that she was doing well. She'd say she was sorry she'd taken everything from the savings account her mother had foolishly opened in both their names, and she'd be paying it back as soon as she got a job. She'd put just the right catch into her voice, and her mother would melt.

She still had the card tucked in her purse. The photographer, the one who had taken those artistic photos of her wearing nothing more than an old curtain, had told her that if she ever came to New York, she could find work as a model. Mary Ellen had read enough about people being paid a fortune for doing nothing more than standing there, looking beautiful. That was something at which Mary Ellen had a great deal of practice. She didn't need to check the card; she remembered the address. The signs in the bus terminal told her she was already close. She could walk. It was only midday on a Friday, and she'd been sitting for fourteen hours. She could certainly walk.

## Chapter 2

When it came to women, Michael Dubrovnik was a careful man. Not that he was frightened, mind you. Nasty, terminal diseases were no more of a threat to him than palimony suits. He considered himself invincible, his borders defended on all sides. He'd been stabbed in the back too many times to give his trust easily, and if he took the time to think about it, which he usually didn't, he realized that at that moment there was no woman on earth he trusted. And there were damned few men.

One of those trusted men stood before him, his lined face creased into impassivity. Zach Armstrong had been with Michael for the last eighteen years, and he was everything Michael wasn't. Twenty-three years older than his boss, Zach was a devoted family man, with a wife and two daughters who were almost more important than business. He came from the gentlemanly South, while Michael had fought his way out of the ethnic slums of the big, rough, northeastern city of New York. Zach was patient, compassionate, yet with his own ruthless streak, and together he and Michael made a good team. Zach could dispense the softer qualities when Michael closed in for the kill. And if sometimes Michael went too far, then Zach could clean up the mess, leaving everything tidy and neat.

He wasn't having much success with the current mess. "I warned you," Zach said amiably enough. "Ms. Winston is as stubborn as a mule in labor. I could have made her an offer five times bigger and she wouldn't have budged. She sent you a message, too."

"Well?" Michael's limited patience had reached its end.

"She said to tell you you can flirt with her mother, marry her mother for all she cares. But you aren't putting your filthy hands on the Glass House."

"Oh, really?"

Zach grinned. He'd known what his old friend's reaction to that challenge would be, and he was already looking forward to the fireworks. "She said to tell you she'd turn it over to the ASPCA as a home for orphan cats before she let you touch it."

"It sounds to me as if the lady needs to be taught a lesson," Michael said, his tone even.

"I don't know, Mischa. In this case you might be the one to end up with your tail between your legs."

Michael's icy-blue eyes frosted over for a moment. "Are you suggesting there's a chance I won't get what I want, Zach? Fortune 500 companies have collapsed with a single word from me. There's never been anything, anything that I've wanted that I haven't been able to get. Do you really think for one moment I'm going to let some little Park Avenue blue blood beat me?"

Zach grinned. He knew perfectly well how Michael, whose sense of humor was definitely at a low ebb, would respond to that grin, and he gauged it carefully. "You haven't met Laura Winston yet."

"I've met her mother. A useless, overbred parasite. Is the daughter any different?"

"You'll see."

Michael sank back into his chair with a weary sigh, and a belated, rueful grin played around his thin mouth. "I suppose I'll have to. If you can't get me what I want, there's nothing left but face-to-face negotiation."

"I knew you'd see it that way. But don't count on instant surrender. Laura Winston will give you a run for your money."

"You think I won't win?" Michael was more curious than affronted.

"Of course you'll win. They don't call you the Whirlwind for nothing. But it won't be easy."

"I don't like things that are easy."

"I know that. And in that case, you're going to like Laura Winston."

"I doubt it," Michael said. "This delay is costing me tens of thousands of dollars every day. I sincerely doubt I'm going to like the woman at all." He tapped the slender platinum pen against the alabaster-topped table. "Get me the car."

"Now? It's after six. You're due at the mayor's in forty-five minutes."

Michael shrugged his wiry shoulders. "The mayor will have to wait. Have my assistant call me the Bentley."

"Your assistant is gone. Amid tears and lamentations, I'm afraid."

"Thank God," Michael said devoutly. "I'd forgotten. Anyone to take her place?"

"I've given you my Ms. Anthony. Don't have her fall in love with you, please. She's too good to lose."

"It's not my fault. I don't go out of my way to be charming."

"I don't think you know how to be charming. Besides, Ms. Anthony is a grandmother. Maybe she'll be able to resist you."

Michael stood up and stretched, energy still humming through his lean, muscled body. He'd been up since four that morning and wouldn't be going to bed till well after midnight. Then he'd wake up at four to start the hectic pace all over again. And not for a moment was he going to feel even a moment of weariness. "As long as Ms. Winston doesn't."

"Don't tell me you think you're going to charm the Glass House out of her!" Zach protested. "Haven't I told you you don't have any charm?"

Michael grinned. "If I did, it sounds as if Ms. Winston would be impervious to it. I'm going to be sweetly reasonable. I've read the reports on Laura de Kelsey Winston. She lives high. That modeling agency she runs is very trendy but not what you'd call a blue-chip investment. I think I can make her see reason."

Zach shook his head. "I'm looking forward to it."

"Susan, darling, when are you going to get me another TV spot?" Frank Buckley's beautiful face settled into mocking, discontented lines. "I think we agree that I don't do my best work in print, and you keep coming up with magazine layouts. I need animation, mobility, to come across."

"You're a little too animated, Frank," Susan said, stifling the unconscious yearning that swept through her every time she looked up into Frank's haunted, turquoise eyes. She knew better than anyone that Frank wasn't really haunted, that it was merely an astonishing combination of bones and coloring that gave him the look of a troubled prince.

A man shouldn't have cheekbones like Frank's, Susan thought wistfully. A man shouldn't have eyes that color, with their totally mendacious hint of sadness. Nor should he have an impossibly sensual mouth that curved into a mocking, teasing smile that told a woman she was irresistible. A man shouldn't have tawny-blond hair hanging to his broad, well-muscled shoulders; he shouldn't have a body that, if it wasn't absolutely perfect, was the closest a thirty-three-year-old could come. And a man shouldn't hang around someone like Susan, flirting, teasing, when he had a woman of unsurpassed beauty waiting at home.

"I'm going broke, Susan," Frank said, throwing his graceful body into the pink leather sling chair and grimacing. Unlike Emelia, Frank didn't worry about wrinkles. He knew that each added line only enhanced his almost unearthly beauty. And he knew, as Susan did, that worrying did little good. "Do you have any idea what the rent on a loft comes to nowadays? Not to mention taxis, food, theater…"

"You could always take the subway. Eat at McDonald's, instead of Lutèce. You could even lower yourself to go to the movies instead of something on Broadway."

"I'd rather dig ditches," he said with dignity. "We all have our standards, Susan, my pet. Even if you like traveling with the great unwashed and eating fast food, I don't."

"What about Tracey? She made two covers last month—she must be earning enough to pay for you a while." Susan couldn't think of the astonishingly gorgeous Tracey Michaels without picturing her in Frank's arms, and the little knife twist of pain in her stomach was an old friend.

"She does indeed. Unfortunately she moved out last month."

"Frank, I'm so sorry," she said, trying to stifle her pleased grin.

He grinned back. "I know, you never liked her. Sometime I'll find someone worthy of me, I promise. But right now I've got the full rent on the loft, plus bills up to my eyebrows."

"But such nice eyebrows, Frank."

"I can't make any money if they throw me in debtors' prison."

"There is no such thing as debtors' prison any more. That went out with Charles Dickens. I've got Laura working on it, Frank. Something will turn up, I promise. In the meantime, if you're really serious about earning some money, there's some catalog work available...."

Frank just looked at her, and once more Susan marveled at the fact that all that wonderful, haughty beauty, that expressive, gorgeous face, just didn't make the leap beyond the camera lens. In person Frank Buckley was beguiling, enchanting, impossibly sexual. But seen through the medium of glossy print, he was nothing more than passably attractive. Film wasn't much of an improvement. Frank needed the eye contact, the physical presence to come across. He used that presence to talk his way into job after job. But the mediocre results were becoming well-known, and the jobs were getting scarcer and scarcer.

"No catalogs," he said, and there was just the faintest trace of his native Kentucky filtering through the deep, rich voice that was a perfect match for his face. "I'm not that desperate." He moved out of the chair, coming to the glass-topped table and placing his strong, beautiful hands on it as he leaned forward, his face only inches from Susan's deliberately uncommunicative expression. "Find me something, Susan. Please."

"I'll put the thumbscrews on Laura. She won't let you down."

"Laura doesn't like me."

"Of course she does. She doesn't have any clients she doesn't like," said Susan, knowing perfectly well what Laura resented about Frank. "And even if she didn't like you, she'd still work her tail off for you. Laura's like that."

"God bless us, everyone," Frank said faintly. He was still only inches away from her, and his perfect mouth brushed hers. "Do what you can for me, angel. I'll be sitting by the phone."

He moved away, and Susan, her expression as impassive as always, nodded. "You mean you'll deign to check the messages on your answering machine. I'll get something for you, Frank. I promise."

He always kissed her. There were times when Susan wondered whether Frank knew of the deep, illogical passion that lurked in her maternal breast, but then she dismissed the idea. To be sure, he never kissed Laura. But Laura would probably knock him back onto his beautiful buns if he tried it. And he certainly kissed everyone else. No, the kisses meant nothing to Frank. They meant everything to Susan.

"Was that Frank?" Laura strode through the glass doors at her usual headlong pace, stopping only long enough to kick off her impossibly high-heeled shoes.

"It was."

"Desperate for money, I suppose. It's a good thing he doesn't do drugs. He'd be even more impoverished."

"Indeed. You don't keep clients who do drugs, and no

one else would be able to find as much work for him," Susan stated.

"Oh, I don't know. Maybe it's my fault Frank isn't working much. Maybe he just hasn't found the right photographer."

"We both know it isn't that. Frank knows it, too."

Laura grimaced, wiggling her toes in the thick, gray carpeting. "I'll say one thing for Frank. He has more brains than most of my other clients put together. Even if he doesn't bother to use them." As she peered at Susan, her brown eyes were far too observant beneath her glasses. "How's his love life?"

"How should I know?"

"Don't waste my time, Susan." Laura dropped into the leather sling chair that Frank had deserted.

"Tracey's moved out. I gather he's temporarily alone."

"Then now's your big chance, lady. Go for it."

"Don't be ridiculous! Frank sees me as a mother figure. Or at least an older sister. Someone to pat him on the back and listen to his troubles and tell him he's wonderful," Susan said, a bitter edge creeping into her voice.

"Mother figure? Older sister? You're five years younger than he is," Laura protested.

"Maybe in years. Frank's a charming little boy. I'm a woman."

"So what are you mooning over him for?"

Susan shook her head. "Midlife crisis?"

"Forget it. I'm having mine first. But at least something good has happened today. Remember the girl Davelli told me about? The one from Kansas?"

"Vaguely."

"She turned up today when you were out. And she's every bit as good as he said she was. Maybe better. I think we've got something here, Susan. Something really big."

"We could use it. We haven't had a major talent since Emelia hit twenty-eight."

"Wait till you see her! I've put her up at a nice hotel for now, but I'll need you to find her a classy sublet. Talk someone into it for as little money as possible, at least until we see how industry response to her is. I think she's going to be dynamite."

"What's her name?"

"Mary Ellen Murphy. We're going to change that. Something exotic, I think. Just one name. What do you think of Marita?"

"Pretentious."

Laura stuck out her tongue at her assistant. "She likes it. If I can just get her pulling in some reasonable money, I can get a decent-size loan. This place is expensive."

"And you're not giving it up."

"Haven't we had this discussion once already?" Laura said wearily.

"You're about to have it again."

"Spare me."

"I would if I could. But it's not up to me. Michael Dubrovnik is on his way up to see you."

"You're kidding!"

"The mountain is coming to Mohammed. Are you still going to tell him no?"

"With great pleasure."

"This I want to see."

"It might not be a pretty sight."

"Who says I'm into pretty sights?"

"Your passion for Frank says so."

"Right now I'm in the mood for a little blood and mayhem. Do you want me to stall him? Long enough for you to get your battle dress in place?"

Laura looked down at her spare body. The red leather

mini was barely decent, the black silk shirt was open, the spiky red heels lay on the floor beside her small, narrow feet. She slipped on her shoes and stood up, squaring her shoulders. "I'm as ready as I'll ever be. This should be interesting. I've never met a whirlwind before."

Michael Dubrovnik slid out of the classic Bentley, one of the few toys he indulged himself with, and stared up at the Glass House. He'd passed it often enough, of course, and he even had a full color photograph of it sitting in a file that had been pending for far too long. He looked at it, at its graceful, almost art deco lines, the deep bronze trusses, the smoky glass that came from another era and was probably an enormous safety hazard. He recognized its singularity, its beauty, a fitting tribute to the genius of Laura Winston's great-grandfather, and his reaction was admiration mixed with exasperation. It was going to cost a fortune to tear the damned thing down.

One more delay, he thought, his mouth tightening. They'd probably have to clear the entire street while they demolished twelve stories of glass. It was a royal pain in the butt, that was what it was, and if he'd only foreseen what trouble it was going to be, he would have opted for the second-best location.

Except that he'd stopped accepting second best years ago. He was used to challenges, he thrived on them. If the fact that his current challenge was nothing more than a stubborn young woman irritated him, it also gave him a measure of infrequent amusement. It reminded him of an elephant being terrorized by a little mouse. He had no intention of running scared, however. He had every intention of squashing her flat.

It was well after six, the doorman-cum-security guard

was busy reading a magazine. He didn't even notice as Michael walked past him to the narrow bank of elevators.

Three of them, all open. He hadn't thought there'd be an office building in New York with only three elevators. Without hesitation he stepped into the streamlined gray Otis. It wasn't that he didn't trust the glass and gilt lifts. He just preferred the familiar and unadorned. If he wanted works of art, he'd look at the walls of his apartment.

Even a decrepit building like the Glass House had full tenancy. He'd reviewed the file, tucking everything away in his almost photographic memory. The top two floors were kept by the owner. Laura Winston ran her modeling agency out of the twelfth-floor penthouse, and she lived one floor beneath it. Everything else in the building was commercial, from the literary agency on the second floor, the employment agency on three, the import-export business on four to the various dealers, brokers, agents and buyers. He was particularly interested in floors nine and ten. They'd been rented from the Winston family since World War II. They held the editorial offices of a small but flourishing trade journal. Michael had no doubt whatsoever that they'd be happy to relocate to one of his buildings farther downtown, and he already had Zach looking into that possibility, if Laura Winston proved as difficult as word had it.

He didn't really expect it to come to that, Michael thought as the Otis carried him swiftly, silently upward. Zach was a master at negotiation, but no one, absolutely no one, could twist and manipulate, intimidate and cajole the way Michael Dubrovnik could, when he set his mind to it. He intended to bring all his very considerable talents to bear on Laura Winston, and if he failed, he would be very much surprised.

There were two women sitting together in the softly lighted reception room of Glass Faces. They were turned toward the elevator, watching his approach, but Michael didn't know the meaning of the word self-conscious. He took his time, surveying the lay of the land with a connoisseur's eye. A thick, gray carpeting past the priceless kilim in the hallway, pink leather furniture from Milan, even a Picasso nude in a treasured spot. He dropped his gaze to the two women, for a moment mistaking their identity. He'd heard from her not terribly devoted mother that Laura had been a plain, plump child, with as much sense of style as a bag lady. Neither woman fitted that description, though one of them, the one behind the desk, was endowed with a generous bosom, simple, soft clothes and a wary expression. He almost risked greeting her as Laura to give himself the upper hand, when a sixth sense that had served him well in the past stopped him.

The other woman lounged in a pink leather sling chair. She was small, bordering on tiny, with long, narrow legs exposed by a tiny scrap of miniskirt, a skinny, boyish body, and a hairdo that reminded him of some twenties actress. He knew immediately that the glasses were merely for show—you could tell by the way light reflected off them that they were flat glass. Her face was deliberately, clownishly pale, the mouth wide and painted a shocking red, and the black pearls in her ears and around her slender neck were absolutely real. She looked up at him with no more interest than if he'd been a messenger, and he immediately understood why Zach had come back empty-handed. It took an expert to see that Laura de Kelsey Winston was an adversary worthy of his mettle, and Michael was an expert. Laura looked up at him, slowly, lazily, her dark eyes glinting with malicious amusement. "May I help you?" she inquired, not moving, swinging her silk-clad leg back and forth over the side of the chair. She knew exactly who he was and why he was there, and she wasn't going to give an inch.

He could appreciate that. He could appreciate her. She was the kind of woman he never allowed himself to get involved with, the kind with brains and savvy and a dangerous determination that, while a challenge in the boardroom, grew emotional and tedious in the bedroom. Not that she'd be interested in going to bed with him, any more than he was interested in sleeping with her. The cool challenge, the glint of hostile amusement, told him that she knew an enemy when she saw one.

And they were enemies, there was never any doubt of that. He couldn't imagine a world where it would be otherwise, even if an anachronism like the Glass House didn't exist. If they had come across each other in the normal course of events, they would have found something else to battle over.

"You aren't what I expected," he said, his rough voice a deliberate contrast to the lush pink and white interior.

Laura raised an artful eyebrow. "I'm not?"

"Your mother said you were fat and plain and shy." For an opening salvo it should have been remarkably effective, but she didn't even blink.

"As you can see, my mother doesn't know me very well. Don't count on her for assistance, Mr. Dubrovnik. You'll be wasting your time."

The woman behind the desk had moved by then, as if by silent signal, heading toward the door behind her without even acknowledging his presence. She had a soft mouth, now tightened in rage. If Laura Winston hadn't minded the insult, her friend minded for her.

"I never waste my time," he said softly. Laura didn't offer him a seat, and he didn't take one. He had no problem standing while she lounged with such studied negligence in the pink leather chair. Towering over her had its own advantages.

"You're here, aren't you?" she observed sweetly. "That's a waste of time, if ever I've heard of one."

"I suppose it's useless to come up with another offer."

"Absolutely."

"To appeal to your kinder instincts? To point out the compromised condition of this building?"

"Save your breath."

He smiled then, a faint, satisfied smile. "All right."

That got to her. She shifted in the chair, her dark eyes narrowing behind the phony glasses, and the blunt shingle of hair swung around her face. "That's it?"

"That's it."

"You're giving up?"

His laugh was soft, genuinely amused. "Don't be ridiculous. I've never given up in my life, and I'm not going to start with a snippy little girl like you."

"There's not much else you can do."

"Don't kid yourself, Laura." He used her name deliberately, caressingly. "I didn't get where I am today by being a gentleman. I fight dirty. You're about to find that out."

She rose then, and he noticed he'd been right in his initial assessment. She was short, coming just up to his chin. She was quivering with tightly suppressed rage, and he realized that despite the rail-thin model's body she had breasts. Breasts that were rising and falling in fury. "I can fight dirty, too," she said, her voice tight.

His nod was the essence of gentlemanly behavior. "I'm looking forward to it."

# Chapter 3

It was eleven o'clock at night. Back home in Kansas it would be just after ten. Mary Ellen's mother would be sound asleep in front of the TV, her mouth open, snoring, the half-empty glass of sherry by her side. Jeff would still be awake. He'd be sitting in the kitchen of his small, spotless ranch house, the house he'd bought to share with her. He'd be drinking coffee, and he'd be thinking of her.

But she, Mary Ellen Murphy—no, Marita—she was in a luxury apartment in The Plaza. She'd looked around her when that funny little Ms. Winston had brought her here, hoping to see someone famous. But Ms. Winston, Laura, didn't want her to stray too far from the apartment. She didn't want anyone seeing Mary Ellen before she was ready.

That was okay with Mary Ellen. During her long walk from the bus terminal she'd quickly seen that her clothes, while stylish enough for Rigby, Kansas, were unspeakably dowdy for the heart of New York. Her hair, her long, straight blond hair that hung down her back like a curtain, was equally outmoded. In this case Laura Winston was right. The fewer people who saw her in her current countrified look, the better.

She'd spent the last two hours walking about the bedroom suite, touching things, savoring the elegance. She stopped now and stared at her reflection in the huge mirror that took up half the bedroom wall. She stared, and a small, mysterious smile curved her mouth. Perfection. Her face and body were a work of art, one she lovingly tended. To do less would be sacrilege. God, or whatever power existed, had given her this remarkable combination of bones and beauty. To ignore it would be ungrateful.

She stood there, practicing her facial expressions. Haughty, meek, solemn, noble. Her face shifted from one emotion to the next, smoothly, perfectly, so adeptly that she almost convinced herself. She'd always had that gift, had always been able to arrange her features in the proper expression and bring forth exactly the response she wanted. Her mother, not to mention her teachers and friends, had always been complete suckers and she'd used both it and them, until they had nothing more to give her.

She lifted her thick blond hair above her head and let it fall, admiring the curve of her breasts, the narrow hips, the slender, delicate waist. Someone other than decent, boring Jeff Carnaby, some very wealthy, generous man was going to get all this perfection, someone who wanted to show it off. Some very lucky man. And whether Laura Winston knew it or not, she was going to find that man for her. Mary Ellen Murphy saw her beautiful smile curve in the mirror, as her bright blue eyes shone smugly.

Susan Richards pulled her nightgown over her head, the soft flannel the perfect defense against the chilly autumn air and the loneliness of an empty bed, and then paused to stare at her reflection. She forced herself to look unflinchingly, assessing her few good and many bad points.

Beneath that soft flannel she was fifteen pounds overweight. She always would be—God knows, she'd tried everything in the world to get rid of those despised extra pounds. Modified fasts, walking, running, pumping iron, starvation, diet pills. She'd even considered liposuction, but the doctor had blithely informed her there was no fat to suck away. She was just built along more curvaceous lines than other women, than the skinny, borderline anorexic models she worked with, day in and day out. She was strong, healthy, well-muscled, smooth-skinned. She might as well accept the fact, the doctor said. Not everyone could have perfect cheekbones.

She'd reluctantly accepted the doctor's pronouncement. If only she could have accepted herself as easily. She stared at her rounded, pretty face. And she thought of people like Tracey Michaels, wandering through the backrooms at Glass Faces, or Emelia Millhouse, or any of the other women without an ounce of spare flesh on them, women with tiny breasts and nonexistent hips, with flat masculine buttocks and endless legs. Women with cheekbones.

She turned toward her bed, away from the frustrating reflection. If only Tracey hadn't walked out on Frank. She could deal with it all if he seemed firmly out of reach, involved with some impossibly beautiful woman. The thought of him, alone in his bed some twenty blocks away, was a torment that wouldn't end. She could only hope he'd get involved with someone new quickly. Then she could put her fantasies safely away, and continue being his kindly older sister. Then maybe she wouldn't die a little inside whenever he gave her those kisses that he handed out so freely.

Turning out the light, she sank into her queen-size bed, sliding against the Laura Ashley sheets. She was a Laura Ashley sort of person, she thought, even if she had to buy the largest size of the clothes they made. Frank didn't belong in Laura Ashley sheets, he didn't belong in a Laura Ashley life. She'd wanted him for more than four years. It was time she learned to let go.

Laura stripped off her clothes and dumped them onto the floor, kicking them out of the way. Pulling on the oversize silk T-shirt she usually slept in, she stopped to stare at her reflection, unflinching, like a technician checking a jet before takeoff. She had about as much emotional involvement with her small, spare frame as a mechanic. As long as it served her well, she ignored it. When it malfunctioned, she took it to a doctor to have it fixed. It provided her with energy and hard work. And no pleasure whatsoever.

She knew that she was no longer fat. There was no spare roll of flesh around her stomach, her breasts were small but well shaped, her hips narrow, her legs trim. It always took her a moment to realize that she wasn't the plump, miserable adolescent, cursed with a beautiful mother and two indecently handsome brothers, the ugly duckling in a family of swans. If she closed her eyes partway she could see that girl again, the spotty complexion, the soft, double chin, the braces, the thick glasses, the limp, soft brown hair.

She'd ruthlessly gotten rid of all that, starting the day she found out that Jilly, her embarrassed, distant mother, had paid Jack Chambers to escort her to the Junior Assembly. Had even gently, delicately suggested that her plain daughter might be pathetically grateful for a little physical affection on the side. It might help her take an interest in her appearance.

What Jack Chambers had provided her in his parents' deserted Fifth Avenue apartment had little to do with affection. He didn't force her, didn't hurt her. He merely mocked and tormented her into complying with something that was so humiliating, so messy, so ultimately degrading that she'd never tried it again. And never planned to.

Rapidly she blinked at her reflection in the mirror. She wore extended wear contact lenses now, ones that made her warm hazel eyes an almost wicked green. She paid Gregorio a fortune for her hair, and only he knew the soft brown color it really was beneath the jet-black dye and ruthless styling. She occasionally worked out, not because she wanted an attractive body, but because she wanted the fitness and the energy, and because she knew, no matter how much Jilly hated the fact, that she'd always be younger than her mother. And her body, which no one was allowed to touch, would always be better.

It was a small enough revenge for years of gentle torment, but it was enough.

Laura turned and climbed into the huge bed that had never held more than one small body. She liked plenty of room, and loved the sense of having all that space to herself. No one else would ever invade it; it was hers, inviolable.

"God, I feel terrific!" Laura announced, breezing into Glass Faces at half past eleven on Monday morning. "Suddenly everything seems under control. I think I can even face your coffee."

"It would serve you right if I bought instant," Susan grumbled.

"Oh, please, please, punish me." Laura leaned against the beveled glass tabletop. "I think we're saved."

"Oh, you do, do you?"

Laura looked at her assistant and best friend, one of the few people she allowed herself to care about. "What's wrong with you? Not enough sleep?"

"Nightmares."

"About Frank?"

"Don't be nasty, Laura. Tell me about our savior."

"The mysterious Marita. She's even better than I thought. I took her to Gregorio this weekend...."

"You took her to your precious Gregorio? I thought you were going to start following a budget."

"I'm afraid any Winston is constitutionally unable to follow a budget. Besides, I think I can hit up my brother Tony for some money. All I have to do is tell him Jilly's trying to twist my arm and he'll give me a blank check."

"Maybe. So Gregorio worked wonders?"

"Indeed. Particularly when he had such a glorious creature to begin with. Then I took her to Gianni for a photoshoot, which might have been a mistake. She could go all the way, she doesn't have to start even one step down, but I figured I owed Gianni for steering her toward me. When I think she might have ended up at Ford or Elite, my skin crawls."

"Certain things are meant to be. How did the photography session go?"

"Spectacularly well. I waited long enough to see the shots. I wanted to make sure we didn't end up with another Frank." She waited for Susan to flinch, but Susan, as always, looked serene, only the shadow of sleepless nights dimming her soft blue eyes.

"So what's our next step?"

"We wait."

"Wait?" Susan echoed. "I thought the wolf was at our door."

"The wolf is trying to buy our door out from under us," Laura said grimly. "But there's nothing he can do. I told him no, and he simply has to accept it."

"I've never heard of Michael Dubrovnik taking no for an answer."

"What else can he do? I don't owe any huge debts at this point. He's tried to get to me through Jilly, a major mistake on his part, I might add. He's offered me ridiculous sums of money for the Glass House, money I refuse to take. He'll simply have to accept defeat."

"Maybe," Susan said, clearly unconvinced. "By the way, why didn't you tell me that the people renting floors nine and ten were moving out?"

Laura could feel some of her buoyant optimism start to fade. "I didn't know they were. They have a twenty-year lease. Are they planning on breaking it?"

"I called your lawyers. Apparently they're subletting."

"Can they do that?"

"Absolutely."

"Where are they moving?"

"You aren't going to like this."

"I'm sure I'm not. Where?"

Susan bit her lip. "Dubrovnik Court."

"Hell," said Laura bitterly. "Hell and damnation." A sudden, horrifying thought struck her. "Who did they sublet to?"

"I haven't been able to find that out yet."

"I can just imagine. Dubrovnik Court has a waiting list a mile long. Someone must have pulled some strings to get them in there on zero notice. Who do you think is going to be ending up on the ninth and tenth floor, Susan? Toxic waste specialists? A halfway house for sex offenders?"

"We'll find out soon enough. The floors are already empty. They started moving at six this morning, Luis said."

"Why can't we afford a decent doorman, who'd advise the owner of these things?" Laura wailed.

"You're probably overreacting. They may have been on Dubrovnik Court's waiting list for years. They've probably sublet to something innocuous."

"As long as they don't install working models on the ninth floor. I don't think I am overreacting, Susan. This is just a little too coincidental, on top of the Whirlwind's visit. I'm expecting the worst."

The phone rang, its discreet, musical note as jarring as a buzz saw. Susan answered it, her voice a polite murmur, and by the time she replaced it, her expression had gone from serene to lugubrious. "You're right," she said. "Your new tenant is moving in."

"And?"

"It's not toxic waste or sex offenders. At least, I don't think so."

"Who is it?"

"Michael Dubrovnik himself."

Michael wondered how long it would take her to find out. He expected a couple of days at least. Word had it that she was so caught up with some new model that she wouldn't be paying much attention to her beloved albatross of a building. He expected he'd have more than enough time to get settled, before she realized what had happened.

He was wrong. He was standing in the middle of the

huge, deserted tenth floor of the Glass House, watching the workmen smash through the cheap partitions, when a pint-sized termagant, dressed this time in a green suit and high-heeled boots, came storming up to him. She was still wearing those glasses, and her coal-black hair practically bristled on her small, well-shaped head. He watched her approach with a cool smile on his face.

"What the hell do you think you're doing?"

"I've sublet these two floors," he replied, mildly enough.

"So I've been informed. I want you out of here. Now."

"Sorry. I'm staying."

"You don't want to be here. I know for a fact you have more real estate in New York than anyone. This is hardly your style...." She winced as a heavy partition crashed to the floor beneath the machinery of an eager workman.

"But this way I get to oversee my investments. I own all the property surrounding you...."

"I know that. And that's all you own. You can camp on my doorstep, you can throw wild parties that keep me up all night, you can do your damnedest, but it won't do you any good." As another wall came crashing down, she shrieked, "Stop that!"

"I'm afraid I have every right to renovate this place. Check with your lawyers, if you don't believe me."

"Oh, I believe you. But what about building permits, that sort of thing? It takes weeks, months..."

"Not when you have the right sort of friends," Michael said softly. "Check with my contractors, if you don't believe me."

"Damn you." She took a deep breath, clearly trying to control her fury, and once more Michael found himself admiring her. Not his sort of woman, he reminded himself. But attractive in a feisty sort of way. Maybe, once she accepted defeat, he might find a place for her in his organization. Bright, fierce, dedicated people were hard to find.

Laura Winston wouldn't take her certain defeat at his hands with much grace, however. And he couldn't see her accepting anything from him, once that battle was over. It was a shame, but he, unlike Laura, knew when to accept the inevitable.

"I hope the workmen won't disturb you. They'll be finished by tomorrow evening."

"Finished what? Destroying my building? What the hell are you going to put on these two floors? You have more than enough office space available to you in the buildings you own—you don't have to invade mine."

"The word is sublet, not invade," he said, gauging his smile to goad her. "And I'm going to live here."

That silenced her. She stared up at him, mute with horror, and he wondered whether she was going to cave in that easily. He almost hoped she wouldn't. Despite the costly delay, he didn't want to see Laura vanquished too easily. It had been a while since he'd come across a foe worthy of his considerable expertise, and he didn't know if he'd ever come up against such a determined woman.

"The hell you are," she said finally.

"The hell I am," he agreed. "Don't worry, I'm a very quiet client. I'll be having a small cocktail party the day after tomorrow, to celebrate my new headquarters. I hope you'll come."

Was it Rumpelstiltskin who got himself into such a rage that he vanished? Michael hadn't had time for fairy tales when he was growing up, but that particular story rang a bell. He wouldn't be surprised if Ms. Laura Winston disappeared in a puff of smoky anger.

Once again he'd underestimated her. She took a deep

breath, managing an icy smile. "You think you can get New York workmen to get this place redone in time?"

"I can get anything I want, Laura. I just have to find the right price."

"The Glass House doesn't have a price."

"Not in dollars and cents, apparently. Though my last offer still stands. No, I'm simply going to have to find other ways to apply pressure. How are the foundations in this old place?"

She glared at him. "I don't know if they'll stand up to a strong breeze. We'll have to wait and see. Are you planning to blast?"

"If I have to go that far."

"You do. You can blast until the whole building collapses in on itself, with you in it, I trust. And I still won't sell to you." She spun on her heel and headed toward the elevators.

"Can I count on your presence Wednesday night? I was planning on having you as the guest of honor."

She paused, looking over her shoulders. "It sounds more like you were planning on having me for hors d'oeuvres. I'll come to your party, Dubrovnik. If I can bring someone with me."

He frowned. "I thought you weren't involved with anyone."

"I'm involved with a great many people. You haven't done your research properly. I can recommend a decent private detective who's much more thorough. I'd like to bring my newest model. You have a passing fondness for models, as I remember."

He grinned then, momentarily entranced. "You think you're going to bribe your way out of the mess you're in?"

Laura's answering smile was dangerous. "Anything's worth a try. And you haven't met Marita."

"I haven't even heard of Marita."

"You will, Michael," she said sweetly. "You will."

# Chapter 4

Even the freight elevator was preferable to the spanking new Otis. Laura rather liked the way the old lift jerked and bounced its way up to the twelfth floor of the Glass House. Her companion wasn't nearly as pleased, a fact which amused Laura. The spectacularly beautiful Mary Ellen Murphy had taken to elegance like a duck to water. Nebraska or wherever it was she'd come from was ancient history to her, and her perfect nose was wrinkled in distaste at the padded walls, the stained floors, the uneven ascent.

Laura took pity on her. She'd already ascertained that she didn't really like Mary Ellen. In the last five and a half days they'd spent almost every waking hour together, working on the enjoyable task of turning Mary Ellen into Marita. During those hours Laura had discovered that there wasn't really anything of Mary Ellen to like. Certainly she put on an excellent front. Her gorgeous, slightly oversize mouth could smile beguilingly, her huge eyes were warm and sincere, her gratitude and compliments neither stilted nor effusive. She hit the right note every time, and yet Laura could see the secret coldness, the go-to-hell shadow in those magnificent eyes. The camera could see it, too. And that—that subtle anger that bordered on cruelty—was what was going to make Marita the face of this decade.

"Sorry about the elevator," Laura murmured, letting her eyes run over her creation. From the tousled strands of silver-blond hair down the long, beautiful body draped in one of Bob Mackie's creations, Marita was a sight that would stop Michael Dubrovnik's crowded cocktail party cold. Laura had chosen the dress with due consideration—something deliberately trashy to set off the girl's flawless beauty. Laura was already reveling in her triumph.

"Oh, that's perfectly all right," Mary Ellen murmured, her low, sweet voice almost sincere. "All the other elevators were so busy with the party...."

"There's that," Laura agreed. "But I also didn't want anyone to have a glimpse of you ahead of time. You're going to make quite a stir, Mary Ellen. I don't want to blunt the impact by having anyone get a sneak preview."

Mary Ellen preened. "Don't you think you'd better start calling me Marita? That is, if you want to," she added shyly, her eyes calculating.

Laura's own smile gave nothing away. "You're absolutely right," she said, adding, "Marita."

The twelfth-floor offices of Glass Faces were softly lighted, illuminating the two figures waiting for them. Susan had that determinedly calm expression on her face, and inwardly Laura cursed. Susan only looked that serene when Frank was around, upsetting her hormones.

"God!" Susan gasped, her eyes widening as she took in all of Marita's astonishing elegance.

Laura knew that her own fatuous smile was nothing short of maternal, but she didn't care. "Didn't I tell you you'd be amazed?"

The first glimmer of real emotion lighted Marita's extraordinary eyes with a feline smugness that was nevertheless oddly appealing. She twirled faultlessly on heels that would have tripped most women, and admired her reflection in the mirrors. "I do look wonderful, don't I?"

"You do indeed." Frank stepped out of the shadows, dressed in a severe black tuxedo. His blond hair was artfully tousled, and his chiseled face was as bemused by Marita's appearance as was Marita with her own reflection.

Laura glanced at her friend, taking in the swift passage of emotions, of despair, rage and acceptance, all racing across her face with the speed of storm clouds and vanishing immediately.

"They make a perfect couple," Susan observed in a carefully neutral tone.

"What the hell are you doing here, Frank?" Laura demanded tartly.

"Laura, my sweet," Frank protested, unmoved by her irritation. "You know Susan can't keep any secrets from me. She told me the mysterious Marita would be making her public debut tonight. You couldn't expect me to miss that?"

"In a tuxedo?"

"I happened to see your invitation from the great Dubrovnik himself. He said bring along any of your favorite models. And I," he said modestly, "am one of your favorite models."

"Not tonight you aren't. I don't like being hustled, Frank."

"Darling Laura, it's not you I'm intent on hustling." He cast a look of sensual longing toward Marita, a look so classic that it bordered on parody. Marita's stony, beautiful eyes looked right through him with no interest whatsoever, and Laura found it difficult to hide a smile.

"You're wasting your time on Marita," she said. "This, by the way, is Frank Buckley." Her introductions were curt, and Marita's regal acknowledgment would have dented a lesser man's confidence.

Frank, however, merely shrugged. "I need work," he said, his usually melodic voice flat. "I'm broke. I thought I could kill two birds with one stone. Escort two charming ladies to the Whirlwind's cocktail party, and drum up some business on the side. I realize you've been doing your best, but the wolf is no longer at the door. He's walked right in and sat down at the table."

"Three charming ladies," Laura corrected him. "Susan's coming, too."

"No, I'm not..." Susan began to protest, startled at her last-minute inclusion, even more rattled by the genuine pleasure on Frank's face.

"Of course you are, darling," he said, advancing on her. "You're the only one who'll be nice to me."

"You can come, Frank," Laura agreed. "But don't try manipulating me again. You try it, and you'll be out of here on your cute little buns so fast..."

Frank smiled at her, all innocent beguilement. "I love it when you talk dirty. Don't you want to face your nemesis with a little moral support?"

"That's why I'm bringing Susan."

Frank's sigh was mocking and resigned. "Then think

of me as a fashion accessory for Marita. I go well with Bob Mackie."

Marita shrugged, her beautiful eyes barely seeing him. "I have no objections," she said, bored.

"Ladies, you're doing wonders for my ego." Frank shook his head.

"I still love you," Susan said sweetly, lightly.

"Thanks, darling." He leaned over and kissed her. "I know you do."

Laura considered pushing Frank out one of the smoked glass panels of the building. Didn't he realize what he was doing to Susan?

"Let's go," she said curtly, controlling her murderous impulse. "I want to see what happens when a whirlwind runs out of steam."

"You're putting a lot of stock in Marita," Susan said, casting a worried glance at the new model.

"She can carry it off. We've got it all planned, haven't we?"

"Certainly," Mary Ellen replied. "I'm going to dazzle Michael Dubrovnik."

"And what if he doesn't fall for her?" Frank asked, his voice wry.

"He will," Laura said, leading the way to the elevators. "He has to. After all, she's going to be the face of this decade."

She paused, letting Marita precede her to the gilt elevator, and Frank's sotto voce comment drifted to her ears.

"Then it's going to be a long, cold decade," he muttered to Susan. And Susan, abandoning her usual tact, laughed.

Where was she? Michael kept the cool, almost feral smile firmly in place, as the cream of New York society, social, business and artistic, milled around him. He didn't have to work the room—with Michael Dubrovnik, the room worked him. He remained in one spot by the expanse of smoked glass windows, one eye firmly fixed on the bank of elevators. He'd torn out the walls of the hallway, so that the elevators opened onto one vast room. He expected that to cause a furious reaction from his reluctant landlady. She'd have an even bigger fit when she saw the hairline cracks in the famous smoked glass panels in the living quarters, one flight below this extremely noisy party. He wasn't quite sure how he was going to get her down there, and if the workmen hadn't managed to inflict a satisfying amount of damage on the building, he wouldn't bother. But if he'd read Ms. Laura Winston properly, the only way to get what he wanted was to keep at her, torment her, in big and little ways.

"Didn't I tell you you didn't have any charm?" Zach appeared at his elbow. "Stop grinning. It looks as if you're going to eat someone for breakfast."

"Just Laura Winston."

"Is that why you keep staring at the elevators?"

He didn't bother to deny it. "You think she's going to show?"

"She'd be a fool to miss it. And Laura's no fool. As a matter of fact, I think she's here."

Michael was suddenly alert. "Where?" he demanded, peering over the noisy crowd that was drinking his liquor, eating his food, and tearing him to shreds.

"She's too short to see beyond all these giants," Zach said. "But there's an extremely beautiful young woman causing quite a stir by the elevators, and I thought I saw the young woman who works for Winston with her. I imagine Laura's somewhere around."

For the first time that evening Michael pushed himself away from his safe perch by the smoked glass walls. He ignored his grateful guests as he threaded his way through the crowd, his steely gaze intent on the tall woman with hair the color of sunlight. When he reached her side, he barely glanced at her.

Laura was dressed in seemingly demure black, a perfect foil to her gaudy companion. The dress was high-necked, ending in a priest's collar, the back was nonexistent, and the skirt was slit to the tops of her thighs. Her shingled black hair swung neatly around her face, and her brightly painted mouth held a mocking smile. He wanted to spank her.

Instead he smiled back, a slow, savage grin that sent his employees running for cover. She didn't even blink. "I'm glad you decided to show up," he murmured, his voice rasping. "I thought you might have chickened out."

"I wouldn't have missed it for the world. Allow me to introduce my companions. You've already met Susan Richards, my assistant. This is Frank Buckley—" she gestured to a man who was far too pretty for her "—and this is Marita."

For the first time Michael took in Laura Winston's secret weapon in all her glory, and he couldn't deny that she was glorious indeed. Her tawny mane of hair rippled and flowed down her narrow, perfect back, her mouth was wide and sensuous, her eyes were slumbrous and daring, her skin, her body utterly flawless. He stared, bemused, looking for an imperfection and finding none. With spiked heels she was just slightly taller than him, a fact that bothered him not in the slightest. He looked directly into her eyes, recognizing the deliberate challenge lurking there. He was never a man to resist a challenge.

"Marita." He acknowledged her presence, knowing

he should make a move before the hungry hordes surrounding them attacked her. He opened his mouth to say something, but instead he turned back to Laura, to the look of smug pride in her eyes. "How do you like the renovations so far?"

If she was disappointed that he hadn't made more of a fuss over Marita, she hid it admirably. "I'm deciding whether to sue you or not," she said pleasantly, nodding toward Marita. The tall model moved off through the room, and the crowd surrounding them followed, leaving Laura and Michael temporarily isolated. Even Frank and her assistant had disappeared, though Michael could still see Frank's blond head atop the perfectly cut tuxedo.

"Is he your lover?" He hadn't meant to ask that. He couldn't understand why he had, unless he'd simply wanted to startle her. The private investigator's report hadn't mentioned any romantic or sexual involvement, but as she'd already pointed out to him, the report had missed a few important details.

"Frank?" she echoed, highly amused. "No. Why do you ask?"

His first mistake, he chided himself, his expression giving nothing away. He'd have to recoup his losses. "What about Marita?"

"I believe both of them are at present uninvolved." She glanced over the crowds with deliberate care. "I doubt it will stay that way for long with Marita. She's caused quite a stir."

"I noticed," he said wryly, not bothering to follow her gaze.

"You aren't interested?" There was no anxiety in her face, only a mild curiosity, but Michael wasn't fooled. "I thought you liked beautiful women."

"I do. And Marita is very beautiful indeed. I just don't think there's any rush."

"Don't you?"

"I'm not really vain, Laura, but how many unmarried multimillionaires are there who are younger than forty? And I'm considered passably attractive, besides."

Her eyes widened for a moment, just a tiny start of shock that he couldn't quite interpret. "Maybe you can afford to wait," she conceded.

"Besides, I'm more interested in you right now."

"You're more interested in my building right now," she corrected him. "I'll blow this place up myself before I let you have it."

"Why?"

She looked genuinely startled, as if she'd never considered the question before. "Why?" she echoed.

"I mean, is it just me, or is it developers in general, or anyone not devoted to your sainted great-grandfather's heritage, or what?"

"All of the above."

He was suddenly very, very angry. "Lady," he said, biting off the words, "you are going down in flames."

"Mister," she said, her manner just as deadly, "I'll take you with me." And without another word she spun on her high heels and swept away. Within seconds she was gone, her tiny figure swallowed up by the crowd, vanished as if by magic.

It took him a moment to remember that she knew this building better than anyone. She knew, for example, where the freight elevators and utility staircases were. She could disappear faster than a magician, but there was no trick to it at all.

And then he realized that while a great number of people were trailing around after the mysterious Marita, there'd been still enough guests left to follow his brief conversation with Ms. Laura Winston with great interest.

If he'd been a man with less self-control, he would have ordered out all the curious, chattering parasites. But he hadn't let either his emotions or his anger get the better of him for close to fifteen years, and he would be damned before he let a supercilious little girl like Laura make him lose his cool.

There were a great many tall men and women in the room. After all, his guest list had included the rich and powerful, and a great proportion of them were tall. But no one had a curtain of sunlit hair, no one moved with such mysterious grace. His eyes narrowed as he took in the crowd surrounding her. He would have preferred to continue sparring with his nemesis, but that option had been summarily removed. For once he'd have to settle for second best. And if second best looked like Marita, it wasn't such a hardship, after all.

"Where do you think you're going, darling?" Frank's voice was lazy in her ear, but the hand on her wrist surprisingly strong and inflexible.

"I'm going after Laura," Susan replied, tugging uselessly at his grip. She hadn't realized Frank was quite so strong.

"Laura's a big girl. She can take care of herself. Relax and enjoy the party."

She looked at him in surprise. "Shouldn't you be working the room?"

"I'm not in the mood for it."

"Neither am I." She tugged again, and this time he released her. "I really do think I should see how Laura's doing."

"I really think you should forget about work for a

change." He reached for her again, slipping an arm beneath hers and steering her toward the elevators. "Let's go find something to eat, and I can tell you all my troubles."

"I thought you didn't have any money," she said, allowing herself to be convinced.

"I don't. But you have, don't you, darling? You can treat a poor starving model to dinner?"

"If you like McDonald's."

"Susan!"

"I'm kidding. We'll go to someplace nice and middle-class and eat home cooking."

"I'd rather die. We'll go to a place near my apartment. A vegetarian place. Maybe I'll even be generous and go dutch."

Susan looked up at him in mock admiration. "You're a prince." She shouldn't go, she knew it. She'd worry about Laura, and two or three hours of Frank telling her about his love life and treating her like a sister would be at best a mixed blessing. It was, however, one she couldn't resist. For tonight Laura would have to survive on her own. She cast one last, worried glance toward the center of the room and Marita's tall, graceful figure. "I'm not sure about Marita. She's not used to New Yorkers...."

"She can handle herself," Frank drawled.

"She's really quite young and unsophisticated," Susan said earnestly, shocked by Frank's unsympathetic tone. "Maybe we should keep an eye on her."

"If you think she's coming along, you can forget it. Trust me. Mary Ellen Murphy can take care of herself. She's got an innate sense of self-preservation that not even the toughest New Yorker is going to be able to dent. I'd worry more about the other people here."

Susan could see Michael Dubrovnik's dark head bent close to Marita's, his narrow, clever face seemingly rapt.

"At least Laura's getting what she wanted," she murmured.

"Is she?" Frank asked cryptically. "Come on, sweetheart. I need to unburden my boyish heart, and you're
the perfect listener."

"Everyone's mother," Susan agreed, half under her
breath as she stepped onto the elevator.

Frank heard her. The gilt and glass box was crowded,
pushing him against Susan, and the expression in his
aquamarine eyes was thoughtful. But he never said a
word.

## Chapter 5

Laura usually slept till nine, waking slowly, grumpily, sipping black French roast coffee until her eyelids were propped open. It took her half an hour to even contemplate anything more demanding than her coffee, and she was seldom dressed before eleven. The morning after Michael's party she was particularly in need of sleep. Alone in her wide bed, she'd tossed and turned all night long, listening to the sound of traffic far below, listening for the sound of voices one flight below. She'd finally drifted off sometime around three, cursing Michael Dubrovnik and his assembled ancestry.

At seven-thirty that morning her eyes flew open, her hands reached out to grip the side of her bed, and her heart pounded against the cool cotton sheets. For a moment she lay there, dazed, not knowing what had ripped her from the thick cocoon of sleep.

The sound came again, thunder rumbling in the bright

morning sky, shaking her bed, shaking the building. She stared in horror as the hairline cracks in one panel of glass slowly, gracefully glided upward.

She sat up, instantly, furiously awake. Jumping from bed, she grabbed the mauve silk kimono, pulled it around its matching teddy and ran from her bedroom in rage, her bare feet scurrying across the thick carpeting.

She slammed back her door, leaving it wide open for potential thieves and muggers, and ran down the utility stairs, two flights, her anger white-hot, blotting out any rational sense of who and where she was. She pounded on the ninth-floor door with both fists.

"Dubrovnik!" she shrieked, her voice hoarse with early morning fog. "Open the damned door, you creep! Open it!"

She kept pounding, making too much noise to hear the footsteps approach on the other side. The door open, she stumbled in, and it took all of the tiny bit of self-control she still possessed to keep from pounding on Michael Dubrovnik.

He was wearing a smug smile, a towel around his hips, and nothing else. "Good morning," he said, his voice even. "Can I get you some coffee?"

She slammed the door shut behind her, and the spidery network of cracks in the glass panels spread in response. "What the hell do you think you're doing?"

"I was taking a shower. Now I'm going to have a cup of coffee. Can I get you anything?" Another rumble punctuated his polite question, and Laura clenched her fists, clenched them so tightly that she almost drew blood.

"Stop them," she said.

"Stop whom?"

"Don't play games with me. You're having people blast too close to the Glass House. Don't you realize what you're doing? Can't you see the damage you've already caused?" She gestured toward the cracked glass.

"I'm not doing that. The building is unsafe—it should have been condemned decades ago. Just because you've managed to pull strings doesn't mean it can go on forever. This building is half glass, and that glass is old and dangerous."

"The glass facing the street has been replaced," she defended herself.

He moved closer, a brave move, considering she was close to murder. "Not good enough, and you know it."

"I don't have the money to replace the rest of the glass."

"I know you don't. You own a safety hazard, and you're holding on to it from sheer stubbornness. Face it, Laura, the time for this anachronism is over. Give it up."

"Go to hell, Dubrovnik."

"Watch your mouth, lady," he said, his tone dangerous now. "I don't like being cursed at."

Another rumble shook the building. "You don't, do you?" she replied. "You slimy, sleazy, soulless, heartless snake. You can take your likes and dislikes and put them where the sun don't shine. You son of a—"

He stopped her mouth—by the simple expedient of grabbing her silk-covered arms, hauling her against his shower-damp body, and kissing her.

She was too shocked to do anything more than stand there, feeling his hard, strong hands digging into her upper arms, feeling the dampness of his chest against hers, feeling the unfamiliar, shocking heat of his mouth on her own.

He released her a moment later, having taken her lips but not her mouth, and she stood there, silenced for the first time in years.

"Why did you do that?" she finally demanded, her rage replaced by confusion. He'd moved away from her, pouring himself a cup of coffee, pouring one for her, too.

"It seemed the best way to shut you up," he said, handing her the coffee.

She took it without realizing what she was doing. "Try that with my lawyer," she said, "and he'll deck you."

He grinned. It was the first time she'd seen him smile, and it made him suddenly more human. "I have better tactics for lawyers."

For the first time she really looked at him. She would have thought he'd be covered with a pelt of black fur, but he was smooth-skinned, only a thin matting of hair covering his chest and disappearing into the monogrammed towel that encircled his narrow hips. His body was lean, wiry, almost vibrating with energy, and Laura absently thought that she could see why women would find him so attractive. Women who liked sex, that is.

She took a sip of coffee, more to give herself time to think than to actually partake of his hospitality in any way, shape or form. A small, sensual moan of pleasure escaped her lips. "French roast," she sighed.

His grin broadened. "I have a machine that's more of a computer than a coffee maker. It roasts the beans, grinds them and brews the coffee, all without me having to do anything."

She should put the coffee down, she knew she should, but there were some things that were simply too much to ask of flesh and blood. She took another sip, just managing to stop moaning in delight again. He was looking at her over the rim of his own cup, his dark blue eyes speculative, and she suddenly realized she was wearing a thin silk teddy and matching wrap, both of which came to the top of her thighs, and nothing else. Not even the high heels she always wore to bring herself up to a height where she could deal with threats like Michael Dubrovnik.

The blasting had stopped, at least for the moment, and she considered being reasonable. "If you destroy this building, you might very well be in it," she said calmly.

"I'm willing to take that chance. I have my own engineers on the job. They know when to stop."

"Just before the building needs to be evacuated."

Michael only smiled. It was an attractive smile, and Laura recognized the wolf behind it. Ready to rip into the throat of the first innocent victim who stood in its way.

She, however, was no innocent victim, and she was used to dealing with wolves. "My lawyer will get an injunction. New York City is full of rules and regulations. Once the city finds out you're endangering lives…"

"Then they'll know this building is unsafe, has been unsafe for years, and they'll condemn it," he filled in smoothly.

She drained the coffee, setting down the cup. "You think you've got me beat."

"I know I've got you beat."

She shook her head. "It's not going to be that easy. I'll take my chances with an injunction. It takes bureaucrats forever to check into things. They won't get around to condemning this building for weeks. Weeks of costly delay, Mr. Dubrovnik. And I can be very creative in a few weeks."

"Give it up, Laura."

"Over my dead body. If it's condemned, I'll sell it to someone else."

"There's no one you can sell it to who won't accept my higher bid."

There was no way she could refute that. She looked

around her, at the spare, almost monastic feel of the apartment. There was nothing there of a personal nature, just a leather sofa, a vast walnut desk littered with papers and the kitchenette. Through the doorway she could see a huge, rumpled bed and nothing else.

"Do you always live this sparsely?" she asked. "Or are you expecting to have to camp out for just a few days?"

"A little bit of both."

Her own smile was just as dangerous as his. "You'd better bring in a few comforts of home, Mr. Dubrovnik," she said, heading for the door. "It's going to be a long haul."

He reached it before she did, putting his hand on the doorknob. Once more she cursed her lack of shoes as she felt him tower over her. "You may as well be a little less formal. Call me Michael."

"I've already called you a great many informal names. Open the door."

"Call me Mischa," he suggested. "Dubrovnik's too long a name."

"We're not going to be friends," she said.

"My enemies can call me Mischa," he murmured. "I don't open the door until you say it."

"Mischa," she replied promptly. "Open the door."

He opened the door with a flourish, and she wished she could wipe that smug look off his face. She turned and was about to say something else, anything that would put a dent in his damned sense of triumph, when the elevator door slid open. Zach Armstrong stepped off, Susan Richards stood inside. Both of them stared in astonishment at Michael and Laura.

Laura's reaction was a muttered curse under her breath. "Hold the elevator, Susan," she said, slipping past Michael and his associate without a backward glance,

pulling the silk wrap around her body. The door slid shut,
closing her in with her shocked assistant. "Don't say a
word," she said, as the elevator moved upward.


"Don't say a word," Michael warned, ushering Zach
into the apartment and closing the door behind him. "Coffee's ready. I'm going to get dressed."

"I think that's a wise idea," Zach observed in a neutral voice. "Are you sure you know what you're doing?"

"Not this time," Michael muttered under his breath,
tossing the damp towel onto the floor and reaching for
his clothes. Why the hell had he kissed her? That was
the damnedest, stupidest, most quixotic act he'd ever per-
formed.

Of course, it had worked out rather well. She'd been so
taken off balance by that kiss that she hadn't realized he
was equally astonished, both by the act and his own reaction to it. If he was going to go around kissing all his female competitors, he was going to run into grave trouble.

Maybe he was going through a midlife crisis after all,
he thought, shrugging into the Egyptian cotton shirt and
buttoning it. If he was going to get distracted by someone
like Laura Winston, he was going to run into big trouble
when he went up against the heavyweights who'd like
nothing better than to see him fall.

He'd already decided that he needed to be married
again, that he needed children. He should have paid more
attention to Marita, he thought, reaching for the jacket
of his silver-gray Armani suit. At first glance it seemed
as if she would fill the bill perfectly. Decorative, silent,
mysterious enough to be entertaining, she would make
the perfect wife. He'd been a fool to send her home in
his Bentley without even making a pass.

Or maybe he hadn't. Marita knew what she wanted,

and he knew how to go about getting it. And with Laura Winston in her corner, coaching her, she knew what she was doing. He'd known that the moment he looked into her soulless blue eyes. He could respect that single-minded tenacity. She would have turned down a pass, gracefully, regretfully, but thoroughly.

"Damn," he said out loud, running a hand through his thick black hair in a ruthless gesture. He couldn't get Laura out of his mind.

Zach appeared in the door, lounging against the molding. "They want to know when to start blasting again. They followed your instructions, blasted for seven minutes, and they're waiting for the word to continue." His expression was knowing. "Did you realize you were going to get Ms. Winston in the sack when you ordered the blasting?"

"If you'd used your eyes, Zach, you would have realized that we didn't just come from a night of unbridled sex. Our landlady heard the blasting and headed down here to throw me out one of her damned cracked windows."

"Uh-huh."

"Think about it, man. Is Laura Winston my type?" Michael demanded irritably.

"No. Marita's your type. But I've never known you to draw the line at anything you wanted. If you thought bedding Laura Winston would get you the Glass House faster, you'd have her on her back in ten seconds flat."

"Don't."

"Don't what? Don't tell me you're becoming chivalrous in your old age? The woman's a menace, we both know it. She's standing in the way of the biggest real estate deal of your life. I can't believe you're going to let good manners and sentiment get in the way."

"You would."

"Yes, but we've already accepted the fact that I'm a Southern gentleman with outmoded values. You're a pirate. You do the dirty work, I clean up after you."

Michael paused in the act of knotting his black silk tie. "Are you planning to clean up Laura Winston?"

"After you get through with her, I doubt there'll be much left. That is, if you're running true to form?" It was a gentle question, one Michael could ignore if he wanted to.

"I'm running true to form," he said, staring at his reflection in the mirror. The man he saw there looked cold and cruel, the blue eyes just as lacking in soul as Marita's magnificent ones. They'd make a good pair, he thought without pleasure. "Just be ready with the dustpan and broom."

"I always am, Mischa."

Michael winced at the name. No one called him Mischa but his closest friends. No woman ever had, apart from his mother and sisters. Why the hell did he suggest Laura Winston use it?

"Good," he said. "It won't be long."

"I'm sure it won't," Zach agreed smoothly. And only his oldest friend recognized the skepticism in his words, kept well below the surface.

"Don't start on me," Laura warned as Susan followed her off the elevator toward her eleventh-floor apartment.

"You didn't sleep with him, did you?" Susan demanded, ignoring Laura's words.

"Of course not! That snake, that wolf, that weasel!"

"I wouldn't call him a weasel," Susan said fairly, shutting the door behind her. "Did you leave the door open all night?"

"I told you, I wasn't gone all night. I didn't sleep with him. That monster had people setting off dynamite at the crack of dawn. Crack…" she murmured, remembering, and her pained gaze took in the long, graceful streaks in the smoked glass panels. "Damn him," she muttered.

"Did he promise to stop?"

"Of course not. Call Phil Dobbins while I get dressed, would you? If my lawyer can't get an injunction, I don't know what I can do."

"Phil can stop him. At least for a while. We may be in over our heads this time, Laura. Michael Dubrovnik is the major leagues, the big time. How long do you think we can hold out against him?"

"Forever," she said fiercely, stripping off her clothes and heading for the shower. "Or until he loses interest."

"Those two things might be the same," Susan muttered. "Want any coffee?"

"God, no! Not unless you want to sneak back down to his apartment and steal some." She paused in the doorway of her bathroom. "The man has one redeeming feature. He makes great coffee."

"Having seen him in only a bath towel, I'd say he has more than one redeeming feature," Susan drawled.

"Get your mind back to business, woman," Laura snapped. "Call Phil before Dubrovnik blasts this entire building down around our heads."

"Aye, aye, sir."

Damn Susan, why did she have to mention the bath towel? Through her confrontation with Dubrovnik she'd been entirely unaware of their scantily clad bodies. Now it was all she could think of. Particularly after seeing the knowing looks in both Zach's and Susan's eyes.

Susan was right, of course. He did have a good body. After all, both women were in the business of bodies, and they'd have to be blind not to recognize a good one when they saw it. Maybe, if the Fates were kind and turned the tables on that rapacious creature, she could offer to find him some work. Underwear ads for catalogs would do nicely, she reflected, grinning at the thought. If only such sweet revenge were even remotely in her grasp.

She wasn't going to bring him to his knees. The best she could hope for was to hold out long enough, so that he'd lose interest in the project. She wasn't going to give in; she wasn't going to sell her birthright and see it tumble into the dust like so many other bright and beautiful buildings, only to be replaced by shiny boxes. She was going to fight to the bitter end, and then she'd fight some more.

By the time Laura reached the twelfth floor, Susan had things humming along nicely. The lawyer was already filing for an injunction, the coffeepot was filling with oily, horrible-tasting liquid, jobs had been found for three of Laura's teenage models, and Maxheimer had called with their usual request for Frank.

"Maybe this won't be such a horrible day, after all," Laura said, sipping the black coffee with a shudder. Caffeine, even in its present poisonous state, was a necessity of life. Maybe she could find out the name of Michael's coffee maker. It seemed as if it might even be Susan-proof.

"Maybe. I left a message on Frank's answering machine." Susan's voice was carefully neutral. "I imagine he'll get it sooner or later."

Laura immediately forgot her own worries and focused on Susan. "What happened last night at the party? Did he score?"

"No. He was reduced to going home with me."

"Susan!"

"It's not what you're thinking. We had dinner at a vegetarian restaurant near his loft. He graciously allowed me to pay for his meal while he told me all about his love life."

"Oh, Susan," Laura said with real sympathy. "That man ought to be gelded."

"But what a loss for womankind." Susan managed a wry smile. "Besides, it was very interesting. I had no idea he'd been involved with Emelia."

"Frank's been around. He's not exactly promiscuous— he just enjoys women."

"So I gather." Susan sighed. "We talked until midnight, he gave me a peck on the cheek and sent me home in a taxi. All very sweet and brotherly."

"Can't you get over him?" The question was gentle, the answer preordained.

"I've been trying for four years," Susan said, staring out over the New York skyline through the network of cracks in the smoked glass. The telephone rang, and both of them looked at it.

"Phil?"

"Frank," Susan said, putting the receiver against her shoulder. "I'll tell him about Maxheimer. At least he'll be in a good mood."

"That makes one of us," Laura said sourly, giving in and taking another sip of coffee. She moved over to the cracked glass panel, staring down into the vacant lot beside the building. She could see workers moving around, their hard hats glinting in the bright autumn sunlight. The blasting must be over, at least for now, or they wouldn't all be wandering around in such an aimless fashion. Dynamite has the tendency to make people move quickly, she thought, leaning her forehead against the cool glass.

"Call Marita, will you? I think we've got to up the ante a bit."

"I thought you were going to be circumspect."

"How can I be circumspect with that monster blasting our foundations out from under us?" Laura shot back, spinning on her heels. "How can I...?" Her voice trailed off as an elegant apparition stepped from the elevator. "Oh, no!" she moaned. "As if today weren't bad enough."

Susan followed her gaze to the front hallway. The woman walking toward them had once been as beautiful as Marita, perhaps even more so. The years had treated her kindly, as had her plastic surgeons. Her beautifully boned face showed not a trace of her fifty-two years, her black hair was thick and glossy and knotted at her graceful nape in a severe style that only the very beautiful can carry off. Her body demonstrated the years of exercise, her carriage reflected the years of money and power. She practically floated into the room, making Laura feel like a small, awkward, fat little girl. As always.

"Hello, precious," the woman said, her voice low and delightfully musical, a perfect match for her face and body.

"Hello, Mother," Laura said without enthusiasm. "Slumming again?"

# Chapter 6

"Susan," Jillian Margot de Kelsey Winston Petrovini McAllister von Kempel purred, ignoring her daughter's jibe as she glided into the offices of Glass Faces with as much grace as Laura's most successful client. "You're looking wonderful. That color is marvelous on you. So slimming."

Susan's polite smile never faltered, but her eyes met Laura's for a brief, knowing moment. "It's good to see you, Baroness," she murmured. "It's been a long time."

Jilly's expression held just the right combination of regret. "I'm afraid my daughter finds me a bit of an old crock. Don't you, dear?"

Laura winced. No one in their right mind would ever call Jilly von Kempel an old crock, and well she knew it. "Yes, Mother," she said politely. "What can I do for you?"

Jilly's magnificent dark eyes chilled for a moment, but her warm smile remained fixed. "If I might have a few moments alone with you? I'm sure Susan will excuse us."

"There's no need…" Laura protested, but Susan was already escaping, the rat, leaving her to her mother's tender mercies.

"I have a few phone calls to make," Susan murmured, disappearing into the back room with more haste than grace.

Jilly watched her go, her expression speculative. "I realize Susan is a dear friend, Laura. But don't you think you could do better? If you must run a modeling agency, don't you think you could present a trendier image?"

"You didn't come here to talk to me about Susan. Get to the point." It didn't take much effort to control her temper. She'd already expended the bulk of it on Michael Dubrovnik, and she had more than enough experience in deflecting her mother's gentle barbs.

But Jilly was clearly taking her own sweet time. She glanced around her, her expression a perfect combination of pity and distaste. "I hate this place, do you realize that?" she said suddenly. "I wish to God that Mother had sold it years ago. It reminds me of everything I'd rather forget."

"It's a beautiful building," Laura protested. "It was great-grandfather's finest work."

"It caused his death," Jilly said flatly. "I don't need to remind you of the sordid details, do I? I doubt a single person in all of New York has forgotten."

"You don't need to remind me."

"Then surely you understand why I want this building gone, leveled, blasted out of existence?"

"No."

"Laura, a madman named Henry Q. Johnston shot my grandfather dead in the lobby of this building!"

"I've always known that," Laura said patiently. "I've also known that Great-Grandfather was having an affair with Johnston's wife, which the juries considered to be extenuating circumstances."

"That man spent eighteen months at a luxurious prison farm," Jilly said, her voice rich with the tragic note she'd perfected long ago.

"And died a war hero. End of Henry Q. Johnston. You were two years old when your grandfather was killed, and you don't even remember him. So don't try to tell me that the loss of your precious grandfather scarred you for life. I won't believe you."

"So hard," Jilly murmured sadly. "So very heartless, the young are."

"Grandmother left the Glass House to me because she knew I'd watch over it and keep it intact as long as possible. You would have sold it the first time you needed a little extra spending money. I would think, Mother, that when you go through so many husbands, you might at least have the sense to pick ones richer than you are."

That snapped Jilly out of her tragic queen mood. "Since you brought up the subject of cold cash, darling, I might point out to you that I have nothing to gain when you sell the Glass House. It's yours entirely—I have no ulterior motive."

"I have no doubt whatsoever that that snake downstairs has offered you a bribe if you can get me to sell to him. Sorry, Mother, it won't work. You say you hate this place. Let me assure you it'll be blasted into rubble before I let Michael Dubrovnik profit from it."

"He's here? Downstairs?" Jilly murmured, momentarily diverted from her single-minded goal.

"Hadn't you heard? He got some of my tenants to vacate and he's moved in, lock, stock and coffee maker." Laura knew her mother well enough to recognize the speculative expression on Jillian's lovely face, and felt a curious, unnameable sinking in her stomach. Michael Dubrovnik wasn't that much younger than Jilly's current, soon to be ex-husband, and her taste in men had gotten more and more youthful. Laura had seldom seen any man able to withstand Jilly de Kelsey's considerable charms.

"I suppose you've been churlish, as always," Jilly said tartly. "Honestly, darling, don't you know that you can accomplish a great deal more with charm? A smile instead of a scowl, a compliment instead of an insult?"

"Sorry, Mother. I never learned the fine art of manipulating people. Even with such a marvelous example in front of me."

Jilly shook her head. "Laura, Laura. There are times when I despair of you." She crossed the room, graceful as always, and gently flipped her daughter's bobbed hair. "Couldn't you do something about this abominable hairstyle? Something softer? And why can't you be like everyone else and get contact lenses?"

Laura looked at her mother through the double barrier of contact lenses and clear glasses. "Because I'm not like everyone else."

"No, indeed." Jilly's sad little laugh was a masterpiece, Laura thought sourly. It was a shame she lacked an appreciative audience for her belated mothering. "Well, if you refuse to be pleasant to Michael, then at least I can try to mend fences. He's not a good enemy to make, darling."

"Too late, Mama. We're already at each other's throats." Out of the blue, the memory of his mouth, his lips on hers, shot through her brain, and she immediately slammed it away.

Not before her mother noticed something. Jilly wasn't an intellectual woman, but when it came to the nuances of human emotion she was a genius, and she'd caught the flash of reaction that had sped across her face, Laura just knew it.

"Go and flirt with him, Mother," she said, turning away. "If you can distract him from trying to flatten me, then I'll be eternally grateful."

"Well, of course I don't want him hurting my baby...."

"I know perfectly well you'll do everything you can to help him," Laura said coldly.

"I love you, Laura."

Laura didn't move. For once Jilly's voice was devoid of artifice, and for some strange reason Laura believed her. Not that Jilly had ever exhibited love for her changeling daughter, but Laura knew that Jilly was just sentimental enough to possess a trace of maternal feeling.

"I know," Laura said gently, not turning back. A moment later her mother was gone. Off to the wolf's lair, she thought bitterly. So much for mother love.

Susan reappeared, her normally placid face creased with worry. "We're in trouble, Laura."

"You're telling me," Laura sighed. "What is it now?"

"That was Maxheimer. Frank called in."

"And?"

"Those fools told him it would be his last shoot. That they've decided to go for a new look, but they felt they owed him something for old times' sake."

"Oh, God. What did Frank say?"

"Nothing that could be repeated over the phone, apparently. The people at Maxheimer are royally put out. You'd better call and soothe them. They're going to want someone new, and you don't want to throw away the commission simply because they're heartless."

"Much as you'd like me to?" Laura guessed. "We knew this was coming, sooner or later. So did Frank."

"They could have handled it better," Susan said, her usually soft mouth tight with suppressed rage.

"Life doesn't work out that way. I'll talk to the people at Maxheimer, tell them I don't like the way they do business. They'd better do it through me in the future, and if they don't like it they can take a flying leap into the East River. What about you?"

"I don't want to take a flying leap into the East River," Susan said, with just the ghost of a smile.

"Go see him if you want. Tell him we can find something, at least temporarily. We have a responsibility to him."

"And he needs someone's shoulder to cry on. You sure you can handle the office?" Susan was already pulling her purse from the desk.

"I'm tough. If I can handle the Whirlwind, I can handle anything. Tell Frank I'm sorry."

Susan paused by the door. "He'll leave, won't he?"

"If everything else dries up, we won't have anything to offer him," Laura said gently. "I'm sorry, Susan. I don't know what else we can do."

"I knew this had to come sooner or later. It's probably all for the best. As long as he's around, out of reach, I can't get over him. Maybe once he's gone I'll be able to get on with my life."

"That's the right attitude."

"Do you think I believe it?"

Laura's grin was rueful. "Not for a moment."

"You know me too well. You sure you can handle things?"

"I've already told you I can. Out of here, Susan. I don't want to see you again until you're certain you want to come in. Okay?"

"Okay."

Laura watched her go, a little twist of sympathetic pain inside her. Thank God she wasn't prey to those sorts of emotions, thank God she'd never ached for someone so

badly that she thought she'd die from it. Her heart, such
as it was, was encased in ice, only melting around children, puppies, good friends and haute couture. Her sex
drive was nonexistent, burned out of her by a heartless
preppy with a nasty streak. Her life was her own, and
she gloried in every moment of it.

Unthinkingly she brushed her mouth with one hand.
That had been definitely odd. No heterosexual male
had kissed her since she'd been old enough to duck. She
would have expected her reaction to be rage, humilia-
tion, disgust.

It hadn't been. Of all things, it had been curiosity. If
it had been…interesting…to be kissed by a man she despised, how would it feel to be kissed by a man she liked?
Found attractive? Might it not be even more interesting?

She was thirty-two years old, getting older by the minute. Emelia, with her absorption in her own beauty, might
not think that would matter to someone like Laura, but
it was beginning to matter very much indeed. Too many
of her married friends had gone through hell and back,
trying to conceive. If she wanted to have children of her
own, she was going to have to do something about it, and
soon. And she desperately wanted children. Her nieces
and nephews simply weren't enough to fill the hole in
her heart where she allowed no one else.

She didn't really need a man. There were any number
of programs in New York to assist a woman in need of
conception and nothing else. She'd been thinking more
and more about it, the decision still eluding her. It wasn't
an easy decision—how could you tell your child she'd
been conceived in a doctor's office? That her father was
nothing more than a vial of fluid?

Laura had never had much of a father. Jefferson Winston had been a cool, demanding man, never allowing a

grubby, affectionate daughter to climb into his lap, never showing any emotion for his family other than cold impatience. When his mother-in-law had bypassed Jilly and left the Glass House to Laura he'd been temporarily paternal, until she made it very clear that she had no intention of following his advice and disposing of the old albatross of a building. He'd walked away from her then, and within a year of her nineteenth birthday he'd been dead of a heart attack.

No child needed that kind of father. They were better off with a single mother and no paternal heritage. Still, maybe she'd been too rigid in her vision of the future. Maybe there was room in her life for a gentle man, a kind man. One who wouldn't interfere in her life, one who would take care of the children, cook dinner. God, what she needed was a wife, she thought with amusement. A nice, old-fashioned, docile wife. She could think of any number of men among her acquaintances who could fit that description, but she also wanted one capable of and interested in fathering a baby.

What she needed was the antithesis of Michael Dubrovnik. At the moment she couldn't think of anyone who fitted that description, but then, she hadn't been looking. Maybe it was time to broaden her horizons a bit.

The phone rang, and she answered it, dealing with business with her customary cool efficiency. And only she knew that half her brain was wondering which designer she would get to do her wedding dress…

"What's our next step?" Michael found he didn't want to look into Zach's knowing eyes, so he concentrated on a satisfyingly dark glass of cheap Scotch in his hand. He had expensive tastes, and he liked to indulge them, but every now and then he liked to remind himself where he came from, and the thick, peaty taste of bargain basement Scotch brought back the lean years, when things had been so much simpler.

"She's got the injunction. You can't blast until the hearing, which is four weeks away."

"Can you get the hearing moved up?"

"I'm already working on it. I can't guarantee results, but I expect if I call in a few favors, we can have it within two weeks."

"Better than nothing." He set down the glass and leaned back in his chair, staring at but not seeing the others in the Plaza bar. "What else?"

"We can do some digging. Bulldozers and backhoes can do all sorts of damage if improperly run."

"It's a shame I didn't get more experienced workers," Michael murmured.

"A damned shame," Zach echoed. "The fines might be considerable."

For a brief moment Michael's dark blue eyes met Zach's. "Am I in some sort of financial difficulty that you've failed to mention to me?"

"You're disgustingly solvent."

"Then I don't think I'll spend too much time worrying about the fines."

"What about Marita?"

Michael frowned, and his long fingers tightened on the glass. "What about her?"

"Is that part of your plan? Sabotage Glass Faces and leave Laura Winston with no alternative but to sell?"

A faint smile played around Michael's face. "You know, I hadn't thought of that. You can be very devious, Zach."

"I've learned from watching a master."

"Flatterer." He took a deep swallow. "Actually, my interest in Marita has nothing to do with the Glass House. I was thinking it was time to get married again."

"Isn't this a little sudden? You just met her yesterday."

"I'm not planning on jumping into anything. She might not do. But it isn't sudden. I've been thinking of getting remarried for several years. I want children before I'm too old to enjoy them. I want someone to leave all this to."

"Sounds reasonable. What makes you think Marita will be the lucky girl?"

Michael shrugged. "She's very beautiful. She doesn't talk much. And there's a certain mystery, a certain air of secrecy about her that appeals to me."

"And you want to solve that mystery?" Zach prompted.

"Not at all. I don't want to wallow in anyone else's psyche, not even my wife's. I expect if I knew what lay behind that beautiful face, I'd be thoroughly bored. No, she can keep her secrets, carry them to the grave as far as I'm concerned. As long as she provides me with what I need."

"That's what I like about you, Mischa. You're such a romantic."

"Thirty-nine is a little old to be romantic, don't you think?"

"Speaking from the advanced age of fifty-eight, I'll inform you that thirty-nine is exactly the age to be romantic. But you won't believe me if I tell you—you'll have to find it out for yourself."

"You think I should fall passionately in love with Marita?" He didn't bother to hide his amusement at the notion.

"No. I think you should wait and find someone you can't live without."

"That day isn't going to come."

"That day's going to come sooner than you think, old man. Trust me."

Michael shook his head. "You're full of crap, you know that? Have you been reading romance novels in your spare time?"

"Have you ever read one?"

"No."

"Maybe you should. You might learn a thing or two about love and passion."

"I haven't had any complaints so far."

"Perhaps, but that doesn't mean…"

Michael held up a hand. "Let's not talk about my love life, Zach. It bores me. I'm much more interested in Laura Winston right now. Once I deal with her, we can sort out my affairs of the heart." He didn't like Zach's grin.

"Okay," his associate said. "We'll talk about Laura Winston and not your sex life. Are you sure the two aren't connected?"

"God help me, do you think I'd be interested in going to bed with Laura Winston?"

"True enough. She's not very pretty."

Why did he feel the need to defend her? "Don't be an idiot, Zach. Not everyone can look like Marita. A hell of a lot of men would find Laura more appealing than a Barbie doll like Marita."

"But not you?"

"Don't play games with me. I like tall, leggy, beautiful women in bed. Laura Winston, despite her attractive qualities, is simply not my type. I'm more interested in smashing her than sleeping with her."

"So do it. You know you can. I've never known you to be squeamish before."

"I'm not being squeamish now. I just think I can get

the Glass House away from her without destroying her life." He signaled for a refill, a double this time.

"You haven't done your homework, Mischa. Once she loses the Glass House, her life will be destroyed. Don't kid yourself."

"Then maybe she needs a new life." He took a deep swallow of the fresh drink.

"Is that for you to decide?"

"It's none of my business. All that matters to me is getting that building away from her, as soon as possible. And it's taking too damned long."

"I'll turn up the heat," Zach said.

"Do that," Michael muttered, thinking illogically of the startled expression on Laura Winston's face when he'd foolishly kissed her. "Do it fast."

"I can't find him, Laura." Susan's tone was bordering on the frantic. "I checked at his apartment, at the bars he usually frequents, at the club. No one's seen him, and he's not answering his cell."

Laura leaned back in her chair, holding the telephone against her cheek. Night had fallen, the early twilight of autumn, and she hadn't bothered to turn on any more lights. The dusky half-light illuminated the empty offices of Glass Faces well enough, and she liked the sense of isolation. "Calm down, Susan. Frank's not going to do anything foolish. He has too much ego."

"It's just been effectively trashed." On the other end of the line Susan sounded close to tears.

"Do you really think Frank's going to hurt himself?"

A pause. "I suppose not."

"He's probably out getting drunk."

"Not in his usual places."

"His usual places are trendy night spots, Susan. Not

the place for a man to do a bit of serious drinking. He'll probably drown his sorrows and head on home. Just leave a message for him and wait."

"He probably won't go home alone." The misery in her voice was at its peak.

"No, he probably won't," Laura admitted.

"Damn it, Laura, I wanted to help him."

"He's probably too big a fool to accept it. Go home, darling. Take a drink, a shower and go to bed. Frank's a big boy now. He'll be all right. You know that, don't you?"

There was a long pause at the other end. "I know it," Susan said finally. "I'm just not sure about me."

Laura was left sitting there as the phone went dead. She'd kicked off her silver spiked heels and her stockinged feet were up on the glass-topped desk. She pulled off the glasses and tossed them onto the desk, wearily running a hand through her hair. Why did everything have to fall apart all at once?

There was a benefit at the Guggenheim tonight. She'd promised the Graham twins she'd go, but right now all she wanted was peace and quiet. Her energy level had sunk dramatically. What she needed was another cup of Michael Dubrovnik's coffee.

What she needed was Michael Dubrovnik out of her life, she reminded herself. Despite her earlier fantasies, what she needed was blessed solitude.

Which she wasn't about to have. She heard the creaking of the ancient elevator long before it reached her floor. The sight of a male figure silhouetted in the hallway started a sudden, unreasonable panic inside her, until she realized it couldn't be Dubrovnik. He'd take the Otis— he'd never waste his time on the gilt and glass elevators.

The man approached the glass doors and opened one.

She still couldn't see more than his general outline. He was taller than Dubrovnik, and much more massively built. His hair was very short and a light color, and his clothes lacked style.

"Miss Winston?" His voice was flat, warm and Midwestern. Not for one moment did Laura worry. This wasn't a psycho, a rapist, a druggie. He stepped into the pool of light, and she looked up into a handsome, fresh face, clean bone structure, worried brown eyes. He looked like someone from Kansas, and Laura instantly thought of Marita.

"You're looking for Mary Ellen?" she questioned gently.

The man, who must have been in his thirties but still looked like a boy, smiled. "Yes, ma'am," he said. "Have I come to the right place?"

A tall, blond, handsome farmer, Laura thought hazily. Someone who could have stepped out of a Frank Capra movie. Clean and honest and Republican. The perfect husband and father.

"Yes," Laura said, her smile absolutely dazzling. "You've come to exactly the right place."

# *Chapter* 7

The telephone purred quietly in the dimly lighted loft. After two rings the answering machine clicked in; he heard a voice, loud in the silence, thick with panic and tears.

"Frank? It's me again. Susan. Where are you? I've been everywhere, called everywhere. Tell me you're all right. Laura's worried about you. I...I'm worried about you. For God's sake, Frank, pick up the damned phone." There was a long pause filled with only the sound of tear-laden breathing, then a short, obscene curse, and the phone clicked off.

Frank sat there in the darkness, a faint smile lighting his face. He wouldn't have thought Susan would even know such a word, much less use it.

He should have gotten up and answered the phone. He should call her back. That was the third message in an hour, and she might have left any number of earlier ones that he'd simply erased, never bothering to check them. But the fact of the matter was, he couldn't.

Couldn't get up, that is. He was gloriously, splendidly, stinking drunk, and if he tried to make it to the phone, he'd fall flat on his beautiful face. Not that that face did him much good, he thought, tipping back the bottle and letting the warm whiskey burn its way down his throat. If he did make it as far as the telephone, he doubted he could come up with a coherent sentence. If Susan heard him stumbling and mumbling, she'd be down there in a flash. And in his current condition he'd be no good to either of them.

No, Susan was going to have to worry a little bit longer. The thought of Susan worrying about him made him shed a few drunken tears, which he quickly wiped away. He wasn't used to drinking this much, and it always made him maudlin. Tomorrow he'd have a miserable headache, a sick stomach, and the sour certainty that he'd punished no one but himself. Even tomorrow he wouldn't be in much better shape to deal with Susan, to tell her what he'd finally accepted.

So why wait till tomorrow, he reasoned, rising to his feet with inebriated dignity. He swayed for a moment, looking across the apartment to the telephone. Before he could move, the phone rang again, and after a few seconds Susan's voice once more pierced the darkness.

"Frank, I didn't mean it. There's a job tomorrow, if you want it. It's not much, but it's money. Down at the Seaport—they'll have everything there. Ten o'clock. If you get back in time, just show up. Frank, I'm sorry. I…" The rest of it was muffled, and the phone clicked off.

Frank blinked in the darkness. "I love you too, babe,"

he said. And then he pitched forward, passing out on the moth-eaten Persian carpet by his bed, a beatific smile on his handsome face.

Now that she'd found him, she didn't quite know what to do with him. Laura looked at the man, keeping her face bland and innocent while she sized him up. The first thing she wanted to do was buy him new clothes. Not Armani—Michael Dubrovnik favored Armani and she didn't want there to be any comparison. With his broad shoulders, big hands and handsome face he looked like a man of the people, a man of the country. Denim and leather and maybe just a touch of tweed, she thought, eyeing him with a professional air.

She leaned back in the leather and chrome chair, half of her mind already bemused with her wedding plans. They'd have good strong children together, she thought. Blond-haired, blue-eyed, freckle-faced. Three of them, two years apart. If she could get him away from Marita. "I'll give Mary Ellen a call. What did you say your name was?"

"Jeff," he murmured. "Jeff Carnaby. But don't call her."

Laura left her hand on the phone, schooling her expression to one of quiet interest. "Why not?"

He sank onto the pink leather sling chair, looking absurdly out of place. "She doesn't want to see me," he said morosely.

"Why don't you tell me all about it?" she suggested. "I promise I'm a good listener. By the way, I'm Laura Winston. I run Glass Faces."

For a moment his misery lightened with real surprise. "You aren't what I would have expected."

"No?"

"I would have thought you'd be old and ugly," he said ingenuously. He was smiling at her—a warm, attentive smile that Laura returned with full force—until he remembered why he was there, and his smile vanished. "Mary Ellen and I were engaged," he said. "Had been since she graduated from high school. I thought she'd be happy with me. She told me she would, until she suddenly disappeared. She left a note for me and her mother, telling us it was for the best and not to worry, but I got to thinking she wasn't ever coming back."

Laura didn't know what to say, so she wisely said nothing.

"Mary Ellen called her mother a couple of days ago from a hotel in New York. She wasn't supposed to tell me, but Gretta Murphy couldn't keep a secret if her life depended on it. So I flew in, went straight to the hotel, and then followed her while she went out to lunch with some fancy-looking hoodlum."

Laura grinned at the apt description of Michael Dubrovnik, then she considered the ramifications. "Did he see you?"

"He didn't. She did. But she looked right through me like I was a sheet of glass. I never thought she could look like that. Cold and hard as ice."

"She's starting a new life," Laura said gently. "A very busy, exciting life. I'm sure she didn't mean to be cruel."

"Maybe," Jeff muttered.

"I still don't understand. What do you want?"

"I guess I need to talk to her, to make sure it's over. I can't go on with my life, waiting for her to call, waiting for her to come home. I need to know if she's just been telling me a pack of lies, if she ever loved me at all."

"People change."

"She's only been gone a week and a half."

"She could have been changing right under your nose, and you might not have noticed it. When would you like to talk with her?"

"I don't know."

"I'll arrange something," Laura said, taking charge with her customary energy. "In the meantime, do you have a place to stay?"

"I've got a room at the Holiday Inn. I didn't know Holiday Inns could be so expensive."

"I'll tell you what. Why don't I set a meeting with Marita for tomorrow afternoon? We can meet for lunch ahead of time, you and I, and discuss things."

"Marita?"

"That's Mary Ellen's professional name."

"I don't like it."

"It's going to become a household word."

"Like Mr. Clean," Jeff muttered.

Laura stared at him in surprise for a moment, then giggled. He was showing more and more possibilities all the time. "Do you love her very much?" she asked softly.

"I love who she was. I love Mary Ellen. I'm not so sure I'm in love with Marita."

Better and better. "Go back to your hotel, get a good night's sleep, and we'll work on this tomorrow."

He smiled at her. He had a terrific smile, Laura thought. Lots of straight white teeth, sparkling blue eyes, and real warmth, the likes of which she hadn't seen in New York City since she didn't remember when.

"You've been very kind."

Laura smiled. "Let me walk you to the lobby. It's late, and I've been sitting here for far too long."

"I'm sorry." Jeff jumped up, towering over her. "I've been keeping you from something important."

"I had nothing planned." It was a gentle hint. She'd

already invited him for lunch—it was up to him to think of dinner tonight.

Unfortunately Jeff Carnaby's thought processes weren't as far-reaching as Laura might have hoped. He just shook his head in surprise, following her out into the hall way. "A pretty lady like you without a date?" he murmured. "New York's a darned strange place."

She hadn't heard anyone say darn in at least fifteen years. She smiled up at him. "It certainly is," she agreed, stepping into the elevator. It was the Otis, but this time she couldn't afford to be picky. They rode down smoothly, speedily, smiling at each other, and she luxuriated in the feeling of him towering over her. Life seemed to have once more shifted a good ninety degrees on its axis, and while the notion seemed faintly disturbing, it was also very exciting indeed.

Her little cloud of well-being lasted halfway across the art deco lobby of the Glass House. Lasted until she came up against Michael Dubrovnik hurrying toward the abandoned Otis, pulling at his tie as he went.

He stopped, staring at Laura, staring at her companion, but the last thing Laura wanted was to mess with introductions. What could she say? Marita's former fiancé, meet Marita's future fiancé? It would have been extremely awkward. And while Jeff seemed the most reasonable of men, he might have aggressive tendencies. Like all New Yorkers, Laura thought anyone born west of the Mississippi had hidden cowboy traits. She didn't even know if Kansas was west of the Mississippi, but she wasn't going to take any chances. She didn't want to see Jeff decked in her pristine lobby.

For a brief moment she stopped to consider why she was so certain that it was Jeff who'd end up decked. He was several inches taller than Michael Dubrovnik and much broader. He appeared to be a man who worked with his hands and body, unlike Michael, who used his mind. And yet she would be more than willing to place bets on the outcome, if the two of them ever decided to settle their differences in a fight.

"Who was that?" Jeff questioned as she hustled him out into the cool night air.

"Who?"

"The man in the lobby. The one who took Mary Ellen out to lunch today."

So much for playing innocent. "His name's Michael Dubrovnik. He's an entrepreneur…."

"Even in Rigby, Kansas we've heard of the Whirl-wind," Jeff interrupted, a pensive note in his voice. "What was he doing with Mary Ellen?"

"Uh…"

"Stupid question. Is she seeing anyone else, or is he my major competition?"

Laura was signaling for a taxi, praying for one to show up quickly and end this tricky conversation. As usual, when you really needed one, none was in sight. She turned to look up into Jeff Carnaby's warm blue eyes. "I don't think he's your major competition," she said frankly. "I think Marita is."

For a moment he didn't say anything. And then he nodded. "I'll pick you up at noon," he said, as the long-awaited taxi finally responded to Laura's desperate hand-waving.

"I can swing by the Holiday Inn…."

"I'll come get you," he said firmly. "And I'll take you out to lunch. You pick the place, but I'm paying. Is that understood?"

"That would be very nice," she said gently, leaning

a little as he squashed his big body into the cab. "Good night, Jeff."

She was whistling as she walked back through the empty lobby. Dubrovnik was nowhere to be seen, and she breathed a sigh of relief as she watched the lights above the Otis travel to #9. She'd been afraid he'd by lying in wait, ready to pounce on her. She should have known he'd have better things on his mind.

She punched the elevator button, the glass and gilt doors slid open, and Michael stood there waiting for her, his jacket off by this time, his shirt half unbuttoned, his dark hair rumpled across his forehead.

"I should have known," she said bitterly, stepping into the cage with the hungry lion. "Why'd you send the elevator up to your floor? You didn't have to go to such elaborate ends. I'm not afraid of you."

"You don't strike me as someone who's afraid of anything," Michael rumbled, pushing the ninth-floor button and leaning back against the elevator wall. "I'd gotten on the elevator and pushed my floor before I changed my mind and decided to find out who that man was."

"Why should you care?" She reached over to push #11, but his hand shot out and stopped her.

"Because I spent most of a very uncomfortable lunch having him glare at me, that's why," he said.

"I'd think you'd be used to having people glare at you. Comes with the territory." He was holding her wrist. His fingers were long and slender and very strong, and they wrapped around her small wrist with space to spare, like a human bracelet. She hadn't been held against her will since she was eighteen, and she didn't like it. "Would you let go of me?" She struggled to keep her voice free of the panic and anger that were simmering beneath the surface; a distant, separate part of her was ready to fight, to kick and scream if necessary.

It wasn't necessary at all. He released her immediately, and she noted with surprise that there was no mark on her arm. He hadn't been holding her that tightly, after all.

"I thought you might stop by my floor and have a drink," he said mildly enough, as the doors slid open at the ninth floor.

"Why should I do that?"

"To find out what the enemy has in mind," he suggested affably, holding the doors open with one of those strong, slim hands.

"And what do you have to gain?"

"The same thing." If his grin was supposed to be welcoming he hadn't looked in the mirror recently, Laura thought. Michael Dubrovnik was a wolf if ever she'd seen one, ready to devour any little lamb fool enough to stray into his lair.

But she was no little lamb, she reminded herself. And she wasn't afraid of the Whirlwind, not one tiny bit.

She stepped off the elevator, noticing as she passed him that he wasn't as tall as Jeff, nor as wide, yet for some reason he was much more intimidating. She smiled sweetly, waiting as he unlocked the thick oak door that still had "Swimming Pool News" stenciled across it. "How did you like the restraining order?" she murmured, stepping into his apartment and deliberately shutting away the memory of what had happened the last time she'd been here.

"I didn't," he said, tossing his jacket and tie across the leather sectional sofa and heading for the bar. He began mixing drinks, and without another word turned and handed her a Lillet on ice.

She took it, albeit warily, and sank onto the leather. "How did you know I drink Lillet?"

The wolf's grin again. "I know everything about you, Laura. You may have disparaged my private detectives but they don't really miss much. Not much at all."

She refused to let him intimidate her. If she thought about it, there were things she'd rather die than have him know, but she had no control whatsoever over it. Better not to think about it. He was wrong about one thing, at least. She liked her Lillet with a twist of orange.

"I forgot to get oranges," Michael said, sinking beside her, too close.

"I'll survive."

"So who was that huge man, and why does he hate me?" Michael took a sip of his own drink, something dark amber and whiskey-smelling.

"He's Marita's former fiancé." She waited to see how he'd respond. She was taking a chance in being honest, but she wasn't certain she'd be able to control a confrontation farther down the road, if she didn't make the rapid progress she was hoping for. At least this time she could control the information.

If she expected Dubrovnik to show jealousy or displeasure she was disappointed. "Then why was he staring down at you like he'd just been given Super Bowl tickets? Did you promise to get Marita back for him?"

"Do you care?"

"It's too early to care. I'm most curious. Whom does he want, you or Marita?"

Laura choked in the midst of taking a sip of her drink. "Is that a serious question?"

"Do I look like a frivolous man?"

No, he didn't, Laura thought, staring at the man sitting no more than eighteen inches away from her. With those chilly, dark blue eyes, the broken nose, the hard jaw and Slavic cheekbones, he looked dark and dangerous and determined. Not the sort of man to ask silly questions or accept silly answers. Not the sort to accept anything but exactly what he required.

"He wants Marita," Laura said, intimidated despite herself. "He's going to have to settle for second best. I don't suppose that's something you're familiar with, is it? Settling for second best?"

"I don't," he said, draining his drink. "And in this case you're assuming you're second best?"

"A cocky assumption, I know, but the man seems willing to be distracted." She should get up and leave, she knew she should, but the couch was comfortable, and flirting with danger, with the wolf, was dangerously seductive. She glanced around her, at the sparse, elegant furniture, the plain walls. "Don't you think you should move in some more things? You're going to be here for quite a while. I'd think you'd get tired of camping out."

His grin acknowledged the hit. "I'm not much for Victorian clutter. My mother was a hoarder. I don't think she ever threw out anything in her entire life, and the apartment I grew up in was crammed with knicknacks, embroidered pillows, religious icons, old photographs, crocheted table covers. Just walking from the front door to the kitchen was like running an obstacle course."

"So you vowed to be completely different. You didn't like your mother?"

"My mother was the most wonderful woman who ever lived. She and my father had a perfect marriage, and they luckily died within days of each other. I don't think either of them could have lasted alone. But my mother was very much old country. Smothering, both in her apartment and in her mothering. Which is fine in a mother, but not in a wife."

"What kind of wife do you want?" This was a strange conversation, but Laura was too comfortable, too involved to stop it.

"Someone decorative. Intelligent, but not intent on proving it all the time. Someone who'll give me babies and take good care of them. A good hostess, an interesting companion, but not someone who makes impossible demands all the time. Someone who's good in bed."

"A charming list. You're one of the last all-time sexist pigs, you know that? What kind of impossible demands?" She reached up to push her glasses further up her nose, and then realized with dismay that the glasses were still upstairs.

"I don't want a wife who needs constant attention and reassurance. She'll need to fend for herself. I'm too busy a man to spend my time holding hands."

Laura shook her head, clucking in mock sympathy. "Poor man. A little hand-holding can do wonders for your level of stress. You ought to try it sometime."

"Like this?" He caught one of her hands in his, and for a moment she tried to yank it away. But the fingers wrapped around hers were strong, and any struggle would be undignified. Besides, it was her fault. She'd goaded him deliberately, ignoring the likelihood that he must have held a lot more hands than she ever had.

She plastered a cool, unruffled expression onto her face, leaning back against the soft leather and leaving her hand where it was. "Something like that," she agreed. "But you're wasting it on me."

His thumb was traveling gently across her palm, his long fingers entwining and cupping hers, caressing her knuckles, the narrow back of her hand, skirting the gold and silver rings she wore in abundance. "You may have a point," he murmured, his voice low. "This could be both soothing and stimulating." He placed his palm against hers, his long fingers curving over her own. "I'm just curious about one thing."

"Yes?" She managed to keep her voice flat and bored.

"Why is your hand trembling?"

She snatched her hand away, clenching it into a fist that she would have loved to send into Michael's jaw. "I'm tired," she said. "I'm going upstairs."

"Actually, I'm afraid I have to leave first." He propelled himself out of the cushiony sofa and away from her. "I have to be at a party uptown in twenty minutes. Why don't you stay here and finish your drink? You've barely touched it."

He moved into his bedroom, stripping off his shirt as he went. She allowed herself a furtive glance at his strong, tanned back, before turning to stare fixedly at her drink. "You trust me alone here?"

"Of course." His mocking voice floated into the room. In a moment he was back, buttoning a fresh shirt, a new, darker tie over his shoulder.

Laura didn't like sitting there, watching him tie his tie with a few quick, precise motions, she didn't like watching him tuck his shirt inside his pants and pull on his jacket. It all felt too damned domestic.

"Make yourself at home," he said, heading for the door.

She still hadn't moved. "Enjoy yourself," she said.

She never would like that grin. "You too."

The night air had grown cooler by the time Michael Dubrovnik stepped onto the sidewalk. His Bentley was waiting, Zach and Connie were inside, and he looked down at his suit with a resigned shrug. He should be wearing a tuxedo. He hadn't wanted to take the time to change completely, however. He'd been afraid he'd scare Laura away. He'd managed to get her as far as his apartment, and the trap had been baited. Now he simply wanted to see if she was going to nibble.

Zach leaned out the open door of the Bentley. "What's up?"

"I'll be ready in a minute," Michael said, staring upward. In only a moment he got the answer he was waiting for. The lights on the darkened tenth floor flicked on, as Laura Winston gave in to temptation and searched his offices.

His grin lighted the interior of the limo as he slid inside, dutifully kissing Connie on her patrician cheek. "Nice night, isn't it?" And as they headed off toward uptown he was chuckling to himself.

# Chapter 8

It was more than clear that Michael Dubrovnik wasn't planning to spend much time in the Glass House. Now that the tenth floor was empty of the noisy, chattering crowd, Laura could see that very little occupied the vast room that had once held the slightly seedy offices of the trade journal. A desk, a computer, a leather chair and a bank of telephones sat in front of the smoked glass panels overlooking the city. He had a perfect view of the city. He probably found all the skyscrapers inspiring, Laura thought sourly, pausing on one foot and massaging the other. She'd left her shoes on the narrow metal service stairs. There was no telling if Michael might suddenly return, and she didn't want her impractical footwear to slow her down. Ginger Rogers might be able to dance backward in high heels; Laura Winston hadn't yet perfected even a short sprint in the damned things. But she was not going to spend her life being five foot one and a half around people like Michael Dubrovnik, even if she had to endure podiatric torture.

The desk was absolutely bare. She headed straight for the computer, sinking into the comfortable chair and turning it on, but the computer had been rigged to protect its secrets. No sooner had it warmed up than it demanded a password. Laura made a few desultory guesses; at the third incorrect one the machine turned itself off in an indignant huff.

Laura Winston wasn't one to give up, but she had also never been the sort to waste her time pining after something that was out of reach. No wonder Michael Dubrovnik had been so cavalier about leaving her alone in his den. His secrets were well protected.

Moving over to the windows, she looked down to the vacant lot beside the Glass House. The earth-moving equipment was a set of silent, bulky, evil shapes in the city-lighted darkness. Tomorrow or the next day they'd start in again. She couldn't be certain of what they were doing, but she wouldn't have been surprised if Dubrovnik, or whoever was next in his chain of command, had ordered the bulldozers and backhoes to spend their working time driving full force into the already compromised foundations of the Glass House. If the building was going to collapse, she could only hope that Michael Dubrovnik was trapped inside when it went.

She was about to head for the door, temporarily vanquished, when she decided to try the computer one more time. She stood in front of the intelligent beastie, turned it on, and watched as the amber screen haughtily demanded the password. "Whirlwind," she typed. The machine made a rude noise. "Glass House."

With a whir and a buzz of machinery, the computer

went into gear, and a menu appeared on the screen. She searched around his files and found one entitled Payoffs.

She sank bank into the chair, letting out a silent whistle of shock and appreciation. There in front of her was a list of payoffs to city officials, from minor bureaucrats up to the mayor's office itself. Enough shameful information to put Michael Dubrovnik out of commission for a good long time.

It took her a moment to figure out how to run the sleek printer. It took her another few minutes to turn the machines off and make certain everything was exactly as she'd found it. Clutching the paper in her hand, she sped out of the room, onto the metal stairs and up the next flight to her apartment, practically sizzling with triumph. She had Michael Dubrovnik exactly where she wanted him, clutched in her angry fist, and all she had to do was tighten her grip.

She threw herself onto her couch, chuckling to herself. For the time being she wasn't going to do a damned thing about it. The restraining order would keep Dubrovnik at bay, and when it was up she'd simply present her information to the right officials and watch the fur fly.

Of course, she could always try blackmail. Instead of taking her damning information to the city government, she could present it to Dubrovnik himself, offering him immunity if he'd just leave her the hell alone. The idea had merit, but a thousand drawbacks. If Michael knew she had that information, he could take steps to cover his butt, rendering her ace in the hole useless. On the other hand, she didn't necessarily want to see the man jailed and disgraced. Slapped down, yes. Destroyed, no.

She'd have to wait and see. Timing was everything in this, but fortunately that restraining order had given her the leisure to figure out her best defense. He might decide to retire from the battle gracefully, and she'd never have to use the dirty tricks. Of course, his bribing of city officials was a fairly nasty trick in itself, and the man didn't deserve her misguided protection. He'd managed to get to a few surprising people, including the city comptroller, her honorary uncle Jake Feldstein. When she'd first seen Uncle Jake's name in the midst of all those bribe-takers, she'd let out a silent whistle of dismay. If she turned in Dubrovnik, she'd be turning in Uncle Jake. She wasn't quite sure if she was ready to do that.

Maybe the best thing was to deal with Michael Dubrovnik himself, rather than turn in the list of payoffs. That way she could protect her Uncle Jake from his one slip into sleaziness, and protect Dubrovnik at the same time. Not that the Whirlwind needed her protection, she reminded herself. Not that he deserved it. But if she was able to keep him away from the Glass House, she didn't really care whether he paid for his wicked ways or not. She'd just as soon he was safely out of her life, making mischief elsewhere.

And now she had the information to ensure that he would do just that, she thought, rolling off the couch and heading toward her sound system. She chose a song, cranked up the volume, and knew a moment's regret that Michael wasn't down below to be bothered by the noise. With a mischievous grin, she began to dance around her apartment, spinning and whirling, leaping onto the sofa, bouncing off the chairs, kicking against the white plastered walls. For once in her life, the future looked very sweet indeed.

At a quarter past two in the morning Michael Dubrovnik quietly walked up the utility stairs between the two floors he rented in the Glass House. His apartment was just as he'd left it, as he'd expected it to be, and he wondered briefly whether the trap he'd laid had been too cunning. Maybe he'd overestimated Ms. Laura Winston. Maybe she wasn't the nemesis he was beginning to view her as.

The pair of high, high heels lay just outside the hallway door. He picked one up, staring at it meditatively. He knew she couldn't still be inside—the wall of windows had been dark when he'd returned from a midnight supper with Zach and Connie. She must have forgotten her shoes, Cinderella after the ball. She had very small feet, not much larger than his hands. And her red leather, high-heeled shoes were very sexy.

He shoved them into the pocket of his jacket and headed into the tenth-floor office. Nothing had been moved, nothing had been changed. He went straight to the computer and turned it on, noting with pleasure the flashing amber message. "Security breached," it read.

He turned to check the printer. The paper with its infinitesimal mark was gone. She'd found what she'd been looking for, printed it and left, forgetting her shoes in her excitement.

"Gotcha, Miss Laura Winston," Michael Dubrovnik said quietly, a look of almost satanic pleasure lighting his dark face. "And you don't even realize it."

Marita kept her face an astonished blank as she looked down at the tiny woman opposite her. It was after ten in the morning, and she'd already grown accustomed to sleeping late, but Laura Winston had sounded so adamant when she'd called an hour ago that Marita decided it would behoove her to be conciliatory. At least for now. Later she wouldn't need Laura Winston. At the moment she'd better watch her step.

"Jeff Carnaby is here?" she echoed, knowing exactly how she'd look. She'd practiced the expression and a dozen others in the mirrors, and she'd gotten this one down pat. Innocence, surprise, puzzled concern. She could see by Laura's reaction that it was working. And Laura was no easy mark.

"He followed you to the restaurant yesterday. He said you looked right through him." Her tone was faintly skeptical, but Marita wasn't discouraged.

"I didn't see him. God, I can't believe he'd follow me all the way to New York. He's such a sweet man. I never wanted to hurt him." She laughed ruefully.

"You were engaged?" Laura prodded.

"Not really. We just sort of…dated. He read something more into it than I did, and I tried to let him down easy when I left Rigby. Unfortunately my mother always encouraged him." She shrugged. "It was wrong from the start. I should have seen he wouldn't want to let me go. I'm sorry he bothered you."

"Oh, he didn't bother me," Laura said instantly. "As a matter of fact, I found him quite charming. And I think he's more than ready to let you go. He just wants to hear it from you."

A small frown creased Marita's face before she quickly erased it. "I'm glad he's being sensible," she said smoothly. "I'd be happy to talk with him."

"He's taking me out to lunch. I'll bring him by afterward and you can sort things out. You're certain you don't want him?" Laura prodded again.

Marita stared at her in amazement. "Do you?"

Laura's grin was answer enough. "I might. That is, if you're sure it's over between you two."

"It's over," Marita said firmly, not sure if she liked this new development. "It never existed." All the while her mind was working feverishly. Could Jeff, her faithful, doglike, devoted Jeff be that ready to turn to someone new? Someone like the tiny, trendy, cynical Laura Winston, after he'd spent the last few years devoted to someone who epitomized grace and beauty and gentle femininity? It didn't seem possible.

Until a week ago Marita had had him convinced that they'd be married in the spring and have three or four babies by the time she was thirty, and Jeff had believed her Norman Rockwell picture of the future.

Marita had no intention of having children for a long, long time. Maybe later, when she was safely married to a man with enough money, so that she wouldn't need to bother with the messy little creatures until they were old enough to be civilized. But farmers, even those whose careers bordered on agribusiness, couldn't afford nannies and nursemaids.

Nevertheless, she certainly wasn't pleased about the ease with which her faithful lover was accepting his dismissal. Even if he'd followed her halfway across the country, it seemed he'd only done so to make sure he was free.

She was half tempted to crook her perfectly manicured little finger and call him back—just to reassure herself that she still had the power to do so. But that would be a foolish mistake, and Marita didn't make foolish mistakes. She didn't want him, and Laura Winston did. If she played her cards carefully, this could be of great benefit.

She gave Laura Winston her best smile. "I'll be more than happy to see him. Anytime you want."

Laura nodded, seemingly satisfied, though the woman was darned secretive. Marita could never be sure if her newfound mentor was reacting as she was supposed to. "I'll have Susan give you a call," Laura said. "I was thinking of setting up some go-sees, but it might be wiser to wait."

"Go-sees?"

"A necessary evil, Marita. The people who will hire you want to look you over. It's pounding the pavement, basically."

"I thought we weren't going to do that? I thought we were going to wait and have them come to us?" A real thread of panic speared her. Was her incipient triumph crumbling before it even came together? She didn't want to be just a model. Laura had whetted her already voracious appetite for fame and money. Marita wasn't ready to settle for anything less than the top of the profession, and she had every intention of starting out there.

Laura's smile was hardly reassuring. "I haven't made up my mind yet. Susan will give you a call." And with an airy wave of her small, delicate hand the woman was gone.

Marita turned to stare at her reflection in the huge mirror. She was beginning to hate her luxury suite at the hotel. She'd hardly been out at all. Once to a party at the ridiculously antique-looking building where Glass Faces resided. Another to lunch with Michael Dubrovnik. She'd been terrified when she'd looked up and seen Jeff glowering at her. But her luck had held. Jeff hadn't come over and punched her date on the nose. Michael had been suitably flattering, and she'd seen that look often enough in men's eyes to recognize it. Dubrovnik wanted her. Not badly enough, not yet. But he would. And when she was ready, she'd make sure he paid for it. After all, he could afford it. And she was worth it.

Michael Dubrovnik was in a foul mood. Ms. Anthony, a stern, grandmotherly type who stood no nonsense from irascible millionaires, had burst into tears at the end of the day. Michael had had to apologize, since Ms. Anthony was the best secretary he'd had in decades, and that apology had made him even grumpier. By the time Zach showed up just after eight, he was ready to tear heads off.

"You're late."

"Go to hell," Zach said genially, shutting the ninth-floor door behind him and heading for the bar. "You keep me very busy." He poured both himself and Michael a tall, dark glass of whiskey and thrust it into his associate's hand. "Drink this, calm down and tell me what's eating you."

Michael did as he was told, leaning back and glaring at Zach even as the whiskey burned its way pleasantly into his stomach. "You know damned well what's eating me. Laura Winston."

"I thought you had her under control. Didn't the trap work?"

"Oh, it worked just fine. Right now she's the smug owner of a piece of paper incriminating me in all sorts of illegal bribes and payoffs. She'll be so busy holding what she thinks is her trump card that she won't take the necessary precautions. When she least expects it the bottom will drop out, and she'll have no choice but to hand over the Glass House to me and be glad I'm still willing to pay her such an exorbitant amount."

"Then why are you in such a bad mood?"

"I'm tired of waiting. I'm tired of messing around with this decrepit building, I'm tired of being bested by a snippy little girl. What's happening tomorrow?"

"Same as before. They'll do foundation work, maybe make a few mistakes here and there. I'm assuming you don't mind paying for overtime. Most people don't work on weekends."

"Most people don't work for me. They know what they're doing?" Michael snapped. "I don't want lawsuits on my head. I don't want this damned building to come crashing down and kill dozens of people."

"We've got the best people in the business. I've got half a dozen men and women on the job with nothing more to do but watch for the first signs of collapse. We'll get the building cleared in time if it comes to that."

"It might have to. I don't think that phony payoff list is going to be enough."

"Mischa, she's just an overage New York debutante playing at a career. She can't possibly hold out against you."

"That's what you think. The woman's a menace. She keeps throwing Marita at my head, and while I might normally be interested, right now I'm too involved in squashing Ms. Winston to give a damn about beautiful women."

"So what's bugging you right now? If anything, you're closer to your goal. What's put you in such a foul mood?"

Michael considered the question. "I think it's the fact that she's busy chasing after some damned man as if she hadn't a care in the world, while I can't even spare an evening out with the most beautiful woman I've met in ages."

"You could spare the time," Zach said. "You just don't want to."

"Maybe I don't."

"And maybe you don't resent the fact that Laura Winston has the time and energy for a little on the side. Maybe you resent the fact that Laura Winston is interested in anyone at all."

Michael laughed, genuinely amused for the first time in hours. "Very funny. If you think I'm sexually interested in a sharp-tongued waif, then you've been wasting the twenty years you've known me."

"She's the heir to a building worth a fair number of million dollars," Zach pointed out. "I'd hardly call her a waif."

"You ever hear the expression 'land-poor'? Ms. Winston is in deep trouble financially, as you well know. All we have to do is tighten the screws."

"You want me to see to it?"

Michael considered it for a moment, then shook his head, rising from the sofa and heading for the door. "Not yet," he murmured.

"Where are you going?"

He paused at the door. "We're finished for the night, aren't we? There's nothing new to report?"

"Nothing new. I repeat, where are you going, Mischa? I know you too well."

He considered giving Zach a well-deserved put-down. And then he grinned, reluctantly. "The damnable thing about you, Zach, is that you're right too damned much of the time. I'm going to badger Laura Winston. I can't stand sitting around here and doing nothing."

"And you insist you're not interested in her." Zach was patently skeptical.

"The day I prefer a feisty little harpy to someone like Marita," Michael said, "is the day the Whirlwind runs out of steam. See you tomorrow." And without another word he headed up the utility stairs, whistling tunelessly.

## Chapter 9

She had absolutely no right to feel as she did, Laura chided herself. Things were going very well indeed, if she just stopped to look at them in perspective. Marita was giving up all claim to Jeff Carnaby. The fact that they were having dinner tonight as a farewell gesture was a drawback, but one Laura could put up with. After all, she needed him free of any strings. She couldn't compete with someone of Marita's staggering looks, not unless Marita was willing to let go.

So that was going well. She had Michael Dubrovnik's list of payoffs in the safe in her apartment, tucked in beside her grandmother's gaudy, nineteenth-century emeralds and the perfectly matched pink pearls that her unloving father had given her on her debut. She never had been, never would be a person who could wear pink pearls, even ones of such rare beauty, and the gesture from her father had been too little, too late. If things got really bad she'd sell them, along with the emeralds, but she knew perfectly well that that would only buy her time, and not much of it. Besides, on nights when she was feeling particularly bitter she liked to take the pearls out and feel sorry for herself.

Even Susan's quiet misery would have an eventual benefit. She was mourning the loss of a dream, an unattainable dream. Everyone had to let go of their dreams sooner or later, Laura thought. Susan was lucky she'd managed to hold on to them into her late twenties. Laura's had been ripped away the night of the Junior Assembly.

She didn't want to think about that again. Think about Susan, she reminded herself. Her assistant had packed up all of Frank's papers, his portfolio and the check that had just come in. He still wasn't answering his phone, but Susan had a key to his apartment.

"Are you sure you want to do this?" Laura had questioned her gently. The only person in the world she was gentle with was Susan.

"I'm sure. The sooner I get his things out of here, his file closed, the sooner I can start behaving like a normal human being again." She managed a wry, self-mocking smile, but Laura wasn't fooled. "I'm a bit too old for teenage crushes, don't you think?"

"That doesn't mean you have to settle."

Susan's smile grew a little braver. "I know. That's why I'm getting rid of things. Including his key. I'm not going to be bringing him chicken soup when he gets a cold anymore. I'm not going to pick up his mail and water his plants when he's out of town on a shoot."

"Sucker," Laura chided.

"I know, I know. I've seen the light, I'm ready to move on with my life. I just need to tie up some loose ends."

"What if he's there?"

"I can't imagine he would be. He doesn't seem to have been in his loft for more than a few minutes in the last seventy-two hours. But if he's there, it'll be even better. Then I can say goodbye. A sense of closure is important, don't you think?"

"I suppose so. What if he doesn't feel like losing his plant waterer and chicken soup maker?"

Susan shook her head. "You never liked Frank much, did you?"

"That's where you're wrong. I liked him very much. I just didn't like what he was doing to you."

"And that's where you made your mistake. He wasn't doing anything to me. I was doing it to myself. He didn't need me to make chicken soup for him. There were half a dozen women willing to do the same. Women just tend to want to do things for Frank."

"He's a user."

"Maybe. But not an ungrateful one. And if people kept throwing things at your head, do you really think you'd have the moral stamina to refuse them?"

"Probably not."

"So," said Susan, hoisting the box in her arms. "I'll say goodbye to him for you if I happen to see him."

"Don't cry," Laura advised.

"Are you kidding? I'd rather die."

Maybe, thought Laura. But she wouldn't place any bets on it.

She moved through the spacious offices, flicking off lights. She couldn't understand why she felt so restless. Maybe it was the weather. It had been a hot, muggy September day, and heat lightning sizzled in the thick city air. She could see it snaking across the sky through the smoked glass panels. If there was any justice in this life, that lightning would find Michael Dubrovnik and strike him dead.

However, with her luck the lightning would find Dubrovnik safely ensconced in his ninth-floor apartment. The Glass House had withstood blasting, enraged bulldozers, two world wars, blizzards, hurricanes, and the vicissitudes of the de Kelsey family fortune. At this point in its venerable life it might not withstand the wrath of God in the form of a lightning bolt.

She locked the door behind her and headed for the utility stairs, rubbing the narrow bridge of her nose behind her glasses. She slammed into Michael Dubrovnik before she realized what she was doing.

His hands righted her. Strong hands, first holding, then immediately releasing her. "What the hell are you doing here?" she demanded sourly, dropping her glasses back onto her nose and staring at him defiantly through the clear lenses. The safety door swung shut, leaving the two of them cocooned on the narrow landing.

St. Clair de Kelsey had been a thorough man. Even the utility stairs in the Glass House had elegance. The space was lighted by Italian bronze wall sconces, the railing and stairs were of wrought iron, the walls a now faded but once glorious shade of peach. The light was muted, playing with the shadows as Laura glared up at her nemesis.

"Looking for Cinderella," he replied, unmoved by her displeasure. He held up her red leather shoes, and she noted with an odd, uneasy feeling that her size five and a half shoe fitted far too well into his large hand.

She snatched them away, belatedly remembering where she had left them. Outside his apartment. "Thanks," she said with little grace.

"Did you enjoy yourself last night?"

"What do you mean?"

"When I left you alone in my apartment. Did you give in to temptation and search the place, or were you honorable and noble?"

"Hell, no. If I tried to conduct this battle with honor, you'd probably stomp me into the ground. I searched your apartment, and then I searched your office," she said frankly. "As you very well know, I couldn't find a damned thing."

"Not even on the computer?"

"I could barely turn the damned thing on," she lied. "I don't know much about computers. And yours wanted a password!" Her indignation at the memory wasn't feigned. "I tried one or two possibilities, but your computer didn't like them and shut itself off." That much at least was true. When you lie it's always best to stick as close to the truth as possible, Laura had learned long ago. And since she spent a certain amount of time lying, she'd learned to do it right.

Dubrovnik was looking at her with a veiled expression in his dark blue eyes. What had Jeff Carnaby called him? A fancy-looking hoodlum? At first it had seemed amusingly apt. Now Laura wasn't so certain. With his narrow, unforgiving face, Michael didn't look so much like a hit man tonight. He looked just slightly like a tired businessman, with his Armani jacket rumpled, his shirt unbuttoned, his tie loosened. He looked human and vulnerable, not like the wolf at all.

"How about a truce?" he asked quietly.

She was disappointed. She didn't believe for one moment that he was ready to call off their war. He wasn't going to give in that easily, not unless he knew she now held the trump card. And there was no way he could know that, unless his damned half-human computer was a snitch as well.

"Permanent or temporary?" she asked.

"Temporary, of course. More of a ceasefire, actually." he ran a weary hand through his thick black hair, rumpling it, and Laura had the sudden insane, irrational urge to smooth it down again. Rumpled hair made the Whirlwind seem real, touchable. She wanted him tough again. "For tonight. For dinner."

"You're asking me out to dinner?"

"I hate eating alone."

"I'm sure you can find a dozen women who'd drop whatever they were doing to go out with you."

"I don't want half a dozen women. I don't want to be charming, I don't want to flirt, I don't want to banter."

"So you thought I'd do?" She should be outraged. Instead she was amused. "Some men think I'm worth flirting with."

"I didn't say you weren't. I just said that with you I didn't have to."

"It would be a waste of time," she agreed. "I suppose if I come out with you, you think I'd let something slip. Something you could use against me later."

"Maybe. But the same thing could happen with me. Why don't you see if I can't be a little indiscreet after my second Scotch?"

She considered the notion, and Dubrovnik himself, for a moment. Her restlessness, her malaise, had vanished. Jeff Carnaby and Marita were a million miles away; even Susan's troubles were now her own responsibility. "All right," she said finally. "But if you say anything useful, I'll eat your computer. You didn't get to where you are by being indiscreet."

"No," he agreed. "But I haven't come up against too many Laura Winstons in my time."

"Lucky for you."

"Indeed. Do you need a coat?"

"On a hot night like this? No."

"An umbrella? There might be rain."

"I don't own one."

"All right," he said, holding out his arm like a proper gentleman. "Let's go."

She looked at him. Being a gently reared child of private schools, cotillions and Edgartown summers, she was used to taking a man's arm. She wasn't used to touching someone like Michael Dubrovnik. The few times she had, she'd felt the energy humming through him—an energy she found oddly threatening.

But she couldn't let him know that. She put her hand on his forearm, lightly, so that she wouldn't have to feel the bone and muscle beneath the rumpled linen jacket. "Let's go," she agreed, tossing her head back recklessly. "I'm very, very hungry."

His dark eyes glowed as they swept over her small, narrow body. "So," he said, "am I."

Susan clutched the cardboard box to her chest as the taxi careened down Second Avenue. She should have headed straight to Frank's apartment when she left work, but she couldn't quite work up the courage. For all that she'd insisted to Laura that she wanted to say goodbye, when push came to shove she couldn't quite bring herself to do it. If she faced Frank she would cry, she knew it. And the whole miserable situation was degrading enough.

So she'd gone home, taken a shower, poured herself two glasses of Chardonnay, and called Frank's number to make certain he was out. As usual the answering machine had clicked on, and Susan knew that she was safe.

It was a warm night, and she dressed accordingly in a blue-flowered shift. It was one of her favorite dresses;

she looked soft and sweet and innocent in it, and clearly not the sort of woman for a man like Frank Buckley. She tucked her hair into a loose knot at the back of her neck, put on just a trace of makeup, because no woman worth her salt steps outside her door in Manhattan without makeup, and grabbed the first taxi she saw, before she could change her mind.

The windows in Frank's third-floor walk-up were dark. Only after the taxi disappeared around the corner did Susan realize she should have had him wait for her. Taxis didn't cruise in this area, at least, not often. She'd have to call for one. At least his apartment was empty.

She rang his doorbell just to make certain, then rapped sharply on the door. When she let herself in, the familiar smells assailed her. Spices. Leather. And the faint, enticing scent of Frank's cologne. He was the only man she knew who used it. He'd been part of that very expensive advertising campaign, and he'd taken a liking to the stuff. It was subtle, enticing, but unfortunately both for the manufacturer and for Frank it had never caught on.

Lucky for herself though, Susan thought, flicking on the lights and closing the door behind her. She'd never smell that cologne without feeling her heart twist inside her.

Frank's apartment was half of an old loft, one huge, untidy room cluttered with paraphernalia. The bed, a sprawling affair in the middle of the room, was covered with dark-patterned sheets and exotic-looking throws. The floor was booby-trapped with Oriental carpets in various stages of decrepitude, and the walls were hung with more Oriental wall hangings. The entire place looked exotic, sensual, foreign. A far cry from Susan's patchwork quilts and stenciled borders.

With a sigh she set down the box on a low table, look-

ing around her one last time. She ought to leave him a
note, but couldn't quite bring herself to do it. Besides,
she'd already made enough of a fool of herself on his answering machine. The box and the key would be enough.

She headed back for the door, noticing for the first
time that there were no pictures on the walls. In particular, no pictures of Frank. When she'd visited before, when
Tracey Michaels had been in partial residence, the walls
had been hung with pictures of Tracey looking haughty,
seductive, innocent et cetera. Of course those were gone,
but Frank didn't have any of his own to replace them.
Curious. She'd never been in a model's apartment before
where the walls weren't covered with photographic im-
ages of the occupant.

It wasn't so much ego, she'd always thought. It was a
reminder of who and what they were. Apparently Frank
didn't need reminders. Or maybe he'd just gotten rid of
them.

She heard the key in the door when she was only a
few feet away from it. Panic sliced through her, and she
looked around in sudden desperation for a back door,
for a window to dive out of, for a closet to hide in. Before she could do more than that the door opened and
Frank walked in, looking weary, unshaven and absolutely beautiful.

He looked up and saw her standing there, holding her
breath. And then he smiled, a warm, welcoming smile
that could have melted her bones. "Thank God it's you,"
he said, shutting the door behind him. Locking it. Three
times. And putting the chains and safety bar on. "I was
afraid it was someone I didn't want to see."

She refused to allow herself to take pleasure in that
statement. She'd been pathetically grateful for crumbs

before. She simply had to let go. "Do that many people have keys to this place?"

"A fair number." He moved across the room and began opening windows to the hot night air. Outside lightning crackled, mixing with the street sounds. "Sorry I can't put on the air conditioner, but my hydro bill is already close to the national debt. Sit down and I'll get you a drink."

"I can't stay," she said. "I just brought your stuff. The check came in from your last shoot, and I rushed it through. I thought you might need it."

"Bless you, darling." He walked past her into the kitchen, and returned moments later, with a glass of white wine for her and beer for himself. She was still standing there, feeling stupid and lost, and he put the glass into her hand, took her by the shoulders and gently pushed her down onto the lumpy old sofa. "Sit," he said. Susan sat.

He dropped beside her, stretching out his long, jean-clad legs, one thigh touching hers as he yawned, running a hand through his hair. "It has not been my best week," he said, tilting back the beer and taking a long swallow. Then he turned to look at her, and his turquoise eyes had a strange light in them. "What about you?"

"Me?" Susan's voice came out squeaky, nervous.

"Yes, you. How was your week?"

"Incomparably rotten."

He grinned. "Partners in misery, then. At least you don't have a hangover. I have the Cadillac of hangovers. If I drank as much as I think I did last night, it's a wonder I was able to make it to that early-morning call."

"When did you get in?" She shouldn't ask him, but couldn't help it. In her unaccustomed nervousness she took a large swallow of her wine, forgetting she'd already had more than her allotted portion for the night.

"Oh, I never went out last night. I spent the entire time drowning my sorrows until I passed out on the floor by the bed. I dreamed about you."

She managed a laugh. "That's because you must have been hearing my phone messages while you were asleep."

"I heard them when I was awake," he said.

There was an uncomfortable silence. She couldn't remember for sure what she had said during all those panicked phone calls. Too much, of course. If she hadn't told him she loved him, she'd come too damned close. And she wasn't going to stay here and let him feel sorry for her.

"I've got to go," she said, draining the wine and standing up.

Frank caught her wrist and pulled her back down again before she even realized what he'd planned. "No, you don't."

"Frank," she said, her voice pleading, almost desperate.

"Susan," he mocked, his eyes alight with something she didn't dare believe. He released her wrist, put his hand at the back of her head, and held her still as his mouth dropped onto hers.

She'd been used to his kisses. To the friendly, lingering brush of lips, to the casual hugs, to the gentle teasing. She wasn't expecting his mouth to open against hers, hot and wet and seeking; she wasn't expecting the surge of desire and despair that swept over her, shaking her to her very bones.

It took only a moment for her to gather her resolve, only the touch of his tongue against hers. She tore herself away, shoving him, and scrambled for the door, knocking over her wineglass as she went.

He caught up with her as she was fumbling with the

locks, his strong arms on either side of her, trapping her there. She had no choice but to turn around and face him, but she kept her head down, refusing to look him in the eye. "This is ridiculous, Frank," she said in a low voice. "We're friends, for heaven's sake."

"We're about to become lovers." His voice was equally low, beguiling, and it ripped into her heart.

"I don't need a charity ball, Frank. I don't need your pity."

She could feel the sudden tension that rushed through him. "Is that what you think this is?" he demanded. "Is it?"

She couldn't help it; she had to look up. His beautiful face looked almost brutal in the dimly lighted room, and the anger in his eyes was unmistakable. "Frank, you don't really want me." If her voice was nothing less than a miserable wail, there was nothing she could do about it.

The anger left his eyes, and a faint smile tugged at the corner of his mobile mouth. "I don't?" he asked flatly. "If you say so." And leaning his elbows against the door, he plastered his body against hers and kissed her, his long fingers cradling her head and holding it still.

This was no gentle preliminary, no idle flirtation. His mouth was open and hungry and demanding, his tongue thrust into her mouth in a gentle, unbearably erotic demonstration of what he intended to do with his body, and the heaviness of his arousal pressed against her stomach. He rocked against her, lightly, making certain she was aware of just how much he really did want her, and with a helpless little moan she slid her arms around his neck.

"That's it." He murmured his approval against her face as his hands deftly unfastened the tiny buttons in the front of her cotton dress. His mouth caught hers in short, teasing little kisses, kisses she clung to, kisses she returned. "I'm not that crazy. Of course I want you." He finished with the last button and began to push the dress from her shoulders. It landed in a heap on the floor, and she was standing in his arms wearing nothing but a pink silk teddy.

She didn't even have time to get self-conscious. "You have the most beautiful body," he whispered, his mouth traveling down, brushing the tops of her full breasts as his fingers slid the narrow straps down over her arms, pushing the silk away from her body to land on the floor. She was standing naked in his arms, and shyness washed over her body in a dull pink haze. She tried to turn from him, but he wouldn't let her, and the hands that ran up the length of her were gentle, almost worshipping. "I love your breasts," he whispered, his hands brushing their softness, so that she wanted to cry with longing. "I love your hips brushing against me, I love your arms around me, I love your mouth under mine, I love your legs, I love…"

She kissed him before he could lie. She'd been noble, she'd been careful, she'd been oh, so wise. The time had come for foolishness, for taking what she wanted, no matter how much it ended up hurting her. She was going to be hurt, anyway. She might as well take the pleasure as well as the pain. Sliding her hands between their bodies, she unfastened the buttons on his shirt. She pushed it from his shoulders, and then his chest was bare against hers, all his beautiful, golden flesh, hot and firm, the light crinkling of hair pressing against her breasts, the tightly muscled arms holding her. She dropped her hand to the waistband of his pants and hesitated. His hand covered hers, pushing it lower to the steely length of his arousal, and she moaned into his mouth with longing and a faint apprehension. But before she could change her mind he'd scooped her up, carrying her across the room with effortless ease and dropping her onto the decadent bed.

She watched him as he stripped off the rest of his clothes, and in the few seconds it took him to shuck his pants, second thoughts assailed her. "I'm making a big mistake," she murmured, not moving.

His grin was elemental, male, and frankly possessive. "Maybe you are," he said. "I'm doing the first smart thing I've done in years." And with fast, almost feline grace, he sank onto the bed, catching her mouth with his for a swift, silencing kiss. He kissed her breasts gently, almost worshipfully, he kissed her navel, and before she realized what he intended he'd set his mouth on the heated, longing center of her being.

She tried to push him away, but only for a moment. First her hands rested lightly on his shoulders, then tightly, then fiercely, as her body arched beneath his mouth.

He didn't give her time to come down. Within seconds he'd sheathed himself in her clenching body, riding out the storm. When the tremors finally passed he began to move, slowly at first, pushing in deep. "Wrap your legs around me," he whispered, and she did so, pulling him in closer, still shaking from the aftermath of what he'd given her. She opened her eyes, watching him as he moved against her. His body was rigid with tension and covered with sweat, and she waited, willing, aching to receive his climax, when his gaze focused for a moment and a ghost of a smile twisted his mouth.

"If you think you're all done for the night, babe," he whispered, "you're wrong." And putting his hand between their bodies he touched her, deftly, deliberately, as he surged forward once, twice, three times.

She heard the muffled cry from a distance and knew

it was her own. His mouth covered hers, drinking in her cry, as his body pushed her over the edge into places she'd never even dreamed existed. There was only rippling darkness, his body pulsing within hers, as every muscle, every cell in her body convulsed. It went on forever, a timeless, impossible eternity, and when she finally returned to the mattress beneath her and the man above her, the room and the noise and the New York City night, her face was wet with tears.

She tried to say something but couldn't. His hand brushed her face, smoothing away the tears, his mouth gently brushed hers. He moved away, and she was asleep even before he pulled her body into his arms.

# *Chapter 10*

Laura pushed a fork in desultory fashion through her smoked duck ravioli with sweet red onion. It was close to eleven o'clock and the after-theater crowd had just surged into a trendy little restaurant a mere two blocks from the Glass House. She hadn't bothered to ask Michael how he managed to get in without one of the de rigueur reservations. People like Michael Dubrovnik didn't need reservations; they just blew their way through life, knocking everything down that stood in their path.

"What's that sour expression for?" Michael murmured. He'd already finished his steak, devouring the blood-rare meat with almost cannibalistic gusto. He was now on his second Scotch, the moment when he'd suggested he might be indiscreet. Laura could see no signs of his guard dropping.

"I was thinking that I hadn't seen anyone eat red meat

in ages," she observed. "Don't you know it's bad for you? It'll clog your arteries and bring you to an early grave."

He grinned. "Don't count on it. At least, not before Dubrovnik Plaza is in place. Not unless you sprinkle arsenic over the top of my steak. Besides—" he leaned forward across the table "—did you ever doubt that I'd be a meat eater?"

"Not for a moment." She pushed back her plate, and the perfect waiter whisked it away before she had time to blink, returning with a matching glass of Scotch. "I didn't order this," she said to Dubrovnik. "I was just thinking how much I'd like one, but I'm sure I didn't order it."

"I did."

"Don't!" she begged, shuddering. "I'm having troubles enough with you. Don't start reading my mind."

"Just anticipating your needs, Laura. It's the duty of a good host."

"You also think I'll let something drop if I have a drink. Don't count on it. I learned to hold my liquor at a very early age. I can drink most men under the table." She took a sip of the Scotch, shivering slightly as it burned its way down her throat.

Michael's dark blue eyes were alight with amusement. "Is that true?"

"No. But it sounded good. Actually I get emotional and silly when I drink too much. Just like everyone else."

"I don't get emotional and silly. I get morose."

"It's your Russian blood. Besides, when was the last time you drank too much?"

He shook his head. "I don't remember."

She sighed. "It just proves my point. You aren't human. All evidence to the contrary, you're simply a machine. Sort of like 'the Terminator goes to Wall Street.' It's no wonder I'm out of my depth with you."

"Are you?" he countered swiftly. "Why don't you simply give in, then? Why keep fighting, if you can't possibly win?"

For a moment they seemed cocooned in space. The noise, the crowds surrounding them vanished. She could feel the icy coldness of the drink in her hand, still taste the sting of the peat on her tongue. She looked up at him, for once not guarding her expression. "Because I'm a fighter," she said simply. "Whether it's a lost cause or not, I won't give in. I may not be able to keep the Glass House out of your hands in the long run, but I can make it as time-consuming and frustrating a process as possible."

She half expected fury. Instead he simply shook his head, smiling wryly. "You have a real talent for that," he agreed. "If it's a losing battle, why waste your time? Why don't you just drop everything and go have babies?"

"Sexist pig," she said genially. "Not every woman is a baby machine. Why do you always come up with sexist remarks when you're trying to irritate me?"

"It usually works with women. Sneak attack. Don't you want babies?"

She slipped off her shoes and curled her legs beneath her on the banquette. "Why do you have this fixation with babies?"

He appeared startled. "Do I? I suppose it's because I want them."

"Not with me, you don't."

He laughed. "I wasn't suggesting it. I imagine I'll probably take you up on the offer you've been throwing at my head. Marita would have lovely babies."

She stared at him in sudden dismay. "Are you always this calculating?"

"By calculating do you mean cold and unfeeling? I try to be. It saves a lot of wear and tear on the emotions later on," he murmured. "What about you? You don't strike me as someone who wears her heart on her sleeve. How much do you let emotions and hormones rule your life?"

She thought of Jeff Carnaby, busy having what she hoped was a farewell dinner with Marita. She thought of Susan's red-rimmed eyes. And she remembered what had happened when Michael kissed her. "Not at all," she said flatly. Believing it.

"You see? We're two of a kind. There's a time and a place for having a family, there's a time and a place for having sex."

"Usually the two go together."

"Wise of you to point that out. That's why I'm planning to get married again. I want a beautiful, entertaining wife and a good mother to my children."

"Marita is beautiful," Laura agreed. "And I suppose it depends on your definition of entertaining. But she's a little young to be having babies."

"She's twenty-two. She's in her prime."

"Physically, perhaps. What makes you think she'll be willing to give up that physical prime to become your baby machine?"

"The knowledge that she'll be more than well compensated for it."

"Why don't you just hire a surrogate mother?" Laura snapped.

"You know as well as I do the trouble you can get into when you do that. Besides, I want a wife and a mother for my children."

"Back to that, are we? Don't you believe in love?"

"Do you?" he countered swiftly.

"Touché."

"I believe in sex. In the exchange of physical pleasure between two mutually consenting adults. Do you?"

The ice in her drink had melted. There wasn't much left of it, and what there was had gone from deep amber to a pale honey. She looked up and met his all too discerning eyes. "I imagine you know the answer to that, if you're bothering to ask. Your private investigator must be better than I thought."

"I hired a new one."

She drained the watered-down whiskey. "Then you must know that I live a life of pious chastity."

"So it would appear."

"Are you fishing for answers? In this case, appearances are correct. I think sex is a messy, highly over-rated business. It weakens the willpower, distracts the mind and turns women into victims." The second drink appeared in front of her. She hadn't noticed Michael signaling for it. Her mistake. She couldn't afford not to notice everything about him.

"What do you think it does to men?" He took a sip of his own drink, watching her out of enigmatic eyes. Dangerous eyes.

"Gives them too much power."

"If it's messy and overrated, why would it give men power? Why wouldn't women simply say no?"

"Biology, for one thing. Nature played a nasty trick on women. They want babies, they want nests, they want providers. Even if their brains know better, their instincts are turning on them."

"You've given this a lot of thought."

She smiled serenely, taking a sip out of her new drink and then pushing it away. "I've had plenty of time. Enough to know that I'm not going to let my biological instincts betray me into making any more mistakes."

"And you called me calculating."

"There's a difference in being calculating when you're

in a position of power, and when you're in what essentially is a position of weakness. You have to use everything you can when you're nature's victim."

"I don't see you as anyone's victim."

She looked at him across the table. At times like these it was hard to remember that he was the enemy, that he wanted to destroy what she cared most about. "Michael..."

"Mischa," he corrected in a quiet voice.

"Mischa," she said, not liking the sound of it in her husky voice. Not liking the ease with which her tongue slid around it. "I never will be again."

She'd had too much to drink. Only a drink and a sip of whiskey, but she had to be drunk. There couldn't be strands and tendrils of emotion twisting between them. He couldn't be looking at her with such a predatory expression on his face, one that was frankly sensual. He couldn't want her. He was a sensible man. He wanted Marita.

She shook her head, clearing away the mists, and the man across from her was once more her nemesis, a man after her beloved building and nothing more. "It's late," she said. "I need to get back home."

He didn't say a word as she slipped her four-inch heels back onto her tiny feet and headed with perfect steadiness for the front of the restaurant. She was half afraid he'd put his hand at the small of her back, but he didn't. He didn't touch her at all, and for reasons she didn't care to examine too closely, she was profoundly grateful.

"Do you ever get the feeling that people are watching you?" Laura murmured.

"They are." They headed out of the door, standing under the awninged portico. "Because I have a lot of money, people are interested in what I do. Whom I eat dinner with."

Laura's reaction was short and succinct. "I should have thought of that."

"Next time you can eat at my place," he said.

"Next time?" She considered it for a moment. "My place would be better. That way I could sprinkle arsenic on your bloody meat without you noticing."

"I'd notice." He looked beyond her, out into the New York City night. "Speaking of noticing, it's pouring. Come back inside and I'll call my driver." This time he did reach for her, but she scuttled out of his way with more speed than grace.

"For two blocks? Don't be ridiculous! A little rain won't hurt you."

Michael looked at her askance. "Have you ever walked in a New York City rain? It's probably pure toxic waste."

"I always walk in the rain, and I never leave the city. Come on, Mischa, don't be a sissy. It's a beautiful night." And without another word she spun out into the downpour, lifting her face to the steady rain.

He tried to grab her, to pull her back under the protective awning, but she danced out of his way, graceful on her four-inch heels, laughing at him.

He stood there, glowering at her. "Are you really going to do this?"

"Absolutely. Do you want me to call you a cab?"

"No one," he said, "calls me a sissy and gets away with it." And he stepped out into the downpour after her.

"Good for you, Whirlwind." She stopped and slipped off her shoes. "Take these."

The rain was pouring down around them, plastering his black hair to his well-shaped skull. It ran in sheets down the contours of his face, illuminating the stark bone structure, the high Slavic cheekbones, the hard jaw, the slightly tilted eyes, the mobile, almost cruel mouth. Not the face of a man to play games with, Laura thought absently. Not the face of a man to dance in the rain with.

"Lighten up, Mischa," she said. "You're only thirty-nine years old."

"Old enough to know better than to walk barefoot in Manhattan," he said dourly, pocketing her small shoes and following her down the rain-drenched sidewalk at a sedate pace.

"You know, I don't think you should marry Marita after all," Laura said, waiting for him at the corner. "You need someone to make you do crazy things." Her short black hair was dripping around her face, and she couldn't see through her rain-splattered glasses. She took them off, as well, tucking them into her purse, shrugging off their lack of protection. Michael had already seen her without them, and he hadn't attacked her in a frenzy of lust. He was hardly going to come on to her again when he was soaking wet.

"That's exactly what I don't need. I know why you're doing this," he said, crossing the street with her. "You're trying to make sure I get pneumonia." Almost on cue he sneezed, and belatedly Laura realized that the late-night rain was bordering on chilly. "It's a waste of time. I could be on my deathbed and still be able to close a deal."

"Actually I hadn't thought of that, but it's a good idea. You might be able to close a multimillion dollar deal on your deathbed, but I bet you can't even answer your own telephone when you have a cold. Men are such wimps."

"No one calls me a wimp and gets away with it, either," Michael snapped.

Laura stopped in the middle of the empty sidewalk,

shoving her wet hair behind her ears and grinning at him. "I just did."

He lunged for her, but she dodged nimbly. "Do you want me to mug someone for their umbrella?" she inquired solicitously.

"Don't bother." His tone was low and threatening as he advanced on her, and she suddenly doubted her ability to escape.

"What are you planning to do?" She stood her ground, letting the rain sluice over her as she watched him approach.

"I'm tempted to shove you in front of a taxi," he muttered direly. "But I don't think one's going to show up. So I have only one option."

"What's that?"

"Race you home." He took off, leaping ahead, but Laura was fast on his heels. What she lacked in the length of her stride she made up for by being shoeless. She caught up with him at the corner, passed him by the deli, and was leaning against the glass panels of her beloved building when he reached her.

She'd sprinted and was out of breath and laughing at him as he stopped, breathless himself, no longer grim, no longer angry. But still, even to Laura's untrained eye, very dangerous.

He was too fast for her. Before she had the faintest idea what he was going to do, he'd pulled her into his arms. Her laughter faded into silence as his mouth covered hers, wet from the rain, tasting faintly of whiskey.

She was too startled, too breathless, to react as she should have. Instinctively she put her arms around him, and suddenly he lifted her, swinging her around, away from the shelter of the building and out into the pouring rain again. She clung to him, half out of dizziness, half out of a sneaking, self-destructive streak she couldn't fight anymore. Damn it, she wanted to kiss him. And kiss him she did, opening her mouth to his as the rain poured down around them.

It was over too soon. He released her mouth, released her body, letting it slide down his length, the soaked, ruined silk of her dress rubbing against the soaked, ruined fabric of his suit until her stockinged feet rested once more on the sidewalk. "Better watch those animal instincts, Laura," he whispered, his eyes dark and glittering in the light from the street. "I think you need to slap them down."

"I think I need to slap you down," she said, the tremor in her voice scarcely audible. She stepped back. "Shoes, please."

He fished them out of his pockets and handed them to her. "No bare feet allowed in the Glass House?" he questioned.

"I have to stop in at the deli," she said demurely, slipping on her shoes.

"I'll come with you."

"You aren't getting another good-night kiss, Mischa," she warned walking away from him.

"Was that what that was?" he murmured, catching up with her at the door of the small, overpriced store that stayed open all night. "It felt more like hello to me."

"Wrong." She headed straight for the back of the store, grabbed what she needed and plopped the items onto the counter, overwhelmingly aware of Michael's scrutiny.

"Three boxes of sugar?" he said. "What the hell are you going to do with it all? Make jam?"

"Do you use that much sugar to make jam?" She was momentarily diverted from her course of action. "How would you know that?"

"My mother always made jam."

"My mother doesn't even eat jam."

"Jilly isn't my idea of a mother."

"She isn't anyone's idea of a mother, hers included," Laura said without a trace of bitterness.

"So what's the sugar for?"

"Susan and I like our coffee very sweet."

The sour-looking woman who ran the place punched the cash register, and Laura reached for her purse. Michael was already ahead of her, pulling bills out of his leather wallet and setting them on the counter.

"I shouldn't let you do that," Laura murmured, trying to keep her expression sober. "But in this case I think I will."

"Good. I don't expect it'll work as much of a bribe. You're not going to let the Glass House go for three boxes of sugar."

"I'm not going to let the Glass House go for love or money." Unfortunate choice of words, she thought, her mouth still feeling the imprint of his. But he merely grinned.

He left her at the ninth floor, pausing to hold the elevator door open. "No good-night kiss?"

"Call Marita if you want one," Laura suggested politely.

"I thought she went out with her fiancé."

"Ex-fiancé," Laura corrected him.

He paused, something in her tone of voice alerting him. "You aren't thinking of having anything to do with that boy, are you? You'd eat him alive."

"He's very sweet and charming and handsome." There was just a hint of defensiveness in her voice.

"I'm considered handsome," Michael offered, a diabolical light in his eyes.

"I wasn't aware that you were in competition for me."
She'd managed to startle him. Or he'd managed to startle himself. "I'm not," he said, with more haste than tact.

Laura grinned at him, clutching the sugar to her chest, once more in control of things. "Try to remember that, would you, Mischa?" she suggested. "Things are confusing enough. Good night." She pushed the Door Closed button, and the rude buzzer startled Michael into releasing his hand. He was still standing there, a bemused expression on his face, as the doors slid shut.

It took Michael a good half hour to get back his equilibrium. He took a long hot shower, washing the grit from his hair, washing the chill from his bones. He usually slept nude, but tonight, with the rain still lashing against the glass panels of the building, he needed extra warmth, and he dressed in a sweat suit, made himself a glass of Russian tea, and stretched out on his oversize, empty bed.

He hadn't been paying proper attention, of course. That was the real danger with Laura de Kelsey Winston. She threw him off balance. He'd never met anyone quite like her, and tended to get distracted by her. If someone had told him he'd run through a heavy downpour just for the hell of it, he'd have thought they were crazy. If someone had told him he'd kiss Laura, and enjoy both kissing her and her startled reaction more than he'd enjoyed anything in years, he would have taken bets against it.

But he had run through the rain. He had kissed Laura, again. And if her prosaic words hadn't stopped him, he would have tried to get her into his bed. Or followed her into hers.

He must be out of his mind. He didn't really want a short, sharp-tongued, determined gamine like Laura Winston. While she was attractive enough, even enticing

in a piquant, mischievous sort of way, he'd always preferred serene, statuesque women. Not feisty little ones
who were completely unimpressed by his money and
power.

Of course, he thought, stretching out on the bed and
watching the rain run down the cracks in the window,
Laura had done exactly what he'd hoped she'd do. She'd
exposed far too much of herself, and it hadn't taken even
half a glass of whiskey. He knew where she was vulnerable, knew it more by accident than design. When it
came to sex, Ms. Laura de Kelsey Winston was almost
powerless.

It was the perfect angle to play upon. What he'd started
out of boredom and an unlikely fascination could turn
into the one weapon against which she'd prove defense-
less.

It wasn't a weapon he'd ever used against a woman.
But then he'd never run up against a woman with Laura's stubbornness. He'd warned her he was no gentleman;
he'd warned her he was going to get what he wanted by
fair means or foul. The question was, how rotten could
Michael Dubrovnik really be?

He viewed it dispassionately, warming to the idea even
as his intrusive conscience tried to come up with warnings. He doubted that Marita would have any qualms if
he used sex to best Laura. Marita struck him as someone infinitely practical. If she didn't like it, there were
other women, other elegant, graceful beauties who'd be
less squeamish.

And he'd actually be doing Laura a favor. He didn't
know who'd done such a rotten job of initiating her into
the pleasures of the flesh—his private investigator hadn't
come up with any concrete information when it came to
her celibate state. But even if her heart and emotions were

temporarily bruised, she'd end up living a more complete life. For all her railings against nature, you couldn't cheat animal instincts for your entire life and expect any happiness. She'd be much better off with a man, with a husband and babies, than with this decrepit mausoleum.

His mouth curved wryly as he reviewed the series of self-justifications. If he made the mistake of bedding Laura in the battle of the Glass House, he'd end up regretting it for the rest of his life. Enticing as the fantasy was, he'd have to keep this battle vertical, at least. No more kisses, no more erotic daydreams. Tomorrow he'd take Marita out to dinner and maybe to bed, if it seemed that the time was right. And then maybe he'd stop thinking about the woman upstairs, who at least knew how to wage a fair fight.

At that moment Laura wasn't thinking about fair fights at all. She'd changed into something dry, had put her boxes of sugar into a shopping bag and started slogging through the mud in the pit beside the Glass House. The earth-moving equipment still sat there like a family of ugly, evil bugs, huge prehistoric insects ready to devour the earth and her poor, wounded building.

It took her a long time to find the gas tanks on the machines. Her fingers were numb with cold, her teeth were chattering by the time she managed to get the cover off the gas tank on the third, final piece of machinery and pour the last box of sugar into the fuel. She didn't know whom Dubrovnik had hired for nighttime security, but whoever it was didn't fancy watching over expensive equipment in a downpour at three in the morning, and she was able to work in peace. It wasn't as if Michael wouldn't know who'd done it. She just didn't want him to have any proof.

She carried the empty boxes back into her building, her boots leaving muddy footprints all the way into the elevator. She'd have to call and have her motley maintenance crew take care of them before the Whirlwind rose from his ill-deserved rest. She hoped he wouldn't sleep too late. She wanted to be close enough to hear his scream of rage when he found out what she'd done.

## Chapter 11

"What in God's name are you wearing?" Jilly strode into the front room of Glass Faces, her mink coat flying around her tall, whippet-lean figure.

"Good morning, Mother." Laura looked up from her position at Susan's desk and pushed her glasses farther up her nose. "What are you doing up so early?"

"Celebrating my divorce. We signed the papers this morning, thank heavens, and I thought you'd like to celebrate with me. You always hated Franz."

"I haven't liked any of your husbands, and I doubt I'll like the next one any better. It's too early for champagne. I'll take you to lunch at the Four Seasons if you can bear to wait another hour. Susan hasn't come in yet."

"I can wait." Jillian threw herself onto Laura's leather sofa and assumed a long-suffering expression. "Is that why you're dressed like a country girl? I hate to tell you, dearest, but the rustic look isn't you. All that frilly cotton looks absurd on someone as short as you."

Laura looked very calmly into her mother's eyes. It had taken years before she'd inured herself to the maternal barbs, but she now had an effective defense system that nothing could penetrate. "You hate me in leather, Jilly. And you weren't very flattering about my denim stage. What should I wear?"

Jilly gave the question the consideration it was due, somewhere near the weightiness of world peace, Laura thought wryly. "I don't really know, darling. You've insisted on going into business. Now if you'd married, busied yourself with children and charities, then I'd have plenty of suggestions...."

"I run a modeling agency, Mother. I'm not a wife, or a mother or on the board of a charity." It was an old argument, one Jilly never tired of. Laura sat back, ready to remind her mother of the ground rules, when the door opened and Susan almost ran in.

"I'm sorry I'm late," she said, her eyes not meeting Laura's sharper ones. "I overslept."

Laura simply stared. "Mother," she said without taking her eyes off her flustered assistant, "go find something to do. Go down to my apartment and rummage through my private papers or something. I'll be ready to go in an hour."

Jilly brightened at the thought of a distraction. "I do hate to be a bother. Maybe I'll see if you have any champagne in your refrigerator."

"I don't."

"Darling, no de Kelsey should be without a chilled bottle of champagne for all occasions. We do happen to have some standards."

"We do indeed," Laura said, aware that the irony in her voice was sailing right over Jilly's head.

"As a matter of fact, I was looking for the de Kelsey

emeralds. You don't happen to have them, do you?" her mother artlessly inquired as she headed toward the glass doors.

"They're locked away, Mother, and they're mine."

Jilly pouted. "They shouldn't be. My own mother, leaving them to you instead of her own daughter. They're too gaudy for you, dearest."

"They're mine. Why don't you go down to the ninth floor and see if Dubrovnik has some chilled champagne? I'm sure he'd be happy to toast your divorce."

Jilly's pout vanished. "Maybe he'll come to lunch with us."

"No. We celebrate your divorce à deux or not at all. Is that understood?"

"Spoilsport. Exactly what is going on with that man?"

"I'll tell you over lunch," Laura said, the lie coming easily. "It's not very interesting."

"Don't think you're going to fob me off with fairy stories," Jilly warned. "I'll get the truth out of you, if I have to spend all afternoon drinking champagne."

"Yes, Mother," Laura said with mock politeness.

"Brat," her mother genially replied, heading for the Otis elevator.

Laura moved away from the desk, allowing Susan to scuttle behind it. She looked up, long enough for Laura to notice her red-rimmed eyes. "What in heaven's name are you wearing?"

"I stole it from you. Don't you recognize your own clothing when you see it?" Laura demanded, allowing herself to be temporarily diverted. She knew exactly how absurd she looked. Susan was a good five inches taller than she was, and a great deal rounder. The French blue shift flowed around Laura's spare body and drifted over her ankles. The gathered sleeves drooped over Laura's bejeweled hands, and the yards and yards of cotton swirled around her whenever she walked. The contrast with her jet-black, shingled hair, bright red lipstick and oversize glasses was almost clownlike. She'd even foregone her high heels for flat black Mary Janes and white stockings.

"I recognize the dress," Susan said wryly. "And I never thought I'd see the day, but I look a hell of a lot better in it than you do. The question is, why? Please don't tell me this is your new look!"

"Trust me, it's temporary. I'm trying to look innocent, and nothing in my closet fitted the bill."

"Innocent of what?"

"That's where we come to you, my dear," Laura said, turning the tables. "Where were you at three o'clock this morning? While I was out committing foul deeds, bereft of a partner in crime, you were somewhere out of reach. Where?"

"What foul deeds?"

"After you tell me where you were. You have whisker burns on your cheeks."

Susan's reddened cheeks darkened further. "What if I said it was none of your business?"

"Is it none of my business?" Laura asked calmly, refusing to be offended.

"It was Frank."

"Good heavens!" she exclaimed, astonished. "I'd assumed you'd gone off to drown your sorrows with someone else. It really was Frank?"

Susan's eyes were trained on the desk in front of her, and Laura had to take it on faith that her mumbled response was in the affirmative.

"Well," said Laura, shoving the papers off the sturdy glass-topped table and levering her flounced body on top of it. "Tell me everything. Was he any good?"

"Laura!" Susan shrieked, shocked out of her misery.

"That's better. So what was it, a one-night stand or the love of a lifetime?"

"A one-night stand."

"Says who?"

Susan bit her already swollen lip. "He wasn't there when I woke up, Laura. He was gone. He didn't even leave a note."

"Don't jump to conclusions." Laura leaned back, staring at Susan in unfeigned surprise. "You really slept with him?"

"I really slept with him," Susan muttered.

"What is that old saying? Something about those whom the gods would destroy, they first make crazy? Or those whom the gods would make crazy, they give them exactly what they want. Or those that the gods would make crazy, they make fall in love? I wish I could remember it."

"It's all of the above," Susan said gloomily.

"Was it worth it?"

"Worth what?"

Susan looked miserable enough; she didn't need Laura's prying. But Laura couldn't help it. Despite her friend's current state, she had to know the answer. "Was making love with Frank Buckley worth the heartache and the misery you seem ready to envision?"

Susan's huge brown eyes filled with unshed tears. But her mouth curved into a sudden, wicked grin. "Every second of it," she said.

Laura shook her head. "I don't know, Susan. I think love is nothing but trouble. Everyone would be better off without it."

"You're probably right. Right now I'm busy worrying about whether he made love to me out of pity."

Laura hooted with laughter as she climbed off the desk. "Frank may be a prince of a fellow, but he's not that noble. Take my word for it, Frank went to bed with you because he wanted to."

"That's what he said. I wish I believed it."

"Go look at your reflection in the mirror, Susan," Laura offered kindly. "You don't look like a woman who's the object of sympathy. You look like a woman who's been extremely well—"

"Laura," Susan protested.

"Well, you do," Laura insisted.

"Well," said Susan, "I was. So let's leave it at that, okay? I spent years mooning after something I couldn't have, I ended up getting it, and now it's over. Why don't you tell me what hideous crimes you committed? It has to be something pretty dire to get you that outfit."

"It was. But first…" Her voice trailed off as the elevator door slipped open. It wasn't an avenging Whirlwind coming toward her. It was a smugly beautiful Marita. And on her arm, looking totally bemused, was Jeff Carnaby.

Laura allowed herself a moment to watch them. They made an attractive couple. Tall and clean-limbed and all-American, they seemed made for each other, she thought with a pang.

"Who's that with Marita?" Susan whispered.

Laura didn't answer, moving across the room at her usual speed, ignoring the unaccustomed weight of the yards of cotton swinging around her. "Good morning, Marita. Hello, Jeff. We weren't expecting you. How was your dinner last night?" And how was your night? she added inwardly, keeping her face bland. Did you sleep with him, Marita? Did you change your mind?

Marita's beautiful face wasn't giving anything away.

"We had a wonderful time. I thought I'd come in with Jeff and see whether you wanted me to go out on interviews. Go-sees, didn't you call them?"

"I thought we were going to keep Marita under wraps," Susan said, clearly perplexed. "We've already got Estée Lauder drooling over the photographs, and Revlon's made a decent, if unspectacular offer. Why should she go out?"

"Just a thought," Laura murmured, cursing her voluble assistant. She gazed at the woman towering over her. No whisker burns on her pale, perfect skin, no love bites on her neck, but that was no proof. Had everyone but herself spent last night in bed with someone?

Why should she care? Wouldn't she rather spend the early-morning hours slogging through mud than writhing beneath a demanding male body? That was not what she wanted, was it? She turned to smile at Jeff, testing her reaction like someone prodding a sore tooth. Again, all she could come up with was a mild attraction. A lack of fear. If Marita had kept her beautiful, long-fingered hands off him, he might still be the answer to her frustrations. Someone safe enough to fall in love with.

He smiled back, clearly at a loss. "You look wonderful today," he said, ignoring the woman at his side. "I like that dress."

"Oh, dear," Susan murmured in the background, barely audible.

There was no time like the present for a little education. "It's not really my style," Laura pointed out.

"Oh, no, I think you look beautiful," Jeff protested, absolutely serious.

Laura grinned, suddenly relaxed as she turned to the enigmatic Marita. "I love this man. Let me know when you're finished with him, and I'll take him off your hands."

Marita's answering smile held just the right amount of shared humor. "You can have him." She leaned over, kissing him on his strong, smooth-shaven jaw. "Just be good to him. He deserves it."

With an effortless grace she had to admire in herself, Laura moved between the two erstwhile lovers, put her hand on Jeff's strongly muscled arm and moved him away. "You've been dumped, darling. Let me help you drown your sorrows. I'll take you to dinner and soothe you."

He stared down at her, clearly entranced, ignoring the world-class beauty watching them. It had been years since Laura had entranced anyone, and she liked the feeling. "I can't," Jeff said.

"You can't?"

"I'm going back to Kansas. I'm booked on an afternoon flight. There's no reason for me to stay any longer."

Isn't there, Laura thought. "Susan," she said out loud. "See if you can arrange an airline strike."

He laughed then. He had a thousand beautiful white teeth and a dimple. God, a man with a dimple, Laura thought. His babies would have dimples. "You wouldn't want to do that. Think of all the trouble you'd cause."

"I'm ruthless when it comes to something I want."

She'd really startled him that time. He licked his lips, cleared his throat, and stared at her. "I could always change my flight," he said.

"You do that," she murmured, testing her voice, seeing if she could make it shy and seductive at the same time. She could. "Susan will help."

"You've had an offer from Revlon?" Marita waited until Jeff was busy on the telephone. "Why didn't you tell me?"

"It's not anything we're going to move on. They want

you as part of a group picture. Just another pretty face. We're going for more than that, and the best way to go about it is to use mystery. Make them hungry for you. Of course, if you want to work your way up...?"

"No." Marita's smile was dazzling. "I trust you completely, Laura. I'll do anything you say."

Laura wished she could have found that declaration more reassuring. "You don't mind me taking Jeff out? You don't want to join us?" Don't you dare, she added mentally.

"I'm going out with Michael Dubrovnik. He called first thing this morning. He is such a forceful man, isn't he?"

"He is that," Laura agreed wryly, ignoring the sudden, irrational pang somewhere in the region of her solar plexus.

"I've heard," said Marita, leaning closer and enveloping Laura in a cocoon of Opium, "that he's absolutely voracious in bed."

"I wouldn't know." Laura kept her voice polite, kept herself from stepping back from the miasmic cloud.

Marita's smile was small and smug. "I imagine I'll find out soon enough."

Laura opened her mouth to say something, then shut it again. Had Rigby, Kansas, really produced this exotic creature? This was no Barbie doll standing in front of her, this was a black widow ready to devour its mate. She'd need someone like the Whirlwind to stand up to her. They'd make a perfect pair, Laura thought grumpily.

"It's all set." Jeff had come up behind her, his voice rumbling from some point over her head. "I can take the five forty-five tomorrow instead of today."

Idiot, Laura thought to herself, not bothering to consider if she meant Jeff or herself. "Then we'll have to make a night of it," she murmured, batting her spiky black eyelashes at him, ignoring the ringing of the phone and Susan's quiet voice.

Jeff stared back at her, transfixed, and Laura was beginning to feel like a black widow spider herself, when Susan interrupted. "That was your mother. She said she'll take a rain check for lunch."

"Typical," Laura muttered. "She must have come up with a better offer."

"She said to warn you that Michael Dubrovnik is going to eat your liver. She said she'll come back when the dust settles."

Laura grinned. Things were lurching and staggering along, not exactly as she'd planned, but they were at least moving in the right direction. "That means I'm free for lunch," she said to Jeff, knowing she couldn't afford to waste one minute. "Why don't we…?"

"Don't count on it," Susan said. "Here comes the Whirlwind, and I think he's out for blood."

Laura looked up, startled, as Michael stormed into the office, and her hand tightened on Jeff's arm. Jeff's quiet yelp told her that she was digging her fingernails into his arm, and she carefully released him, greeting Michael with a serene smile.

It didn't take him long to assimilate the situation, she had to grant him that. His dark blue eyes swept over the motley group of people, taking in Susan's red eyes, Marita's instinctive preening, Jeff's faint and totally unwarranted air of possessiveness. And then his gaze swept over Laura from the top of her shiny black hair down the length of the frilly dress to the flat black shoes, and the thunder left his gaze, replaced by something that was uncomfortably close to amusement.

Then the polite veneer was back as he greeted Marita

with instinctive charm, tolerated an introduction to Jeff and bestowed a surprisingly sweet smile on Susan. At Laura he crooked a finger in an arrogant male demand that she treated with stony noncompliance.

"What?" she asked, with more truculence than grace.

"We're late for lunch. Come along, Laura."

"I'm not going to lunch with you. I've already promised to have lunch with my mother to celebrate her divorce."

"Your mother has stood you up for my thirty-three-year-old assistant, Peter McSorley. Try again."

"We were just discussing lunch." Jeff stepped forward, ready to be assertive.

"Discuss it with Marita," Michael said flatly. "Laura and I have business. If you think Laura puts anything before the Glass House, you have a lot to learn. Are you coming?" Impatience was eroding his earlier amusement, and Laura would have given anything to have simply told him no. Anything but the Glass House.

"Coming," she said demurely. After all, she was going to have to face him sooner or later, listen to his threats and his fury over the damage done to his expensive machinery. Might as well get it over with.

He didn't say a word as the elegant old elevator carried them down the twelve stories to the street below. When they stepped out into the lobby he simply took her arm, guiding her past the dried, muddy footprints that she'd forgotten to have eradicated. She could see the Bentley waiting out on the street, and began to feel the first tendrils of uneasiness.

"Where are you taking me? To jail?" she muttered, knowing she was betraying herself, no longer caring.

"Without passing Go or collecting two hundred dollars. I'd love to, but as you well know, I have no proof."

He stopped just outside the door. It was a warmish fall day with just a hint of crispness in the air, and the breeze immediately ruffled Michael's longish black hair. "And if you think I'm going to be fooled by those ridiculous clothes, you might as well forget it. I'd say you looked like a little girl dressing up in her mother's clothes, but even I know Jilly wouldn't be caught dead in something like that."

Laura caught her full skirts in one hand and swirled them gently. "I think I look adorable."

He glowered down at her feet. "You're too short."

"That's nothing new."

"Get in the car."

"I don't trust you."

"I don't trust you. Get in the car, or I'll pick you up and throw you in."

At that she grinned. "Go right ahead," she said amiably. "Then I can charge you with assault, get some nice new restraining orders and not have to worry for ages."

"Don't count on it. And don't count on my temper remaining this mellow."

"This is a mellow temper? I'd hate to see you when you're riled."

"Believe me," Michael said grimly, "you would. Get in the damned car."

"Not until you tell me where we're going."

"I'm going to introduce you to homemade jam."

"I beg your pardon?"

"You said you didn't know people actually made jam. My sister still does. I'm taking you up to her apartment for lunch. I'm sure it's an area of New York you've never seen. Consider it an educational excursion."

"Why?" she demanded suspiciously.

"Why not? But first—" he whipped out a white silk

handkerchief "—we have to make you look a little more presentable. My sister is quite a bit older than me and very old-fashioned. She'll probably think those stupid clothes are just charming, but she won't like the lipstick." Holding her chin in his ruthless grip, he took the hand-kerchief and scrubbed at her brightly painted mouth. He eyed her defiant face with a critical air. "You're too pale," he decided, and rubbed the lipsticked silk against her cheekbones.

She batted at him, but he was quite amazingly strong, capturing her hands with his one free hand. "And these," he said, filching her glasses, "have to go." To her horror he took them and flung them over the top of the Bentley, under the tires of the oncoming traffic.

Laura's reaction was brief and colorful. "You rotten, overbearing, manipulative son of a..."

"Try that with my sister and she'll wash your mouth out with soap." He shoved her into the Bentley, followed her, almost landing on top of her before she scuttled out of his way, and tapped on the smoked glass panel in front of him. "My sister's place, George. She's expecting us by one."

"As you say, sir." The Bentley pulled into the traffic, Laura, who was in the midst of trying to scramble out the other side, was thrown back into Michael's lap, and within seconds they were careening up the street.

"I'll get you for this, Dubrovnik," she snarled, as his hands unaccountably held her in place.

"I'd say you already did," he drawled.

# Chapter 12

Laura decided that a sulky silence would serve her best as the Bentley dodged and darted its way through midtown traffic, heading northward. During her thirty-some years she'd been through every section of New York City, including the murderous South Bronx, but she hadn't ventured outside her own, familiar neighborhoods too often. As they crossed the park and headed up the West Side, the streets grew narrower, more ethnic looking, the buildings older, the stores tinier, the whole area pulling in on itself, huddling against the bigger, noisier presence of midtown Manhattan.

She stole a glance at Michael's averted profile. He was looking out the window, a distant, abstracted expression on his face.

"Did you grow up here?" she asked, her husky voice breaking into the silent ride of the limousine.

He turned to her, and the faintly surprised expression

in his eyes told her he'd forgotten her presence. "Yes," he said. "As a matter of fact, I was born in the apartment we're going to. My mother didn't make it to the hospital."

"You mean the same apartment's been in your family for forty years?"

"I'm thirty-nine." His smile was wintry. "And the same apartment has been in our family since my father emigrated to this city from Moscow. He escaped after the revolution and came here. He always wanted to see the west, see cowboys and Indians. I don't think he ever got west of New Jersey."

"Did he die young?"

"Hell, no." Michael leaned back against the leather seat, a reminiscent smile softening the usually harsh lines of his face. "He was fifty when I was born. He made it to eighty-three, and he would have lasted longer if my mother hadn't died. He didn't want to live without her, so he didn't."

"I don't remember reading anything about your family in the magazines...."

"That's why I'm going to end up with the Glass House. I do my homework, and I pay attention to minor details. I can tell you the names of everyone in your immediate family, where they went to college, and, more importantly, how much money they have."

"So I'm making a vain, noble effort at keeping this battle on a straightforward, businesslike level."

"Putting sugar in the gas tanks of machinery with a combined value of close to a million dollars isn't my idea of a straightforward, businesslike level. I wouldn't call it noble, either."

"So sue me."

"My lawyers are looking into it."

Laura hoped he didn't notice her cringe at the thought.

"Tell me about your family. Don't waste my time with useless lawsuits."

Michael's expression was faintly skeptical, but he seemed willing to comply. "My parents left Russia in their late teens. They had five children, Piotr, Magda, Aloysha, Sonya and lastly Mikhail. I was more of an afterthought. My mother was forty-four and thought she was going through menopause when I showed up."

"That must have scared the hell out of her."

"I've been known to have that effect on people," Michael agreed. "The others have moved to various parts of the country. Only Sonya wanted to stay in New York." By this time they'd stopped outside an old, crumbling brownstone. Laura looked up at the spotless, lace-curtained windows, noting the general seediness of the area. Down the street she could see the onion domes of a Russian-style church; the writing on the storefront window nearby was Cyrillic, and two of the old women shuffling down the street were wearing babushkas. She couldn't help thinking that Michael Dubrovnik could afford better for his sister.

"Nice neighborhood," she murmured, as Michael climbed out, holding the door for her.

He didn't miss her implied criticism, but didn't blink. "It's home."

"Mischa!" The woman who greeted them at the door of the third-floor walk-up looked more as if she could be Michael Dubrovnik's mother than sister. She was dressed neatly but modestly, in a dress that would have come from any department store, Laura decided. The marcelled gray hair completed her dated look. She was somewhere in her late fifties or early sixties, and her Slavic cheekbones and faintly tilted eyes were her only resemblance to her more dashing younger brother. She flung her strong arms around Michael, embracing him fiercely, then turned that uncomfortably familiar dark blue gaze on Laura, taking in the ruffled clothes, the uneasy stance.

"Mischa," she said, "You're getting married again!" And without another word she pulled Laura into that same, crushing hug, not bothering to release her brother.

Laura didn't know whether to struggle, to protest or to cry. Pressed against Michael, pressed against the maternal bosom of this powerful woman smelling of vanilla and flowers, she was suddenly, irrationally reminded of just how much she'd wanted a mother. Jilly had never embraced her in her life.

"Sonya," Michael said patiently. "This is not my fiancée."

Sonya immediately released them, stepping back to take a closer look at Laura. Laura could feel her cheeks flush, but she met the intense gaze stoically enough.

"Who is she, then?" Sonya demanded.

"A thorn in my side. Laura de Kelsey Winston, meet Sonya Dubrovnik O'Reilly. My sister."

"How do you do?" Laura was beginning to feel like Alice in Wonderland. O'Reilly?

"How's Tim? How are the children?"

"Tim is thriving, as well you know," Sonya said, still not taking her eyes off Laura. "And the children are doing you proud. Seamus loves Harvard Law School, Fiodr is entering his last year at Stanford, and Jane is crazy about Bennington. You are too generous."

"What else is money for?"

Sonya was still staring at her, bemused. She shook her head. "So who are you going to marry then? Some tall, skinny, useless girl again?"

"I'm not planning on marrying anyone right away."

"You're getting old, Mischa. You need children."

"I was born when Father was fifty-three."

"Well, if you want only one…" Sonya conceded. "I think you're wrong, Mischa. Marry this one. She'll give you lots of babies."

The color in Laura's cheeks had just begun to fade. Michael gave his sister an affectionate push. "Enough matchmaking. You promised us lunch and Russian tea. Go cook."

"You see," Sonya announced as she headed down the dark, narrow hallway of the apartment. "Already you're protective of her. She's the one to marry, Mischa."

"You did this on purpose," Laura hissed as she followed Michael into the apartment.

"Not really. I should have realized she'd jump to that conclusion and warned you ahead of time."

"Why did you bring me here?"

He stopped in the middle of the crowded living room. "I'm not quite sure. At the time it seemed the best alternative to strangling you."

"I'm not going to be impressed that you're sending your nieces and nephews to the most expensive colleges in the country," she said stonily. "You could afford to send several dozen to Bennington and not even notice the cost."

"You're right, of course. Sit down."

"No."

"You're in my sister's house, and you're damned well going to be polite." Michael didn't raise his voice, but the message was chillingly clear. Laura sat, jumping up again as a beaded pillow prodded her backside. His glare didn't allow her even that much respite, and she sank back, more carefully this time, and looked around her.

There wasn't a bare section of wall anywhere. Furniture was crammed into the room, old, heavy furniture, tables draped in scarves, whatnot shelves, even a grand piano was stuck in a corner, covered with a fringed scarf and a dozen silver-framed pictures. The walls were similarly loaded, with dark portraits of gloomy-looking people, old photographs, religious icons and the like. The effect should have been overpowering and depressing. Instead, Laura felt like curling up on the surprisingly comfortable sofa and kicking off her shoes.

Michael was watching her, and probably reading her reaction. Before he had time to say anything, however, Sonya swept back in, her impressive bulk now swathed in a floral cotton apron bearing a tray of tall glasses set in silver holders.

"Two glasses, Sonya?" Michael questioned, moving over to an overstuffed chair trimmed with antimacassars. "Aren't you joining us?"

"You're the one who isn't joining us, Mischa. Father Dmitri wanted to talk with you about the afterschool program. I called him and told him you were coming. He's expecting you."

"Sonya…"

"Don't worry, little brother. I'll do exactly as you asked. I'll show Laura how the Russians drink tea, I'll tell her how I make jam, and we'll talk about you. Come back in an hour."

Laura sat there fascinated as Michael hesitated. Never would she have imagined that someone as overbearing as Michael Dubrovnik would take orders from a cozy-looking matron. But take orders he did. "An hour," he agreed, still reluctant.

Sonya didn't even acknowledge his departure, busying herself instead with the tall glasses of tea. "I prefer raspberry jam," she said, stirring a teaspoon of the thick red stuff into the glass of amber-colored tea. "Though blackberry jam will do. If only Mischa had given me more warning, we could have made jam together."

"Exactly what did Michael tell you?" Laura accepted her glass of tea with all the aplomb of a true coffee drinker. There was no potted palm conveniently close at hand to dump the tea into—she'd have to drink the stuff.

"That he was bringing a young woman up to drink Russian tea with me. Nothing more. I was hoping…but then, you know what I was hoping. Instead he says you're his enemy. I can't believe it."

"Can't believe that Michael has enemies? I'm sure that he has more than his fair share."

Sonya nodded. "What do they call him? The Whirlwind? He was always like that, even as a little boy. Determined to get what he wanted, blowing over everything in his way. He was never deliberately cruel, though. Just a little thoughtless sometimes. When he saw that he'd inflicted pain, he always did his best to make amends. What I find hard to believe is that *you're* his enemy."

"He wants a building that I own. I won't sell it to him."

"Why not?"

"It was designed and built by my great-grandfather. My grandmother left it to me, in the hope that I would keep it intact. Any other member of my family would have sold it, the first chance they got. I'm going to hold onto it, no matter what."

Sonya shook her head. "No, you aren't. Not if Mischa wants it. My brother hasn't gotten where he is today by taking no for an answer. The only one who tells him no and gets away with it is me."

"Then tell him no for me."

Sonya shook her head. "I don't think it's that easy. Even I have a battle when Mischa's made up his mind. He was determined to move us out of the old building, the old neighborhood. He bought us a condominium on Park Avenue, twice the size of this old apartment. He wouldn't listen when we told him we didn't want to live on the East Side. We like it here, in the old neighborhood."

"What happened? He must have finally accepted the fact that you didn't want to move."

"My Mischa is not one for fighting fairly, I warn you of this. When we refused to leave, he bought this building and served us with our eviction papers."

"No!" Laura breathed, horrified.

"Yes!" Sonya declared.

"What did you do?"

"We had no choice. My Tim works for the post office. He didn't want any of the jobs Mischa offered him. He wants to be his own man. We couldn't afford any alternatives, so we moved into Mischa's fancy condominium and were completely miserable. Five months later Mischa gave me the deed to this building for my birthday and sold the condo, putting the money in trust for the children. He's a good boy, he just needs a little push every now and then. Drink your tea."

Fascinated despite herself, Laura drank, noting with surprise that it wasn't nearly as nasty as she'd thought it would be. As a matter of fact, it was rather good.

"I don't think that tactic would work in my case. For one thing, he wouldn't care if I was completely miserable months later. For another, even if he did, the Glass House would already be buried beneath the foundation of Dubrovnik Plaza."

"Oh, dear," Sonya murmured. "It's in the way of the Plaza? That's been Mischa's dream for years. I don't think there's any chance of making him see reason."

"Neither do I."

"But I think you're wrong about him not caring if

you're miserable. Mischa likes to leave everything tidy. If he razes a building, he relocates the tenants. If he takes over a corporation, he either makes sure everyone's job is secure, or he has people to see that the employees find other jobs. He's got a conscience."

"There's nothing he can bribe me with. I won't give up my great-grandfather's building."

Sonya nodded. "Mischa should understand that. He knows how important family and tradition are."

"Not when they get in the way of his ambition." Laura found she had drained her tea and was, in fact, wishing she had more.

"Perhaps not. I think you should marry him. He needs a wife to temper that ambition. Then when you help me make raspberry jam next summer you can be carrying a baby."

"I'd love to help you make raspberry jam. And I'd love to be pregnant. But I'm going to marry someone else." Laura liked the cool sureness in her voice.

Sonya's shrug was philosophical. "I'm happy for you, but sorry for Mischa. I think he needs someone like you."

"He's going to marry another model, like his first wife." Laura finally remembered something from the magazine article she'd read about him. "Someone tall and elegant and beautiful. That's what he needs."

"That's what he thinks he needs," Sonya said darkly. "He doesn't listen to his sister, that's his problem. Tell me about the man you're going to marry. Not a tall, skinny model?"

"A farmer."

Sonya's dark blue eyes widened in surprise. "That's not what I would have picked for you, and I'm accounted to be something of a matchmaker around here."

"He's big and strong and gentle," Laura said, hoping to keep the defensiveness out of her voice. "He's a good man."

"So is my brother."

"Your brother doesn't want me." Not strictly true, a nagging little voice whispered in Laura's ear.

"Then he's a fool," Sonya said flatly. "If you're going to marry a farmer, then it will be even more important that you know how to make jam. Come back to me in the spring with a farmer's baby in your belly, and I'll show you how to make jam. Unless you've already moved away."

"We'll be living in New York."

"What will a farmer do in New York?"

Laura hadn't thought that far ahead. "Maybe we can have a roof garden on top of the Glass House."

"Laura," Sonya said gently, "you won't own the Glass House."

"Yes, I will."

Sonya opened her mouth to refute Laura's claim, then shut it again. "I hope you're right. My brother shouldn't get his way in all things. Come with me and we'll set lunch on the table. Father Dmitri promised he'd keep Mischa long enough for us to talk and then send him back. He's going to try for an hour, but I expect my brother will be back sooner. Did you like your tea?"

Laura rose, following Sonya's graceful bulk toward the kitchen. "Yes, I did."

"Surprised you, didn't it? We'll have more with lunch. Mischa says no one can make it like I do." She pushed open the swinging door into the large, old-fashioned kitchen, and a medley of heavy aromas enveloped them. "I wish Mischa had given us more warning. Tim would have arranged to come home for lunch. He'd like to meet you."

"Why?" Laura kept her voice deliberately suspicious as she accepted the enveloping apron Sonya handed her. "I told you there's nothing between your brother and me."

"I think he'd like to see a woman who could say no to Mischa and get away with it." She lifted the lid off a pot on the old-fashioned white porcelain stove and took a deep, appreciative sniff. "I would like to give you one piece of advice. I probably shouldn't...."

"Please," Laura said, hoping for a key to Michael's character, a clue to besting him. "Anything."

Sonya looked at her, planting meaty hands on her ample hips. "Those clothes are terrible on you. Throw them out when you get home."

Laura was still laughing when Michael walked in moments later. They made it through lunch peacefully enough, the three of them seated around the old white metal table in the middle of the kitchen. Laura waded through borscht, some sort of meat and rice dish, and even a third, totally optional glass of Russian tea, this time with blackberry jam. She could feel Michael's eyes on her, but she ignored his gaze, knowing from experience that she'd be unable to interpret it. It wasn't until they were ready to leave, and she was loaded down with half a dozen jars of homemade jam, that things got a little iffy.

"Come back and see me again, Laura," Sonya said at the door. "Don't wait for Mischa. He forgets his family...."

"I do not!" Michael protested.

"You could do better, Mischa," Sonya said sternly. She turned her back on him. "Bring your husband next time, Laura. I'd like to see who you'd prefer to this businessman of mine."

"Husband?" Michael didn't raise his voice, but the walls seemed to shake anyway.

"She's marrying a farmer," Sonya said, not bothering to look at him. She smiled at Laura, and to her new friend's amazement, winked. "She knows what's important in this life. Family is important. And the land."

"For a woman who's spent her entire sixty years in New York City, you're a fine one to talk about the land," Michael drawled, putting a hand under Laura's elbow and steering her out the door.

"Women understand these things."

Michael's response was short and to the point, but his sister was unruffled. "Show some respect, Mischa. If your mother was alive, she'd wash your mouth out with soap." She pushed her brother aside and enveloped Laura in her maternal embrace. "I wish you'd change your mind," she whispered. "My brother needs you more than any farmer."

Laura simply shook her head, returning the hug. Michael had stomped past the two women, heading down the narrow stairs in a patently foul mood. With a shrug and a smile, Laura followed. "Don't let him win," Sonya called after her. "He needs to learn about losing sometimes."

Laura paused at the top of the stairs. "I'll do my best to teach him a lesson," she said. "Count on it."

When she arrived back down on the sidewalk Michael was leaning against the Bentley, his hands in his pockets, his gaze abstracted, staring at his old neighborhood without seeing. "What did she say to you?"

"That I shouldn't wear long, frilly dresses," Laura replied with complete truthfulness.

Michael snorted with laughter before following her into the back seat of the Bentley. "I've got to get you back downtown. I'm late for a meeting, and I'm taking Marita out tonight."

"So I gather." Her voice was completely tranquil as her beringed fingers clutched the jars of jam she was still carrying. "As a matter of fact, I've got quite an evening planned myself."

"With the farmer?"

"Exactly."

"Don't you know you shouldn't get involved with someone on the rebound?"

"Then why are you going out with Marita?" she countered.

"I hadn't noticed that Marita's heart was broken. I'm not convinced she even has a heart."

"That'll be convenient for you. Nothing to entangle you with untidy emotions. You can have your bloodless marriage."

He said nothing for a moment, but Laura could see a pulse ticking at the base of his neck. Not too thick, not too thin, smoothly tanned, it was a nice neck that rose above the crisp white linen collar. She had the odd, totally irrational desire to press her mouth against that pulse.

"I can't see you with a farmer," he said finally.

"It's none of your business."

"I don't want to see you make a mess of your life."

"Why?"

He looked at her, his dark blue eyes wintry. "You're going to have a hard enough time living without the Glass House."

"I'm not going to live without the Glass House. You are."

The Bentley had accomplished the ride back downtown with admirable speed. They'd already stopped outside the building, but Michael made no move to open the door. "I'm tired of arguing with you," he said quietly.

"Then give up. Admit when you're defeated."

He grinned then, a sudden, oddly lighthearted upturning of his mouth. "I never give up."

"Neither do I."

"Have fun with your farmer."

Laura gave him her sexiest smile. "I have every intention of doing so. Enjoy your model." And she slid out of the car, still clutching her jam jars to her breast.

Susan was alone in the twelfth-floor offices, looking only marginally more cheerful than she had that morning. At least her eyes weren't currently red-rimmed. "Anyone call?"

"Emelia's got her screen test," Susan said.

"She must be bouncing off the walls." Laura set the jam jars on the table and ran her fingers through her thick black hair.

"She told me to tell you she loves you. I sent Jacki, Marlann and Melvin over to see the people at Dior. They called and are going to take them."

"You don't even need me," Laura murmured, wandering over to the windows and looking down at the construction site beside them. The huge pieces of machinery were just where they'd been left, a swarm of technicians working on them with the intensity of a team of brain surgeons.

"I need you."

"What about Frank? Any word?"

"Nothing." Susan quickly changed the subject. "This came for you." She held up a sealed envelope marked PRIVATE.

"What is it?"

"I didn't open it. I thought you deserved some secrets."

"I don't. Deserve them, or have them." She took the envelope from her assistant's hand, staring at it for a moment before tearing it open. "It's probably just an advertisement for a new deli or..." Her voice trailed off as she stared at the flimsy piece of paper in front of her. The words were cut from a newspaper; their message was horrifyingly clear.

"What is it?" Susan demanded. "You look white as a ghost."

"I guess I do have some secrets after all," Laura said numbly, crumpling the paper in her hand.

"Are you going to tell me what's in that letter?" Susan demanded. "Or am I going to have to wrestle you for it? I'm five inches taller than you and God knows how many pounds heavier."

"Yes, but I fight dirty," her boss replied with a ghost of a smile. "I'll tell you tomorrow. I have to think about it first."

"Laura..."

"Tomorrow, Susan. In the meantime, you can help me find a place for all this jam."

Susan knew when to let something be. "What are you going to do with all this, for heaven's sake?"

"Make tea," Laura said with a ghost of a smile. "Make tea."

## Chapter 13

This damned building was getting to him, Michael thought three hours later as he rode upward in solitary splendor. He looked around him at the ornate art deco brass swirls in the elevator, the polished oak floor beneath him, and cursed. He didn't trust the ancient elevator, but the Otis was out of order, and he wasn't in the mood to hike up nine flights of stairs to the floor he was using as his headquarters.

He leaned back against the walls, feeling the vibrations pulse through him as the cage bore him upward. He had to admit, as far as elevators went, that it was a pretty one. He wasn't a complete philistine—he could appreciate beauty in functional objects. But he couldn't afford to be distracted by beauty, by the beauty of an elevator, of an old, obsolete building, of a feisty young woman dressed in little girl's clothes.

She didn't realize how damned sexy she was in those

ridiculous clothes, Michael thought, stepping off into his hallway and unlocking the door that still said "Swimming Pool News." He already had a very good idea of what her body looked like beneath all that voluminous cotton— he'd seen her in micromini skirts, in scanty night clothes, in low-cut blouses. He knew she had surprisingly long legs, nice breasts, a small waist, and the most distracting rear end. He'd been sitting in a meeting, a meeting he'd been late for, much to the shock of everyone there who knew his obsession for promptness, and instead of listening to the all-important six-month projections, he'd been fantasizing about those long legs wrapped around him, the calico skirts spread beneath her.

Damn, he was doing it again! He slammed the door behind him and headed straight for the bar, pouring himself a generous dollop of whiskey with one hand as he loosened his tie with the other. This whole affair had taken too long, become too important to him. No wonder he was letting himself get distracted by a minor irritation like Laura Winston. He'd learned early on not to let all his energies get diverted into one project. There were always too many variables—he'd had to accept his share of defeats in the early years, and he'd always made sure he had something else going on at the same time, something he could turn to if the first project fell through.

The problem was, he hadn't had to face defeat in years. He'd forgotten that some things were simply beyond his control, the irrational stubbornness of the female mind being one of them.

He laughed, thinking how Sonya would beat him about the head and shoulders for that sexist thought. She'd liked Laura. He'd known she would, but unfortunately he couldn't compare that liking with anything in the past, since he'd never before taken a woman up to see his sister. Sonya had taken one look at his ex-wife and refused to allow her to visit the run-down but spotless apartment building on the Upper West Side.

She'd invited Laura back. Without him. He still couldn't quite figure out why he'd taken her up there. He'd been so furious when he heard about the damage to the earth-moving equipment that he knew he'd strangle her. Sonya's calm presence had managed to restrain his murderous impulses, though he was still sorely tempted to spank Laura.

The stupid thing about it was that he felt betrayed. After their dinner, their late-night dash through the rain, he'd felt an odd kinship with her, an undeniable attraction that he'd been too smart to act on. Or too slow, he reminded himself, thinking of Laura's laughing speed in escaping him. That she could have returned his kiss in the pouring rain, and then crept out to damage a fortune in equipment was something that rankled deep inside. Sooner or later he was going to have his revenge, and that revenge included razing her beloved building to a pile of rubble and broken glass. It wasn't his fault if it felt as though he were overreacting.

Marita. He needed to concentrate on Marita. Someone with the looks of an animated Barbie doll. Mile-long legs, tiny feet, tiny waist, spectacular breasts. Not to mention perfect blue eyes and a glorious mass of blond hair. And something behind those eyes, something both mysterious and fascinating, that he couldn't quite fathom. As he told Zach, he probably didn't want to know the answer to the mystery. Its resolution was unlikely to be as interesting as the question.

What he ought to do was sleep with her tonight. Granted, he'd only been out with her a couple of times—it would be rushing things. He'd never been one to rush into relationships—it got too messy if things weren't thought out thoroughly. But he needed distraction from Miss Laura Winston, and who better to provide it than the owner of the face of the decade? If he made his move in that direction, it would wipe out the absurd temptation to sleep with his nemesis, and maybe the whole mess would resolve itself sooner.

So why couldn't he get more excited about the idea? Why couldn't he work up even half the enthusiasm for Marita's perfect body that he could for Laura?

It must be a midlife crisis. That, and the fact that he was facing the remotest possibility of defeat for the first time in more than a dozen years. It was enough to shake anyone. Particularly when he knew that the only reason he might have to accept defeat, the only reason this was taking so damned long, was because he was too squeamish. He couldn't crush Laura Winston with the speed and strength he usually used in ridding himself of obstacles. And as long as he was hampered by this unexpected conscience, the future of Dubrovnik Plaza was still uncertain.

Draining his whiskey, he pushed himself out of the chair and headed for the shower. He was dutifully telling himself all the delightful things he'd do to Marita's body, when a sudden, unpleasant thought wiped away any nascent desire. Hadn't Laura said she was going out with Carnaby? Hadn't she told Sonya she intended to marry the man? He'd ignored that as the canard it was, but mightn't it be possible, just possible, that Laura Winston was having the same thoughts he was? And that she'd come across the same solution to her problem?

If Jeff Carnaby touched her with his big farmer's hands, he'd break his wrists. And that was just for starters.

"So what does a modern woman do when she's about to embark on a love affair?"

Susan looked at her. "You're asking me? One three-month relationship two years ago and a one-night stand do not make me an expert. Why don't you ask your mother?"

"Not my mother." Laura made a face at her reflection in the mirror. "Come on, Susan, give me a break."

"Who is going to reap the benefit of your sudden fall from chastity? Please don't tell me it's Marita's ex-boyfriend."

"You probably think I'd be better off with Dubrovnik."

"Did he offer?"

"Of course not. Michael wants my surrender in a lawyer's office, not a bedroom."

"If you say so. Jeff Carnaby's too nice for you."

"Thanks a lot," Laura said, miffed.

"I mean it. You have a bulldozer of a personality. You need someone to stand up to you, not a gentleman."

"But I want a gentleman!" Laura wailed, frustrated beyond bearing. "I don't want someone to stand up to me. I want someone who is sweet, thoughtful and doesn't always want his own way."

"In other words, you don't want someone like you."

"I'm not in the mood for this, Susan," Laura warned. "I'm facing one of the most difficult nights of my life, and I need support, not criticism."

"If you expect me to support you in your seduction of Jeff Carnaby, you might as well save your breath. Why don't you show your usual good sense and forget about this whole ridiculous idea?" Susan took one last run at making her see reason. "Jeff Carnaby isn't the man for you."

But Laura wasn't interested in seeing reason. "So you're not going to make this easier on me?"

"Not if I can help it. Don't do it, Laura."

Laura looked at her watch. "I'd better go down and

change. One thing's for certain—I'm going to have to do something about his taste in women's clothing. Any man who thinks I look good in a frilly floral dress needs a few basic things pointed out to him. Even Sonya knew these clothes were terrible on me."

"Sonya?"

"Sonya Dubrovnik O'Reilly. Michael's sister. No, don't ask," she said, forestalling the question. "I'm going to change. Can you close up here?"

"I ought to leave it open to muggers and lowlifes."

"The only danger to this building is already in residence. Give me a break, Susan."

"Tomorrow we'd better start thinking of taking on some new clients," Susan said, tacitly ignoring the plea. "It's one thing to have an exclusive clientele, but if you expect to make any sort of profit, you're going to have to diversify. Representing the best hands in the business is not going to pay the rent."

"I don't pay rent, remember? I own this building. For now, at least."

"Then Marguerite Valmy's hands won't support your legal fees. You need someone to take Frank's place." Her voice didn't even waver.

Laura bit back the sympathy that rushed up. "You're right. We'll have open call on Tuesday and see what we can come up with. Does that make you happy?"

"It's a start," Susan said.

Laura was already at the door. "If Jeff shows up, send him down to the eleventh floor."

"If Jeff shows up, I'll direct him to the nearest elevator shaft," Susan growled.

"Don't you want me to experience the same misery you are?"

"No. Stop looking so cheerful. Go downstairs and change out of my clothes."

"I'm not cheerful, I'm nervous. I always grin when I'm nervous. Wish me luck."

"Break a leg."

"Why do I suspect you really mean that?" Laura asked the ceiling. "I'll call you tomorrow and tell you all about it."

Susan watched her leave, watched the little skip in her step as she disappeared down the utility stairs to her apartment. Her gaze shifted to the six jars of jam. While the thought of adding it to hot tea moved her not one bit, she hadn't eaten a thing all day. Susan had had the vain hope that misery would enable her to lose a few pounds, but that stage had already passed. What she needed was food.

Tossing one of the jars into her purse, she cleared her desk and locked the door, hoping that Jeff Carnaby wouldn't know how to find Laura. She knew that hope was a vain one, but couldn't keep from wishing that Laura didn't have to make such an obvious mistake.

Who was she to worry about other women's mistakes, after she'd made such a major one? Funny, though. Despite her misery, her depression and despair, she still didn't regret it. Maybe that would come later.

The first thing she did after she got home to her tiny apartment was to head for the kitchen. Drowning her sorrows in food seemed an excellent idea, and she took the baguette she'd bought from the French bakery down the street, split it sideways and slathered it with butter and Sonya Dubrovnik's raspberry jam. She then committed the unpardonable sin of pouring a generous dollop of Drambuie over ice, and wandered back into the living room, kicking off her shoes as she went. She curled up on the sofa as the autumn night closed in outside her windows, and had just brought her self-indulgent sandwich to her mouth when a shadow appeared in her bedroom doorway.

She almost screamed, immediately certain a thief had broken in. The last person in the world she expected to see was Frank Buckley, barefoot, his pale gray designer pants making his aquamarine eyes seem very dark. Without a word he came and sat down beside her, warmth and amusement glinting in those eyes. "Hungry?"

She started to put down the sandwich, but he took it from her, biting into it with strong white teeth. "God, that's good," he murmured. "I don't blame you for wanting the whole loaf. And I don't even have to think about my diet anymore. I can eat anything I want. I'll probably gain fifty pounds in a week. Will you still love me when I'm fat?"

She finally gathered enough self-control to say something. "Who says I love you now?"

He didn't say a word. He just looked at her, a slow smile curving his beautiful mouth, and she wanted to hit him. But how could she hit a man for knowing the truth, when she'd made it painfully obvious? Instead she changed the subject. "Where were you this morning?"

His smile faded, his eyes clouded and he leaned back, taking another bite of her jam-and butter-slathered baguette before passing it back to her. "I have a little tiny bit of a problem," he said.

Susan took a bite of the baguette, allowing herself a small moan of appreciation while Frank swallowed half her Drambuie. "A tiny bit of a problem?" she prodded when she'd finished chewing.

"Just minor," he said. "Did you hear the telephone ring this morning?"

Susan blushed, remembering that she'd been lying naked in this man's bed when she heard the phone ring. "Yes," she said, staring intently at the half-eaten loaf of French bread. "Was it a job?"

"Not exactly. I'm afraid, Susan my love, that I am being blackmailed."

Laura was having a hard time working up any enthusiasm for tonight's activities. While the red roses Jeff had brought were beautiful, she'd always hated red flowers. And though he was clearly responding to her, she was busy battling an almost terminal case of cold feet. Getting that anonymous letter hadn't helped.

But she wouldn't think about that. She couldn't afford to, not right now. If someone had the gall, the absolute stupidity to think they could blackmail her and get away with it, they were in for a rude awakening. But that was going to have to wait till tomorrow. There was nothing she could do about it now, and she had more important things to concentrate on. Namely the man beside her.

"You're a wonderful cook," he said, when they ended up back on the couch after finishing the sumptuous seven-course meal she'd had secretly delivered to her kitchen. He looked at her over his glass of brandy, his eyes blue and warm and guileless, and reached over and captured her hand in his. "Such a small hand," he murmured, caressing it.

Why did he have to hold her hand? she wailed inwardly. Why couldn't he do something Michael hadn't done? Certainly Michael hadn't done much—there was a realm of possibilities. He could nuzzle her neck, put his hand on her breast, or even push her down onto the sofa and climb on top of her. But he seemed damnably content just to sit there and hold her hand, and she could do nothing but compare the feel of his hand, with its calluses, its broad palm and thick, spatulate fingers, with Michael's hand. She tried to tell herself that Michael's hands were those of a wimp, a man who didn't do anything more physical than an occasional game of racquetball. It didn't do any good. Quixotically she was still more moved by Michael Dubrovnik's elegant hands than by the sturdy, workman's hand holding hers right now.

She shifted, pulling up her legs underneath the black silk skirt that had hitherto exposed those admittedly enticing legs, and thought about the trouble she'd gone to that night. Apart from ordering the dinner and shifting everything to her own dishes, she'd put her poor body through a series of tortures that should have made her acceptable to a Middle-Eastern pasha, much less a Midwestern farmer. She'd shaved her legs and her armpits, rubbed perfumed cream into her skin. She'd flossed her teeth, plucked her eyebrows, scrubbed her entire body three times over, first with a loofah, then with the rough Finnish towels she always preferred, then with the softest of French cotton terry. She'd updated her pedicure and manicure, sprayed every square inch of her body with Eternity, and then spent hours agonizing over what to wear.

She'd finally settled on a black taffeta dress, silk clocked stockings and four-inch heels. Her underwear was whisper-thin silk, and she'd had the astonishing courage to wear a black lace garter belt. If she could just manage to get those large, scrupulously clean hands partway under her skirt, she was counting on the garter belt to do the rest.

The room was too bright. She had music playing softly in the background. Usually she liked classical, but the tinkling on the piano was making her want to scream. Jeff's completely relaxed pose wasn't much comfort. She told herself she was glad he found her so easy to be around, but she lied. She wanted to excite him. Now that she'd finally decided to fall in love with someone, to have an affair that would with luck lead to marriage, she was in a hurry for it to happen. Especially since the longer it took, the more she was doubting her decision.

It was already after eleven. If he didn't make a move by midnight, she was going to give up. She had better things to do than wait around for him to realize she was available. Better men than he had been panting at her heels for the last fourteen years. He didn't realize what he was being offered.

She drew back, draining her brandy with less than the respect it deserved, working herself into a snit. The least he could do was kiss her. She needed to make sure it wasn't just Dubrovnik's kisses that sent her mind spinning into the twilight zone.

"Penny for your thoughts," Jeff murmured, and Laura controlled her immediate wince. She didn't know people still said things like that. Another thing she'd have to change about him.

Still, he had very kind eyes. And broad shoulders, sturdy legs and a trusting disposition. He hadn't even suspected that that fancy dinner hadn't been prepared by her lily-white hands, even when she'd made up totally absurd names for the exotic dishes.

And did she really want a man who lunged? Wasn't his diffidence, his unwillingness to push her, part of his charm? He was waiting for permission, and the best thing she could do was grant it.

"I was wondering when you were going to kiss me," she murmured.

He moved with flattering speed, leaning over and

pressing his lips against hers. They were nice lips, firm, warm. And closed. Michael's mouth hadn't been closed when he'd kissed her.

She sighed, leaning back, and softened her mouth beneath his. He took the cue, opening his mouth over hers, and she waited for his tongue.

Nothing. Just his wet, open mouth on hers. His hands were now on her bare shoulders, his thumbs rubbing against her arms, and she very shyly put her tongue to his lips. He jerked, clearly startled, but made no move to respond to the caress.

All right, Laura thought. So he didn't use his tongue when he kissed. It was sort of an intimate business, anyway. Maybe they don't do that in the Midwest.

He moved his mouth away, sitting closer and sliding an arm around her shoulders, holding her there. Like a couple sitting on a porch swing, Laura thought with misty sentiment.

"This is nice," he murmured, his voice deep and rumbling in his chest. "I wish I didn't have to go home tomorrow."

"Do you?" She let a hand trail over his wash-and-wear shirt, her fingernails fiddling with a button. She wondered whether he had hair on his chest. Not too much, she hoped. The amount Michael had was just about right.

"I'm afraid so," he said. "But I'll never forget you." And to her absolute shock he removed his arm, stood up and headed for the door.

She sat there dumbfounded as he pulled on his jacket. It took her a moment to move, but she was at the door before he'd opened it. "Remember this," she said, sliding her arms around him and pressing her body against his. She kissed him, pulling his head down to her own, being careful not to repeat the mistake with her tongue, and waited for his response.

It was a little slow in coming, but not bad. His arms encircled her, pulling her tight, and if it was more like a bear hug and less like an embrace, she had to remember he was a strong man. "I want you," she whispered into his ear. "I want you to make love to me."

He slid his hands down her back, cupping her buttocks and yanking her against his body. She could feel the beginnings of arousal through his suit, and almost gnashed her teeth in frustration. She'd thought she would have been flat on her back, the dirty deed accomplished, by this time. Chambers had certainly been quick about the business.

"Oh, honey," Jeff murmured thickly, his tongue sloshing in her ear. "I can't believe this. You're so smart and so sophisticated. And you can cook, too." And with that he scooped her up into his arms and started across the room. "Where the heck's the bedroom?"

That did it. "Stop," Laura said, pushing him away. He dropped her, and she tripped, falling against him. "I can't do it," she said. "I can't sleep with someone who says heck." And without another word she turned and ran from her apartment, along the hallway and down the utility stairs in her stocking feet, leaving Jeff alone, confused, and just slightly relieved.

# Chapter 14

Susan lay in bed, staring at the play of shadows on her ceiling. New York City nights were never still—even at this late hour they were a ballet of light and sound and people, invading her apartment through the tightly shut wooden shutters and enveloping calico priscilla curtains. She turned her head, watching the tendrils of light invade the darkness of her bedroom, and thought back to the strange events of the earlier evening.

"You're being blackmailed?" she'd echoed, staring at Frank in horror. "You call that a little tiny bit of a problem? What qualifies as a major disaster?"

"Losing my livelihood." His voice was flat, unemotional, but Susan immediately bit her lip. "Besides, the whole thing's ridiculous. I'm being blackmailed for something I never did. A few years back the merest hint of it would have scuttled my career, but since that's already vanished, I don't really have anything to worry about.

What I am worried about is who's blackmailing me, and who else this person has decided to hit on. Not to mention where they got their information."

"What are you being blackmailed for?"

He grimaced. "When you start out in the modeling business you aren't too choosy about getting jobs, and you're not too particular about your body. It's a tool of the trade, used to sell things."

"I don't think I want to hear this," Susan began, starting to get up, but Frank pulled her back.

"Sorry, but I don't exist simply as part of your fantasy life. I'm real, I'm human and I've made mistakes. If you prefer your lovers to be faultless, you picked the wrong man."

The hand on her arm was too strong, the lines around his mouth were too deep, belying the bland expression, and suddenly Susan was ashamed of herself. "You forget," she said. "I've known you for four years. I'm already aware of one or two faults."

He grinned, and the tension in his body faded slightly. "This is a bit more than an excess of narcissism or a tendency to forget bills. I was in a porn movie."

Susan took a deep breath. "Okay. What else?"

"God bless you, darling. I wasn't even doing anything in it. Just part of the crowd scene in an orgy. They wanted good-looking bodies, and I had one. Unfortunately I wasn't much use to them except for scenery. That sort of thing just doesn't excite me."

"I wouldn't have thought that was all that hideous. A little sordid, perhaps, but nothing criminal."

"That's where it gets a little iffy. I was in the one scene, just standing around watching. But later scenes involved things that were more than sordid. They were disgusting. And criminal. And while there's no way to prove that I was anywhere around when they shot those later scenes, any prospective employer would think twice before hiring someone who'd appeared in a movie like that. And no, I'm not going to tell you what was in those scenes. I tried to watch it once, and I threw up. I expect your stomach is even a little more delicate."

Susan managed a shaky smile. "Who knew about this?"

"Laura."

"You don't think she...?"

"Of course not." He offered her the half-empty glass of Drambuie, then drained what was left. "She knows better than anyone that it's now just an empty threat. I don't have any money, and I don't have a career to jeopardize."

"I don't understand why she didn't tell me."

"I went to her in private when this first came out. A friend of mine with bent tastes happened to see the movie at a private showing, and he told me about it. I figured I owed it to Laura to warn her what might happen. I offered to let her out of our contract." He leaned back, running his hands through his sunlit hair. "Of course she told me not to be ridiculous. If it came out she'd stand beside me, bless her heart. It never did, thank heavens."

"But why didn't she tell me?"

"We decided it might upset you too much. Also the fewer people who knew, the better. Laura had her lawyer send a letter to the movie's distributors, demanding that they either withdraw the film from the limited circulation it was enjoying, or else disguise my face so that I wouldn't be recognized. They opted to do the latter, so only my former lady friends would recognize me. And actually, given my state of boredom, maybe even they wouldn't know me."

"This isn't something to joke about," Susan said sternly.

"What else can I do? I certainly can't come up with ten thousand dollars by tomorrow morning."

"Ten thousand dollars? That doesn't sound like very much."

"Maybe not, but I don't have it."

"No, I mean it doesn't sound like very much for blackmail money. Whoever is doing this doesn't have any idea of the kind of money a model can usually command. Since he doesn't know you're not working, he should think you'd be able to come up with a lot more money."

"An interesting point. Academic, however, since I'm not entirely sure I can come up with ten dollars at this point, much less ten thousand. And of course, there's no reason to pay."

"If you were still working, would you have paid?"

"I doubt it." Frank leaned back on the sofa, stretching his lithe body. "I don't like the idea of someone taking my money for nothing. With my face disguised, they would have had a hard time proving anything."

"But someone must have a copy of the film which hadn't been altered to disguise you. Otherwise how would your blackmailer have known about it? Unless you told someone…?" The thought of petulant, beautiful Tracey Michaels entered her head, but she dismissed it, knowing it was the product of jealousy rather than justifiable suspicion.

"No one knew. The friend who mentioned it to me died last year, and I doubt it made enough of an impression on him to have mentioned it to anyone else. No, that's not where the information came from. It came from Laura's office."

"Don't be ridiculous. I know every square inch, every

piece of paper at Glass Faces. If I didn't know about it, how could someone else find out?"

"Darling, I don't know. All I know is that Laura had a copy of the legal agreement we made with the film's distributors. The blackmailer sent me a photocopy of it."

"Have you talked with Laura about it?"

"She keeps disappearing. Every time I've tried to catch her, she's been on the run somewhere. You have any idea what's going on?"

"She's in love," Susan said glumly.

"With whom?"

"She thinks she's in love with Marita's ex-fiancé. She's been so busy chasing him that she hasn't had a chance to notice that she's really in love with Michael Dubrovnik."

Frank let out a long, low whistle. "That doesn't sound very promising."

"It's doomed. She's probably better off chasing after Jeff Carnaby."

"Unless the face of the decade decides she wants him back."

"Why should Marita do that? She could have her choice of a dozen men, men of power and influence and money. Why should she settle for a Midwestern farmer?"

"Maybe those choices will evaporate."

"I can't imagine why they should. She'll only get more famous, more sought after as time goes on. You don't like her much, do you?"

"Not much," Frank said, his voice flat and noncommittal.

"Why not?"

"Look into her eyes sometime. Look really deeply, and you'll see what I mean."

"When did you look really deeply into her eyes?" She couldn't help sounding jealous, but Frank simply laughed, stretching out on the sofa and pulling her down on top of him.

"It's easier to see if you're used to it, my sweet. I didn't get any closer than five feet, and that was close enough. Besides, it's you that I'm concentrating on."

She made a very slight effort to struggle. Not enough to free herself, but just enough to let him know it wasn't going to be that easy. "But what about your blackmailer?"

"As Scarlett said, I'll think about that tomorrow. I have an idea or two."

"But…"

He stopped her mouth with his, a slow, leisurely kiss that left her breathless and mindless, the specter of Frank's blackmailer fading in the early-evening twilight. When he finally lifted his mouth from hers, his eyes were bright with warmth and laughter. "You were saying?" he prompted.

It took her a minute to regain her senses, especially since one of his hands was cupping her breast through the frustrating layers of clothing.

"Frank…"

"Yes?" He was rubbing his thumb over her nipple, distracting her further.

"Frank, what are you doing here?"

He laughed, sliding his arms around her and pulling her close against his taut body. "Making love to you, dearest. Where else would I be?" He looked down at her, some of the humor fading. "Didn't you think I'd be back?"

"I didn't know." She tried to stare down at the carpet, but his hand beneath her chin forced her face up to his.

"Susan, we're friends," he said. "We've been friends for four years, and damned good ones at that. I'd hate to think that last night changed that."

"Of course it changed it. It changed everything. You can't have sex and then assume that everything is just as it was. It isn't that simple. It…"

He cupped her face with his long-fingered hand, his thumb touching her lips lightly. "It wasn't sex, Susan. If we'd had a nice, casual roll in the sack it might have been, but it didn't end up that way, and you and I both know it. I don't think I've ever felt that way before. But I don't want to lose you as a friend. I'm greedy, I want both. I want your friendship and I want your love. Is that so much to ask?"

Susan shut her eyes for a moment, drinking in the sound of his words, the feel of his thumb against her lips. "Oh, God, Frank, you have it already," she whispered. "But what are you offering me in return?"

"All of the above," he murmured. "I want to marry you. I want to have babies with you. I want to get old and fat and saggy with you. But don't panic. I won't rush you into anything. We can live together for a few months beforehand. Your place or mine?"

"Frank."

"My place is bigger." He considered the matter, ignoring her scandalized expression. "But your location's better, and you don't have cockroaches."

"Everyone in New York has cockroaches," she said faintly.

"Well, yours aren't as big as mine. Mine could bite your head off. When you get pregnant, let's move out to the country. I bet they don't have cockroaches in Connecticut."

"Don't count on it," she said faintly.

"Don't count on the cockroaches? Or don't count on you?"

She couldn't fight it anymore. No woman could, not

when everything she ever wanted had been dumped into her lap. She was afraid, mortally afraid he was going to break her heart. But if she refused to take a chance, to risk the pain for the sheer glory of it, then she deserved to be miserable.

"Frank," she said. "If you break my heart, I'll kill you."

He grinned at her. "Same to you, darling. How about a Christmas wedding?"

Running away was never a good idea. For the first time Laura could understand why cowardice was a mistake. She was on the third-floor landing of the utility stairs, barefoot, no purse, no money, no coat, no key. Upstairs waited a man she'd rather die than face. And she had no options.

Well, almost no options. The Petronelli Employment Agency had been in the building for decades—old Mr. Petronelli was still in command, though his savvy young daughter was probably going to revitalize the business, the moment he finally retired. He still left a key over the ledge of the doorway, innocently secure in his faith in mankind and in the Glass House's night watchmen. She could go in there and hide for a while. Long enough to regain control of her stupid emotions, her hammering heart, her ridiculous panic. Besides, Gina Petronelli was a coffee snob. There was an espresso machine that was kept in perfect running order. A cup of coffee and a few minutes of peace were all that Laura needed to regain her equilibrium.

Unfortunately the Petronellis' office was on the east side of the building. She had a perfect view of the ugly pit of the excavation beside her, the squat, malevolent shapes of the bulldozers shrouded in moonlight. She

could make out at least two figures moving around—
the Whirlwind had decided to lock the barn door after
the horse was stolen. Beefed-up security wouldn't help
him, Laura thought, sipping her espresso. She'd simply
have to go at him from another angle. That is, if she was
able to deal with the threat that had crept up behind her.

The blackmail letter had been short and succinct.

*If you don't want Dubrovnik to see the Williams
Engineering Company's report on the Glass
House, you will have ten thousand dollars in
small, unmarked bills ready for me. Instructions
will follow.*

Hell and damnation. That report was locked up tight
in her private file—no one, not even Susan, had access
to what lay in there. Not that she'd suspect Susan, even
for a minute. She'd as soon suspect her mother.

As a matter of fact, her mother was a likely suspect.
Jilly never had enough money, and she certainly had no
qualms about going through her daughter's belongings.

But Jilly wouldn't have been naive enough to ask for
a measly ten thousand dollars. She knew that her daughter could liquidate any number of holdings in fairly short
order, up to and including the Glass House. The sale of
that building would have suited Jilly just fine, and ethical
considerations wouldn't have slowed her down for even
a second. Jilly wouldn't ask for ten thousand dollars, any
more than she'd ask for cab fare. She always played in
the major leagues.

Then who was it? It couldn't be Michael—he had
nothing to gain. Once he got his hands on that damning report, it would be all over. The building would be
closed as a safety hazard until the stress points could be

evaluated, she'd be fined for covering up, and she'd have to surrender.

She knew one person who needed money quite desperately, and who had unlimited access to her office. She didn't even like to consider it, and Susan would kill her if she knew what she was thinking, but Frank Buckley was the only likely suspect she could come up with. He was desperate for money, his career had dried up in front of him, and he knew better than anyone about the locked file in her office.

But ten thousand dollars seemed puny, even for Frank. And while she didn't pride herself on being a particularly good judge of character, she couldn't really believe that Frank would do that to her. To Glass Faces, and to Susan.

She wasn't going to pay ten thousand dollars to an anonymous bully. She was going to stall, stall like crazy, until she could figure out who was behind this. If worse came to worst she could always hock Grandma's emeralds, but she would hate to do it. Her grandmother had loved the Glass House, despite its history. She wouldn't have minded her jewels being sacrificed in its defense.

All Laura could do was wait and see. Too much had happened today, and she was desperately tired, vulnerable beyond belief. All she wanted was to go and hide in her own apartment, to be alone.

She could hear the elevators in the vast stillness of the almost empty building. She didn't know who was using them—her own security, what there was of it, took the stairs. She had no guarantees that Jeff had done the decent thing and taken his leave, sparing her the embarrassment of ever facing him again.

Life wasn't usually that kind or convenient. And she couldn't spend much more time in the Petronellis' office, swilling espresso. She was wired enough as it was.

She needed her own apartment, her own view, high up, looking over the lights of the city. She needed peace, for just a few short hours. Though she suspected that her thoughts would refuse her that peace.

Leaving a note for Gina, she switched off the silver espresso machine, filling her cup and taking it with her as she started back up the stairs. Her stockinged feet were silent, and six flights later she wasn't even winded. She seldom bothered with health clubs—her stairs gave her workout enough.

She passed Dubrovnik's floors with her face averted. She knew where Michael was. In Marita's bed, most likely, Laura Winston and the Glass House miles from his consciousness. With luck he'd be so bemused by Marita's charms that he wouldn't be able to concentrate on his pet project.

Strangely the thought made her feel more like the madame her mother sometimes accused her of being and less like a businesswoman. And she couldn't help but feel like a woman who'd stabbed herself in the back.

A neat trick, she thought with a wry smile. Only a contortionist could manage such a thing. Please, God, make Jeff have left already. Please let my apartment be empty.

He answered the second part of her prayer. Her apartment had to be empty, because coming down the stairs from her apartment on the floor above was a decisive pair of male legs.

He'd just turned the corner, the tall male figure obscured in shadow, when Laura's voice halted him.

"Don't come any farther," she said, her voice tight with strain. "Why don't you go back upstairs and take the elevator? I really don't think I can face you."

He didn't move, and Laura turned around and sat on the bottom step, her back to the figure on the landing. "Please, Jeff. I'm sorry about tonight. It was all my fault. A stupid mistake on my part, and I'm sorry you got caught in it. Let's just leave it at that. Nice to know you, have a good trip home, and goodbye."

Still not a word, not a movement from the man behind her. Laura sighed, setting down the coffee on the step beside her and drawing up her knees close to her body. "You want an explanation?" she guessed, frustrated by his refusal to just leave. "I suppose I owe you that much. I thought we could be right for each other, but I was wrong. I thought you'd be the perfect man for me, someone I could fall in love with, someone who wouldn't demand anything of me, someone who'd give me babies and let me run my business. A friend and companion who wasn't too demanding.

"God, I sound like Dubrovnik. I told him he was cold and calculating, but I'm just as bad. I'm just like him," she said, testing the notion and finding it unpleasantly applicable. "I don't want to be, but I am. No, maybe I'm not quite so bad. I couldn't go through with sleeping with you. Not when I realized that it wasn't you I wanted at all. It was him."

The man behind her moved, but she held up her hand, forestalling him, her eyes trained on her stockinged feet. "I know just how ridiculous that sounds. Susan tried to tell me, but I refused to realize it. I can't understand how I could prefer a cold, ruthless wolf of a man to someone who's kind and gentle and decent. How I could be falling in love with a man who wants to destroy me, and running away from a man who'd give me everything a woman could want?

"But I am. It doesn't make sense, but I am. So instead of making one of the major mistakes of my life and sleeping with you, I'm going to continue with my life of celibacy. I'm smart enough not to go to bed with you, and I'm smart enough not to go to bed with Dubrovnik, even if he offered. If I just don't think about it, if I concentrate on what a rotten, deceitful snake he is, then maybe I'll forget all about falling in love with him."

Still the damned man didn't leave. The coffee beside her was cold, the twist of lemon peel spinning and floating like a dead leaf on the wind. For a moment that was what she felt like. The helpless prey of fate, twisting and turning in the wind. But she wasn't. She was Laura de Kelsey Winston, strong, invincible, mistress of her own fate, owner of the Glass House, in control of her own emotions.

She rose, feeling very small without her heels, very tired of the battle she'd been waging in her own soul. "Goodbye, Jeff. I'm sorry I used you, but I won't be using you again. I'm not going to bed with you."

She turned, looking calmly up the stairs at her stubborn guest, expecting Jeff Carnaby's mild eyes. Instead she found she was looking into Michael Dubrovnik's blazing blue ones.

He was only a few steps above her. He was wearing jeans and a cotton sweater open at the throat, and he looked very dangerous indeed. "Oh yes, you are," he said, his voice low and rumbling.

She was immobilized with horror and embarrassment. If she hadn't felt like such a fool she would have moved, would have run before he could reach her. She could have hidden once more in the Petronellis' office, and in the light of day this whole, surreal confession would cease to have any power. But he moved down the steps so swiftly that she only had time to take a step before he caught her, his hands hard and unyielding as he held her arms.

For a moment she was beyond rational thought. She

hit at him, struggling, but he was inflexible, subduing her without much effort at all. She'd be bruised tomorrow, she thought distantly. Maybe she could charge him with assault.

"Why didn't you say something?" she hissed, glaring up at him.

"And miss that interesting confession? You have a much higher opinion of my sense of honor than I would have thought. I'd been wondering what you were doing with Carnaby. Now I know."

"Just what you were doing with Marita," she snapped.

There was a small, reckless smile playing about Dubrovnik's mouth. "Exactly. I left her at the door of her hotel room, without even a kiss. Did you kiss Carnaby?"

"None of your business!" His hands were like manacles on her wrists. The more she struggled, the tighter they grew.

"No, I suppose not. Since you're ending up in my bed, not his. Still…" Before she realized what he intended, he pulled her into his arms, tightly against his body. He was far more aroused than Carnaby had ever been, and the tension and strength vibrating through him effectively wiped out any other considerations. When his mouth met hers she was absurdly ready, hungry for him despite all her better judgment.

She moaned when his tongue touched hers, pushing him away with her freed hands as her mouth answered his. Ignoring her hands, he cupped her face, holding her still for the scorching power of his kiss, and her fists grew feebler, batting at him weakly.

Scooping her up into his arms, he started back up the stairs, toward her apartment. "We might as well use your bed. It's all set for a seduction, isn't it?" Her apartment door was open, left that way by the thoughtful man she'd been fool enough to reject, and Dubrovnik kicked it shut behind him. The music was still playing, the dishes still littered the walnut table by the smoked glass panels. "Very nice," he muttered. "You'll have to do this for me sometime. Where's the bedroom?"

"Put me down and get out of here," Laura said, her voice shaky with emotions she didn't dare define. That was the second time a man had held her in his arms and asked that question. This whole evening would seem ridiculously unreal, if it weren't for the heat and muscle of the arms carrying her.

Dubrovnik ignored her demand, heading with unerring instinct for the bedroom door. "We shouldn't waste such a setup. Unless you'd rather come down to my place?"

"I'll have you charged with assault and rape," she hissed. "It'll give me just the ammunition I need to stop you."

He halted by the huge bed, letting her down slowly, her silk-clad body rubbing against his. "Oh, really?" His hands were already on the zipper at the back of her dress.

"You'll lose every chance you've ever had at the Glass House," she said, trying to ignore the hands at her back, their touch scorching her chilly flesh.

"What if you stop objecting?"

"I'll lie. If you do this, you'll lose everything."

His expression was reckless and determined as he pushed the dress off her shoulders. "It'll be worth it," he murmured, baring her breasts. "More than worth it."

## Chapter 15

Laura stood there in her darkened bedroom, her arms trapped by the silk dress Michael had pushed down. Looming over her he seemed huge, dark and dangerous, and she had a sudden moment of complete and utter panic. She'd delayed this moment for almost fourteen years, the trauma of her rough initiation wiping out any desire to repeat the experiment. She'd always known that sooner or later she'd try it again, preferably later. She'd always thought she'd pick someone gentle, sweet, pliant. Someone who could work up to it in stages, take no for an answer, woo and court and flatter and cherish her.

She hadn't expected to get caught up in a whirlwind. And caught up she was. The distant, rational part of her brain was protesting, fighting, manipulating. But the rational part of her brain no longer had any connection to her mouth, to her lips, to any other part of her body. While the sensible parts of her said no, the rest of her said yes…yes….

Michael pushed the dress the rest of the way, so that it settled in a silky puff around her ankles, leaving her wearing nothing but black clocked stockings, a black lace garter belt and a thin wisp of silk panties. She could feel a flush start across her cheekbones, and looked up at Michael out of dark, haunted eyes.

"To think you almost wasted this on Carnaby," he muttered. His hands came up to touch her breasts, to cup them with surprising gentleness, and she shivered in response, leaning into him slightly. His fingers were deft, stroking her, and she felt her nipples harden against his hands, felt a knot of desire tighten in her stomach, felt the heat of longing burn between her legs. His hand left her breasts, sliding around her as he kissed her, her body pressed against the soft cotton sweater, and his mouth opened on hers, demanding a response.

She still wasn't ready to give it. She stood passively enough in the circle of his arms, initially unprepared for his next move. He pushed her down and across the high wide bed, but she was too fast for him. She started to scramble away, out of his hypnotic reach, but he caught one ankle, yanking her back, moving to cover her body with his fully clothed one, trapping her beneath him. She bit her lip rather than give in to him, but he ignored it, covering her mouth with his, coaxing, teasing, until it opened beneath his, allowing his tongue the entry it demanded.

With a moan she gave in, putting her arms around his waist, holding on, shaking with both fear and anticipation. It was no longer her choice. He wouldn't let her leave, he wouldn't stop, therefore she didn't have to take responsibility. It was up to him, everything was up to him. He'd either prove to her that she was right in avoiding sex, or he'd show her what was missing. Either way, it was no longer her decision.

Her hands were trapped between their bodies. He must have sensed her acquiescence, for he released her mouth, angling his body off hers, enough to free her hands. Now that she had them back, she wasn't quite sure what to do with them. She wanted to touch his hair, the thick, black pelt that tumbled over his dark blue eyes; she wanted to touch his chest, that smooth, golden, muscled flesh she'd seen all too briefly. She wasn't sure if she wanted to touch anything else at this point. Sooner or later she'd have to, but she didn't think she was quite ready....

Taking her hand in his, he placed it on the insistent bulge beneath his zipper, holding her there when she tried to pull away. He felt hard, heavy under her hand, powerful in ways she didn't know how to deal with. Slowly she allowed her fingers to relax, to gently trace the rigid outline, curiosity and the confusion of desire burning away her fear.

The growl in the back of his throat signaled his approval even as he shifted his body out of her reach. He moved his own hand down her legs, stopping at the rosette-studded garters. He unsnapped them one by one, his mouth kissing the flesh beneath as he deftly rolled down her black silk stockings, and she could hear her own moan in the quiet of the bedroom. Reaching behind her, he unfastened the garter belt with the skill of a man with either great manual dexterity or too much practice. She didn't want to think about that. She just wanted to think about the mouth that had moved from the top of her thigh to the triangle of her panties, nibbling at her through the thin silk.

And then the silk was gone, stripped off her legs before she even realized it, and she was lying naked, vul-

nerable on her bed with a man who was fully clothed and
frighteningly powerful. She no longer had the inclination to try to escape—she'd accepted her fate, willing to
find out if she'd been missing anything. But for a moment Michael pulled back, sitting up and watching her,
his shadowed eyes unreadable.

"Aren't you going to ask me to leave you alone?" he
asked, his voice a deep growl. "Aren't you going to plead
one last pitiful time? It'll be easier to make the charge of
rape stick if you put up some form of protest."

Somewhere she found her voice. "I'll lie."

A ghost of a smile lighted his face in the darkened
room. "Why don't you ask me to go?"

Her lips were suddenly dry as she realized what he
was demanding of her. Something much worse than the
physical surrender he was expecting. He wanted more
than a tacit agreement. And she didn't know if she had
the nerve to give it.

Her bedroom had never felt so foreign. She'd spent the
last ten years of her life sleeping in this room, alone in
this bed, the smoky glass panels letting in the lights of
the city below, the tall buildings around her, the moonlight overhead. Now her space, her privacy and eventually
her body would be invaded. And he wanted her soul, too.

He couldn't have it. Gathering all her determination,
she looked up at him, her eyes far more eloquent than
her words. "Go," she said.

He stood up, swift and graceful, and headed for the
door. She had to bite her lip to fight back the moan of
protest, but even so he stopped at the open doorway to
look back at her. His face was lost in the shadows, but
hers was illuminated by a shaft of moonlight. She didn't
move, didn't care that she lay sprawled naked across the

huge bed, her clothes scattered around her. He was going to leave, and she had never felt so bereft in her entire life.

She shut her eyes against the sudden sting of tears. The quiet closing of the door released the final hold on her tenuous self-control, and a small, miserable sob escaped her—only to be swallowed as she heard his footsteps approach the bed.

She looked up again, trying to school her expression into one as enigmatic as his. "I thought you were leaving."

He looked down at her for a moment, then stripped the sweater over his head and tossed it onto the floor. "I was waiting for you to tell me not to leave."

"I won't ever do that."

"Yes, you will." His hands dropped to his pants, and with one swift move he shucked them.

She quickly shut her eyes again, waiting for the expected weight of him on the bed. Still nothing. He couldn't walk out on her stark naked. Or could he? There was nothing a man like Michael Dubrovnik wouldn't be capable of doing.

She opened her eyes, keeping them trained on his face and shoulders, biting her lip.

"That's better," he murmured. "Don't tell me you've never seen a naked man before—I won't believe you."

Briefly she let her eyes drop before yanking them upward again. "I've seen scores," she said flatly. "I run a modeling agency, remember. The human body holds no mysteries for me."

"Uh-huh. So why are you looking like Bambi when his mother was shot? It's just a body." He dropped onto the bed beside her, too near, not near enough. He put out a surprisingly gentle hand, pushing her spiky black hair out of her face. "Is it me you're afraid of, or sex in general?"

Now wasn't the time to lie, much as her pride demanded it. "Both," she said.

"Why are you afraid of sex?"

She wanted to nuzzle against that hand like a kitten starved for affection. "It's been a while since I've been involved with anyone," she said lamely, hoping that would cover things.

"How long?" He'd moved closer, his mouth gently nibbling at her neck, his breath warm and tingly on her skin.

"Fourteen years." His hand was on her arm, gently stroking, drawing it over himself to rest lightly against his waist. The shock of his bare skin made her start to pull away, but then she let her hand drop, let it rest against the smoothness of his flesh.

He didn't seem shocked by her answer. He was too busy nibbling on her shoulder. "And what did this involvement cover?" he whispered.

"Once."

"One night?"

"No. Once."

She could feel his mouth against her skin, could feel the unexpected grin. When he lifted his head to look down at her he was still grinning, an expression both possessive and rampantly sexual. "Good."

"Mischa…" The name came easily to her tongue. "Please be gentle with me."

He appeared to consider the notion. "Did this other man rape you?"

"He was just a boy," Laura supplied with the last traces of bitterness. "No, he didn't."

"Did he hurt you?"

"No. It just wasn't very…nice."

Michael shook his head. "Sex isn't nice, Laura. And it isn't always gentle."

"It would have been with Jeff," she protested lamely.

"Then why did you run from him? Why are you here with me?"

"Because I'm an idiot."

"Wrong answer. For once in your life you're showing some brains. You're with the man you want, not the man you think you should want. No, Laura, I won't be gentle with you. I'm not a gentle man, and you know it." And his mouth dropped onto hers, drinking in any protest as his tongue thrust deep into her mouth. Instinctively her arms went around his neck, pulling him closer, and her tongue answered his.

His hands swept the length of her body, deft, arousing hands, dancing over the fevered silk of her flesh softly, teasingly. He moved his mouth away from hers, capturing one tightly budded breast and drawing it deeply into his mouth, suckling hard. She cried out as a knot of desire spasmed through her, and one of his hands slid down her flat stomach, curved around her narrow hip, and moved between her legs.

For a brief moment she tried to close her legs to him, but he ignored her attempt. His fingers found her, the damp, heated center of her, and his first touch made her arch off the bed in surprise and panic. She reached down to push him away, but he ignored her, his mouth moving to her other breast as his fingers began to stroke her, taking possession of the most private part of her body, making it his, so that instead of trying to pull his arm away, her hands were clasping his wrist, her fingernails digging in, and she felt the unbearable, wonderful sensations begin to spiral out.

He released her breast, and her skin felt damp and cool compared to the feverish flush that covered the rest of her body. "This is a game for two players, Laura," he said, his voice rasping in the darkness. "Touch me."

She released his arm, reaching up to tentatively caress his shoulder. He was covered with a fine sheen of sweat, and she could feel the tension pulsing through him. "No," he said, his voice hard. "Touch me."

She couldn't pretend not to know what he meant. And suddenly she wanted what he wanted. She wanted to feel that heavy male power in her hands, wanted to know what would soon be a part of her. Running one hand down his chest, she let it slide across his taut stomach, down the crisp curl of hair. And then she touched him, the silken length of him, the satiny-smooth flesh, the heat and desire and dampness and sheer size of him. She wanted to draw away in panic, but she couldn't, her fingers fascinated with the feel and texture of him, even as her mind panicked.

"You see how much I want you?" he murmured into her ear, as his hand still continued its inexorable invasion between her legs.

"You're too...too big," she whispered.

"Don't worry. I'll fit."

"Mischa," she said. "I'm afraid."

He levered his body over hers, holding her legs apart as he settled between them, the steely power of him resting against her, dampness against dampness, heat against heat. "I know," he said, his hands sliding beneath her to cup her buttocks. He gave her no false promises, no reassurance. "I know," he said, and pushed into her.

For a moment she panicked, trying to push him away from her, tightening up against an invasion she wasn't sure she wanted. "Don't fight me," he murmured, but she couldn't hear him, lost in her own unexpected alarm. The sharp pain on her shoulder startled her into a shriek of dismay. Michael took advantage of his deliberate distraction, pushing in deep, filling her with his strength and masculine power. She shuddered, accepting him, and when she looked up, her eyes were glazed with tears.

"You bit me," she whispered.

"Needs must when the devil drives," he murmured, running his tongue over the teeth marks on her soft white shoulder. And he began to move.

She whimpered slightly, expecting pain. But there was none. Just the aching emptiness of his withdrawal, the richness of his filling her once again. He moved slowly, letting her accustom herself to him, and as her fear faded, her tension built. She found she was clutching him, her hands clinging to him with nothing short of desperation. Something was stirring within her, some teasing, tangling twist of wanting that was building, not steadily, but in odd fits and starts, warning her of something beyond her control.

She sighed, her mind drifting in unexpected pleasure, when he suddenly pulled away, out of her body, poised just out of reach. In desperation she tugged at him, but he was maddeningly distant. "Don't leave me," she whispered.

She didn't need his small smile to know that he'd won. It no longer mattered. He returned to her, thrusting deep and hard, and his voice in her ear was just a reminder of her weakness. "I told you you'd beg me not to leave you."

Deep in her body he was holding still, and she had no choice but to respond. "You're a manipulative bastard, Mischa."

"Yes." He reached down, took her legs and wrapped them around his waist. "But I'm honest about what I want. And I want you."

She didn't understand her body, or the shimmers of re-action that were radiating from her. She didn't understand how he managed to make her feel this way, didn't under-stand what was happening to them. She no longer cared. "Shut up and take what you want," she said fiercely. And reaching up, she kissed him hard on the mouth.

He'd been honest. He wasn't gentle with her. He was fierce, demanding, driving into her with a force and power that left her weak, clinging to him, longing for more. They were both slick with sweat, breathless, striv-ing for something that Laura didn't even comprehend. All she knew was that she wanted him, more and more and more of him, again and again, deeper and deeper. Her fingernails raked across his back, but he ignored them, his hands bruised her wrists, but she ignored them, clinging to him with her arms, her legs, her body, hold-ing tight and reaching…reaching….

"Look at me," he said, his voice hoarse, his muscles standing out with exertion. "Open your eyes and look at me, Laura. I want to watch you when you come."

She opened her eyes. "I'm not going to," she said faintly. "I'm not…"

"Yes," he said. "You are."

And suddenly she did, convulsing around him, shock and surprise spinning into blind sensation as she was swept away, caught in a whirlwind of dark desire that was twisting and turning her, tossing her into a night where nothing existed but sheer sensation. She felt him convulse in her arms, his body rigid, and clenched her-self ever more tightly around him, wanting to scream with the joy, with the power, with the fear. For a mo-ment she was alone, and then he was with her, and the fear was gone. Together they rode the storm, whirling in the wind, soaring through the darkness into light, into shadow, back to the wide bed with the New York City night all around them, shining through the smoky panels of the Glass House.

He pulled away from her, rolling onto his back, his breath coming in shallow rasps. She could hear her own heart hammering away at her rib cage, her face wet with sweat or tears or both, her body still trembling, shivering. Lying there she felt so alone, and yet she was afraid to say anything, was afraid to touch him.

Was he going to get up and walk away without a word? Was she going to spend the rest of the endless night alone in her huge bed, a bed that was no longer inviolate? Did he make love to her…no, call a spade a spade, did he have sex with her in order to get her to give up fighting for the Glass House? Was it all part of his devious, manipulative plan?

He'd said he was honest. That he wanted her. Did she dare believe him? Now that he'd had her, did he still want her? What was she doing lying there, still wanting him, when her body hadn't yet recovered from the power of his possession?

Very shyly, very tentatively she moved her arm across the bed, so that her fingers just brushed his arm. She was unprepared for the speed of his response. His hand gently wrapped itself around her wrist, and she was pulled up and over his body, sprawling across him, her flesh absorbing the heat and strength of him, reveling in it.

He put a hand behind her neck and pulled her down for his kiss. It was different from before, deep and careless and oddly lighthearted, and she sank into him, her bones melting over him as she kissed him back, fully, freely, for one brief moment banishing fear. There were enough things waiting to bring her down, to smash her to the pavement eleven flights below. For now she was content to ride the whirlwind.

"I don't believe it!" The voice was much too loud and rich with amusement. It was also far more disturbing than the bright shaft of sunlight that had been warring with Laura's tightly closed eyelids for the past hour. "If I didn't know you better, I'd think you must have gotten royally drunk last night. Did you?"

Laura had no choice. She opened one eye, taking in her mother's tall, elegant figure as she lounged in the chair beside her bed, her long legs crossed at her perfect ankles, her beautiful, unlined face nothing short of smug.

"No," said Laura, sitting up, pulling up the sheet around her shoulders as she went. "I didn't get drunk last night." She cast a furtive glance around her. Her clothes were still littering the floor, but that didn't mean anything. She'd never been a particularly tidy person. There was no sign that a male had occupied the room or the bed, no telltale depression on the pillow beside her. She doubted his head had touched the pillow during the entire, active night.

"Darling, are you blushing?" Jilly inquired solicitously. "If I didn't know my saintly, judgmental daughter better, I'd think you'd had a night of riotous sex. But then, you're saving yourself for marriage, aren't you?"

As a matter of course Laura ignored Jilly's barbs. "What time is it?"

"Eleven-thirty. I wouldn't have thought you'd sleep so late with the wolf at your door."

"The wolf at my door?" For a moment she was mystified.

"Dubrovnik. His bulldozers are hammering away at your foundations, and you lie here sleeping like a baby.

I'm glad to see you're taking a more reasonable approach to the problem. After all, a man with Dubrovnik's resources is bound to win in a fair fight."

For a moment Laura didn't move. Then she pulled herself out of bed, wrapping the sheet around her nude body, and stalked over to the window panel to look down at the foundations below. Sure enough, the machines were moving again. From that distance she couldn't tell whether someone had been able to circumvent the effects of the sugar in the gas tanks, or whether Michael had simply ordered in new machines. It didn't matter. Either way she felt betrayed.

"This isn't a fair fight, Jilly," she said in a stony voice as she turned and headed for the bathroom. "It's dirty and nasty and mean. Why are you here?"

"I was going to let you take me out to lunch. We still haven't celebrated my divorce, have we?"

"No, we haven't. I suppose I'd better move fast, or you might get married again."

"I'm never going to get married again," Jilly announced. "Five times is enough for any woman."

"Once is too much for any woman," Laura said, looking at her reflection in the bathroom mirror as she waited for the deep marble tub to fill. It was a lucky thing that Jilly was so self-absorbed. Anyone else would have noticed the luminous expression in Laura's eyes, the swollen lips, the whisker burns that flushed her cheeks. Anyone else would have looked at Laura and known this was a different woman from the one they'd known just yesterday. But Jilly was too busy chattering about her plans.

"I think I'll go to Tortuga. Michael has a villa there that he's put at my disposal. I haven't been to the Caribbean in ages—I think a little sunlight and sea air will do me wonders."

"It's hurricane season," Laura said sourly. "Michael who?"

"Dubrovnik, of course. He's really been quite charming to me, Laura. For a while I thought he might be interested, and I was quite torn as to how I could let him down gracefully."

This was enough to lure Laura from her depressing perusal of the mirror. She stood in the bathroom door, staring at her mother. "I don't think people turn Michael Dubrovnik down."

"You have," her mother pointed out, ignoring the evidence right in front of her. And then the famous eyes narrowed. "Darling, are those bruises on your wrists?"

Laura ducked back into the bathroom, slamming and locking the door behind her. "No," she called back through the door, dumping her sheet on the floor and heading for the steaming, scented water of the bathtub.

"Laura!" Jilly was pounding on the door with a surprising amount of force. "Did something happen to you? Did someone hurt you? Answer me!"

Laura paused by the tub; the running water was drowning her mother's demands. She looked down at her nude body, turning to examine it in the steamed-up mirror. Michael had left plenty of evidence of his possession. He wasn't a gentle lover, though there was a certain savage tenderness about him. And he hadn't been satisfied with once or twice. As one thing blended into another she'd lost count, but they'd probably made love four and a half times. Maybe five.

The bruises on her wrist were rather daunting, if one didn't take into account how pale Laura's skin was, and how easily she bruised. If she decided to fight him as down and dirty as he fought her, she could make the charges of assault stick. At least for a while.

All she had to do was drain the water out of the tub, send her mother away, and call Susan. Jilly would be a lousy accomplice, but Susan was always reliable. And it would be far too easy to drum up a good bout of hysterical tears.

She reached for the drain on the tub, staring down into the water for a long moment, contemplating. Deciding. Turning back, she rummaged through the shelf of crystal-bottled perfumes, picking up the Eternity she'd worn last night and dumping it into the trash. Then she took her bottle of Poison and poured half of it into the tub.

"I'm fine, Jilly," she said finally. "You know me—if anything was wrong I'd scream about it, loud and long."

"Perhaps." Jilly's voice was unconvinced. "Are you certain you're all right? No one hurt you?"

"I'm fine."

"Then hurry up, darling. I'm hungry."

"So am I," Laura said, sinking into the tub, washing the scent and feel of him from her skin. She'd thought she was as bad as Michael. As low-down and dirty, as willing to fight for what she wanted, no matter what the cost, as he was.

But she wasn't. She couldn't sink that low; she couldn't lie and destroy what had gone between them last night, even if he could. Even if it had meant nothing more to him than the means to an end, a way to get her off balance while he continued his pursuit of the Glass House, it didn't matter. Even if she'd gone to bed with the wrong man, a man who could turn around and attack what she held dearest, at least she knew that she liked it. Liked the way her body could feel, liked sharing it with someone. She only hoped that feeling could be transferred to someone a little worthier than Michael Dubrovnik.

She could feel the occasional faint tremor ripple

through the building whenever the bulldozer moved too close, she could feel the pain sear through her heart in counterpoint. With the pain came anger, pure, cleansing anger, and with it her sickness disappeared, replaced by sheer energy.

She'd told Michael she would never be a victim again. And she wouldn't. She wouldn't let Michael's possession of her body destroy her determination, and she wouldn't let an anonymous blackmailer demoralize her. She was a fighter, and the battle was far from over. They might be starting the final round, but the outcome was still in doubt. And she was determined to win.

## Chapter 16

Michael Dubrovnik sat behind his desk on the tenth floor of the Glass House, picked up his cup of coffee, and hurled it at one of the smoked glass panels beside him. The cup shattered, the coffee spewed across the glass, covering the freshly painted walls between and dripping onto the newly installed pale gray carpet. Without moving he began to curse with great inventiveness and remarkable obscenity in English, in French, in Russian. Zach walked in on this tirade, took in the mess on the wall, and helped himself to a cup of coffee without a word.

"What the hell are you doing here?" Michael demanded furiously.

"It's going to be a day like that, is it?" Zach said coolly, sitting down opposite his angry associate and taking a sip of coffee. "It's not that bad, you know. You didn't have to throw it. You could have added more cream."

"I'm not in the mood for humor, Zach."

"I noticed. Maybe these will cheer you up." He dumped a thick sheaf of papers onto the teak desk.

Michael didn't even bother to look at them. "What are they?"

"Purchase and sale agreement for the Glass House. Deed, warranty, all the papers for closing. I even filled in the higher amount you suggested last week. All you have to do is get the little lady in here and make her sign, and you're home free."

"All I have to do…" Michael echoed bitterly. "Hand me your coffee, Zach."

"Why?"

"I want to throw it at you."

"What's got you in such a snit? Your damned machinery's chewing away at the foundations. The Winston woman is in the palm of your hand if you just cared to use your full strength on her. All systems are go. What's the problem?"

Michael looked at him. "The problem is that I feel like a royal bastard. A rotten, despicable snake, to quote someone of my acquaintance."

"This isn't like you, Mischa. You can't afford a conscience in your line of work," Zach chided.

Michael leaned forward, glancing at the legal papers for a moment, then raising his eyes to Zach's. "I'm one of the fifty richest men in the country," he said. "Heading toward the top ten. If I can't afford it, who can?"

"You want to drop this whole thing? Let Laura Winston have her crumbling building? That's not the answer and you know it. If you don't get her, time will. Or some other financial shark who hasn't developed a latent case of scruples. Face it, Mischa, she's going to lose the place, one way or the other. You may as well gain from it."

"I intend to. I can't drop it. Too much has gone into this project—I'm not about to terminate it and lose a bundle, just because I feel sorry for the woman."

"This is all brought about by pity?" Zach was incredulous.

From somewhere Michael summoned up a wintry smile. "God, Zach, I don't know. All I know is that I wish I'd never heard of the Glass House and Laura Winston."

"Okay." Zach knew when to leave things alone. "Did you have a good time with the model last night?"

"I beg your pardon?"

"Word gets around. I hear you dragged Marita out of Maxim's at a dead run. Connie would love to help you plan a wedding."

"Have I ever indulged in locker-room gossip, Zach?"

"Not usually. But you're in a damned strange mood. Are you getting married again, Mischa?"

Michael stared at him for one long, troubled moment. "Good God," he said. "Maybe I am."

"Let me be the first to offer you congratulations," Zach said, rising and clapping him on the shoulder.

Michael looked up at him gloomily. "Sympathy might be more appropriate. Let's drop my impending nuptials for the moment, okay. What's on tap for today?"

"Have you decided what you want to do about the extortionist?"

It took Michael a moment to return to more mundane matters. "I'd almost forgotten. What was it he wanted?"

"Ten thousand dollars in exchange for the engineering report on the Glass House. The one we bought two months ago."

"I don't want to call the police. For one thing, I don't want Laura to realize we have the report. I'm not sure that it's enough to close her down, and I don't want to waste it."

"So what do you intend to do?"

"Wait and see. Maybe our friendly extortionist has something else up his sleeve."

"Maybe he'll come up with something on you," Zach suggested.

"Impossible. I'm as innocent as a babe."

"Tell Laura Winston that."

"I don't think I'm going to be able to tell Laura Winston anything," Michael said, as the building shuddered from a bulldozer's too-near pass. "Not for a while."

"Whatever you say. When's the wedding? Connie will want to help."

"God only knows," Michael said, staring out the coffee-splattered window. "I haven't even asked the lady yet. She might hand me my head on a platter."

"Marita strikes me as an intelligent human being."

"She does, doesn't she?" Michael murmured, deliberately noncommittal.

"Let me know."

"You'll be the first, Zach. Thanks for the papers."

Zach grinned. "Use them wisely."

"Let's just hope I get to use them fast."

A stack of instructions was awaiting Laura when she finally turned up at Glass Faces three hours later. She'd had too much champagne with her mother, her body felt worn out and tingly in places she didn't even want to think about, and she couldn't rid herself of the totally unfamiliar urge to burst into tears. For the first time she really understood what Susan had been going through over Frank, and had every expectation of their crying on each other's shoulders when she finally showed up at the office.

Susan sat behind the desk, a beatific glow on her face that caused Laura's throat to tighten up once more. The smile she flashed at Laura was brilliant, mocking the stern words.

"Where have you been all day? You wouldn't answer your phone all morning, and when I finally went down to try to find you, you were gone."

"I slept late," she said, dropping into the chair and rubbing her head. "Do you have anything for a headache?"

"Looks like your plans worked out just fine," Susan said, casting a critical eye over her. "Where's Carnaby?"

"I expect he's back in Kansas by now."

"Did he take the Wicked Witch of the East with him?"

"You don't mean Marita?"

"I don't like her."

"She's going to be bringing in the money to pay your salary," Laura pointed out.

"Maybe I could live with a pay cut. So it wasn't over the rainbow, after all?"

"Maybe I'm not as dumb as I look. I didn't go to bed with him, you'll be pleased to know."

"Then who did you go to bed with?"

"Who says I went to bed with anybody?" She tried for a casual laugh, but it came out as a defensive growl. "God, I can never fool you."

"Why should you want to?"

"I'm as big a fool as you are. Falling in love with a man who disappears the next morning and probably doesn't give a damn about..."

"I resent that." Frank appeared in the doorway of her inner office, his easy, sexy grin belying his words.

Laura looked from Susan's glowing face back to her

former model. "I should have realized," she said with a sigh. "I'm glad something's going right. Uh...what were you doing in my office, Frank?" Her earlier suspicion came creeping back, unworthy as it was. If Frank turned out to be her mysterious blackmailer, she might just consider paying up rather than watching Susan's heart break again. An expression like Susan's was worth almost any price.

"Looking through your private papers, love," Frank said with complete candor. "Did you realize your lock had been broken?"

She held herself very still. "Why were you looking?"

"Because someone was blackmailing me over that stupid movie I made, and I figured they could only have gotten their information from here."

"You too?" Laura gasped.

"Don't tell me," Susan said. "That's what that mysterious letter was yesterday."

"Exactly. Someone wants ten thousand dollars, or they'll give Dubrovnik a copy of the engineer's report on this place."

"Is it that bad?"

"Bad enough," Laura replied.

"Whoever it is, they like the ten-thousand-dollar figure," Frank said. "Seems sort of paltry to me, but then, I suspect our blackmailer's a paltry sort of person."

"Do you have any idea who it is?"

"Yup."

Both women stared at him, but it was Susan who spoke first, with an asperity only slightly softened by complete adoration. "Who?"

Frank only smiled, a mysterious smile that should have sold a million dollars worth of cologne. "Let me think about it a little bit more. I have to figure out if it's just because I dislike the person, or whether I really have any reason to suspect them."

"Are you going to pay?" Laura asked.

Frank laughed. "You know my financial situation, love. I couldn't pay for a Dove bar at this point, much less a blackmailer. What about you?"

"I haven't made up my mind yet. I'll wait till you tell me who you think it is."

"You may not have the time," Susan said. "This came for you, and unless I miss my guess, it's from the same source." She held out a plain white envelope.

Frank took it before Laura could. "Do you mind?"

"Go ahead."

He tore it open. "You're supposed to leave ten thousand dollars in unmarked bills on the fourth floor of this building."

"Whoever it is knows even more than I thought. Their lock was broken, and I can't get a locksmith in until the middle of next week. Damn."

"You've got a while to make up your mind. It is now two forty-five. You're not supposed to drop it off until seven, and then you're supposed to leave the building."

"That's stupid. I can come back in the service entrance and wait to see who picks it up."

"I don't think our blackmailer is overloaded with smarts. Otherwise they would have picked better marks and asked for more money," Frank said.

"They?" Susan echoed. "Do you think there's more than one?"

"Just a generic term, lovey. I think it's one very greedy, fairly short-sighted person. And I've got a pretty good idea who it is."

"Stop saying that if you're not going to tell me," Laura

snapped. "Where are you supposed to leave your pay-off?"

"Same place, different time. I only have till five o'clock."

"You, however, don't have anything to lose."

"I do if I intend to use my long-lost M.B.A. in anything nearing respectability. Blue-chip companies frown on their executives appearing in porn movies."

"I forgot you had an M.B.A.," Laura said momentarily distracted. "If I ever get rich and famous, I'll hire you as Susan's assistant."

"You are rich," he pointed out. "And famous."

"Not rich enough. Ever heard the term 'land-poor'? It doesn't just apply to farmers in the Midwest."

"Speaking of Midwestern farmers, you never did tell me who you slept with?" Susan piped up.

Frank immediately looked very interested. "Yes, who did you sleep with? I thought you didn't go in for that sort of thing?"

"Shut up, both of you!" Laura snapped. "Any more mail?"

"Marita's photos came in from the studio. You might want to check them. Want some coffee?"

Laura thought of the pictures, curiously loath to look at the perfect face of the girl who was much better suited to a Whirlwind than she was. "A glass of tea," she muttered, retiring to the pink leather sofa. "With a spoonful of jam in it."

Susan just looked at her. "It must be love," she muttered.

"Or the horribleness of your coffee," Laura retorted, resigning herself to look at the photographs.

The room fell into silence, broken only by the whistle of the teakettle, the clink of glass and teaspoon, the rustling of clothing as Frank and Susan touched every time they got close. Laura took the proffered glass of tea with a murmured thanks, noting with a trace of amusement that her two companions were drinking the same brew, before she returned to her perusal of Marita's burgeoning career.

It was almost an hour later when she declared: "I'm going to let Marita out of her contract," she said flatly.

Susan had been sitting in Frank's lap, and she almost fell off in her surprise. "You're crazy. She's the hottest thing to arrive on the scene in years. Lancôme's about to come up with a huge offer. You can't just throw that away."

"I can," Laura corrected her.

"She's going to be the face of the decade!" Susan wailed.

"You haven't looked at her pictures."

"Sure I did. They were fabulous."

"They were very, very good. She'll go to the very top of her profession. But she won't go with me," Laura said. "I finally realized what was so mesmerizing about her. It's not just her beauty. There are a lot of beautiful women in the business. It's the expression in her eyes. Beneath that sultry gaze there's nothing but a cold, dead contempt. It's hatred for the world. If that's the face of the decade, I don't want it."

No one said a word. After a moment Susan gave a reluctant nod. "I'll trust your judgment. I admit, I haven't been comfortable around her, but I thought I might warm up to her later."

"Frank doesn't like her, does he?" Laura said shrewdly.

Frank smiled. "Frank doesn't like her at all," he replied softly.

Laura's eyes narrowed. "You think it's her, don't you? You think she's the blackmailer?"

"The thought had crossed my mind. Problem is, I have no proof. Just a gut instinct. And the knowledge that she's a stranger who's had access to this place."

"She's never been alone here..." Susan began hotly, then blushed. "Yes, she has. For about an hour, last Wednesday. She must have gone through the files then. You weren't aware of anything wrong?"

"The box was in the back of the closet. I don't usually notice it," Laura said. "The question is, how are we going to prove it?"

"Lie in wait," Frank suggested. "What has she got planned for today?"

"Nothing. It's Sunday, remember? She went out with Dubrovnik last night, so I didn't arrange any appointments." She could feel the telltale blush darken her face.

Susan's eyes widened. "You mean it was Michael Dubrovnik? He abandoned Marita for you?"

"Hard to believe, isn't it?"

"You're worth a dozen of Maritas, and you know it," Frank said calmly.

"Yes. I just don't expect anyone else to realize it." She managed an impish grin, feeling momentarily lighthearted.

"So what are we going to do about this mess? How do we catch her red-handed?" Frank continued.

"We're going to and wait for her. All of us," Laura said flatly. "And I get to be the one to deck her."

"She's a lot bigger than you are," Frank pointed out.

"I'm a lot madder than she is. God, if life gets any more complicated, I'm going to scream."

"Fair warning," Susan said. "Life is about to get more

complicated. Michael Dubrovnik just stepped off the elevator."

Laura's back was to the hallway, and for a moment she considered strolling into her private office and locking the door without a backward glance. But now wasn't the time for cowardice. Besides, if she could judge by the sound of his footsteps on the marble floor, he'd probably break the door down with one knock.

"You've got trouble," he said flatly, his voice rough.

Slowly she turned, schooling her face into her blandest possible expression. It wasn't her fault that her cheeks were flushed with the memory of the night before. "Do I really?" she countered smoothly, trying to keep the surprise out of her voice. he didn't look like a callous seducer; he didn't even look like the Whirlwind. He looked harassed, confused and angry.

"Can we talk in private?"

"My friends can hear anything you have to say." She didn't trust herself alone with him. She was too vulnerable, too desperate.

He was keeping his temper in check only with an extreme effort. "Well, if you want to talk about birth control with an audience, that's fine with me," he snapped.

"My office." She preceded him, her cheeks flaming even brighter, sitting at her desk, glaring at him as he shut the door behind him.

"Someone's trying to blackmail me," he said without preamble.

She stared at him in astonishment, forgetting her embarrassment. "What?"

"Someone has your engineer's report on this building. They offered it to me for ten thousand dollars."

Laura shut her eyes. She might as well give up—the game was over. "Damn."

"When I informed the extortionist that I'd bought the report months ago for a hell of a lot less and had no intention of making it public, he changed his tune."

"He?" She picked up on the pronoun. "It was a man?"

"Actually I don't know. The first contact was by letter. The voice on the phone was disguised—it could have been a man or a woman, old or young. Why do you ask?"

She didn't answer. "Why haven't you used it?"

"Despite what you seem to think by that gloomy expression on your face, it's not airtight. I couldn't be sure I could get the building condemned simply on the strength of one engineering firm's concerns. I was waiting until I had more ammunition."

"Nice of you."

"I'm not nice. I'm thorough. You know that."

"I know that," she agreed. "What did your friend say, when you told them you weren't interested?"

"They suggested that if I didn't want to pay ten thousand dollars to use the information, I might want to pay ten thousand dollars to suppress it."

"That's ridiculous! We'd already figured the blackmailer was stupid, but I didn't think it was this bad."

"You mean you know about it?"

"I mean someone's been blackmailing me about the same report. They seem to have an affection for ten thousand dollars. Supposedly if I ante up this evening, you won't ever know of the report's existence. So much for false hopes. And if Frank Buckley comes up with a similar amount, his involvement in an unfortunate situation won't come to light, either." She shoved a hand through her hair, wishing she'd had even half an hour of sleep the night before. The man standing in front of her had been... relentless.

She looked up at him, determined not to show any emotion. "What did you tell her?"

"Her?"

"Marita." There was no use pretending. Only Marita would know of Dubrovnik's involvement with her, of his irrational, quixotic affection for an enemy.

"That bitch," he said succinctly. "I told her I'd think about it. I was going to leave it up to you."

She stared at him in astonishment. "Why? Wouldn't it have fallen into your plans perfectly?"

"I don't like being blackmailed," he said.

She nodded. "Well, we're busy working on revenge. Do you want in on it?"

He was too close to her. Despite her better judgment she wanted to lean against him, wanted his strong arms wrapped around her, wanted to go back downstairs to her rumpled bed with him. She stayed where she was, waiting.

"I wouldn't miss it for the world," Michael Dubrovnik said fiercely.

A sudden horrifying thought came to mind. "What did you mean by that crack about birth control?" she demanded. "I thought you did something about it."

He grinned. "Just wanted to scare you. You look so ridiculous when you blush. It doesn't go with your image."

"Whereas low blows fit your style perfectly."

"Touché. That's the only reason I left when I did."

"What is?"

"I ran out of my supply. And I was more than well prepared."

"You're a beast." She could feel the color mounting on her face once more.

"And you're amazing for such a prude," he murmured

in return. "Don't worry. I won't run out again. What time do we confront the blackmailer?"

Next time? There was nothing she could say to that, so she wisely ignored it. "Six-thirty. Come up to my apartment and we'll all go down together."

"All of us? Won't that get a little crowded?"

"Marita might have accomplices."

"I can take care of them."

"Don't be disgustingly macho. Frank has his own score to settle. Susan will stay near the telephone, in case we need to call the police. Or an ambulance," she added hastily.

"Sounds delightful. The papers are ready."

"What papers?"

"For the sale of the Glass House to Dubrovnik Enterprises. I had Zach bring them over. Anytime you're ready to sign, they'll be down there."

"You can have Zach shove them—"

"Now, now. What would my sister say if she heard you saying such things to me?" he mocked.

"She'd probably say 'Bravo.'"

"She probably would. Six-thirty. And then we need to talk."

"I don't want to talk to you."

"Tough. I'm bigger and stronger than you are, and I always get my way. I presume you decided not to charge me with assault?"

She shrugged. "I figured I couldn't make it stick."

"Liar," he said softly. "We'll talk about that, too."

"Next time I won't be so nice," she warned.

"Next time I'll be even nicer," he said, his voice a low, sexy purr. "See you at six-thirty."

She waited until the sound of his footsteps could no longer be heard, waited until Susan and Frank started talking again in the outer room. And then, laying her head on her desk, she let out a long, miserable moan.

Marita looked around the spacious confines of her hotel room, and her perfect upper lip curled in disgust. She'd come a long way in a few short days. When Laura Winston had first brought her here, she really had thought it was a palace, a fairyland of elegance and luxury.

Now she knew better. She had a room, not a suite. There was no view, and while everything was spotless, the little details were not quite top drawer. Apparently Ms. Winston, for all her flattering words, hadn't thought Mary Ellen Murphy was worth the best. Maybe Mary Ellen wasn't, but Marita was. And Laura Winston would soon learn her lesson.

These New Yorkers and their contempt for the people from the Midwest, she thought with a sneer. Of course she shared that contempt, but she hadn't been impressed by any of the sophisticated big-city dwellers. She was on the verge of besting them all, of forcing them to pay through the nose for their stupidity. She'd felt their condescension, and every glance had rankled. She'd show them who was smarter, more ruthless than all of them put together.

And the best part of it all, the most delightful revenge, was that she no longer needed it. She had a few hours to spare, then she'd be gone, beyond their reach. And whenever she thought of them, she'd laugh.

# Chapter 17

It was raining. Laura stood in her apartment, watching the water streak and slide down the cracked glass panels, shielding the city from her eyes with a layer of tears. She snorted at her own melodramatics. There was nothing to cry about. Even one of the worst mistakes of her entire life had its positive aspects. By going to bed with Michael Dubrovnik she'd discovered that sex wasn't the messy, unpleasant business she'd always thought it. Well, to be completely truthful, it did have its messy aspects. But maybe, years from now, when she thought back on her brief liaison with Michael Dubrovnik, her thoughts would be fond ones. Particularly if she were sitting where she was now, still owner of the Glass House.

He wanted to talk to her, did he? That was the last thing she wanted. She knew without asking that she didn't want to hear anything he had to say. And she didn't trust what might happen once they stopped talking.

Leaving her post by the window, she went back to the telephone and punched out her mother's phone number. After a few moments she slammed the phone down again. Count on Jilly to disappear when Laura needed someone to talk to. She'd begun to have hopes, irrational ones, of course, that she and her mother might finally come to an understanding. Lunch had been more fun than any time they'd spent together in years. Of course, Jilly had spent most of the time talking about Peter McSorley, one of Dubrovnik's middle-management executives, but she'd been attentive enough to Laura's hesitant confessions. After all, if Jilly didn't know about love and sex, she didn't know who did.

"So this man spent the night with you, and you're wondering if he'll respect you in the morning?" Jilly had drawled sipping her way into the second bottle of champagne.

"No," Laura snapped, drinking too much herself. "I'm wondering if I have to worry about him coming back."

Jilly shook her head. "Then why in the world did you go to bed together in the first place?"

"I don't know," said Laura. "Animal lust, I suppose."

"It would take some man to make you feel animal lust, darling," Jilly said with her usual candor. "I know what your problem is, but you aren't going to want to hear it."

"Go ahead. I asked for advice."

"You're in love with him. If you weren't, you wouldn't have had anything to do with him. You're too hard-headed."

Laura looked at her mother in disgust. "I know that. Tell me something new."

Jilly arched a perfect eyebrow. "I suspect he's in love with you, too. Why else would Michael Dubrovnik be courting his sworn enemy?"

"What makes you think it's Michael?"

"I've seen the expression on his face when he's been cursing you. And I know you well enough to know you wouldn't do the conventional thing. Therefore I put two and two together and came up with four."

"It was a fluke. An accident."

"How do two people spend the night together by accident?" Jilly countered. "In my years of experience I've never heard of it happening. Please enlighten me."

"I need sympathy, Mother, not needling."

"Darling, you have all my sympathy," Jilly protested. "Any woman with the misfortune to spend the night enjoying herself prodigiously deserves pity."

"Who says I enjoyed myself?"

"The fact that you spent the entire night with him. And that he isn't in jail right now, charged with assault or whatever other nasty thing you could think of. I wouldn't have put it past you to seduce him, just so you could charge him with rape. Your devotion to that damned building knows no bounds."

"Yes," said Laura, thinking of the choice she'd made earlier, turning down her perfect chance to stop Michael. "It does."

"I really can't give you any advice, darling. I don't know enough of the details."

"And I'm not going to give you any of them."

Jilly's face fell. "And here I thought we were becoming like a real mother and daughter."

"That doesn't include pillow talk."

"I'll tell you about Peter McSorley, if you tell me about Michael Dubrovnik."

"Mother! You haven't gone to bed with him already?"

Jilly shrugged. "I'm not cut out to be alone. Unlike you, I need a man to lean on."

"So you aren't going to be any help?"

"I didn't say that. I'm just not sure what you expect from me."

"I'm not sure, either," Laura said, depressed. "I'll call you tonight when I figure it out."

But that evening Jilly wasn't answering her phone. She was probably just out for cocktails and dinner, Laura told herself. Jilly could, if desperate, pour her own drink and make scrambled eggs, but that was as far as her home-making talents went. Laura realized she'd just have to call her after the confrontation with Marita. After she'd either managed to avoid talking with Michael or survived it.

Frank and Susan arrived first, flushed, laughing, their arms around each other. Laura had no doubt at all as to what they'd been doing just before they arrived at the Glass House, but if she felt a pang of envy, she stifled it. By the time Michael finally arrived she'd worked herself up into a state of perfect calm and unconcern, a state that only slipped for a moment when she looked at the latecomer.

Michael was wearing jeans and a cotton sweater, the same clothes he'd worn the night before when he carried her upstairs to bed. He'd done it deliberately, she knew, wanting to remind her. She could see it from the glint in his eyes, the slight smile that curved his mouth. "Sorry I'm late," he said. "I was meeting with my lawyers."

"I thought the papers were already drawn up," Laura snapped. "Not that they'll do you any good."

"Testy, aren't you?" he said mildly, taking the drink Frank was offering. "Don't worry, this should all go off quite smoothly. And I had them draft another agreement. An extra one. It should be ready in a couple of days—I can wait that long for you to sell me the building."

"You can wait till hell freezes over."

Now his smile was unrestrained, and before she realized what he was doing, he'd reached out a hand and stroked her neck, withdrawing before she could slap him away. His fingers had been cool on her flushed skin, and she wished she could have leaned into them, let them touch her cheeks, her lips, her breasts.

"It's twenty to seven," she said, wiping any lingering erotic thoughts from her brain, though probably not before the too observant Michael had recognized them. "Are we going to stand around and have a cocktail party or go wait for our blackmailer?"

"Calm down," Susan said, touching her arm. "We have Luis watching the front entrance, and the back one is blocked by the earth-moving equipment. He'll call up the moment she arrives."

"I don't trust my doorman. He's let other snakes in before without telling me." She let her hostile gaze rest on Michael for a moment, but he only smiled in return, maddeningly pleased with himself. "Let's go. The sooner this is over with, the better. I have things to do tonight."

"Yes," said Michael, "you do."

She ignored him. The four of them trooped down the flights of stairs, Laura's high heels making a sharp, staccato ring on each step. As Frank and Susan moved ahead, Michael caught her arm, delaying her.

She tried to yank herself free, but as usual he was very strong. "Don't you want to take off those shoes?" he said easily enough. "They're making a hell of a racket, and I bet you won't be able to run in them."

"I don't expect to run, and I don't give a damn what kind of racket they're making. I'm leaving them on. I'm at enough of a disadvantage around you. I'm not going to make myself four inches shorter besides."

"I'm glad you think you're at a disadvantage around

me. Maybe then you won't notice the effect you have on me." Without another word he moved ahead of her, and she had no choice but to take up the rear, puzzling over his words. If he weren't a despicable, manipulating snake, she might almost think he cared about her. That he was as floored by what had happened last night as she was. But that was ridiculous. Wasn't it?

There was no sign of Marita in the empty office. The envelope of money that Frank had left earlier, compliments of Michael, was still there, untouched. "Do you think she's changed her mind?" Susan whispered. "Maybe chickened out? Maybe she realizes we suspect her."

"All the more reason for her to take the money and run," Laura said. "She'd know that she wasn't going to be making any money from assignments through Glass Faces. She'd have to cut her losses. Everybody hide."

"Yes, ma'am." Susan and Frank slipped into the inner office and a quiet giggle could be heard.

"Quiet in there," Laura snapped, dropping her own envelope of play money on top of Frank's.

"Yes," Michael said. "Quit having fun."

She glared up at him, but he still seemed infuriatingly unrepentant, even downright cheerful. "Why don't you go out on the ledge and watch?" she suggested sweetly.

"In a thunderstorm?"

"It's only a four-flight fall. You'd probably bounce off a bulldozer."

"My bulldozers have been through enough. I'll hide here with you."

"No, you won't...." But he'd already grabbed her and pulled her down behind the desk. There wasn't much space between the metal furniture and the wall, and one side was blocked by a credenza. She had no choice but to sit there as Michael pulled her into his lap and wrapped his larger body around hers, but she was fuming by the time he threaded his arms around her waist. "This isn't necessary," she hissed.

"But it makes everything a lot more enjoyable," he murmured into her ear. "I've missed you." He began to nibble on her earlobe, ignoring the diamond stud that was in his way.

"Be quiet," she said, trying to jerk free. Instead his teeth closed gently on her soft skin, holding her there, and she had no choice but to remain still, shivering both with frustration and a reluctant reaction that had nothing to do with anger.

Beneath her she could feel his arousal, and she squirmed against him.

"Don't do that," he whispered. "You're only making it worse."

"Pervert," she whispered back.

"Actually I'm very healthy. It's a normal enough reaction, especially when you're around."

"If you don't shut up, she'll hear us."

"Not another word," he promised, moving up his hands from her waist to cup her breasts through the loose cotton.

She tried to pry away his fingers, but his mouth was on her neck now, kissing her, and somehow she found her hands covering his, pressing them against her as she let her head fall back against his shoulder, giving him better access to the sensitive column of her neck. She was safe enough—what could he do in an office, with two other people and a blackmailer about to appear? She'd take what she could, enjoy it, and walk away with nothing more than a cool smile.

Of course, she hadn't expected his hand to slip down

the loose front of her shirt and cup her breast through the thin lace bra. And she hadn't expected him to unfasten the front clasp, so that her flesh spilled into his hand, warm and straining. She had to bite back the quiet little moan that threatened when he rubbed his thumb against her turgid nipple, and despite her best intentions she snuggled back against him as he unbuttoned the front of her shirt, all the way down to her navel.

"Don't…" she whispered.

"Shh." It was a bare breath of a sound, one she decided she'd better obey. If he was taking unfair advantage of her by running one hand down her stomach while he still cupped her breast with the other, then clearly there was nothing she could do. She couldn't risk warning Marita. All she could do was sit there, trapped in his arms, and feel her skin grow warmer, softer, more sensitive beneath his wicked hands.

His fingertips were toying with the edge of her lace bikini panties. She sucked in her breath in sudden dismay, but it only allowed him better access. Frank and Susan were in the other room, out of sight, out of hearing if she didn't make a fuss, and probably equally absorbed in each other. She tried to jab him with her elbow, but he ignored it, his long, deft fingers reaching the heated center of her, delving deep.

Her strangled gasp reached no farther than her lips. Paralyzed, in shock, she sat there, and before she could gather her senses enough to fight him, the first, demoralizing tendrils of reaction began to set in.

He could feel her response and made a low, almost inaudible sound in the back of his throat, one of approval and encouragement, as he continued his shocking caresses. She whimpered ever so softly and turned to protest, but his mouth caught hers, silencing her as he stroked her.

With a shiver she pulled her mouth away, unable to look at him, unable to stop him, unable to do anything but sit there, wrapped in his body, and give in to the sensations that were pulsing through her.

Her entire body began to quiver. She was covered with a fine film of sweat, her breathing was rapid and shallow, and the pleasure he was giving her was so exquisite, she thought she might die from it. "Stop," she whispered hoarsely, unable to bear any more. "I can't...."

"Yes, you can." His voice was nothing more than a breath of sound on the still night air. And suddenly she did, biting her lower lip as her body convulsed in a reaction that was still too new. He held her tight, prolonging it, prolonging it so that she thought she might explode as tears poured down her face.

Slowly, tenderly he brought her back down, soothing her with suddenly gentle hands, his lips brushing the back of her neck, kissing away the tears from the side of her face, cradling her in the warmth and comfort of his arms. She wouldn't have thought he could offer warmth and comfort, she thought dizzily, sinking back against him as he refastened her bra and began to button her shirt. But he could, and she took it gratefully, and anything else he had to give.

She didn't even notice the time pass. She felt boneless, completely relaxed in the shelter of his arms. If she was aware of the insistent hardness of his body beneath hers, she took a small, smug pleasure in it. This hadn't been her idea, and if he was in torment, it was his own fault. And hers, she thought with rich, feminine pleasure. And hers.

"She's not coming." Frank's voice broke through her dreamy abstraction, and she began to struggle out of Michael's arms. He held her still for a moment, long enough to adjust his own clothing to partially disguise his condition, and stood with her.

"What time is it?"

"Eight-fifteen," Frank said, his handsome face illuminated by the evening city light from outside, his voice rich with disgust. "If she hasn't shown up yet, she's not going to."

"What makes you think that?"

"Instinct. She wouldn't let all that money sit alone in an unlocked office building. She would have been on it like fleas on a dog. Something's gone wrong."

"Maybe it isn't Marita," Laura suggested, hoping she sounded cool and composed.

"I'd be willing to take bets," Michael said, tugging at his jeans. "What's next? Laura and I can stay here while you two go out and reconnoiter."

"No!" Laura's strangled gasp startled everyone, including herself. "Why don't we go upstairs and call the hotel she's staying at? She might be in her room there, innocent of all this."

"Sounds good," Michael said. "Why don't Frank and Susan go over there and give us a call back at Laura's place?" He reached out and touched her mouth, and there was a trace of blood on his finger. "You've cut your lip," he said, his eyes dark with further promise.

She jerked away nervously, hoping the others wouldn't see her blush. "Why don't we all go upstairs?" she suggested desperately. She didn't dare spend any more time alone with Michael. She was close enough to surrendering everything, as it was. If he touched her again, her brain would be well and truly gone.

"Hush up!" Susan hissed. "I think someone's coming."

Everyone immediately dived behind the desk, a tangle of arms and legs and bodies, none of them daring to breathe. Michael had managed to end up directly on top of Laura, and though he scarcely moved, she could feel the insistent pressure of his arousal. She moved her face three inches, nuzzling it against his shoulder, and sank her teeth in.

"Shh!" Susan said sternly, as Michael yelped in pain.

They remained motionless for seconds, while Laura came to the miserable conclusion that her act of savagery had, if anything, intensified Michael's desire. Then the door opened and a flashlight was trained across the room. "Miss Winston?" Luis's voice sounded only slightly more nervous than they felt. "You in here?"

Laura could do nothing more than mumble as the other three climbed off her. "What is it, Luis?" she asked wearily, when she finally struggled to her feet once more.

"A messenger came by with a letter from Miss Murphy. I thought you'd want to see it right away."

"Miss Murphy?" Michael echoed, mystified.

"Marita," Laura clarified, taking the letter from him and ripping it open. "Good God, that little swine."

"Big swine," Michael supplied. "She's almost a foot taller than you are."

"It's her nature that's small," Laura said with dignity. "She's eloped."

"What?" Susan shrieked.

"With Constantine Milopoulos."

"You're kidding?" Frank was the first to respond. "She's eloped with that filthy old man?"

"He's a very rich filthy old man," Michael observed. "Richer than me, and that's saying a lot. Word has it he's more into watching than doing, and Marita's a girl who likes to be watched. Sounds like a match made in heaven. Does she say anything else?"

"Yes," Laura said, crumpling the letter in her hand. "She's holding on to the copy of the engineer's report. She figures it might come in handy someday."

"It'll be academic by the time she returns from her honeymoon," Michael said smoothly. "The Glass House won't even exist by then."

Laura froze. It shouldn't have bothered her—she knew full well that almost every bit of his energy was concentrated on wresting her heritage from her. It still felt like a particularly nasty form of betrayal after their time behind the desk.

"That's that," she said briskly. "You can all let yourselves out." She headed for the door, Michael hard on her heels, but Susan, bless her heart, intervened, forestalling him.

"Where are you going?" Michael demanded, his voice rich with frustration.

"To see my mother. I promised we'd indulge in some long overdue girl talk."

"Your mother isn't…" His voice trailed away as she vanished into the corridor and headed down the stairs. By the time she reached the lobby she could see that the rain, rather than abating, had gotten even heavier. She hadn't paid much attention to the news, but vaguely remembered the meteorologist fussing about a hurricane. It looked like a tropical storm outside, the slender trees bending in the wind. There was very little traffic, and she was willing to bet that what there was of it didn't include any empty taxis.

It didn't matter. Her mother's apartment was only five blocks away. Maybe the rain would wash some of the anger, some of the hurt away.

She was shivering by the time she reached Jilly's apartment. She was livid by the time she realized that

Jilly simply wasn't home that night, despite her promise to be there. She turned and headed out into the night again, when George, the elderly doorman who'd known her for years, stopped her.

"Shall I call you a cab, Miss Winston? It's a nasty night out."

She smiled at him, summoning up the last of her energy. "I don't think even you could find one, but thanks for the thought. When my mother comes in, would you tell her I was looking for her?"

"I would, miss. But she's not expected back for an indefinite period of time."

Laura stopped dead in her tracks. "Where's she gone?"

"To Paris, I believe. With a young man named Peter McSorley. I hesitate to mention this, miss, but she showed me her new engagement ring."

It took all her effort to summon a wry smile. "That sounds like Mother. Good night, George."

"Good night, miss."

She'd always loved rainy nights in the city, but that night she discovered a new advantage in them. She found she could walk five blocks, sobbing like a child who'd lost its favorite toy, and no one would even notice.

She took the elevator up to the eleventh floor. She was half afraid that Michael would be lying in wait, but her apartment was blessedly empty. There were messages blinking on her answering machine, but for once she ignored them as she headed for the bathroom and the deep marble tub.

It took the better part of an hour to soak the chill out of her bones. The better part of another hour to drink three glasses of Chardonnay and decide that she'd die before she let Michael Dubrovnik near her again. And one more hour to slip on her four-inch heels, wrap a silk kimono around her lime-green silk chemise, and head down the stairs to his apartment.

He was coming through the door when she reached his landing, and at the sight of her he stopped, a wary expression on his face. That look surprised Laura. She wouldn't have thought he'd be uncertain about a thing, particularly about her reaction to him.

"Were you going somewhere?" she questioned coolly.

"I was coming up to get you. I thought you weren't coming." He backed into his apartment, and she followed him, holding the peach silk kimono tightly around her.

"I don't remember being invited," she said, as he shut the door behind her, staying very close.

"That's what last night was." His voice was a low, sexy rumble, but he didn't touch her.

"I'm not going to sign those papers," she said fiercely. "I'm not going to sell you this building."

"I don't give a damn about the building," he said. "Not right now. What goes on between us in bed has nothing to do with a piece of real estate."

She looked at him for a long moment, saying nothing. And then she dropped the kimono onto the floor, standing there in the skimpy, transparent shift and her high, high heels.

He smiled then, a tight upturning of his mouth as he surveyed her. "Tell you what," he murmured. "You can wear your shoes to bed."

"You're definitely taller than I am lying down," she said, with just the faintest hint of a smile.

He moved, pulling her into his arms, and she went willingly, her body trembling slightly in anticipation and delight. "I just wish you could trust me."

"I do. To a certain extent. I wouldn't be here if I didn't."

His own smile was crooked. "I suppose that'll have to do."

"It'll have to do," she agreed, sliding her arms around his neck and pulling down his mouth to meet hers. "For now," she added against his lips, so quietly that he didn't even notice.

## Chapter 18

Michael lay in bed, watching the rain sluice down the sides of the building he'd been planning to demolish. It caught in the cracks in the thick smoked glass, and the rivulets turned first into streams, then into rivers. Lightning split the predawn sky, and the entire building trembled. For a moment he considered waking the woman lying beside him, to point out just how compromised the old building was, to be so vulnerable to the vagaries of the weather.

But if he woke her, they'd just end up making love again, with nothing settled between them. And nothing could be settled, until he figured out exactly what was going on in his own mind.

Sleeping with the enemy was a major mistake, and at least for now Laura Winston definitely was the enemy. In this latest financial endeavor, that is. It was hard to believe, looking down at her, lying curled up so trustingly by his side, that she could be just as stubborn, just as ruthless as he could.

Well, maybe not quite as ruthless. But once her initial distrust had relaxed, once she'd accepted the fact that she was in bed with him, she'd proved to be fully as passionate as he'd expected. It was no wonder he couldn't keep his hands off her. Even thinking about her body made him hard again, something that shouldn't even be remotely possible after such an active night. But it was, and all he wanted to do was roll on top of her, bury himself in her warm, clinging body and listen to her sighs and whispers.

Sex he could understand. What still confused him was the peculiar feeling of tenderness that swept over him whenever he thought of her. Little things, like the clear glasses she wore over her contacts, the glasses he'd tossed beneath an oncoming car. The way she'd charmed Sonya. That uneasy, vulnerable expression in her eyes when she thought he wouldn't notice. Her bravery, her stubbornness, her determination.

He wanted to wrap her in his arms and protect her from all the evil creatures who wanted to do her harm. The damnable thing was that of all that threatened Laura Winston's well-being, he was the worst. No one could hurt her as much as he, simply by taking away her accursed building.

And it was too late to change his mind, to pull out of something he'd already committed millions of dollars to, just because he'd developed an irrational, quixotic fancy for one of the stumbling blocks. Zach was right; he could have used that engineer's report as a counter to her restraining order, and she would have been up a very muddy creek without a paddle. But even back then he'd been curiously ambivalent.

He couldn't see any way out of it. He couldn't scrap a project that was so far along, and there was no future for them if he won. They were trapped, and the sexual attraction made it even worse. Hell, whom did he think he was kidding? It wasn't just a sexual attraction. She was most of the way in love with him, despite the fact that she considered him a sneaky, manipulative snake. And he...he'd never felt the way he was feeling, not in his almost forty years. He'd be damned if he'd call it love. But he didn't know what else it could be.

She murmured something in her sleep, turning over and snuggling closer to him. She'd made remarkable progress from that first, shy, almost virginal coupling to her enthusiastic seduction of him a few short hours ago. Everything they did was very new to her, and her wonder and delight made it seem new to him, too.

He couldn't resist. Leaning over, he kissed her mouth, lightly at first, then deeper, as she stirred and slid her arms around his neck. When he drew away she was smiling up at him, her distrust, her defenses temporarily banished. "You," she whispered, "are voracious."

He smiled back. "I try to do my best."

"You succeed," she said in a husky voice as he pulled the cover from her naked body. "You surely do succeed."

Laura heard the pounding on the door from the mists of a deep, deep sleep. The noise seemed to shake the entire building, and she buried her head under a huge down pillow, trying to shut out both the noise and the world. Then voices penetrated, harsh, rapid-fire, excited voices, and slowly, reluctantly, Laura lifted her head.

She was alone in the middle of Michael Dubrovnik's king-size bed, wrapped in a fur throw that had to be sable. She felt decadent, sated and very sleepy, as the lightning flickered behind her eyelids. Then the building shook again, but there was no telltale sound of thunder, and with sudden grave misgivings she opened her eyes.

The lightning wasn't flickering outside. It was the electricity in the building, flashing, sinking into the darkness of a rainy morning and then coming on full force. Laura watched in horror as wide, dangerous cracks sped along the length of the glass panels, as once more the building seemed to shift and resettle.

Michael slammed into the room, dressed in jeans and sweater, soaking wet. "Get dressed, Laura. They're evacuating the building.

"What have you done?" she demanded in a horrified whisper, ignoring the small crew of men beyond the door, their hard hats and slickers shining with rain.

Dubrovnik slammed the door, stalking over to her as she huddled away from him, the sable throw pulled tight against her. "What did I do?" he echoed, his voice edged with fury. "What the hell did you do, damn it? The foundations started collapsing this morning. The whole block is cordoned off, the army corps of engineers is flying in, and there's a man, a good man, trapped beneath your stupid anachronistic heap of glass and rubble.

"Oh, God!" she breathed, as guilt swamped her. "Who…?"

"One of my workmen. A twenty-seven-year-old father of two. They're working as fast they can, shoring up the building, but he hasn't made a sound in the last ten minutes. Get up and get out."

He was covered with mud halfway up his thighs. She had no doubt he'd been down there himself, digging with his hands, trying to get to the man. The horror, the guilt of it threatened to strangle her, and she immediately rejected it.

"If you hadn't been sending bulldozers banging away at the building for days," she said bitterly, "it probably would never have happened."

If she'd hoped to shatter him, she'd underestimated his coldness. "Maybe. You think that exonerates you?"

She just stared at him without a word, sitting naked in the middle of his bed, the bed they'd shared with such mesmerizing results a few short hours ago.

He ran a hand through his wet hair in sudden exasperation. "Listen, we can't talk now. Get your clothes on and get out of the building, and we'll figure out how to deal with this. In the meantime you're in danger..."

"Mischa!" Zach Armstrong stormed through the door, equally wet and mud-splattered, politely oblivious to Laura's presence in the bed. "They've got him out. They're taking him to the hospital right now, but it looks like he's in not too bad shape. I've got a car waiting."

"I'm coming. Get out of here, Laura," Michael said again, with no kindness in his voice. "Go to your mother's place." Without another word he was gone, taking Zach and his crew of workmen with him.

Huddled in the bed she sat very still, watching as the lights flickered on and off. They went off entirely, plunging the room into an unnatural gloom, and still she sat, wrapped in priceless sable, watching the window cracks widen.

She assumed she was alone in the building. If it collapsed, only she would be killed. There was a certain grim justice to it all. It wouldn't be so bad to die wrapped in sable and the remains of a multimillion-dollar building.

The lights came back on, slowly at first, just a dim glow, growing ever stronger. The building was no longer shaking, despite the insistent rain that was dashing against its sides, as if desperate to penetrate those long, dangerous cracks in the glass. And suddenly Laura lifted her head, struck by a strange but unavoidable conclusion.

The Glass House wasn't worth dying for. Her great-grandfather had died for it, murdered by his lover's husband, the poor cuckold who'd financed the building. Now a workman had nearly died for it, leaving his family alone in a harsh, cruel world. He still might, but not if Michael Dubrovnik had anything to say about it. Michael could snatch someone back from the very jaws of death. If he was going to the hospital, there was no way the man could die.

And it certainly wasn't worth the death of a thirty-two-year-old, proud, stubborn fool named Laura Winston. Granted, she'd been so blind and greedy that she hadn't wasted a moment's thought on anyone else's welfare. She'd refused to consider the possibility that the Glass House might have outlived its destiny, had kept her mind rigidly shut until she'd almost brought her world crashing down around her. It was time to let go. For the first time in years, it was time for Laura Winston to admit defeat.

She managed to find her kimono and wrap it around her shivering body. Leaving everything else behind she walked out of his apartment up one flight to his office. It only took her a moment to find the papers. She signed them, each one, with a flourish, not even bothering to check the terms. The price for the Glass House was absurdly generous—it should go toward her legal expenses and leave enough to live on besides.

It took her just over an hour to make a few phone calls and pack up what she needed. If the building survived, she could ask Susan to pack the rest and put it into storage. In the meantime all she needed were warm-weather clothes and her grandmother's gaudy jewels. The rest could tumble into the muddy foundation with the shards of glass.

The list of Michael's payoffs was still sitting in her safe. She stared at it, hesitating, then tore it in half. Tucking it into an envelope, she sealed it, wrote Michael's name on it and left it on her bed. If he got it, fine. If he didn't, that was all right, too.

When Laura stepped out into the rain, Susan was behind the barricades, restrained by the police and Frank's strong hands. She escaped both of them, running across the cordoned-off street to Laura's side, grabbing her hands.

"Do me a favor," Laura said without preamble. "If the place survives, find a spot for Glass Faces. It's still a viable concern—Frank could be an enormous help if he felt like it. It's yours, if you want it."

"Don't be ridiculous...."

"I'll send you ownership papers. Or part-ownership papers," she amended with a wry grin. "I'm going to need some income."

"Where are you going?"

"California. You know Emelia—she always needs someone to hold her hand through these things. If she does well, there's no telling what will happen."

"But the Glass House..."

"I've sold it to Dubrovnik. I imagine it'll be gone in a matter of days."

"Oh, Laura," Susan breathed, sympathy and pain in her voice.

Laura shook back her cropped black hair, smiling determinedly. "It's time. You and I both know it. I'll call after I get settled."

"What about Michael?"

"What about him?" she asked coolly.

"That's it?"

"That's it," Laura said. "I'll call you in a few days." And hoisting her duffel bag over her shoulder, she took off into the rainy morning, without a backward glance at the building that had meant more to her than life.

There was one good thing to be said about Southern California, Laura decided three months later. You weren't as acutely aware of the passage of time, for the simple reason that the seasons never changed. The end of December was only a couple of degrees cooler than midsummer, the rain was still practically nonexistent, and the balmy, smog-laden air was comforting in its sameness.

Comfort was a key word in her life nowadays. Things were settled, even, one smooth day after the other. Not that she wasn't kept busy. Emelia's burgeoning film career required constant attention, and Laura welcomed the challenge. When she wasn't busy arranging interviews, dealing with impossible demands from the studio, holding Emelia's hand or generally trying to make her temperamental client's life run smoothly, she was busy trying to settle into her own little nest.

She'd sublet a tiny cottage in Laurel Canyon, with an algae-covered swimming pool, bugs and rodents in the garage, and a spectacular view of the mountains ringing L.A. She'd obtained an unlisted phone number, and once she'd ascertained that Susan, Frank and Glass Faces were still intact, she'd remained blissfully remote.

Not that people hadn't tried. Jilly, returning from a month-long honeymoon, had left message after message on her answering machine. Laura's response had been warm, friendly and so distant that nothing could reach her. Susan and Frank had flown out for a long weekend, and they'd spent the entire time working out details for a new three-way partnership. Not that Laura really cared. If it had been up to her, she would have given the business to Susan, who, with Frank's expertise, seemed to be making it the hottest modeling agency in the city.

But Susan had been adamant, and Laura was too calm to fight. Nothing had the ability to dent her unruffled calm, not even the news that Marita Milopoulos was on the cover of Paris *Vogue* with an astonishing amount of diamonds surrounding her perfect face. Laura simply smiled and talked of Emelia and how much she loved California, and Susan and Frank watched her with sympathy and frustration.

The one thing she refused to talk about was the Glass House. She'd let it go, turned her back on it with a completeness that was almost brutal. She didn't want to hear about Dubrovnik Plaza, and she most especially didn't want to hear about Michael Dubrovnik.

He knew where she was. His lawyers had been pestering her, telling her there was one last agreement to sign, and she'd always politely agreed to their requests and never showed up at the appointed hour. If something was standing in his way, that was his problem, not hers. Not hers at all, she told herself fiercely.

But there'd been no word. Not of thanks, not of apology, not even to tell her that she wasn't being held responsible for the condition of her building—it had been up to his lawyers to do that. Michael must have pulled some strings to work that, but she wouldn't thank him. She couldn't stand the thought of facing him in his triumph, with the corpse of her beloved building lying between them.

It was the building she was grieving for, she reminded herself. The anachronistic pile of glass and bronze that had been her great-grandfather's crowning achievement.

A thing of great beauty and even greater impracticality, it had owned her, body and soul, and she was mourning its passing. Not the loss of something she'd never had. Not the loss of Michael Dubrovnik.

Even Sonya knew where she was. She'd sent her a triptych for Christmas, the ancient, jewellike colors glowing from the painted wood. It was Laura's only Christmas decoration in her little house, but it was enough. She spent a lovely Christmas Eve drinking Russian tea laced with vodka, toasting the triptych and its Holy Family. And refusing to think about that other family—of Russians in New York.

It was early January when she got the phone call. Susan's voice, breathless, insisted she turn on the television.

"It's only three-thirty in the afternoon, Susan," Laura said calmly. "The news won't be on for hours."

"Well, for God's sake, watch it!" she snapped.

"Don't be so grumpy. Doesn't marriage agree with you? I told you you should have a big wedding. No one enjoys elopements."

"We did," Susan said with the trace, just the trace of a raunchy laugh in her voice. "Besides, we did it for you. We knew you wouldn't come East, and if we couldn't have had you at our wedding, we didn't want anyone."

"Don't make me feel guilty."

"Just watch the news. Then tell me how you feel."

She wasn't going to do it. She'd avoided the news in the three months she'd been in California, had avoided the reality with an assiduousness her mother would have been proud of. It was probably just another puff piece on the wealthy Mrs. Milopoulos. The evil creature was probably expecting twins.

Or maybe it was about another person she'd recently

known far too well. Maybe someone else had married and was now expecting twins.

The suddenness of the pain that split her came as a shock, and she sat on her narrow sofa, breathless, waiting for it to subside. That couldn't be it. Susan would have warned her. She wouldn't have left it up to some anchorman to tell her that the Whirlwind had gotten married.

She almost called the East Coast. Not Susan—she knew her friend well enough to know that she wouldn't say anything more than she'd already said. Jilly might be coerced into talking, but Jilly had never watched the network news in her life.

There was no answer at Sonya's Upper West Side apartment. Just as well, Laura thought, replacing the receiver. What could you say to the sister of the man you loved? Chances were she would have burst into tears at the sound of Sonya's voice.

One thing was certain, she couldn't stay there and watch the clock for three hours. There was no food in the house, and Laura had developed a healthy interest in food. She'd put five pounds on her spare frame, and instead of bewailing the fact, she found the effect rather becoming. Curves were nice, even if there was no one around to appreciate them.

As luck would have it, the traffic leading into the canyon was monstrous. She was late getting back, the news was half over, and she raced into her living room, scattering packages of food as she went, turning on the huge television that had come with the house.

The anchorman's voice, in its customary staccato mode, had just finished the words "Glass House." As she watched in terror and amazement, she saw the grainy, overblown projection of the Glass House on the screen. Not a pile of rubble carted away, not a shiny new box.

Her Glass House, surrounded by scaffolding, surrounded by new buildings going up on either side of it. It was still there.

She sank to her knees in front of the screen, staring numbly. The story was brief and to the point. The famous New York landmark, the Glass House, was serving as the focus of billionaire Michael Dubrovnik's latest project, a huge glass and steel construction known as the Glass House Plaza. The architects' model shown on the screen told the story better than any words. Tall buildings abounded with shiny glass spires, their roofs angled downward so that no light was kept from the centerpiece. The Glass House sat in the middle, a tiny jewel of a building in a perfect setting. Delicate, inviolate, shored up and strengthened to last centuries.

She waited until she stopped crying to call the airlines. They were still in the midst of the post-holiday rush, and she couldn't get a flight for two days. She considered calling him, but knew that wouldn't be enough. She had to face him. To thank him, to exorcize old demons, to get on with her life. If they could meet civilly, the battle between them finished, then perhaps they might be friends. That was the best she could hope for, and for right now, that was ambition enough.

## Chapter 19

"I'm not in the mood for this, Sonya," Michael warned, glaring at her from behind the desk in his makeshift office on the top floor of the Glass House.

"Mischa, you've been like a bear with a sore paw for too long," Sonya said, meeting his glare with one of her own. "For three months, to be exact. Your sister goes to all the trouble of coming down to this terrible mess, just to bring you a Christmas present, and you act as if I've done you a grave injustice."

'You're going to lecture me, and I don't want to hear it."

"I'm the only one around who can lecture you," she returned sternly. "Someone has to point out the error of your ways."

Michael leaned back with a weary sigh. He knew his sister too well to suppose there'd be any escape. She'd put on her best dress, her fanciest hat and the sable coat, the one extravagant present she'd ever allowed him to give her since the debacle of the East Side condo. She was dressed for battle, and he was no match for Sonya on the warpath. "All right, Sonya," he said. "Tell me where I've gone wrong. I have a few minutes to spare."

"You'd need days," she said, sitting down opposite him and placing two jars of homemade jam in front of him. "But I'll start with the mortal sins. We'll go on to the venial sins later."

"Thank you for the jam," he said politely. "You already sent me down a caseful."

"This isn't from me. This is from Laura."

He froze, staring at the two small jars for a moment before taking them into his large hands. He didn't even recognize her handwriting. He'd only seen it once, on the bottom of the legal papers she'd left for him, transferring ownership of this expensive whim of his.

"All right," he said, not noticing that his thumbs were subtly caressing the diamond-ridged jars. "Tell me what a rotten SOB I am."

"I wouldn't demean our mother with the suggestion," Sonya said with great dignity. "You haven't done anything wicked, Mischa. Just stupid. That's not like you." She looked around her, at the sawdust and debris littering the floor, the staging outside the new glass panels that practically obliterated the bright winter sunlight, the skeletons of the buildings surrounding them. "This is good, Mischa. The right gesture. But you haven't gone far enough. You must go after her."

He looked at his sister with fresh exasperation. "Why?"

"You won't be happy until you do. Admit it, brother, you're in love with her. You're stupid to fight what can't be fought."

"Who said it can't be fought?" he countered. "She's not what I had in mind."

"Do you think Tim O'Reilly was what I had in mind? Or our parents? Love has nothing to do with plans, or common sense, or economics. Love is the silliest, most impractical thing that God ever created. But you should know by now when a battle is hopeless, and give in with good grace."

"She knows where I am," he said, his eyes hooded.

"You know where she is."

"We'll drive each other crazy."

"It can't be any worse than it is now."

He just looked at her for a long moment. "The damnable thing about you, Sonya," he said, "is that you're always right."

Sonya beamed at him. "Never forget it, Mischa. You'll go tonight?"

"The next flight I can book."

"You have your own jet. What's the excuse?"

"Tonight," he agreed, grinning at her. For the first time in months he felt a great weight lift from him. He'd hoped the news conference would move her. Every waking minute of every hour he'd waited for her call. Some sign from her, even a paltry emotion such as gratitude would have been something. But in the last two days only silence had issued from that tiny house in California.

Right then he would have given anything just to be certain she hadn't changed her mind and started seeing someone. That she hadn't gotten over him. He needed to know there was something left, some spark he could resurrect. Sonya was right, he couldn't live without her. It made no sense, it complicated the hell out of his life, but it was useless to deny it any longer. And since she wasn't coming to him, he had no choice but to go to her.

He spent the rest of the morning clearing his desk of anything pressing. Chances were he wouldn't be able to find it when he returned. There were times when he considered moving his base of operations over to Dubrovnik Court. Glass Faces was doing very well in the offices he'd set up for them there, and the lure of peace and efficiency was a heady one.

But he couldn't leave the Glass House. Maybe it exerted its own pungent magic. Laura had been tied to it with more devotion than she'd shown any man in her life. Maybe it bewitched people. Maybe he'd been a fool not to tear it down.

Maybe, hell. He knew he was a fool. He'd seen the revised estimates, he knew to a penny the cost of the original architects' drawings that had had to be scrapped. He was out of his mind, and even crazier to go chasing after her when she'd shown no inclination that she still wanted him. Maybe she thought the plaza was a travesty. Maybe she hated him.

The intercom buzzed, and his new assistant's voice announced his California lawyer's name. He sighed, punching a button and listening to the man's excuses.

"She still wouldn't sign the agreement, Mr. Dubrovnik. Wouldn't even look at it. She said to tell you that if you wanted her to sign anything else, you could damn well bring it to her yourself."

"Did she really?" That was the most encouraging thing he'd heard in months.

"Of course, the press conference hadn't been aired then. She's probably feeling a lot more mellow by now."

"Maybe," said Michael in his frostiest tone. He didn't like people to try to explain Laura's motives to him. His sister was bad enough—he drew the line when it came to his lawyers.

"What'll I do next?"

"It appears you've failed," Michael drawled. "I'll handle it from here." And he cut the connection.

It was two-thirty, his jet was set to leave Newark in less than an hour, when Ms. Jackson interrupted him one more time. "There's someone to see you, sir."

He grimaced, mentally cursing Zach for taking back the efficient Ms. Anthony and leaving him to deal with another incompetent. "I told you I wouldn't be seeing anyone else today. I have a plane to catch."

"But sir…"

"No one!" he snapped, slamming down the phone.

He should have installed a lock, he thought dismally as the door to his office opened. Once things were at a stage where he could concentrate on interior decorating, he'd see that he had an automatic lock on his office door, accessible from his desk.

The girl who came in was hesitant, as well she should be, considering he didn't want to see anyone. He glared at her as she approached his desk, his cold blue gaze dissecting her.

She was a woman, not as young as he'd first suspected, maybe in her late twenties. She had soft brown hair that framed her face in loose curls, a narrow, slightly curved body, and small, beautiful hands which she'd clasped together in an attempt to appear casual that only betrayed her nervousness. She was wearing pale lavender, something soft and clinging and surprisingly seductive. He looked down at her feet, at the four-inch heels, and then back to her face in shock.

"Yes, it's me," Laura said with a little laugh that bordered on panic. "I didn't think you'd forget me so quickly."

"You look different," he said, rising from the desk and

heading toward her. She backed away, still nervous, and he slowed his advance. He had to handle this right, he thought. One false move and she might be gone forever. "You look wonderful," he said, meaning it. With the razor-cut black hair, the vibrant, trendy clothes and sharp manner she had been undeniably seductive. Today, with the sharp edges softened, she was well-nigh irresistible. He decided it was just as well half the room stood between them. If she was within reach, he wouldn't be able to stop himself touching her, pulling her into his arms, pushing her down onto the floor and making her moan the way she had a century ago, lying in his bed.

He shook his head, trying to clear the erotic thoughts from a brain already overstimulated. He hadn't even been listening to what she was saying, so bemused was he by her sudden reappearance.

"I wanted to thank you for this," she said. "I don't know what made you do it, but I wanted to thank you anyway. I hope it wasn't guilt. You don't need to blame yourself for anything that happened. It was my fault—I was running around in circles and I didn't realize it. You just got caught in the cross fire."

"Explain yourself. In English this time."

Her smile was self-mocking. "You won the Glass House in a fair fight. It was yours to do with as you pleased. The loss of it didn't destroy me, much as I thought it would."

"Great," he said roughly, thinking of the money he'd lost on this foolish, glorious gesture.

"And it wasn't your fault that I threw myself at you," she continued, her voice cool and precise. "You don't need to feel guilty about seducing and abandoning me."

Anger flared within him. "I sure as hell don't. I didn't do the abandoning."

"As I remember, you were responsible for the seducing part, weren't you?" she retorted with a flash of her old fire.

He was oddly relieved. He liked the new, softer Laura, but he wouldn't want her too sweet. "So I don't need to feel guilty for taking you to bed?" he inquired evenly.

She nodded, pleased that he'd understood. "I realize you didn't care for me, that you just sort of got trapped into it. I just wanted you to know that I understand."

He shook his head in exasperation. "I have never in my life seen anyone trapped into seducing someone. But if it makes you happy to believe that…"

"What else can I believe?" Her voice sounded a little raw by then. A good sign. A very good sign. Moving around her, he walked to the door, opened it, and sent Ms. Jackson home with a glare that brooked no denial. Then he locked the door, turned around and surveyed his delectable prisoner.

She didn't realize she was a prisoner yet. She just looked at him, her chin raised defiantly, waiting.

"You can believe what you want to believe," he said, brushing her body deliberately as he reached across the desk and took the agreement he'd been planning to hand-deliver to her. "You're ready to sign this?"

"Of course." Without even glancing at it, she flipped to the last page, set the agreement on the desk and signed it with a flourish.

"Aren't you going to read it?"

"I trust you."

"Why?"

She appeared startled. "I don't know. I just do."

"Why don't you carry that trust just a step further? Read what you just agreed to."

Her dark eyes took on a wary expression, and the last

of her diffidence vanished. "What have you done, you snake?"

He finally let himself touch her, putting his hands on her shoulders and shoving her gently onto the paper-strewn sofa. "Read, Larushka. Then we'll talk about traps."

She'd been a fool to come. Why in heaven's name had she thought that she needed to face him to exorcise his power over her? All she'd done was succumb anew, so that she could barely look at him without melting. God, she wanted him so much that it was eating into her soul like acid! She had to get out of here without distracting herself. Had he really locked the door?

"All right," she said coolly, crossing her legs and leaning back against the sofa. "But you have no witness. If I don't like what I signed, I'll take you to court."

"Susan will lie. She witnessed your other signatures when you took off to California...."

"That's because I'd asked her to."

"And I'll ask her to do this one. She will, too."

Laura glared at him, flipping back to the first page of the legal document. "We'll see," she said fiercely, staring at the words without seeing. When they finally swam into focus, they still didn't make sense. She looked up at him, astonished. "Prenuptial agreement?" she said, her voice not much more than a whisper. "Are you out of your mind?"

"Yes," he said blithely, standing over her. For the first time she noticed how nervous the implacable Whirlwind was, and her bones began to melt. "Let me just summarize the major points in the agreement. It takes too long to wade through the legalese my lawyers assure me is necessary. In return for sole ownership of the Glass House

Plaza, you will have no claim on any of my other possessions at the time of the marriage. Anything acquired after the marriage would be owned jointly."

"You're crazy."

Michael shrugged. "You might as well accept it. New York is a community property state, anyway. The Plaza is worth a lot more than half my estate right now, and it starts us off on more of an even footing. This way neither of us wins."

"And neither of us loses." She set down the papers, rising from the sofa. "Why, Mischa?"

Now that the time had come, he seemed curiously loath to say it. "Ask Sonya," he said with just a trace of asperity. "She'll be glad to tell you."

"She's already told me, and I didn't believe her. I need to hear it from you."

"Come here."

"No." She shook her head. "Do it the hard way. Without touching me. Tell me."

"What is this, revenge?" he demanded, still fighting.

"No, Mischa. Justice." Her voice was soft, seductive and very sure. A bubble of joy was building inside her, threatening to burst, but she had to hear the words.

He crossed the room, standing in front of her, inches away, so close that she could feel his body heat reaching out for hers, so close that she could feel his tense breathing stir her hair. "All right," he said. "I love you. It doesn't make any sense, but I can't fight it anymore. I'll give you anything I own if you'll marry me, even this damned stupid Plaza that's been an albatross around my neck since the moment I thought of it. You don't even have to love me back if you don't feel like it. We'll work on that part."

Even her four-inch heels weren't high enough. Reaching up on tiptoe, she threaded her arms around his neck, smiling up at him, her heart pounding against his. "You don't have to bribe me," she whispered. "I already love you. And I'll marry you. I'll walk around the world barefoot on coals for you. Just say the word."

He kissed her then, pulling her up into his arms so that her feet slipped out of her shoes and dangled in midair, kissed her with a hunger that nothing would ever sate. When he set her down, his arms were trembling, but he managed a wry smile. "You mean I didn't have to give you the Plaza?"

"Too late," she said with a mischievous grin. "I already signed the papers. It's mine." And with great deliberation she began to rip off his shirt, the buttons flying everywhere around the room.

"Gold digger," he muttered, tugging her lavender sweater over her head.

"Snake," she replied amiably, as they sank to the floor.

"Love," he murmured against her skin.

"Love," she agreed, closing her eyes in pleasure.

And outside, the New York sun glinted benevolently through the smoked windows of the Glass House, gilding the lovers within.

\* \* \* \* \*

Dear Reader,

I'm one of the lucky ones. The love of my life is also my very best friend. Marrying him was the easiest decision I ever made. Learning how to *be* married was a little tougher. (i.e., Should the toothpaste cap be left on or off? Is taking out the garbage a gender-oriented chore or an equal-opportunity event? Just how much information is too much? Or too little?) And though in the early days of our marriage our life together sometimes resembled a Hepburn-Tracy comedy, we eventually achieved a very nice balance and a healthy respect for each other's wants and needs.

This is not, however, yet the case for Cal and Ashley Hart. College sweethearts, pursuing dual careers in medicine, they both expected everything to be just perfect when they finally tied the knot. It wasn't. And neither could figure out why.

The problem? A failure to communicate.

And now Cal and Ashley are on the precipice. Do they cut their losses and prevent further hurt? Or roll up their sleeves, renew their commitment and get to work on the challenging task of making their marriage work in a very fundamental and satisfying way?

I hope you enjoy this story as much as I enjoyed creating it. For more information on this and other books, visit my website at www.cathygillenthacker.com.

Best wishes,

Cathy Gillen Thacker

# HER SECRET VALENTINE
## Cathy Gillen Thacker

This book is dedicated to Charlie, with all my love.

# Chapter 1

"How long is this situation between you and Ashley going to go on?" Mac Hart asked.

Cal tensed. He'd thought he had been invited over to his brother Mac's house to watch playoff football with the rest of the men in the family. Now, suddenly, it was looking more like an intervention. He leaned forward to help himself to some of the nachos on the coffee table in front of the sofa. "I don't know what you mean."

"Then let us spell it out for you," Cal's brother-in-law, Thad Lantz, said with his usual coach-like efficiency.

Joe continued, "She missed Janey's wedding to Thad in August, as well as Fletcher's marriage to Lily in October, and Dylan and Hannah's wedding in November."

Cal bristled. They all knew Ashley was busy completing her Ob/Gyn fellowship in Honolulu. "She wanted to be here, but since the flight from Honolulu to Raleigh is at minimum twelve hours, it's too far to go for a weekend trip. Not that she has many full weekends off in any case." Nor did he. Hence, their habit of rendezvousing in San Francisco, since it was a six-or seven-hour flight for each of them.

More skeptical looks. "She didn't make it back to Carolina for Thanksgiving or Christmas or New Year's this year, either," Dylan observed.

Cal shrugged and centered his attention on the TV, where a lot of pre-game nonsense was currently going on. "She had to work all three holidays." He wished the game would hurry up and start. The sooner it did, the sooner this conversation would be over.

"Had to or volunteered to?" Fletcher muttered with a questioning lift of his dark brow.

Uneasiness settled around Cal. He'd had many of the same questions himself. Still, Ashley was his wife, and he felt honor-bound to defend her. "I saw her in November in San Francisco. We celebrated all our holidays then." In one passion-filled weekend that had oddly enough left him feeling lonelier and more uncertain of their union than ever.

Concerned looks were exchanged all the way around. Cal knew the guys in the family all felt sorry for him, which just made the situation worse.

Dylan dipped a tortilla chip into the chili-cheese sauce. "So when is Ashley coming home?" he asked curiously.

That was just it—Cal didn't know. Ashley didn't want to talk about it. "Soon," he fibbed.

Thad paused, his expression thoughtful. "I thought her fellowship was up in December."

Cal sipped his beer, the mellow golden brew settling like acid in his gut. "She took her oral exam then and turned in her thesis."

Fletcher helped himself to a buffalo wing. "Her written exam was last July, wasn't it?"

Cal nodded. "But her last day at the hospital isn't until January 15," he cautioned. In a couple of days from now.

"And then she's coming back home, right?"

That had been the plan, when Ashley had left two and a half years ago to complete her medical education in Hawaii. Now he wasn't so sure that was the case. But not wanting to tell his brothers any of that, he simply said, "She's looking for a job now."

"Here, in North Carolina."

Cal certainly hoped so, since he was committed to his job at the Holly Springs Medical Center for another eighteen months, minimum.

"If she were my wife..." Mac began.

"Funny," Cal interrupted, the last of his legendary patience waning swiftly. "You don't have a wife."

"If it were me," Mac continued, ignoring Cal's glare as he added a piping-hot pizza to the spread, "I'd get on a plane to Honolulu, put her over my shoulder and carry her home if necessary." His take-charge attitude served him well as the sheriff of Holly Springs, but his romantic track record hardly made him an expert on dishing out relationship advice.

"That John Wayne stuff doesn't work with Ashley." Never had. Never would.

"Well, you better do something," Joe warned.

All eyes turned to him. Cal waited expectantly, knowing from the silence that fell there was more. Finally, Joe cleared his throat. "The women in the family are all upset. You've been married nearly three years now, and most of that time you and Ashley have been living apart."

"So?" Cal prodded.

"So, they're tired of seeing you so unhappy." Dylan

took over where Cal left off. "They're giving you and Ashley till Valentine's Day—"

Cal and Ashley's wedding anniversary.

"—to make thing right."

"And if that doesn't happen?" Cal demanded.

Fletcher scowled. "Then the women in the family are stepping in."

"If you keep this up, people are going to start calling you the Artful Dodger."

The low sexy voice with the hint of Southern drawl echoed through the Honolulu General staff lounge. Her heart leaping with a mixture of pleasure and surprise, Ashley turned to see her husband of almost three years standing in the doorway. Joy swept through her as she hungrily surveyed him.

Cal was wearing a loose-fitting tropical print silk shirt that made the most of his hard-muscled chest and broad shoulders. Pleated trousers nicely outlined his trim waistline and long sturdy legs. His short, traditionally cut ash-blond hair was brushed away from his face, and his smooth golden skin glowed with good health. The hint of a traveler's beard clung to his strong—and exceedingly stubborn—Hart jaw. Taken alone, his features weren't particularly outstanding. His nose bore the scars of a childhood athletic injury. His brows and thick, short eyelashes were so light in hue that you could hardly see them, and his upper lip was a little on the thin side. And yet, together, those penetrating pewter-gray eyes and not-so-perfect features combined to make a drop-everything, he-is-so-arresting man. Not to mention, she thought wistfully, how stealthily he moved—as if all that male power were just waiting to be unleashed. Or how intimately he looked at her, which suggested he couldn't wait to get her back into his arms and into his bed.

"Cal." Ashley stared at him in shock.

"Well that's something anyway." He grinned at her lazily. "At least you recall my name."

Beneath the teasing tone was a hint of hurt that was baffling, since Cal rarely revealed the inner workings of his heart and mind to her or anyone else. Ashley swallowed around the sudden lump in her throat, sensing that was about to change. He had four inches on her, so at five foot ten, she still had to tilt her head back to clearly see into his face.

"What are you doing here?" she demanded, wondering if his sturdy masculine presence and six-foot-two frame would ever stop making her feel tiny. "I thought—"

Cal arched his blond brow. "That I was going to wait until you gave me the signal it was okay to come and get you?"

Aware he was now standing close enough for her to inhale the sea-and-sun fragrance of his cologne, Ashley shoved aside the familiar anxiety bubbling up inside her, ducked beneath a Congratulations, Ashley! banner and went back to pulling things out of her locker and dropping them in a cardboard box. "Who said anything about you coming to get me?" She had wanted to be prepared for this no doubt difficult tête-à-tête. She had wanted to know precisely what to say.

Cal stepped closer. "Exactly. There were no plans made. And yet," he observed, his voice dropping a seductive notch, "your last shift at the hospital was today."

Ashley drew a deep breath and turned to face him. "What's gotten into you?" Feeling the need for some protection from the emotions shimmering between them, she held her rain jacket in front of her like a shield.

Cal took it from her and dropped it into the box of belongings. "What do you mean?"

Her pulse pounding, Ashley whirled back to get a few books. "You're normally so…easygoing and patient when it comes to stuff like this," she said as she dropped them on top of her jacket. Today he seemed anything but that.

Cal's eyes gleamed with a predatory light. He flattened his hand on the locker next to her and leaned in close. "Which is perhaps the problem, Ash. Maybe I'm too good at waiting and not nearly as good at going after what I want."

Oh, my. "Which is—?" Ashley countered.

Cal took her in his arms and swept her close, until they were touching intimately. "For starters, this," he told her as his lips came down on hers.

Their first kiss after a long separation always radiated lots of feeling and passion. And this one, Ashley noted as Cal's lips and tongue laid claim to hers, was no exception. He tasted like the spearmint gum he carried in his pocket. And, as his arms wrapped tightly around her, she felt that she had finally come home. Not that this was any surprise.

Ashley had loved Cal practically from the first moment she had set eyes on him, during her freshman year of college at Wake Forest. Maybe it was because he was four years older than she was—already a first-year med student when they met—but he had always overwhelmed her with his confidence and sexy Southern charm. She felt safe when she was with him. Desired. Every inch a woman.

It was only when they were miles apart, out of each other's arms, that the doubts crept in about their love lasting forever. But when he was kissing her like this,

his lips moving surely over hers, all she could think was how right he felt pressed up against her.

They could have gone on forever like that, wrapped in each other's arms, kissing madly, if it hadn't been for the sound of a door opening behind them. Followed by a discreet cough and laughter.

"No need to ask what you two are doing," the maternity-ward nurse said.

Cal lifted his head reluctantly. "Celebrating!" he said, looking more than ready to do it all over again.

Ashley relaxed in Cal's arms, laying her head on his chest, as the nurse beamed. She looked at Ashley. "You must have told him about the job offer in Maui! Isn't that fabulous?" The nurse turned back to Cal. "Do you know how many of us would give up our vacations to work there?"

Silence fell as the impact of her words sank in. Cal's expression turned troubled, as did Ashley's and then the nurse's. Ashley held up a hand before an apology could be made.

The nurse took another look at their expressions, then smiled again and quite wisely made for the door. "I'll, uh, see you two aren't disturbed," she stated delicately on her way out.

Cal just stood there, looking as if he felt as shut out of Ashley's life as she often did of his. Guilt flooded her. As usual, it seemed she was going to be damned if she did and damned if she didn't. If she declined this job, her parents and Dr. Connelly, her mentor here, and everyone else she worked with was going to be disappointed in her. And Cal wouldn't be pleased with her no matter *what* she did. He expected her to be as successful in her career as he was in his, yet he didn't want any work-related demands interfering with their time together. Given the fact she was an obstetrician and he a surgeon—both of them prone to be called out at any moment on patient emergencies—that was one tough bill to fill. Aware he was still waiting for an explanation, she said finally, "I was going to tell you."

Cal studied her, his gray eyes distant. "I take it this means you haven't turned the position down yet," he replied.

Ashley shrugged, wishing she were clad in something other than blue cotton scrubs and tennis shoes. Maybe if she were dressed like Cal—in sophisticated street clothes—she'd feel more confident. Feeling errant strands escaping down the back of her neck and brushing the sides of her face, Ashley released the butterfly clip that held her hair. She straightened the strands with her fingers, twisted them into a loop and put her hair back up. "I just found out about it last week."

"Your coworkers know about it."

Ashley knew he expected first dibs on news like that. And she would have told him, if she'd had any other job offers to go along with it. But she hadn't because she'd been so busy finishing up her fellowship that she hadn't even had time to really start looking for a permanent position. This one had just fallen into her lap. When she had talked to Cal, she had wanted to have more options to present. So he wouldn't be as disappointed in her as her parents were likely to be to find her lax in her search for employment after all those years of expensive education and training. Cal had had about six job offers waiting his decision when he finished his residency. But then he had devoted the entire first five months of their marriage to making sure that was the case. Whereas she had reserved her precious few days off to spend with Cal, instead of searching for a position.

"Some of the staff just happened to be here when I got the phone call from Maui about the offer," Ashley explained.

A mixture of anger and disappointment flashed briefly in his eyes. "Phones work on the mainland, too," he muttered.

His displeasure cut right through her worse than anyone else's ever had. "I thought it was something we should discuss in person," she said, her voice trembling with emotion.

He regarded her with mounting dismay. "You can't seriously be considering taking it."

"Actually," Ashley hesitated, "I don't know what I'm going to do yet."

Cal nodded and said nothing else.

Realizing he didn't want to have this conversation in a communal staff lounge any more than she did, Ashley continued getting ready to leave.

After Cal helped her gather up the rest of the things, she said her goodbyes to the staff, and they drove back to her apartment.

Located in a high rise that overlooked Waikiki beach, the furnished efficiency was as sparely decorated as it had been the day Ashley had moved in two-and-a-half years ago.

Cal had only been at her apartment a handful of times, and Ashley had been there mainly to shower and sleep. The majority of her time had been spent at the teaching hospital and various clinics served by it around the island.

There was a stack of collapsed moving boxes for her clothes and books shoved along one wall. A pile of mail on the coffee table. The large square room and bath normally felt cold and empty to Ashley. Tonight, with Cal here, it felt suffocating. Almost too small for comfort.

"Aren't you going to ask me anything else about the job I've been offered?" Ashley said, wishing Cal would open up to her more instead of always keeping everything inside. Except, of course, when it came to his desire for her. He was very open about expressing that. As was she, she admitted reluctantly to herself.

"Actually—" Cal set down his small duffel bag "—first, I'd like to go for a swim. We can get into all that over dinner?"

Ashley swallowed. If they were going to fight, she just wanted to do it already. "But—"

He cut her off with a derisive look. "If there's bad news coming, I think I'd rather wait until later to hear it, if you don't mind."

The decision made—as far as he was concerned anyway—Cal methodically emptied his pockets. No sooner had he unclipped the cell phone from his belt than it began to ring. He glanced at the caller ID and tossed the phone to Ashley. "See what Mac wants, would you?"

Cal grabbed his swim trunks from his overnight bag and disappeared into the bathroom. Ashley was left holding the still-buzzing phone. By the time she figured out how to use it, the call went over to message. She waited for it to finish and then retrieved it, using Cal's password.

"Well?" Cal said. Emerging from the bathroom, he tossed his shirt and slacks onto the back of the sofa. "What did Mac want?"

Despite her quickly mounting irritation from the message she'd listened to, Ashley couldn't resist admiring his tanned, muscular physique. "Actually, the message was from all four of your brothers and your brother-in-law." Defiantly, she kept her gaze from wandering below the waist of his loose-fitting tropic-print swim trunks.

Cal tensed, but his expression did not change. Hence,

Ashley couldn't tell if he had been expecting this "fun-filled call" from his brothers or not.

"Go on," Cal demanded.

With pleasure, Ashley thought, as she caught her husband's gaze and held on for all she was worth. "Mac reminded you that 'a woman appreciates strength in a man.'"

"Fletcher said, 'There's nothing more seductive than making someone laugh.'" *Hah! As if Cal had ever needed help getting her into his arms and his bed!*

"Dylan said, 'When it comes to women, patience is a virtue that is highly overrated.'" Since when had Cal waited for anything he wanted from her? It was more his style to conquer first and ask questions later.

"Joe suggested you think 'offense' this time around." *Offense for what?* Ashley wondered. *Their marriage? That made it sound like a game!*

"And Thad suggested that 'you not forget to listen.'" Which was, Ashley considered, actually something Cal needed to do more of.

Her diatribe over, Ashley tossed the phone back to Cal. "So," she fumed. "Do you want to tell me what that is all about? Or should I just guess?"

# Chapter 2

"They're just clowning around," Cal said lamely, as he opened the sliding-glass doors to her balcony and stepped through them.

"And that's it?" Ashley prodded warily, joining him on the lanai.

Here was his chance to tell her his whole family was worried about them. Ready to step in and help, if need be. But sensing she would not take this news well—Ashley had never really gotten how close the Harts were, or how much they depended on each other for moral and emotional support—Cal simply said, "The consensus is we've spent so much time apart in the three years since we said our 'I do's,' that we're still newlyweds."

"And in other ways," Ashley sighed, turning her glance to the blue ocean and shimmering white sand dotted with palm trees, "sometimes it seems like we're hardly married at all."

Precisely the problem, in Cal's estimation. "That will all change once we're living in the same house in the same city again," Cal told Ashley confidently. He studied her carefully as the warm tropical breeze fanned across them. "That is still the plan, isn't it?"

Ashley hesitated, much to Cal's dismay.

Resentment roiled in his gut. "You can't seriously be thinking about taking the position!"

To his increasing disappointment, Ashley made a palms-up gesture that reflected her uncertainty. "It's a dream job, Cal. Something I would feel lucky to be offered even ten years down the road. To get the opportunity now is a real coup. One that would make my parents proud. And you, too, I would think." Her voice trembled, despite her strong resolve. "After all, didn't I support you when you landed a position that would allow you to treat members of Carolina's professional hockey team and a lot of the premiere college athletes in the area?"

Cal turned his glare to the beautiful blue horizon. "I never said you didn't support my dreams to be the best sports medicine specialist and orthopedic surgeon around."

"Good." Ashley waited until he turned back to her, then tossed her head. His breath caught at the image of her dark hair falling like silk around her shoulders. "Because I have, Cal."

"But what about us?" Cal demanded, hating the need radiating in his low voice. He tried so hard not to be selfish.

Hope shone in her china-blue eyes. "You could move here in eighteen months, when your contract with the medical center in Holly Springs is up. There are plenty of athletes in Hawaii, and on the West Coast, who would be lucky to have a physician of your expertise."

Cal knew she was avoiding the point. "Your coming to Hawaii was supposed to be a temporary measure," he reminded her coolly. A move made more out of necessity than choice.

Abruptly, Ashley stilled. She looked wary—as if she were afraid to commit herself too fully to him and their marriage again. As if she wanted them to continue the long-distance charade of a marriage. "Things change, Cal," she told him softly.

And not always for the better, Cal thought.

He had never understood why Ashley had withdrawn emotionally from him in the first six months of their marriage. True, it had been a hellishly bad spring and summer. The fellowship program Ashley had been enrolled in had abruptly lost its director and its funding. She'd had to scramble to find a place that could take her as a second-year fellowship student, while he was studying for the medical boards that he had to pass in order to practice orthopedic and sports medicine. A physician in training herself, Ashley should have understood the kind of pressure he was under. She'd certainly said she did. But that whole summer, she'd been on an emotional roller coaster—crying one minute, too quiet the next. First overeating to the point she had gained weight, then barely eating at all.

He'd known she was in a crisis brought on by the potential interruption of her education. But overwhelmed by his own mountain of studying, he realized in retrospect that he hadn't been there for her or helped her as much as he should have. By the time he had completed his testing, she had already secured another fellowship and left for Hawaii.

Cal had tried to make up for his earlier lack of understanding and support by being as enthusiastic as possible about the stellar opportunity Ashley had secured for her-self. But, by then, the damage had already been done. At least emotionally. They had continued to make love, as if nothing were wrong. In fact, a lot of their interludes were even more physically passionate than ever before. But when it came time for them to bare their souls... Well, that just didn't happen. It had been as if a wall were be-tween them—and it had gotten wider with every month that passed. A wall that was impenetrable even now.

"There was no way I could have anticipated being of-fered the position of Director of the Maui Birthing Cen-ter." Ashley sat down in one of the striped vinyl chairs on the lanai and propped her feet up on the rail.

Cal dropped down into the chair next to hers. "How long do you have to decide?" he asked, wishing he could be more charitable. But he couldn't. His patience with this long-distance marriage of theirs was at an end.

"A month."

Ashley fanned her hand in front of her face, as if that would dispel the heat of the late-afternoon sun that pinkened her cheeks and added perspiration to her fore-head. "Of course they'd like my answer sooner."

Cal watched her pull the fabric of her cotton top away from her breasts. "Of course." *Why couldn't you just say no?* Cal wondered. *Why are you even considering this?* Unless his gut fear was right, and she really did not want to be married to him after all.

"Look, I know how little time off you have," Ashley said sympathetically.

Figuring he wasn't going to like this either, Cal tensed. "So?"

Ashley swallowed and brought her feet down off the pastel green metal railing and stood. "We need to be practical here. There's no reason for you to stay while I'm job-hunting and getting ready to move out of this apartment."

Cal bet she wanted him out of the way. But his time for being the understanding husband, with no demands of his own, was over. He grimaced, knowing he hadn't needed his brother's advice to react in a take-no-excuses manner now. He'd had it up to here with the separations and it was time his wife knew it! "I'm not leaving, Ashley."

She blinked. "Excuse me?"

He stood and faced her, legs planted apart, hands braced on his waist. "I'm not going back home without you. Not this time. Nor do I plan to let you make a decision about your professional future without considering the impact that decision will have on our marriage."

"What has gotten into you?" Ashley demanded.

Two and a half years ago, Cal had pushed her to be all she could be. Insisting—just as her parents had—that Ashley take the fellowship slot in Honolulu, rather than face a one-year interruption in her medical education. It hadn't seemed to matter to any of them that she hadn't really wanted to go all the way to Hawaii or be apart from her husband of just five months. The opportunity in Hawaii was worth the sacrifice, or so everyone had told her.

She'd let herself be convinced of that, because she had truly needed time apart from Cal to deal with her own mistakes. Mistakes that Cal and her parents still knew nothing about. And she hoped guiltily, they never would.

Oblivious to her own inner angst, Cal impatiently answered her question. "Let's just say I've finally come to my senses. Living apart for two-and-a-half years is much too long. I'm your husband. You're my wife. Enough of the long-distance marriage, Ash. We need to be together."

If only he had said this to her back then, Ashley thought sadly. She wasn't sure she could trust his sudden devotion to her now. She didn't want to start counting on something that would, in the end, only be snatched away from her by circumstances yet again. Right now they had a commuter marriage that was working, despite the occasional glitch. At least to the point that he still wanted her when they were together. That wouldn't necessarily be the case if they were together day in and day out and she ended up letting him down.

Ashley was afraid that if she returned to Holly Springs, it could be the end of her marriage. After all, what if the members of the Hart clan passed judgment on their less-than-perfect union and it pushed Cal even further away? Right now, she would rather have "half a marriage" than none at all.

"And if I go to Maui tomorrow?" She posed the question to him casually, as if her entire well-being weren't riding on his reply.

Cal gestured, as if the answer to that were a no-brainer. "Then I guess I'll go to Maui with you."

Now he *definitely* was not making sense. Nor was she sure she quite believed him. "What about your family and your patients back in North Carolina?" Ashley asked bluntly.

For the first time, there was a hint of conflict on Cal's face, reminding Ashley how tied he was to his hometown.

Cal shrugged, still refusing to back down. He walked through the sliding-glass doors and into the apartment. "I guess they'll all have to get along without me," he drawled.

Right on cue, her deeply ingrained sense of responsibility reared its ugly head. She couldn't be responsible for Cal shirking his duty, and he knew that. Ashley followed him, then folded her arms in front of her and glared at him. For once she wished she weren't so inherently responsible. "This isn't funny, Cal." She pushed the words through her teeth.

Still clad in nothing but swim trunks, he sank down on the mattress and made himself comfortable on the pillows of her bed, folding his arms behind his head, as if he slept there with her every night. He narrowed his eyes at her and replied, "It isn't supposed to be."

Ashley glided closer, being careful to stay out of easy reach. "You can't just stop working in Holly Springs on a whim!" She planted both her hands on her hips.

Cal's inherently sexy smile widened. "Want to bet?" he tossed right back.

Heat flooded Ashley's face as her glance moved over his sinewy chest, broad shoulders and long, muscled limbs. With difficulty, she forced her attention back to the matter at hand. "You'll get fired from the medical center or sued for breach of contract by the state if you pull a stunt like that," she warned. He wasn't serious. He couldn't be. And yet…he looked as if he was fully ready to do just that!

"Change into your swimsuit and we'll go for a swim, Ash."

She stared at him. Their discussion had apparently come to an end as far as he was concerned.

He patted the mattress. "Okay, if you don't want to take a swim, then come to bed with me."

Ignoring the sexy command, she looked right back at him. "In your dreams," she retorted.

Now it was Cal's turn to be stunned. No matter how rocky their relationship got at times, Ashley had never refused to make love. "All right." He got up lazily, closing the distance between them. He was determined to feel close to her in whatever way he could. "I'll come to you, then."

"This isn't going to work, Cal," Ashley murmured as he took her into his arms and kissed her neck. Ashley splayed her hands across his chest and pushed him away. "Every time we find ourselves alone we end up doing this!"

Cal drank in the intoxicating fragrance of her hair and skin, then drew back to savor the sight of her. With her heart-shaped face, long-lashed china-blue eyes, high sculpted cheekbones and slender nose, she was just as beautiful now as she had been the day they had met, nearly ten years ago. Her thick, glossy dark-brown hair was still shoulder-length, although she now wore it in a sexy, layered style, and her skin had retained its radiant golden glow. The only change, it seemed, was her weight. There was a new voluptuousness to her breasts, a slight thickening of her waist and hips, that hadn't been there the last time he had been with her. He was glad to see she had put a little weight on her tall, willowy body. Last fall and summer she had been almost too thin.

"We *are* married," Cal reminded her, stepping back enough to take in her long curvaceous legs.

Ashley reached for a brush on her bureau and ran it through her hair. "We make love so much when we do see each other it feels like we're having an affair!" She rummaged through her bureau and brought out a turquoise tankini.

Cal leaned against the wall and folded his arms against his chest. "I can think of worse things than trysting with my wife."

Ashley disappeared into the bathroom with her swimsuit. "Making love right now won't solve anything," she called through the door.

"Neither will you not coming home where you belong." Cal waited until she emerged in the demure swimsuit. The sight of her breasts pushing against the confines
of the top confirmed his observation that she had gained
weight.

With effort, he turned his glance away from the swelling curves. He paused as their glances met in a firestorm
of emotion once again. "You want to work things out
with me, don't you?"

"Of course I do," she said hotly. She didn't know why
her husband even had to ask that! The problem was she
was scared that if they tried Cal would discover what she
already knew in her heart—that this marriage of theirs
was a sham.

"Then," Cal continued, moving away from the wall.
He sauntered toward her, all insouciant charm. "I expect
you to do the practical thing and take the next month to
figure out what you want and where you want to live.
And do it while spending time with me."

As he neared her, Ashley felt as if she was being
backed into a corner and she hated that as much as she
hated being instructed what to do or feel or think. "How
do you know I haven't already made up my mind?" she
challenged.

The corners of his lips turned up smugly. "Have you?"

"Well, no, I haven't had time."

A mixture of affection and promise gleamed in his
gray eyes as he took her in his arms once again. "Come
home with me and you'll have all the time in the world."

Ashley didn't like feeling trapped. When Cal behaved
this way, he reminded her of her youth, of growing up
with parents who had everything all plotted out for her,
there had been no time for discussion or dissension. All
the decisions regarding Ashley's life had already been

made for her. Telling her parents that what they wanted was not necessarily what *she* wanted had been futile. They had argued and pushed and prodded until it had been easier just to give in and go along. Her cooperation had made them happy. But it had made her miserable.

Cal didn't seem to realize it, but his relentless expectations had often left her feeling just as hemmed in. The only difference was Cal had not pushed to rule every situation they encountered in their marriage. He had allowed her to do what she wanted, when she wanted. But that freedom had not come without a price. She had seen the disappointment in his eyes when she failed to live up to his dreams of what his wife and lover—and the potential mother of his children—should be. She had felt his hurt, and known she was responsible. And that had been worse to her in many ways than the distress she had caused her parents when she had thwarted their expectations of her.

So Ashley had done the only thing she could to preserve her marriage—she'd put enough distance between them to prevent such clashes on a daily basis. Her hope had been that "absence" would make their hearts grow fonder…and strengthen their relationship.

Only it hadn't worked out that way; they'd become even more emotionally distant than before.

Cal pulled her closer. "We can't keep running from each other," Cal said quietly as the warmth of his tall strong body penetrated hers. He threaded his fingers through the hair at the nape of her neck and tilted her face up to his. "We have to figure out a way to make this marriage of ours work on an everyday basis."

Fear mixed with desire. "And what if it doesn't?" The whispered words were out before Ashley could stop them.

Cal's expression hardened. He took his hand away

from her hair, let it fall back to her waist. "We'll never know until we try."

She couldn't deny the truth of his words.

"It's time we stepped up and confronted the problems that have been dogging us since the moment we said our vows."

"All right." Ashley moved away from Cal. "But we do it on my terms."

He lifted a brow. "Which are?"

"No sex." Ashley bartered the condition she had been thinking about for quite a while.

He blinked in surprise. "Excuse me?"

Ashley held up a cautioning palm. "I mean it, Cal. Sex between the two of us is great, but it never fails to derail us when we are trying to work out a problem. We end up making love and not talking about whatever it is that needs to be dealt with in the first place. So, if I come back with you to North Carolina while I job hunt, then we can't make love."

As Ashley had expected, her husband had to think about that. Hard. Which confirmed all of Ashley's worst fears—that without the sex they really had nothing to hold them together. Nothing that would keep their marriage going for the next fifty years.

A wealth of emotions flickered in Cal's eyes. Finally, to Ashley's relief, he assented. "But I have a few conditions of my own," Cal said firmly as Ashley found her beach sandals and sat down on the sofa to slip them on.

"One, you live with me under the same roof the entire time you are in Holly Springs. And two, you stay until our third wedding anniversary on Valentine's Day and celebrate the occasion with me. You can have your own bedroom—either the master suite or the guest room," he offered expansively. "Your choice."

Ashley stared up at him, her hands braced on either side of her. "That's a whole month, Cal."

Nodding, he held out his palm and helped her to her feet. "Which ought to be long enough to figure out where we go from here."

## Chapter 3

"You've really done a lot to the place," Ashley remarked late the following morning. Despite her wool coat, she shivered a little from the brisk winter air. They had taken the red-eye back to Carolina. And now, some twelve hours later, they were back at the farmhouse he had purchased during the first year she had been in Honolulu. "It was in pretty rough shape the last time I saw it."

"That's right," Cal recalled. "You've only seen the place once." He set their suitcases down in the front hall and went to adjust the downstairs thermostat that had been lowered in his absence.

Ashley felt the chill seep from her bones. "You've obviously worked hard on it. I'm impressed."

The two-story farmhouse had been painted a sunny yellow on the outside. The pine-green shutters and door coordinated nicely with the new slate-gray roof. Inside, the hardwood floors had all been redone. The walls were painted a creamy sand that went well with the white crown moldings and trim. She couldn't help noticing, however, that the parlor and formal dining room at the very front of the house were empty and the walls bare.

"I thought you might like to help me decorate these rooms," Cal told her casually. "So I haven't done anything with them." Looking happy to have her there again at long last, he took her hand and led her back toward the rear of the house.

He continued to show her around proudly. The country kitchen had all new glass-front cabinets and marble counters and was painted a soothing shade that blended well with both. The same color continued into the laundry room at the rear of the house, as well as into the tastefully decorated family room that overlooked the fruit orchards edging the backyard. A big stone fireplace was the focal point of the room. The mantel was lined with photos of Ashley and Cal. Formal engagement and wedding day portraits, as well as casual snapshots of them with family and friends from happier times. Before things got so complicated, Ashley thought wistfully.

Cal moved to the entertainment cabinet and showed her where the remotes for the wide-screen TV, stereo and DVD player were kept. "There's no cable out here—so we've got satellite. I'll show you how to use it whenever you want."

"Later would be fine," Ashley said, wondering at the formality that had risen up between them now that they were physically together again. When had things become so awkward between them they didn't even know how to be in the same house together? she fretted miserably. A house they co-owned as husband and wife.

"Want to see the upstairs?" Cal asked, continuing to play the perfect host.

"Sure." Ashley nodded agreeably. "And then I'm really going to have to crash." She was so fatigued from the flight back, she was nearly light-headed. She turned and looked at the dark circles beneath his eyes that hadn't been there sixteen hours previously. "You must be beat, too." He had flown to Hawaii, and then hours later, turned right around and flown back to North Carolina.

"I am," Cal admitted, stifling a yawn. Logging nearly twenty-four hours travel time in a thirty-two-hour period was finally catching up with him.

He led her past the hall bathroom, which looked as if it had been outfitted for guests and was rarely used, and two empty bedrooms. A guest room was next. It had the big cozy bed they had used the first five months of their marriage and an antique bureau with a mirror that conjured up a lot of memories for Ashley that she wasn't sure she was ready to remember yet.

Next was the master bedroom. A brand new king-size sleigh bed with matching cherry nightstands and antique brass lamps took up most of the space. Two separate walk-in closets had been built. And where the fifth bedroom and bath had been was a brand-new master bathroom.

Ashley gaped at the changes. There were dual pedestal sinks, a sit-down vanity, a separate water closet for the commode, and a whirlpool tub beneath a bay window of privacy glass. But it was the shower that commanded her attention. Pale-green marble covered the floor, walls and ceiling of the six-by-eight-foot space. A high window at one end let in plenty of sunlight, and a long green marble bench was situated beneath it. There were two showerheads—a handheld and an overhead—and the glass shower door stretched all the way to the ceiling.

"This doubles as a sauna," Cal boasted, showing her where the controls for that were.

"Wow," Ashley said. She had never seen anything quite so luxurious.

Cal's gaze drifted over her appreciatively. "The sauna can feel pretty good after a long day or night at the hospital."

As would their lovemaking, the implication seemed to be. Ashley swallowed, pushing away the flutter of desire deep inside her. She had promised herself she would not let passionate sex distract them from the work they needed to do on their relationship. She would keep that vow.

Cal frowned, apparently registering the sudden drop in temperature between them. "Anyway, I know I promised you separate accommodations," he said gallantly ushering her back out into the hall.

And it was good they'd made that agreement, Ashley thought. Otherwise she would have been tempted just to say the heck with caution and fall into bed with her husband once again.

He gave her a hot, assessing look. "So unless you've changed your mind…"

"I haven't," Ashley said, pretending her thoughts weren't traveling down the same ardent path as his.

To Cal's credit, if he was disappointed by her careful outward demeanor, he did not show it. He paused to turn the upstairs thermostat higher. "I'll take the guest room then," he said mildly.

"You don't have to do that," Ashley said, knowing that she'd be more comfortable in the bed she had used before than in anything that had been exclusively his.

He looked at her a long moment, the faint hint of disappointment radiating in his pewter-gray eyes. "I'll carry your suitcase up then," he said quietly. And that was that.

The phone rang at 6:00 p.m. Cal reached for it with a groan, and dutifully talked to his mother on the other end of the line. By the time he hung up two minutes later, he found Ashley standing in the doorway of the master bedroom. Tousled and adorable, she looked as disoriented as he felt after only a couple of hours sleep.

"Everything okay?" she murmured.

Damn, she looked sexy in a thigh-length cotton nightshirt and bare legs, Cal thought as he struggled to shake off his jet lag and sit all the way up against the headboard. Since she had obviously gone right from the shower into bed, her dark hair had dried in thick unruly waves.

"Who was that?" Ashley stifled a yawn with the back of her hand as she padded closer.

Knowing they would both adjust to the change in time zone if they stayed up the rest of the evening and went to bed at the normal time, Cal rubbed the sleep from his eyes. "My mother wants us to come for dinner. I told her I wasn't sure you'd feel up to it. She said, if not, she'd send something over."

"Is the whole family going to be there?" Ashley asked, with the hesitation she always evidenced when confronted with all five of his siblings. And now, thanks to a recent round of satisfying romances, four of them had spouses, too.

Cal shrugged. He didn't want to make things any more awkward than they already were between him and Ashley. "We can always see everyone later," he told her.

Looking as sleepy and out of it as he felt, Ashley perched on the end of the bed and tucked one hand around the sleigh-shaped footboard. "I know everyone wants to see me."

An understatement if there ever was one, Cal thought. Particularly since his whole family had decided to help "fix" his marriage, unless he managed to do it first.

"So we might as well go this evening," Ashley continued practically. "If you feel up to it."

Cal figured it had to be better than staying here alone with Ashley, wanting to make love to her when he had promised to abstain. At least for the time being. He was still hoping she would change her mind about that and realize making love to each other always brought them closer. And now, more than ever, with so many important things ahead of them to decide, they needed to be closer. "We can make it a quick visit," he said. He didn't want to stay long lest his brothers decided to get into the advice-giving business again.

Ashley nodded her assent. "Just give me a few minutes to get dressed."

Forty minutes later, Cal was still waiting for Ashley. When she finally came downstairs she was wearing a jewel-necked, long-sleeved black dress that she usually reserved for cocktail parties.

"I thought you were wearing slacks," he said with a frown, wondering if he should go upstairs and change out of his jeans and cotton shirt into something more formal, too.

"I was. Or I tried."

He looked at her, not understanding.

"I guess I've gained a little weight over the holidays," she said, her cheeks flushing bright pink. "I didn't think I'd had that many Christmas cookies, but...suddenly none of the pants I brought with me want to zip. So it's either this or another dress or the sweats I wore on the plane—

and those need a run through the washer first." Cheeks flushing all the more, she swept past him. "I'm sorry I kept you waiting."

"I'm not. You look great." The black fabric clung to her newly voluptuous curves, and the swirling skirt and high heels made the most of her sexy legs. She'd left her hair down, and it looked as wild and untamed as he knew her to be in her most unguarded moments.

Cal paused to remove her winter coat from the hall closet. "Would it make you feel less self-conscious if I went up and changed?" He knew everyone in his family would probably be wearing jeans, too, but he could put on a sport coat and tie.

"No. It's fine, really." Ashley waved off his concern. She slipped on the long black wool coat and looped a cashmere scarf around her neck. "I'm just going to have to get back to exercising on a regular basis again."

Cal held the door for Ashley. "Well don't lose any weight on my account," he said. He let his eyes travel over her appreciatively. "I think you look amazing. I mean it, Ashley," he continued when she scoffed. "Any extra ounces you have put on are definitely in all the right places."

"And those would be...?" Ashley prodded dryly as he unlocked the passenger door on his SUV and helped her inside.

In answer, Cal grinned and let his gaze touch her breasts, waist and hips.

She blushed again.

"You're perfect," Cal repeated. Wishing—just once— she would believe it. "And I like the glow on your face, too," he added softly. He touched her cheek with the back of his hand.

Ashley wrinkled her nose, and shook her head. "I'm

going to pretend I agree with you…just so we don't have to talk about my embarrassing predicament anymore. It's probably what I get for living in scrubs and lab coats, anyway. All those loose-fitting tops and elastic waistbands…I'll be more careful in the future. Just do me a favor and don't mention my wardrobe crisis to your sibs? I'm embarrassed enough already."

"Don't you look wonderful!" Helen Hart told Ashley when she and Cal walked in to her home behind the Wedding Inn, the palatial three-story white brick inn Cal's mother had turned into the premiere wedding facility in North Carolina. As always, Ashley noted admiringly, Helen's short red hair was perfectly coiffed, her amber eyes as warm as they were astute. Ashley's mother-in-law favored clothes that were classic, not trendy. Tonight she was clad in a cream wool turtleneck sweater and gray slacks perfect for an evening with family.

"You think we look good now, wait until we get some more sleep!" Cal winked at his mom as he helped Ashley off with her coat and went to hang it up.

Ashley returned Helen's hug warmly. Although her husband's siblings could sometimes leave her feeling overwhelmed, she adored Cal's mom. Maybe because the openly loving, family-oriented woman was everything her own mother wasn't. Helen Hart loved and accepted her kids, no matter what. She did not demand they succeed at all cost. She simply wanted them to be good, kind, loving people. Which wasn't to say Helen was a pushover. If the fifty-six-year-old Helen saw one of her brood making a mistake that could hurt someone else, she was always quick to intervene and make sure that the situation was corrected. But she also gave them plenty of room to live their own lives. And as a result of that, her six adult children were a very tight-knit group. The death of Cal's father twenty years ago had made them even more so. They understood the value of family. And they loved each other dearly. So dearly that even after ten years of being Cal's one and only, Ashley sometimes still felt like an outsider looking in.

Oblivious to Ashley's anxiety over the evening ahead, Helen linked arms with Ashley and led her toward the Great Room at the rear of the house, where everyone gathered. "If we'd had more notice, I would've invited your parents to be with us this evening, too," Helen noted cheerfully. "They must be very anxious to see you, too!"

Were they? Ashley wondered.

"When are you and Cal going to visit them?" Helen paused in the kitchen to check the big pot of spaghetti sauce simmering on the stove.

"I'm not sure," Ashley hedged, watching Helen put water on to boil.

"But they do know you're back in Carolina?" Helen ascertained, concern lighting her eyes.

Ashley nodded. "I emailed them my plans before I left Honolulu." And hadn't yet checked to see if there had been a response, largely because she hadn't felt ready to face the constant pressure to achieve that her parents were likely to exert on her when they did see her.

Aware this was a touchy subject with Ashley, Cal motioned them all to the family room, where the rest of Hart clan was gathered around the television, watching two NHL teams do battle on the ice in Montreal. Had the Carolina team been playing that evening, three of the men in the family would have been absent. Janey's husband, Thad, because he was the coach. Dylan, because he was a game announcer, and Joe, because he was one of the hockey players. But since the team had the day off, and the next game was at home, they were all there. As was Janey's twelve-year-old son Christopher—who was petting Lily and Fletcher's recently adopted yellow Labrador retriever, Spartacus. Mac and the newest members of the Hart clan—Joe's wife, Emma, Dylan's wife, Hannah, and Fletcher's wife, Lily—were gathered around, too.

A happier bunch couldn't have been found, Ashley noted, accepting hugs and warm hellos from one and all. And it was then the trouble she'd been anticipating began.

"Something wrong?" Janey asked two hours later as the two of them carried the containers holding leftovers out to the spare refrigerator in Helen's garage.

Besides the fact that everyone there seemed to be keeping a careful eye on everything she and Cal did and said? Ashley wondered.

Ashley figured if anyone understood the five Hart brothers it was their only sister, Janey. "What do you know about the advice the guys have been giving Cal about me?" Ashley asked, opening the fridge. She was willing to bet whatever had prompted the phone message Cal had received in Hawaii was still going on among the men. Sly looks, approving nods, the occasional slap on the shoulder, one brother to another, had been going on all night.

Abruptly, Janey looked like a kid who'd been caught with knowledge she had no business having.

Ashley held up a palm. "I heard it all, Janey. I just want to know what prompted the onslaught of friendly guidance in the first place." Cal was the most private of the Hart brothers. Definitely the least likely to seek advice regarding his marriage.

Janey slid her containers into the spare fridge, then knelt to make room for Ashley's. "They were just worried about you two." Janey kept her head down. "We all were." Even more quietly she said, "Cal's been so lonely while you were away."

This was news. Ashley's heartbeat picked up and anxiety ran through her anew. "Was he complaining to the rest of you?" If so, she wasn't sure how that made her feel! Not good, certainly.

"No, of course not." Finished, Janey straightened. "Cal never complains. You know that." Janey paused to look at Ashley seriously. "But even though he shrugged it off, we all knew he was pretty miserable whenever he wasn't busy working."

Then why hadn't Cal said something? Ashley wondered, hurt and dismayed, instead of acting as if the weeks and months apart were just something to be endured.

"Hey, you're not still upset about the clothes-not-fitting thing, are you?" Cal asked as they turned into the driveway of the farmhouse. He stopped in front of the two-car garage and hit the automatic door button.

"That's the least of my worries," Ashley muttered as she watched the door lift.

Cal steered his SUV into the garage. He frowned as he cut the motor and depressed the remote control. "Did someone say something to you tonight?"

Ashley got out of the Jeep, aware the jet lag she had felt earlier had vanished in the face of her anger and disappointment. She watched his face as she waited for him to join her at the door to the softly lit interior of the house, wishing he weren't so darned handsome and appealing. It would make it so much easier to stay angry with him. "Did you expect them to?"

Cal unlocked the door and held it open for her, turning sideways to let her pass. Their bodies brushed lightly, igniting her senses even more. "I know my family can be a bit overwhelming, all at once."

Ashley put her purse on the kitchen counter and pivoted to face him. She had to tilt her head back to see into his penetrating gray eyes. "Tell me something, Cal. Whose idea was it for you to come to Hawaii early and surprise me?"

The guilt she had hoped desperately not to see flashed across his face. His fingers tightened on the keys in his hand. "You heard about the Hart posse coming to see me," he surmised grimly.

She had now. Wondering just how deep his family's interference in their marriage went, Ashley folded her arms in front of her. "I'd like to hear it from you," she retorted, just as quietly.

Cal shrugged as if the incident were so insignificant it had barely registered on his radar screen. "It was suggested to me that I might want to do a better job of taking charge of our…situation…and bring you home."

Her spirits deflated even more. "So that's the only reason," Ashley presumed, the knowledge blindsiding her.

Cal clamped his hands on her shoulders, preventing her from running away. "No," he corrected with exaggerated patience. "I flew to Hawaii because you're my wife, and I'm your husband. And I thought you could use some help packing up your belongings, shutting off utilities and turning over your apartment."

*How...romantic.* Ashley struggled to contain her zigzagging emotions, even as she wondered when the last time Cal had said he loved her had been. Six months ago? A year? Longer? With effort, she kept the too-casual smile on her face. "Be honest with me, Cal. Would you have come and gotten me if your family hadn't intervened?" she demanded.

Cal released her as suddenly as if she had burned him. He leaned against the opposite counter and watched her in that strong, silent, aloof way of his. "Originally, I was planning to let you come home on your own timetable," he said eventually.

"And then you changed your mind," Ashley ascertained, aware neither of them had yet taken off their winter coats, and yet she still felt chilled to the bone in the cozy warmth of the farmhouse.

Cal gestured off-handedly, not about to apologize for what he had or had not said or done. "Look, I didn't ask for their interference, but what they were intimating made sense."

Feeling the sting of tears behind her eyes, Ashley turned away from him. She didn't know what it was about her lately—maybe it was the wealth of life-determining decisions ahead of her, or her continuing emotional distance from Cal—but she was so much moodier than usual!

"Where are you going?" Cal demanded in a low, gruff voice when she headed for the hall that ran the length of the house.

Ashley shrugged as she removed her black wool coat. "Does it matter?"

"Hell yes, it matters." In three long steps, Cal had overtaken her. He shackled her wrist, stopping her flight. She whirled toward him and they stared at each other in silence. "You don't believe I had our best interests at heart, do you?" he said quietly.

Achingly aware of the warmth of his fingers lightly encircling her wrist, Ashley drew a deep breath. "I think your family wants us to be together—here in Holly

Springs—and you want to please your family." *Just like I want to please mine.* She swallowed around the rising lump in her throat. "So it's only natural—"

Cal's lips thinned. He shook his head at her disparagingly and tightened his grasp on her wrist. Swearing passionately beneath his breath, he steered her through the house to the door leading to the backyard. "Enough of this baloney!"

Ashley trembled as he struggled with the dead bolt on the door and yanked it open. "What are you doing?"

"Exactly what it looks like!" Cal said as he switched on the backyard lights. He took her out onto the deck, down the steps and onto the lawn. "I'm taking *you* to the barn!"

# Chapter 4

"I don't know what has gotten into you," Ashley fumed as Cal charged through the floodlit darkness of the backyard to the barn a hundred yards away.

He gave her a wickedly teasing look. "A little John Wayne perhaps? And for the record," he wrapped an arm about her waist, tucking her into his side, "it's long overdue."

"It is not!" she told him with a determined toss of her head. She dug in her heels, flung off his arm and turned to face him. "And you can *not* do this!"

He lowered his face until they were nose to nose. "Want to bet?"

Ashley's heart pounded in her chest. She stabbed a finger at his chest, trying not to notice what a beautifully sculpted body he had. From his broad shoulders and well-muscled chest to his narrow waist and long legs, there wasn't an inch of him that wasn't fit and toned to the max. "I mean it, Cal."

He inclined his head at her, just as stubbornly. "So do I," he told her in a voice that brooked no dissent. "I don't care if you like it or not, Mrs. Hart." He drew in a slow breath and stayed just exactly where he was. "You're coming with me and you're coming right now."

The next thing she knew, he was swinging her up into his arms and striding across the lawn.

"The last time you did this was on our wedding night!" Ashley said breathlessly.

He grinned with customary self-assurance. "You planning to give me one of those?"

Ashley tried not to notice how the skirt of her dress was riding up her thighs, or how his powerful arm felt clamped beneath her hips. "Not tonight I'm not!" She wiggled in an attempt to get free. "Not after this!"

Oblivious to her machinations, he regarded her with a mysterious glint in his eye. "We'll just see how romantic you're feeling in a minute," he murmured huskily. He set her down in front of the double barn doors and opened the latch.

Once used to store farm equipment and fruit from the orchards, the big, red-sided building had been empty the only other time Ashley had been to the farm. She discovered it wasn't empty now as Cal hit the switch that brought on the overhead lights hanging from the rafters. A lawn tractor, hand mower and edger occupied one corner. But it was what was in the center of the cement-floored space that left her speechless.

"Oh, my..." Ashley stared at the big red heart on the windshield of a red '64 Mustang convertible in letter-perfect shape, from the pristine retractable white top and fancy silver wheel covers, to the candy-apple-red vinyl interior. It looked like the borrowed vehicle they'd had their very first date in.

Still watching her carefully, he took her gently by the hand, and led her toward the car. "Happy early Valentine's Day," he said when they neared. Wrapping both hands around her waist, he brought her close enough to kiss her temple affectionately. "This is for you."

She stared at him in amazement.

"You bought this for me?"

"For us. Yes."

"But we've never done anything this extravagant for each other for Valentine's Day!" Ashley protested. Usually, they exchanged cards, and went out to dinner, and that was about it.

"I know."

"Then why now?" She gazed at him. Was this part of his family's influence, too? Or all Cal's idea?

"Because we used to be closer," Cal told her in a low, sincere voice. Abruptly, all the love he had ever felt for her was in his eyes. "And I know we could be that connected to each other again if we just let ourselves go back to the beginning and start over. And where better to do that than in the car where our courtship began, eleven-and-a-half years ago?"

Ashley had to admit, the Mustang had already generated a lot of good memories in just a few scant minutes.

He regarded her with distinctly male satisfaction. "Want to test drive your new Mustang?"

Her hopes rising about them being able to fix the problems in their marriage after all, she took the keys he handed her. "Absolutely—if you'll come with me."

He winked at her cheerfully, suddenly looking like the carefree, charming med student she had fallen in love with years ago. "Wouldn't miss it for the world."

Cal opened the door for her, and Ashley slid behind the steering wheel. Circling around to the other side,

Cal dropped into the passenger seat. Electricity sizzled between them as Ashley recalled how they used to do a little "parking" in this car, too.

"As much as I'd like you to try it with the top down..." Cal said.

Ashley shivered, just thinking about the wintry air blowing over them. "Yeah. I think it's too cold for that tonight, too."

"But when warmer weather comes," Cal predicted, fastening his old-fashioned lap belt, "we'll have a lot of fun with it."

It certainly sounded as though he was in this for the long haul, Ashley thought, as she fastened her belt, too. She shook her head, marveling at how accurately Cal had targeted her feelings.

To her delight, the motor started easily and ran with a gentle purr. "I can't get over how much this looks like the Mustang we started dating in," Ashley commented as she took it out on the country road and drove it through the moonlit countryside.

Cal draped an arm across the back of the seat. "It doesn't just look like it, Ashley." He leaned over and kissed her shoulder. "This is *the Car.*"

A quick glance his way showed her he wasn't kidding. Ashley turned onto a road that would take them back in the direction of the farm. Enjoying the quick responsiveness of the motor, and the tight command of the wheel, Ashley asked, "How did you manage that?"

"I talked to Marty—the friend we used to borrow it from—and got the serial number and worked backwards from there," Cal told her as she slowed the car and turned into the long, narrow driveway.

"Unfortunately, the guy who owned it last summer didn't want to sell it to anyone because it's such a collector's item now," Cal continued affably. "So Hannah had to help me convince him to part with it. And then she spent the fall putting on a new coat of paint and making sure it ran like a dream."

Ashley guided the car back into the barn and cut the motor. "You were working on this all the way back then?" she asked in amazement. He'd never said a thing!

Shrugging, he released the catch on his safety belt. "I wanted you to have a spectacular coming-home present."

*Spectacular* was the word for it, all right. Ashley couldn't think of a better, more meaningful gift he could have given her. Except the gift he had unknowingly given her and she'd lost, before. The gift he still knew nothing about.

Ashley paused, aware yet again how much she loved Cal. More than anything, she wanted to be close to him again.

Maybe it was time she stopped guarding her heart. Instead, she could concentrate on tearing down the walls between them and building a better foundation for their marriage. Heaven knew this was a remarkable start. Just knowing he, too, wanted things to be better between them made all the difference. For the first time in months, she was optimistic about their future together. Optimistic that it wouldn't be just great sex and their love of medicine holding them together...

She wreathed her arms about his neck and leaned over to kiss him. "This is without a doubt the sweetest thing you've ever done for me."

His lips moved warmly on hers. To her relief...and disappointment, he didn't try to take the caress further. "I'm glad you like it," he whispered, holding her close as she snuggled against him.

"I more than like it, Cal. I love it." Ashley splayed her

hands across the solidness of his chest. As she looked at him, her heart felt lighter than it had in ages. "But you know what this means, don't you?"

Cal shook his head, still holding her eyes with all the tenderness she had ever wanted to see.

"I still owe you a Valentine's Day present. And it's going to have to be a whopper to live up to the gift you've given me."

"Ah, Ashley, don't you understand?" Cal chided her gently, pulling her close yet again for another long, soulful kiss that ended much too soon. He threaded a hand through her hair. "Just coming home with me and spending the month with me in Carolina is present enough."

The next morning, Cal woke at his usual time of 6:00 a.m. Congratulating himself for going against his baser instincts to seduce Ashley back into his bed the night before, he rose and headed downstairs to put on the coffee. And then waited. And waited. And waited.

When Ashley still hadn't stirred five and a half hours later, he went up to check on her. She was curled up on her side, sleeping soundly, one hand tucked beneath her pillow. Knowing she'd never get on Eastern Standard Time unless she made an effort to adapt to the five-hour time difference, he opened the drapes and let the January sunshine pour across the guest bed. "Rise and shine!"

Ashley moaned and burrowed deeper in the covers. "What time is it?" she asked without opening her eyes.

"Almost noon," Cal leaned against the railing at the end of the bed. She appeared to be going back to sleep. He nudged her foot. "Want to go for a run with me?"

Ashley opened one eye. "Mmm." She made a soft, sexy sound low in her throat. "Maybe later?"

Cal was about to coax her further when he heard a

car in the drive. He crossed to the window and saw Ashley's father's Mercedes coming up the lane. This was... unexpected. "Ashley, I think your dad's here," Cal said.

Ashley scoffed and put one of the pillows over her head. "Get real," she mumbled.

Cal plucked the pillow away from her ear. "I mean it, Ash. I'm not kidding. Your dad just drove up to the house."

Ashley started, and ran a hand through her "bed-head" hair. As usual, she looked more apprehensive than pleased when confronted with a meeting with her parents. "I'll keep him company while you get dressed," Cal promised, aware he wasn't much more comfortable with his father-in-law than Ashley seemed to be.

By the time Cal made it downstairs, Harold Porter was standing on the front porch of the farmhouse. Cal hadn't seen Harold for nearly a year but he looked the same as always. His impeccably cut silver hair was brushed away from his forehead in a suave, sophisticated style that didn't move even in the stiffest breeze. His skin bore the perennial suntan of a man who played golf, sailed and skied. Not that those activities were pleasure-oriented. Cal knew that everything Harold Porter did revolved around his work. And sometimes the only place a business meeting could be worked in was on the slope, the deck of a boat or a superbly manicured green. Hal Porter did whatever was necessary to get the job done, which was how he had risen through sales and marketing departments to become CEO of a prominent pharmaceutical company.

"Sir." Cal shook his father-in-law's hand and escorted him inside. Despite the fact it was a Saturday morning, Harold Porter was decked out in an expensive suit and tie.

"I can't stay." Harold shrugged out of his cashmere

overcoat and handed it to Cal. "I've got a flight to Chicago later this afternoon, but I wanted to drop in and see you and Ashley before I headed to the airport."

Cal wasn't surprised. Harold traveled at least five or six days every week. Many weekends, he didn't make it back to North Carolina at all.

Cal hung up Harold's coat. "Ashley will be down in a minute. She's just waking up."

Harold frowned and glanced at his Rolex in obvious disapproval.

"She's still on Hawaii time," Cal explained, wishing Ashley's father wasn't so hard on her. "Can I get you some coffee or juice?"

Harold waved off the offer and regarded Cal soberly. "Actually, I'd like a word with you privately, if I may."

Aware this couldn't possibly be good, Cal led the way past the unfurnished rooms at the front of the house, to the family room at the rear. After Harold sat on the leather sofa, Cal took an easy chair and waited. The curt admonition wasn't long in coming. "I thought I had explained this to you when you asked her mother and me for her hand in marriage," Harold began sternly.

Cal was beginning to think of that conversation as the Devil's Bargain. One he never should have made in order to get their blessing for the union.

"Ashley is very much like her mother and me," Harold continued matter-of-factly. "She will never be happy unless she is free to be all she can be professionally. I know, because for the first six months after Ashley was born Margaret tried to give up her career goals and aspirations and be a full-time mother because she thought that would please me. She was never more miserable, nor was I."

Which meant Ashley couldn't have been happy, either. Cal knew that to have a happy baby—and a happy family—you had to have happy parents.

"I would hate to see you and Ashley walk down that same path, even for a short while."

Resenting the implication that he had behaved less than honorably in any instance, Cal held up a silencing palm. "Sir, with all due respect," he said angrily, "I resent what you are implying here. I assure you I have never done anything to hold Ashley back professionally." Even when that meant biting his tongue when it came to her leaving him for a good two-and-a-half years. "In fact, I've done everything possible to help and encourage Ashley to follow her dreams." *At considerable cost to our marriage.* Cal was sure the time apart had contributed to the emotional distance between them.

Harold lifted a skeptical brow. "Then I don't understand what she's doing here for a month, lazing around and sleeping 'til noon, when she doesn't have a job yet."

Thinking of the emotionally and physically exhausted woman upstairs, Cal's patience waned. "She's earned some time off."

Harold frowned and cast a glance at the doorway, as if he didn't want them to be overheard. "She can take that once she's secured a position worthy of her education and training."

"Thanks for the advice, Dad." Ashley stood in the doorway. The expression on her face indicated she had caught the last of what Harold had said, but no more. And that was good, Cal thought, because he never wanted Ashley to know about the stipulations her parents had put on their blessing for Cal and Ashley's marriage. It was enough that he knew that their concern had not been that he love her with all his heart and soul, but rather that he wouldn't interfere with the stellar career achievements they expected of their only daughter.

Still moving tiredly, Ashley came farther into the room.

She was wearing a pink plaid flannel robe over her nightshirt, and slouchy pink sweat socks covered her feet. Her face was still bare of makeup, but she had brushed her hair and fastened it in a sleek chignon at the nape of her neck. She looked vulnerable and repressed—not at all like the carefree young bride who had been driving a Mustang convertible around country roads at midnight. Cal's heart went out to her once again.

Ashley had no trouble being her own woman when she was away from her parents. But when she was in their presence, she always seemed to shrink a little and fade into some stressed-out realm where Cal could not always reach her.

"Ashley." Harold stood, embracing her in a warm, paternal hug.

Cal noted with some relief that Harold looked genuinely glad to see his daughter. Ashley looked happy to see her father, too. But she was also wary. Nervous. On edge. Which was how she always acted around both her parents, no matter what the situation.

"I take it you haven't accepted the job in Maui," Harold said.

"No," Ashley said simply. Her glance cut over to Cal briefly before she turned her gaze back to her father. "I haven't."

"Well, it's probably a good idea to scout around first," Harold said, his tone gentling amiably as they all took a seat once again. "So where else are you looking?" Harold pressed.

Ashley folded her hands primly in her lap and sat with

her back perfectly straight. "I haven't gotten that far yet, Dad. It was enough to finish my fellowship."

Her father frowned, making absolutely no effort to hide his disapproval about that. "I gather you are planning to job-hunt from North Carolina, then."

Ashley hesitated and this time she didn't look at Cal at all. "Yes." He reached over across the sofa and squeezed her hand reassuringly.

"Makes sense." Harold nodded thoughtfully after a moment. "Travel arrangements would certainly be easier from the mainland." Harold chatted on for several minutes. He gave Ashley a list of potential contacts who might know of suitable positions. Then he rose. "Well, I'd better get going. Don't want to miss my flight to Chicago. I've got a business dinner there this evening."

"Where's Mom?" Ashley asked, also standing.

"She's still in Boston. She won't be home for another seven to ten days. A new semester is a very busy time for the university. As chancellor, she can't afford to be away."

"Right," Ashley said.

If Ashley was disappointed her father had so little time to spend with her, she was not showing it. "Well, travel safely, Dad." Ashley rose on tiptoe and kissed his cheek. Harold hugged her again, even more warmly this time, shook Cal's hand and was off.

Ashley and Cal stood watching until Harold had driven away.

As soon as he was gone, Ashley let out a long breath. Her slender body seemed to deflate. "I'm sorry about that," she said, shaking her head. "He should have called first, let us know he was coming."

"He's family, Ashley," Cal corrected his wife gently. "Your father doesn't have to call for permission first. He's welcome here anytime. In fact, I wish he would come here more," Cal said sincerely. Perhaps if Ashley and her parents spent more time together their relationship wouldn't be so strained. He knew they loved each other. They just hadn't quite figured out how to show it. A lot more interaction, on a more casual basis, might help that.

Ashley looked full of resentment. "If my father'd been coming here on business, he would have called ahead out of courtesy."

"Maybe he thought you'd duck him if he gave you too much notice," Cal teased gently and waited for her reaction. As he expected, it wasn't long in coming.

Ashley turned to Cal, moisture brimming in her china-blue eyes. "I love him."

"I know." Cal wrapped an arm around her shoulders and brought her in close to his side.

"I love both my parents," she insisted thickly.

"I know that, too." He comforted her with a kiss on the top of her head.

Ashley leaned into his embrace, as if soaking in the comfort he was trying to give, then moved away. She threw up her hands in frustration as she paced back and forth. "They just drive me crazy."

Cal knew that, too. "You could just tell your father you don't want to talk about the job search."

"That wouldn't stop him from putting his two cents in," she complained.

*Probably not,* Cal thought and released a long, frustrated breath.

"Anyway," Ashley sighed. She started to run her hands through her hair, the way she always did when she was restless, then stopped when she encountered the sleekly arranged chignon and pins. Looking as if she no longer wanted to discuss this, she eyed him up and down, taking in his ancient sweats and running shoes. "Did you say something about going for a run with me?"

He had, but that was before she was standing in front of him, looking so…wrung out and pale. He didn't want to say so, but physically she didn't look up for a long walk never mind a run in forty-degree weather. "Yeah, but—" Cal paused as the beeper at his waist began to buzz. He looked at the numbers running across the front, grimaced. He glanced at Ashley in apology, aware this was something he'd forgotten to mention. "I'm on call this weekend."

He turned the beeper off and headed for the phone.

"That the hospital or a patient?" Ashley asked.

"Hospital." Which meant it wasn't likely a problem that could be solved over the phone. He picked up the phone and dialed. Ashley was still waiting when he had finished talking. "I've got to go. A sixteen-year-old kid got hurt on an ATV. From the sound of it, I'm going to be a while."

He was already grabbing his keys and wallet. "I'll call you later," he said.

Ashley flashed him a wan smile.

Cal headed for the door then came back, hooked an arm about her waist and pulled her close. Aggravation boiling up inside him, he kissed her soundly. He wished the demands of their profession weren't separating them again so soon. "Damn, I hate leaving you today," he said.

This time her smile was real. And sexy as all get out. "We've got time," she murmured reassuringly. Both hands on his chest, she shoved him in the direction he had to move. "Now, go."

Looking back, Ashley didn't know how she managed it. But she waited until Cal had driven off before she gave in to the nearly overwhelming nausea that had plagued her from the moment she had woken up. She rushed to the bathroom, where she promptly threw up.

Telling herself it was just nerves—and the pressure her parents were exerting on her to find a job "worthy" of her education and training—Ashley forced herself to shower and dress. And then she threw up again.

Wondering if she were coming down with something, she took her temperature, found it normal. Then she said to hell with it, and went back to bed.

By the time an hour had passed, and she had napped a little more, she felt remarkably better. At least as far as the steadiness of her stomach was concerned.

As far as the rest of her went…well, the more she thought about it, the more questions she had. And there was only one way to get the answers she needed. So she got up, grabbed the keys to the Mustang, and went to see an old and dear friend.

## Chapter 5

"Thanks for meeting me at the office on a Saturday afternoon," Ashley told Carlotta Ramirez, a petite beauty with dark hair and eyes and olive skin. Carlotta had been Ashley's "big sister" when she'd entered medical school—the fourth-year student assigned to help Ashley adjust. Now an obstetrician-gynecologist with a thriving private practice in Holly Springs, Carlotta was also married to another doctor, and the mother of three children: one born during her undergraduate years, the next while she was in medical school and the third during Carlotta's Ob/Gyn residency.

"No problem." Carlotta unlocked the door to her office suite, flipped on the overhead lights to dispel the wintry gloom and led the way inside. "I heard you and Cal were back this morning and I've been dying to see you. So how was Hawaii?" Carlotta continued as she shut the door behind them. "Beautiful!?"

Ashley thought about the white-sand beaches, blue skies and even bluer ocean, the lush vegetation and a temperature that never varied much below seventy degrees or above eighty. "Very."

"I envy you the chance to do your fellowship there." Carlotta shook her head in awe. "Talk about paradise."

It had been, Ashley thought. But it would have been so much better if Cal had been there with her. Maybe then she wouldn't have felt such soul-deep loneliness the whole time she was there.

"So how long have you been feeling lousy?" Carlotta asked as they walked through the deserted inner office.

Ashley paused as Carlotta stopped at the linen closet and got out a soft pink cotton gown and a folded linen sheet, and handed both to Ashley.

"I just started throwing up this morning," Ashley said, telling herself that what she was worried about couldn't possibly be true.

"But—?" Carlotta prodded, experienced enough to know there was more.

Ashley confided reluctantly, "I've been tired and overemotional and I suddenly can't fit into my pants."

"Any chance you might be pregnant?" Carlotta asked casually.

Yes, as a matter of fact, there was a slight chance—even though Ashley kept telling herself it couldn't possibly be true. "Cal and I were together in mid-November for a weekend in San Francisco," Ashley admitted with a rueful smile.

Carlotta grinned. "Sounds romantic," she teased.

Romance involved feelings, which Cal and Ashley had both been careful to keep tamped down. "It was certainly passionate, anyway," Ashley joked right back, aware her palms had begun to sweat as she faced finding out the absolute truth of her situation. A truth she wasn't sure she was ready to deal with.

Carlotta paused at another cabinet, and withdrew what she needed to do a screening test for iron-deficiency. "Did you two use protection?"

Ashley blushed as Carlotta tore open an antiseptic packet. An Ob/Gyn, too, she knew these were the kind of questions she should be asking others, not answering herself. "I've been taking oral contraceptives."

"And that's it?" Carlotta asked.

Ashley cleared her throat, embarrassed to find herself in this position. "Right. Which was foolish, I know, since nothing is absolutely foolproof in and of itself." How many times had Ashley counseled her own patients in the women's clinic to use two methods of contraception simultaneously, and not just one, if they wanted to make absolutely sure they did not conceive?

Looking back, she couldn't believe she hadn't followed her own oft-given advice. But she had missed Cal so desperately, and making hot, wild love with him had always been the one sure way the two of them could connect, even when every other method of communication failed abysmally. Not wanting anything between them, she'd told him to forget about condoms and had been a little reckless.

"Well, there's one way to find out." Carlotta swabbed the end of Ashley's third finger with the antiseptic wipe, then pricked her finger. "I can do an in-office urine pregnancy test for you right now and, if that's positive, of course, we're going to want to take some more blood to send to the lab for a complete prenatal workup and screening."

"Sounds good." Ashley watched as a dot of blood appeared on her finger and waited for Carlotta to fill a small plastic cylinder with a sample of her blood for the iron-deficiency screen.

Finished, Carlotta swabbed Ashley's finger again, then gave her a small plastic cup.

By the time Ashley emerged from the bathroom with the cup full, her blood sample was already in the machine that would render the results. Carlotta completed the in-office lab tests while Ashley undressed in one of the exam rooms.

"Well, you're not anemic," Carlotta announced, breezing in. Her cheerful grin confirmed what Ashley already knew in her heart. "And it looks as though the stork is going to be paying you two a visit next August."

Ashley drew a deep breath as her old friend started the physical exam by taking her blood pressure and listening to her heart and lungs.

"You're sure?"

Carlotta nodded. "Even without the test, I would have known. I'm surprised you and Cal didn't pick up on the signs. Your breasts appear swollen and you've got blue and pink lines beneath the skin." Carlotta moved to the end of the exam table while Ashley slid her feet into the stirrups and slid down.

Carlotta donned gloves and continued the physical exam. "Your uterus is enlarged and soft. Yep, you're definitely pregnant, all right."

Finished, Carlotta gave Ashley a hand and helped her sit up.

Ashley sat there, completely stunned. "Why don't you get dressed and then we'll talk in my office?" Carlotta said gently.

A few minutes later, wearing the same comfortable pale-blue sweats she had worn on the plane back from Hawaii, Ashley entered Carlotta's office. "Well," she said, as she sank into a seat. "This certainly explains why I've gained over five pounds in two months and suddenly none of my pants with waistbands fit."

"I take it pregnancy wasn't in the plans you and Cal have been making?" Carlotta said delicately.

Ashley shook her head. "We haven't even discussed children since the first couple of months we were married." Then they had both thought about having a child, except it hadn't worked out, and shortly after that, the troubles in their marriage had begun.

Carlotta handed Ashley a month's supply of prenatal vitamin samples. "You think he doesn't want children?"

Ashley hesitated. She was bewildered to discover she no longer knew the answer to that. "It's just…"

"I understand. It's a life-altering event, no matter how it occurs. But for the record, I think Cal would be very happy." Carlotta paused. "I mean, you are planning to tell him, aren't you?"

Happiness bubbled up inside Ashley, followed quickly by fear, and a disturbing feeling of déjà vu. "Yes, of course I'm going to tell Cal, as soon as I hit the three-month mark and pass the danger of miscarriage."

Carlotta blinked. "You're sure you want to wait that long?"

Ashley knew from her own patients that most women couldn't wait to tell their husbands.

"Yes." For very good reason.

Carlotta did some quick calculations, and grinned as she jumped to the logical conclusion. "Valentine's Day, huh?" Carlotta teased.

Ashley smiled. Now—heaven willing—she knew exactly what she was going to give her husband for Valentine's Day. And it beat the heck out of any car, even a red '64 Mustang convertible. "Promise me." Ashley looked

Carlotta in the eye and did her best to quell her nervousness. "Not a word to anyone, even your husband, until I give the okay."

Carlotta crossed her heart. "You have my word. Now, is there anything else you want to discuss?"

Ashley sobered. "As a matter of fact," she related unhappily as she prepared to fill her friend in on the most private parts of her medical history, "there is."

"You haven't heard a word I've said, have you?" Cal said in frustration several hours later.

Ashley flushed guiltily and looked across the kitchen table at him. They'd been having dinner for a good twenty minutes now, and although he had been talking nonstop about the case he'd seen earlier and the difficulties the surgery presented, she had heard only a smidgen of it. Which had been most unlike her. Usually, she loved hearing about Cal's cases, and vice versa. Medicine was the one thing they could always talk about.

"What's going on with you?" Cal asked, narrowing his eyes at her.

*I'm having a baby—our baby—and my mind and emotions are in awhirl. Ashley swallowed, embarrassed. "What do you mean?"*

"One minute you're smiling like you just won the lottery," Cal observed.

*That's because I feel happier than I've ever felt in my life.*

"And the next you're frowning like you have the weight of the world on your shoulders."

*That's because I'm scared to death that what happened before is going to happen again. And none of this is going to work out the way I want and hope.*

"What did you do today, anyway?" Cal continued as he stood and began to clear the table.

Noting how the gray in the cashmere sweater he was wearing brought out the pewter shade of his eyes, Ashley stood and began to clean up, too. She wished she could think about something besides kissing him whenever they were this close. Especially today…

"I went to see Carlotta," Ashley finally answered.

Cal smiled and held her eyes for a long, breath-stealing moment. "I'm glad you two were able to get caught up."

"Me, too," Ashley said. *Even if I can't tell you everything about that meeting just yet.*

Cal slid the dishes into the dishwasher with the ease of a man who'd done dishes many times growing up. "Then what did you do?"

Ashley edged away from the enticing sea-and-sun fragrance of his cologne. "I drove to the mall to find some clothes that fit and a few how-to books on decorating." *And while I was at it, I stopped and looked at baby things. Lots and lots of baby things.*

Cal wiped his hands on a dish towel, then set it aside. He stood facing her, his back to the counter, hands braced on either side of him. "Is that what's worrying you?" he asked as Ashley backed away from him self-consciously, feeling guilty as all get out once again.

*What's worrying me is the fear that I will let you and our baby down—again—and you'll feel the kind of hurt no parent should ever have to feel.*

"You worried about needing a bigger size in clothing?" Cal continued sympathetically, oblivious to the real reason behind Ashley's distress. He caught her hand and reeled her in to his side. "Because I have to tell you," he confided appreciatively as he wrapped an arm around her waist, "extra five pounds or no, I've never seen you looking more beautiful."

As Ashley looked into his eyes, she had never felt

more beautiful than she did at that very moment. Or more secure in his love. And maybe it was selfish of her, but she wanted it to stay that way. She wanted to get through this next month, and one of the riskiest periods of her pregnancy, and then on Valentine's Day tell him he was going to be a daddy. And by the time she told him the happy news, she wanted all the problems in their relationship worked out.

"You were kind of pale when I left this morning, but tonight your face is just glowing," Cal continued.

*That's because I am about to give you the most wonderful gift a woman can give the man she loves.* Ashley ducked her head and let it rest against the warm solidness of his broad shoulder. "Well, thank you," she said, blushing.

He cupped a hand beneath her chin and lifted her face up to his. "So maybe you should stay this weight," he told her sincerely.

Ashley's lips curved as she imagined how happy Cal was going to be if everything went as she hoped. "I don't think that's going to be possible," she said dryly.

"And feel free to buy yourself a whole new wardrobe," Cal suggested, as compassionate and generous to her as ever.

She inclined her head ruefully and deliberately held his gaze. "If I didn't know better, I'd think you were trying to spoil me," she teased.

He wrapped both arms about her waist and pulled her in until all of her was pressed against all of him. "You deserve spoiling," he muttered huskily

Ashley had known Cal wanted to make a move on her—she had seen it in his eyes all evening. She just hadn't thought, given the agreement they had made to abstain from making love until their marriage was on solid footing, that he would. But now that he was kissing her again, his lips tenderly coaxing and recklessly taking, she realized something else. She needed this connection with him, needed the fierce sensuality of his mouth moving over hers, and, above all else, she needed to be loved by him.

She wreathed her arms around his neck, kissed him back every bit as passionately as he was kissing her and let all the joy she felt over their baby growing inside her wash over her. It didn't matter that she wasn't ready to tell him yet. The baby forged a powerful connection between them that would last their entire lives and she wanted that just as fiercely as she wanted to have his child.

Cal had never been able to read Ashley's heart as well as he wanted to, but he had always known intuitively when she needed him to take her in his arms. And, for whatever reason, she required his physical closeness tonight. He'd seen it in the dreamy, distracted way she had looked at him all through dinner, and he'd felt it in her kiss and in the way her body cuddled against his. Not that he minded holding her. Kissing her. Touching her. Even if their hot embrace was picking up his heart rate and sending blood rushing to his lower half. But when she moaned, soft and low, in the back of her throat, and he felt her nipples budding tightly as they brushed against his chest, he knew he had to stop—now—or break the promise he had made to her. So, reluctantly, he let their steamy kiss come to a halt and drew away from her.

He wasn't all that surprised to see disappointment mingled with pleasure and relief on her face as she trembled and looked up at him. She had to know, good intentions or not, that with them both living under the same roof again it was only a matter of time before their passion ignited.

"So," he said in a low, gravelly voice, determined to be more noble than selfish, at least for this evening, "you want to show me your new clothes?" Maybe that would distract him from the sensual shape of her damp lower lip.

Ashley stepped back a pace. Her hand shook as she shoved her hand through the mussed strands of her dark hair. "I just bought two pairs of slacks." Oddly enough, she looked as if she were keeping something from him. What, he couldn't imagine.

"One gray and one black," Ashley continued, appearing a little embarrassed.

Disappointment swept through him. He had been hoping for a sexy fashion show. The kind she used to give him when they were dating. He quirked a brow, wondering why she had been so frugal when she didn't have to be. She loved clothes! Loved shopping for them, too. "That's all?"

A flash of guilt appeared in her eyes and just as quickly disappeared. "I know my larger waist is only temporary," she stated reluctantly, embarrassed. "I plan to get back into my old clothes. It's just going to take time." She turned her eyes from his once again. "And some dedicated working-out on my part. Which I plan to do."

Cal knew Ashley felt better and had more stamina when she was physically fit—they both did. Maybe he could help her here. Help them both. He walked to the refrigerator and took out a bottle of chilled spring water for each of them. "As long as we're talking about how to decorate the rest of the house, what do you think about putting in a home gym?" he asked her casually.

Ashley appeared surprised and intrigued. "Where?"

"Upstairs." Cal took her by the hand and led her up the back staircase to the second floor. He enjoyed the soft, delicate feel of her fingers clasped in his. "I was thinking maybe we could use the bedroom right next to ours," he told her, unwilling to admit how many lonely nights he had spent dreaming about the things they could do with this place, if only she would join him.

He steered Ashley to the room he was talking about and waited hopefully for her reaction.

Ashley knew Cal wanted her to support his idea wholeheartedly, but she couldn't quite do that. She knew this room next to the master bedroom suite should definitely be the nursery. Beginning to see just how hard it was going to be to keep this news from Cal until another four weeks had passed and she was sure everything was going to be all right, Ashley said instead, "What about the other empty bedroom?"

Cal shrugged. She could see he was a little hurt by her immediate dismissal of his idea. "It's smaller, and it doesn't have as many windows. So the light wouldn't be as good as it is in here."

"Maybe we don't want as much as light." Ashley linked arms with Cal and guided him down the hall to show him the other room.

Cal studied her. "You really think this room would be better?"

"Well. What are you planning to put in here?" Ashley looked at the ten-foot-by-twelve-foot room.

"An exercise bike. Treadmill. Maybe a stair machine or an elliptical trainer. What would you like?"

Ashley thought about the exercises she recommended for her pregnant patients. "A place for a yoga mat. Maybe a TV with a DVD player built into it mounted on the wall. So I can watch it while I work out."

"Sounds good to me," Cal said as he turned to survey the room one more time. "So when do you want to get on this?"

Ashley smiled, glad they had something to occupy themselves with the rest of the weekend. "Right away."

"I have to go back to the hospital," Cal said as soon as he got off the phone Sunday evening.

"Another emergency surgery?" Ashley asked.

Cal nodded as he clipped his beeper back on his belt.

He looked disappointed their evening together was going to be cut short. Ashley knew exactly how he felt. The weekend had gone too fast. But this was the life of a practicing physician. They both knew that, although they were usually a lot better at taking it in stride.

Determined to be the kind of supportive spouse he needed, Ashley touched his arm and smiled at him gratefully. "We had a great day." They'd slept late, gone to 11:00 a.m. services and had lunch with Cal's family, then spent the afternoon finding everything they needed for their home gym. Ashley still had to purchase the things she would need for her pregnancy workouts, but she'd have to do that when Cal wasn't with her.

"I just wish I had Monday off so I could spend it with you," he murmured.

Instead, he was scheduled to work from seven in the morning until dinner time. Which left Ashley wondering what she was going to do. She knew she should be looking for a job, but right now all she wanted to do was stay here and "play house" with Cal. And how weird was that? She couldn't be nesting, could she?

"Promise me you'll miss me desperately," Cal said, pulling Ashley closer for a long, slow kiss.

Ashley sighed and sank into his luxuriant embrace. "I

already do," she murmured back playfully. And to prove it, she kissed him again, even more thoroughly.

Cal smiled and ruffled her hair. "Don't wait up," was the last thing he said as he went out the door.

Figuring the best thing she could do for her pregnancy was get as much sleep as possible in this first trimester, Ashley took one of the prenatal vitamins she had spirited away in her purse, drank a glass of milk, and went on up to bed. She had no trouble falling asleep and slept for six hours straight, not waking until she heard Cal's car in the drive shortly after 3:00 a.m. He came up the back stairs and headed straight for the master bedroom.

Ashley heard him go into the master bathroom, come out again and fall into bed.

From the absence of sound, Ashley figured he'd gone straight to sleep. She was not as lucky. No matter how hard she tried, she couldn't fall back into dreamland. Eventually, her stomach began to growl. She knew if she didn't put something in it soon, her nausea would likely come back.

Ashley pulled on her robe and tiptoed down to the kitchen, where she studied her options for satisfying her pregnant cravings.

## *Chapter 6*

Cal swore he was so tired when his head hit the pillow he wanted nothing more than to sleep until his alarm went off at six-thirty. And perhaps he would have if the aroma of something spicy and delicious hadn't wafted up to tease his senses. He rolled over and glanced at the clock. Four in the morning! What the heck could Ashley be doing up at this hour? And what was that he smelled cooking? Whatever it was, it certainly wasn't breakfast food.

Curiosity overrode fatigue.

He strode downstairs, wearing just his boxers, and found Ashley standing at the kitchen stove. Glossy dark-brown tendrils were escaping her ponytail to frame her delicate heart-shaped face. She was clad in a pair of loose-fitting light-blue cotton pajamas that brought out the blue of her eyes and were the perfect foil for the soft golden glow of her skin and the pinkness of her cheeks.

Her delicate bare feet peeked beneath the hem of her pajama pants, and there was something so sexy about those polished red toenails, it was all he could do to stay where he was. Oblivious to his presence, she was pouring a dark-red spice into the palm of her hand. Satisfied with the amount, she added it to the pot of browning beef and onions. As it hit the sizzling meat and the aroma escaped into the room, his eyes widened in surprise. "Are you making chili?"

Ashley glanced up, for a moment looking like a kid who'd been caught with her hand in the cookie jar. Then she shrugged as if it were the most natural occurrence in the world. "Had a hankering for it," she said, in her best Southern drawl. She went back to the stove, adding salt and fresh-ground pepper to the sizzling meat.

Cal leaned against the counter, watching as she opened a can of crushed tomatoes and poured them into the pan. The kitchen smelled even more delicious. He grinned. "You're not the only one." Now he wanted some, too. He reached over and brushed a lock of hair away from her cheek. "How long until it will be ready?"

She trembled at his touch—evidence that she was no less affected by his presence than he was by hers. Flushing self-consciously, she slipped by him, to the open pantry shelves and returned with a can of ranch-style pinto beans. "Ten, fifteen minutes." She added those, too, and gave it another stir while he appreciated the intimacy of being with her like this. He realized there had been far too few moments such as this since the two of them had been married. More often, they had been hopping into bed and back out again as one of them rushed off to the hospital. Their union had been more like a hot, passionate affair than a marriage.

Which was why it was so awkward now...why, suddenly, as she picked up the tall glass of milk next to the stove and drank deeply from it, that she was having trouble meeting his eyes. "Sorry if I woke you," she said quietly, picking up the notepad on the table. Tearing off the top sheet, which had some sort of list on it, she carried it over to the far counter and slipped it into her shoulder bag. "I was trying to be quiet."

And she had been. He was the one who couldn't stay away from her. But that was hardly a surprise. After all, he'd never been able to stay away from her.

"You're up awfully early," he observed, and watched her cheeks grow ever pinker as an almost guilty look came into her eyes. Wondering what was going on with her, Cal padded closer.

"I went to bed really early." She aimed a trigger finger at his exposed belly-button, before turning her gaze slowly back to his face. "And speaking of bed, shouldn't *you* still be in yours?"

Cal would be—if she were there with him. As it was, he couldn't think of anywhere he would rather be.

Ashley had obviously turned up the thermostat when she had come downstairs, and the kitchen was warm enough not to require additional clothing. Though from the distracted way Ashley kept looking at his bare chest, Cal knew she would have preferred he go and get a robe to cover up. "I'll get back there eventually," he told her, enjoying the ardent look in her eyes as much as the free-flowing electricity between them.

She frowned and looked at him as if she wished it would be sooner rather than later. She went back to stir the pan of fragrant, bubbling chili. She opened the cupboard and leaned across the counter to reach the shelf containing the soup bowls. "Want some?"

"Absolutely." Cal couldn't help noticing the way the

neckline of her pajama top fell open as she moved. Instead of a glimpse of her breasts, however, he got a look at a stretchy white cotton undershirt that came up halfway to her collarbone.

Not that this wasn't sexy, too—especially when he thought about taking both garments off her.

Reminding himself of his promise not to make love to her again—at least not yet—Cal went to get the crackers. Coming back to the table he was surprised to see her take something out of the oven. French fries?

Ashley caught his glance and blushed again. "I had a hankering for them, too," she said.

Obviously, Cal thought. Were these hankerings the reason Ashley was suddenly having trouble with her weight? Not that he minded her new voluptuousness.

He thought she looked amazing. Especially now that she looked as if she were catching up on her rest. "Want some ketchup?" he asked as he opened the fridge.

Ashley shook her head. "Extra-sharp cheddar?"

Cal grabbed it out of the cheese drawer and the milk off the shelf, then shut the door with the back of his arm, and carried both to the table.

He nodded at the paper she had slipped into her purse. "What are you working on?"

"Your Valentine's Day present. And don't even think about peeking," she scolded as she went to retrieve it and tucked it into the pants pockets on her pajamas. "Because you're not finding out what it is until next month."

Cal grinned as they sat down at the breakfast table in front of the bay window. Her working on a present for him had to be a good sign, didn't it? "Since when do you eat fries and chili first thing in the morning?" he asked her curiously.

She shrugged as she grated some cheddar over top of

her chili and then dipped another crispy golden fry into the steaming bowl. Abruptly, he had the feeling in his gut that she was once again withholding every bit as much as she was telling him. Not that this was a surprise. It had been a pattern that had developed in the early days of their marriage.

"Since right now," Ashley said, looking as if she were in heaven as the concoction melted on her tongue. She washed it down with another swallow of icy-cold milk. Suddenly, the teasing look was back in her blue eyes, the flirtatious note in her soft voice. "I take it from the astonished look you're giving me that you've never eaten them together?"

She seemed happy again. Really happy. Maybe happier than he had ever seen her.

"No," Cal said, struggling to keep his mind on the conversation. "And I wasn't aware you had, either." Ashley was usually a lean grilled chicken or fish and healthy fruit and vegetables kind of woman. The carbs she ate were healthy and whole grain. Whereas he…well, Cal always had appreciated potatoes—any kind—and spicy calorie-laden foods like chili. Was her making chili for him now an attempt to find her way back into his heart? To better mesh their lives? Whatever the case, he appreciated her going to all the trouble.

She rested her hand on her upturned chin and regarded him inscrutably. "I thought it might be a good combination."

Cal leaned toward her as she fed him a fry dipped in chili and sharp cheddar. The combination *was* delicious—spicy and rich.

"You like it, don't you?" she teased.

*I like you.* "Actually, I do," Cal said with surprise.

Her blue eyes gleamed with pleasure and pride. "Tell me about the surgery," Ashley said.

He filled her in while they finished eating. "Sounds like it was a challenging case," Ashley noted when he had finished.

Cal nodded. It had been.

"So, shouldn't you be sleeping?" Ashley continued in a soft, wifely tone.

Yeah, Cal thought as he stacked their dishes and cleared the table, he *should* be catching twenty winks right about now. But it was hard falling asleep and staying asleep when she was under the same roof in another bed. It would be so much easier if he at least had her to snuggle with under the covers. He always slept better with Ashley wrapped in his arms. And maybe so did she.

He took her hand and brought her gently to her feet. "You should be in bed, too."

Drawn slightly off balance, she bumped into him, then steadied herself by putting one hand against his chest. "I wasn't in surgery most of the night." She turned away from him and began putting the leftover chili away.

Funny, how his energy came surging back whenever he was around her. "I'm a doctor. I'm used to getting by on little sleep. And so are you." He pitched in to help her finish the dishes.

"True." Ashley wiped down the table, countertops and stove.

"But that still doesn't explain what you're doing up in the middle of the night," Cal continued.

Ashley hesitated, as if trying to think of a reasonable explanation for her insomnia. "Must be the time difference," Ashley speculated finally, looking pleased she had come up with something that sounded logical, when Cal's intuition was telling him her excuse didn't ring true.

Something specific was keeping her from sleeping. She just didn't want to share it with him, he realized, stung.

"After all, Hawaii-time it's only 11:00 p.m. right now," Ashley continued matter-of-factly.

She had a point there, Cal had to concede.

"But you're still on Eastern Standard Time and, as you pointed out earlier this evening, you have to work tomorrow. So you really should go back to bed right now," Ashley said.

He regarded her, reluctant to comply, even when he knew she was right. He could use more rest.

She batted her eyelashes at him flirtatiously. "Come on, doc." She crooked a finger his way. "I'll tuck you in."

He grinned and began to relax as she clasped his hand lightly in hers. "Oh you will, will you?" he bantered back. As they moved up the stairs and paused in the doorway of the master bedroom, Cal murmured hopefully. "I don't suppose I can convince you to join me."

Something akin to the deep and abiding love she used to have for him—and he hoped *still* did—flickered in her pretty blue eyes. "Something tells me neither of us would get much sleep if I were to do that."

"Yeah," Cal agreed, aware all over again as she led him toward the big empty bed how much he liked spending time with her. "But think of the fun we'd have." *Think of how much closer we'd feel. Think about the possibility of me getting you to lower your guard once and for all.*

But, he noted sadly, it wasn't going to happen now. Tonight, she was still holding onto her secrets and private doubts, whatever they were. "How about a rain check?" she countered, easing him down into the sheets.

Cal tightened his grip on her fingers and looked deep into her eyes. The fear that he had somehow unknowingly contributed to the distance between them filled him with guilt. "I'm going to hold you to that," he warned her soberly, letting her know once and for all he intended to make her his again.

She leaned forward and brushed a light kiss to his temple that was as tender as it was playful. "Somehow, Cal, I knew you would."

During lunchtime on Monday at the Wedding Inn, Cal caught sight of his mother and sister-in-law. "Just the two women I wanted to see," he said cheerfully. "Have you got time to have a top-secret meeting with me?"

Helen glanced at her watch. The owner of the premier wedding establishment in North Carolina, she was usually on the run from the time she showed up for work in the morning until the time she left. Joe's wife, Emma, was just as busy in her wedding-planning duties.

Looking as stylish and pulled-together as ever in a pastel-pink business suit, Helen ran a hand through her short red hair. "I've got fifteen minutes," Helen said.

"I can spare you ten," the petite and elegantly pretty Emma said.

The three of them went back to Helen's office. Helen closed the door, insuring their privacy. She slipped behind her desk, her eyes focusing on Cal with maternal concern. "What brings you over here in the middle of a work day?" she asked, perplexed.

"I want to know if you're booked for Valentine's Day."

Emma and Helen chuckled as if that was the funniest thing they had ever heard and shook their heads. "Honey, we're booked three years ahead for Valentine's Day," Helen said.

"How can people book three years ahead?" Cal asked. When he and Ashley had decided to get married, they had only waited six months. He couldn't imagine waiting three years—for anything!

Helen smiled. "Some people just know."

"And are willing to wait for the exact time they want," Emma added.

Cal was willing to wait for the exact woman. He wasn't giving up no matter how long it took to make his marriage to Ashley work the way it should to give them the happily-ever-after they had both always wanted. Which was, of course, why he was here. He had come up with an idea to help speed the process, now that the groundwork had been laid. Especially since he only had three-and-a-half more weeks to convince Ashley they needed a lot more face time with each other than they'd been having.

"I want to have a wedding here on Valentine's Day," Cal told both women.

Two sets of eyebrows raised. "Mind me asking whose?" Emma interjected, with her usual tranquility.

Cal sat down in one of the chairs in front of his mother's desk and stretched his long legs out in front of him. "Ashley's and mine. I want to renew our vows on our wedding anniversary—February fourteenth."

Emma smiled and sat on the edge of Helen's desk, facing both Cal and Helen. "That's very romantic," Emma said approvingly.

Helen's eyes narrowed as if to say not so fast. "What does Ashley think about this?" she asked curiously.

Leave it to his mother to hit the nail on the head, without even trying. "She doesn't know," Cal stated, pretending not to see his mother's obvious reservations about his plan. "I'm going to surprise her."

Helen splayed a hand over her heart. She looked as if she might faint. "You can't surprise a woman with a wedding!" Helen said, aghast.

*Au contraire.* Cal held his ground. "I can if I want to," he said stubbornly.

Emma looked at Helen. Although no words were spoken, much seemed to pass between them. "I think it's a very romantic idea, Cal," Emma said tactfully at last, while Helen nodded in agreement. "But there are so many details that would have to be decided. And usually brides want very much to decide those things."

Cal knew that was true—Ashley had possessed very definite opinions on just about everything the first time around. "Can't we just use the same flowers and stuff we used at our first wedding ceremony?" Cal asked.

"I suppose." Looking reluctant to snuff out such a romantic idea, Helen bit her lip.

"What about the dress?" Emma asked. Again, she and Helen exchanged telltale looks. "Without sounding indelicate…are you sure Ashley will fit into the dress she wore the last time? As I recall it was quite form-fitting."

Cal hadn't thought about that, either. It was a good point. The last thing he wanted to do was point out to everyone else she had recently gained five pounds as well as several inches in all the right places. "So we'll get her a new one," Cal said.

"How?" Helen leaned forward, determined to be practical now. "We don't even have her measurements."

Cal shrugged, not going to let something that inconsequential derail his plans to add even more romance to his flagging marriage. "You know her style. I'm sure between the two of you that you could pick something out that she'd like to wear."

Helen and Emma exchanged trepidation-filled looks, then turned back at Cal.

"I really want to do this, Mom," Cal said before they could argue further.

"And you're sure it needs to be a surprise?" Emma ascertained slowly.

Thinking about how commitment-shy Ashley had seemed lately, he nodded.

"What about the Mustang you bought for her?" Helen interjected curiously. "I thought that was for Valentine's Day."

Cal rubbed the tension gathering in the muscles in the back of his neck. "I already gave it to her. She needed something to drive now, and well...it's a long story," he said vaguely, not willing to go into specifics because of Ashley's pique over the Hart family's involvement in their marital difficulties.

His mother looked at him as if she just bet there was much more to tell.

Emma glanced at her watch again. "Oh, darn, I've got an appointment with Polly Pruett and Peter Sheridan to pick out their reception-table settings."

Cal understood their business was important. He stood, knowing he had to get back to the hospital, too. "Can I count on your help with this? Especially the dress and all that?" he asked Emma.

Emma nodded and patted Cal's arm reassuringly as she passed. "Just get me some undergarments and a dress or a skirt or pair of slacks that fit Ashley well and bring those in to me. We'll run them over to the dressmaker and take the measurements off of those. If you're discreet about it, Ashley will never suspect a thing."

Cal had known he could count on the women in the family to come through for him. "Thanks, Emma." He stood, hugging her briefly.

"You romantic devil, you." Emma stood on tiptoe, bussed his cheek, then slipped out the door.

Helen picked up the pen in front of her and looked at Cal. "Now. Suppose you tell me what's really going on," she said.

Leave it to his mother to cut straight to the chase. "What do you mean?"

Helen got up to close the door to her office, ensuring them privacy once again. "Are you really this insecure about your marriage?" she said.

Too restless to sit, Cal leaned up against the wall and put his hands in the pockets of his slacks. He should have known his mother wouldn't pull any punches. Especially when it came to something this important. But if she thought he was backing out, just because there were logistical details to be worked out, she had another think coming. "I'm being romantic," he defended himself.

Helen sat on the edge of her desk and folded her arms in front of her. She regarded Cal sagely. "Romantic or desperate?"

Ouch again! Cal let his jaw slide forward pugnaciously. "I admit I want her to stay."

Exasperation mixed with the kindness in Helen's eyes. She looked at Cal as if she didn't know whether to hug him or scold him. "To the point you're trying to buy her love?"

Cal tensed. A muscle working in his jaw, he moved away from the wall and began to pace the small confines of his mother's elegantly outfitted office. "That's not what I'm doing." Cal moved to the floor-to-ceiling window and looked out at the elegantly landscaped grounds where many spring, summer and fall weddings were held.

Helen walked over to adjust the elegant red and gold velvet drapes that were so perfectly suited for the century-old inn. "The car alone was a pretty big gift. Now you're talking about throwing yourselves another wedding."

So Cal was generous when it came to his wife? He wasn't about to apologize for gifting Ashley as she deserved. Besides, he had done something like this before—the first year they were married, he'd given her the farm and the house for Christmas.

"Albeit on a much smaller scale," Cal cautioned, letting his mother know the rest of his plans. He surveyed her sternly. "This time around I'd like it to be just family and a few close friends." Not the splashy social occasion it had been the first time.

"Still," Helen shook her head disparagingly, "for someone who is still in the process of paying off his medical school debts, that's a pretty big deal."

Cal knew the gift was impractical. That wasn't the point. "I want her to know I love her," he said firmly.

Helen dropped the pen back onto the center of her desk. Abruptly, she looked as restless and unhappy as Cal felt. "And you think giving Ashley presents will accomplish that?" Helen said, as if it were the dumbest idea he'd ever had.

"Well, God knows nothing else has."

Cal hadn't meant to say the words out loud. But now that he had, they just hung there in the increasingly uncomfortable silence that followed.

Helen stepped nearer and compassion resounded in her low tone. "You really think Ashley questions your feelings for her?"

Cal knew his mother wished he would admit otherwise. But he wasn't going to lie, not now, when he was finally putting voice to some of his own deepest fears. He dropped back down into the chair, suddenly feeling as exhausted—and uncertain—as he had every right to be. Finished pretending, Cal looked up at his mother and reluctantly confessed, "I don't know, Mom. We've said we loved each other dozens of times over the ten years we've been a couple."

Just not recently.

"But?"

"I think she doubts something about us." Cal just didn't know quite what it was.

Helen's mood turned as contemplative as Cal's. "And why would she do that?" she asked gently.

*And wasn't that just the million-dollar question?* Cal spread his hands wide. "Maybe because we lived apart from each other for two-and-a-half years. And you don't have to remind me, I know you told me it was a dumb idea from the get-go to put our careers before our marriage." But they had done it anyway and now they had to live with the consequences.

Cal shrugged again, aware his mother was waiting to hear the rest. He needed to tell someone close to him what was bothering him deep inside. "Because we stopped knowing how to open up to each other what was in our hearts and on our minds. Because there's this *distance* between us, Mom, that sometimes has us feeling more like strangers than husband and wife." Even if Ashley didn't come right out and say so, he knew by the way she looked at him she felt that way. Damn. Listen to him. He sounded like some whiny kid. Cal shoved his hands through his hair. "I'm hoping that if we renew our vows, if we start fresh, we can fix this." Because God knew he needed to make his marriage right.

Helen sighed, suddenly looking as deeply worried and discouraged as Cal. "Maybe you should consider counseling instead," she suggested quietly.

Cal thought about how that was likely to go over. Not

well, to put it lightly. He shook his head. "No. I know Ashley, Mom. If she won't open up to me, she sure as heck won't open up to any counselor. This is the way it has to be."

Cal was sure he was doing the right thing. He and Ashley had to start communicating with each other before they would be able to believe in their future. Putting someone else in between them at this point would be as bad as putting miles between them. The way he saw it, if the car had worked to get her moving toward him, renewing their vows would be even better. "Now, are you going to help me?" Cal looked at his mother sternly. "Or should I be looking for a location other than the Wedding Inn this time around?" he asked impatiently.

Helen went back to her calendar. "Of course you can have the ceremony here, but it will have to be February thirteenth. There's a wedding here earlier that day, but it should be cleared out by, oh—5:00 p.m., or so—and we could set up for yours for the eve of your wedding anniversary, if not the actual anniversary."

Close enough, Cal decided. "That'd be fine."

"And Cal, there's one more thing—"

A knock sounded on Helen's door. "Come in," Helen said.

And much to Cal's amazement and chagrin, Ashley walked in.

Ashley wasn't sure what had been going on between Cal and his mother before she opened the door, but the tension in the room was so thick you could cut it with a knife.

"You wanted to see me, Helen?" Ashley asked cheerfully, deciding this once ignorance was just going to have to be bliss. Because she had enough troubles, trying to keep her pregnancy secret, finding a job, pleasing her parents, and mending her struggling marriage to Cal, without borrowing any more.

Not that this strain was any surprise. Cal had always been among the most private of Helen's offspring, and the fact he wouldn't confide what was on his mind had always made it hard for Helen to help him, as a kid and as an adult. And that was a shame, Ashley thought, because Helen Hart was one of the most understanding mothers Ashley had ever come in contact with. Given the chance…

Helen smiled warmly and gestured for Ashley to have a seat in the chair next to Cal's. "I asked you to come over because I have a favor to ask. You're planning to be here through February seventh, aren't you?"

"Sure." Ashley settled in her chair and crossed her legs at the knee. "Why?"

"Well, we have a wedding going on here that is just a disaster waiting to happen, I'm afraid," Helen confessed, her anxiety apparent. "The bride will be eight-and-a-half months pregnant on her wedding day."

Ashley did a double take as she contemplated that. "Whoa."

"Yes, I know." Helen shook her head, commiserating. "Both Emma and I tried to talk Polly Pruett out of getting married so close to her due date, but Polly was adamant about wanting a big wedding as close to Valentine's Day as possible. Turns out her fiancé, Peter Sheridan, was insistent they tie the knot before the baby was born. And her parents—who are paying for this huge affair—refused to let the wedding happen any closer to Polly's due date than that, so this was the best compromise we could come up with."

"Where do I come in?" Ashley asked, aware that beside her Cal seemed to be relaxing. Maybe because the attention was no longer on him or whatever it was he and his mother had been discussing when she interrupted?

Helen continued, "I was wondering if you would agree to be here on call for any emergency, during the ceremony and the reception. Emma and I would rest easier knowing there was an Ob/Gyn on the premises. You know how stressful weddings are. And how emotional brides can be, under ordinary circumstances."

"That I do," Ashley said, recalling the hoopla surrounding their own ceremony.

Out of the corner of her eye, Ashley could see Cal had a funny look on his face. Why, she couldn't imagine. Struggling to keep her mind on the conversation at hand, Ashley asked, "Who is her regular obstetrician, do you know?"

"Carlotta Ramirez. I would ask her to be here on standby but I know she is stretched pretty thin as it is with a husband and three kids and a solo medical practice."

*Unlike me, who has way too much time on my hands at the moment,* Ashley thought. "I'd be happy to do this for you."

"Thank you." Helen released her breath. Looking relieved, she hastened to add, "The Inn would pay you your hourly rate, of course."

Ashley lifted a hand. This was family. "You don't have to do that, Helen."

"I insist. If we take your time, we compensate you. Otherwise, I wouldn't feel right about it." Helen rose. "Polly and her fiancé are with Emma right now. Would you like to meet them?"

Ashley stood, too. "Absolutely."

Helen looked at Cal, wordlessly inquiring if he wanted to tag along. "I've got to get back to the hospital," he said, rolling slowly to his feet. As Helen's and Cal's glances collided, something unspoken passed between them that left Ashley feeling out of the loop.

Her heart aching that the distance between them would rear its head again now, Ashley forced herself once again to pretend she had noticed nothing amiss.

Relaxing slightly, Cal turned to Ashley and bussed her cheek. "I'll meet you at home tonight, okay?" he said as he squeezed her shoulder.

Ashley nodded. She wondered, even as he was walking off down the hall, what he and his mother weren't telling her.

"Something sure smells good," Cal said when he walked into the house shortly after seven o'clock.

Ashley looked up from the vegetables she was sautéing on the stove. Amazing how her heart could still leap when he entered a room. "Better than the chili and French fries, hmm?" she said, taking in his work appearance. She had gotten so used to seeing him in vacation attire or nothing at all, she had nearly forgotten how good he looked in a coordinating shirt and tie and dress slacks.

"Like you said." Cal wrapped his hands around her waist and brought her close for a long, thorough kiss the moment he had his brown leather jacket off. His face and lips bore the cold of the winter air outside, and the combination of cool lips and hot wet tongue sent a ribbon of desire spiraling through her. His gray eyes glimmered with affection as he gazed raptly down at her, and murmured seductively, "An interesting choice for an interesting woman with a hankering." He bent his head to kiss her again just as the phone rang.

Heart pounding, Ashley slipped from the warm cradle of his arms. Much more of this and she'd forget why she had felt it so important they spend their time talking and working out their problems instead of making love. "Saved by the bell," she said breathlessly as Cal went to answer it.

He grinned in a way that let her know she wasn't off the hook—yet. "Cal Hart," he spoke into the receiver. His smile fading, he said with careful politeness, "Yes, she is. Just a moment, please."

He handed the phone to her. "It's Dr. Connelly from Hawaii."

Ashley's mentor in the fellowship program.

If ever they needed a reality check, this was it.

Aware her husband no longer looked as happy as he had when he'd walked in the door and found her in the kitchen—barefoot and, unbeknownst to him, pregnant!— Ashley took the receiver from Cal. Already tensing, her spine ramrod straight, she walked into the dining room to finish the conversation. When she returned, Cal was standing at the stove, stirring the vegetables Ashley had forgotten about. He had a stoic expression on his face that pretty much matched the abrupt change in Ashley's mood. "So, what's up?" he said, looking at the stove, rather than Ashley.

Ashley moved to take over the cooking duties once again. "Dr. Connelly wanted to know if I was going to take the Maui clinic job."

"And…?" Cal's fingers brushed hers as he handed over the spatula.

Ashley tried not to make too much of the implacable look in his eyes or his newly subdued mood. "I told her I hadn't made up my mind yet, but I was leaning against it."

Cal's expression didn't change. He regarded Ashley cautiously. "And her response was?"

"Unhappy," Ashley admitted, wishing she and Cal had just let the phone ring and kept right on kissing.

Cal's eyes narrowed. "Does that surprise you?"

Ashley shook her head, guilt flowing through her anew. "She pulled a lot of strings to get me nominated for the position." In her mentor's mind, in a lot of people's minds, Ashley was indebted to her for the opportunity, and she should take it and make everyone who had helped train her proud.

Cal loosened his tie and the first two buttons of his starched gray-and-white striped shirt. "What changed your mind?"

Ashley watched him pull out a beer and twist off the cap. "You. This." *The prospect of—if everything went all right this time—having your baby.* She swallowed hard around the growing ache in her throat. "I don't think I want to be so far away from you again."

Cal met her gaze, held it until the familiar mixture of sadness and resentment appeared. "I don't want that, either," he said, very softly.

The phone rang again. Cal sighed. "I wish I didn't have to answer that." But he did because it might be one of his patients or the hospital calling. He picked up the phone, listened and smiled broadly. "Hey, Carlotta. Sure you can talk to Ashley. She's right here." He handed the phone over.

While Cal sipped his beer and sorted through the mail, Ashley listened to Carlotta's dilemma. "Of course. I'd be glad to help. No, it's not a problem. I've got the morning free. The afternoon, too. Okay. I'll see you at seven." She hung up and turned to Cal. He was watching her, an expectant look on his ruggedly handsome face. "Carlotta and Mateo's nanny, Beatrice, had a family emergency. She's boarding a plane to Denver as we speak. They can't find anyone to stay with the kids tomorrow. So I said I'd help out."

"That was nice of you." Cal wrapped an arm around her shoulder and brought her back, so she was cuddled against his body.

"After all she did for me in med school, I owe her. Besides," Ashley shrugged, "how hard can it be?"

# Chapter 7

"I don't like broccoli. And neither do Lizbet or Lorenzo," ten-year-old Juan told Ashley at five o'clock the next evening.

It had never occurred to Ashley that the three Ramirez kids wouldn't like broccoli. She had always loved the nutrient-filled veggie.

Aware she was in way over her head, Ashley did her best to hide her frustration as she regarded them all gently. "Well, how about corn then? Or green beans? No? Brussel sprouts? Um…" Suppressing a beleaguered sigh, Ashley scanned the contents of the freezer section, then turned to the refrigerator. "Carrots? Celery sticks?"

She struck out on all counts.

Juan regarded her glumly. "When is Beatrice coming back?" he demanded.

"I don't know," Ashley said honestly. Like her three charges, she wished the Ramirez's nanny was there.

"I miss her!" Five-year-old Elizabetta burst into tears. Two-year-old Lorenzo joined in.

Ashley picked up Lorenzo and placed him on her hip, but her soothing had no effect.

Juan pinched his nostrils shut. "That—" he pointed to the sweet-and-sour chicken simmering on the stove "—smells yucky, too!"

Elizabetta cried harder.

Ashley turned the controls on the burners to the off position and sat down at the kitchen table. She put the toddler on one leg, and helped his wailing sister climb onto the other. "There, there, now," she comforted both Lorenzo and Elizabetta as best she could, aware she had never failed so badly at anything in her entire life.

"I'll get it!" Juan shouted.

"Get what?" Ashley asked, unable to hear anything above the din of crying children.

"The door!" Juan shouted, already racing off.

"No, Juan, let me answer it!" Ashley said, struggling to get up.

As she moved, the kids cried even harder, and Elizabetta clung to Ashley, refusing to be put on the floor. By the time Ashley reached the foyer, Juan already had the front door wide open, and Cal was walking in, his strong male presence like a port in the storm, two big sacks from a popular fast-food restaurant in his arms. Juan looked as though he'd just been saved from a fate worst than death by the handsome surgeon. Ashley couldn't blame Juan; she felt the same way. She couldn't recall ever having a more miserable day. Not because she didn't like kids— she did. But because they seemed to sense they were in the hands of a rank amateur and were reacting accordingly. In their place, she would have wanted her parents and/or nanny, too.

Cal set the bags on the table. Pausing only long enough to brush a kiss across Ashley's brow, he reached for Elizabetta and cradled her in his big strong arms. He looked down at her tenderly and smiled. As their eyes met, Elizabetta's misery began to fade. "Do you know anybody who likes French fries?" Cal asked her gently.

Elizabetta stopped crying as abruptly as she had started. She remained still as Cal used a tissue to wipe away her tears. "Me," she sniffed. "And Lorenzo, too."

"And me, of course!" Juan hustled to get the ketchup from the refrigerator.

"I wasn't expecting you," Ashley told Cal as Elizabetta and Juan scrambled to take their seats at the kitchen table. But she was very glad he had come.

"Carlotta and Mateo are both going to be late tonight—Mateo's in surgery as we speak, and Carlotta's delivering a baby. So I told 'em I'd come over and give you a hand until one of them got home."

Cal settled Lorenzo in the high chair and gave him a potato wedge cut into toddler-size pieces to keep him busy. In short order, they had plates for all three kids with chicken nuggets, applesauce from the fridge and fries.

"It didn't occur to me you would already have started dinner," Cal said, eyeing what was on the stove with interest while Ashley poured the milk.

"The kids eat early." Or at least that was what Juan had told her. Ashley peered into the sack to see what else Cal had brought. "And for the record, it wasn't a very popular menu," she told him dryly. "So what would you like to eat? Grilled chicken salad or what's on the stove?"

"What's on the stove looks awfully good to me." Cal helped Elizabetta put more ketchup on her plate.

Ashley served them both and sat down across from Cal at the table.

It was amazing how calm the kids were in Cal's presence, and that tranquility continued throughout the evening. "You were wonderful with them," a relieved Ashley said, once all three children were in bed, asleep. She and Cal settled in front of the TV.

"So were you." He brought her into the curve of his arm and looked over at her as if she were the most beautiful woman in the world.

"Not before you got here," Ashley lamented, exhausted. Then, it had been nothing but chaos and disaster, despite her very best efforts. "Lorenzo never did take a nap." Every time she had tried to put him down, he had just sobbed until she wanted to cry, too.

Cal shrugged, experienced enough to be unconcerned. "Lorenzo was probably just upset because Beatrice wasn't here. Kids get used to their routines. And that's especially true for the little ones."

Ashley rested her palm on his thigh. His muscles felt warm and strong beneath the fine fabric of his dress pants. "How did you know what they would want to eat?"

Cal shrugged and covered her fingers with his own. "Everybody knows that..."

"Except me," Ashley sighed. Was she going to be this bad at mothering their baby? Was what had happened before somehow a harbinger of that?

Cal noted her distress. He paused and started over, this time a lot more carefully. "I baby-sat my siblings a lot when I was a kid. And I've taken care of my nephew Christopher, too, since Janey moved back here. From what I've been able to see, French fries, chicken nuggets and applesauce are always a hit with kids of any age. And if it's from a chain restaurant with a trademark clown, even better."

"So how come I didn't know that?" Was she always

going to screw up when it came to family matters, whether it be marriage or children or in-laws or her parents? Was her only real success going to be in medicine?

He gave her a look that warned her not to indulge in self-pity. "You've been around kids."

"Sure, on my pediatrics rotation in med school. And—to a certain extent—in the delivery room. But I realized today I still don't know anything about caring for them in their normal environment."

"You didn't baby-sit as a kid?"

"My parents wouldn't let me. They said it wasn't a good use of my time. They wanted me home, studying. And of course I didn't have any sibs, or even any cousins, since I was the child of two only children, so...today was just..."

"What?"

Difficult, Ashley wanted to say. Very difficult. But couldn't. Not given the fact she was about to become a mother herself. Feeling jittery, Ashley got up and headed for the kitchen.

"Where are you going?" Cal said from the sofa.

"To clean up," Ashley called from the kitchen.

He followed. "There's nothing to clean up in here."

Ashley wiped down the table and counters again, anyway. Cal put his hands on her shoulders, forced her to look at him. "Are you okay?" he repeated, looking into her eyes.

*No, I'm not okay. I'm pregnant and I'm scared to death I am somehow going to screw up again,* Ashley was about to say. And that was when Carlotta and Mateo Ramirez both walked in.

Carlotta smiled and cocked her head, listening. "It's blissfully quiet in here."

Mateo nodded. The accomplished surgeon looked as beat as his obstetrician wife. "Kids asleep?"

"Fed, bathed and down for the night," Cal said. As glad as he was to have the kids' parents home, he wished they hadn't chosen that particular moment to walk in the house. Cal had the feeling Ashley had been on the verge of telling him something important that might explain her jitteriness whenever the subject of kids came up.

Before they had married, she had been all for having a big family. That had changed the first summer of their marriage. Why exactly, he still didn't know.

"We owe you both tons," Carlotta continued as she hung up her coat.

Mateo nodded. "Carlotta and I didn't realize how much we relied on Beatrice until last night."

"How long is Beatrice going to be gone?" Cal asked, curious.

"Three weeks. So I was wondering…" Carlotta paused, drew a breath and looked Ashley straight in the eye. "I know you're supposed to be taking a much-needed rest before you begin job-hunting in earnest, but would it be possible for you to continue helping me out?"

Beside him, Cal felt Ashley tense. He did the same. He didn't want Ashley spending all her time over here. Not when they still had so much to work out, and relatively little time in which to do it.

"You mean baby-sit?" Ashley asked.

Cal applauded the lack of emotion in his wife's voice.

"No. I think we've got that part worked out," Carlotta smiled. "I've found a friend to take Lorenzo during the day for me, another to take Elizabetta after kindergarten. But I'm really going to have to be here in the late afternoon and evening to cook dinner, help with homework, and ride herd on baths and bedtime. But with a full patient load now, I can't just close the office at two-thirty or three every afternoon."

Cal began to see where this was going.

"You want me to help out at the office?" The tension left her body. Ashley grinned at the suggestion.

Carlotta nodded. "I'd love it if you could do the afternoon office hours and take calls for me one night a week. I'll do the other two nights, and my call partners will do the rest. It would help me out enormously."

"Not to mention show me what it's like to work in a small private practice here in Holly Springs," Ashley said.

"Then you'll do it?" Carlotta asked hopefully.

Ashley nodded, smiled. "With pleasure."

Cal's hopes to pick up their conversation where they left off were dashed by a series of phone calls from the hospital and Ashley's fatigue. Tuesday evening all Ashley wanted to talk about was what she had done at work that day. Cal had been only too eager to listen. He loved Ashley in doctor mode and he wanted her to settle down in Holly Springs with him more than anything. On Wednesday they were supposed to have lunch before she began afternoon office hours for Carlotta, but he ended up in surgery instead. That night he was home, but she was on call, and spent most of the night at the hospital, delivering twins. Thursday afternoon was his scheduled time off, so he went home early, changed clothes and went for a run. He had just gotten back to the farmhouse when he heard a car pulling into the drive. Bottle of water in hand, Cal went to the front window and then stepped out onto the porch to greet their visitor.

"Hello, Margaret." At fifty, Ashley's mother was every bit as beautiful as her only daughter. They shared the same elegant bone structure and tall, willowy frame. Margaret's dark-brown hair was threaded lightly with gray and cut in a short, sophisticated, easy-care style. Unlike Cal's own mother, who had a clear delineation between family time and work, Margaret had a crisp, businesslike demeanor that carried over into her personal life. *Warm and fuzzy* were not words he would have used to describe her, even under the most sentimental of occasions. And judging by the cool look in her eyes, this was not one of those.

"Cal." Margaret nodded at him, brow raising at the sweat dripping down his face.

Cal mopped the perspiration with the sleeve of his sweatshirt. "I just got back from a run."

"So I see."

Telling himself not to be offended by the lack of affection in his mother-in-law's eyes, Cal ushered her in and helped her off with her coat. "Ashley didn't tell me you were coming."

Margaret straightened the hem of her tailored jacket. "I wanted to surprise her."

Margaret was going to do that all right, Cal thought. She followed him back to the furnished areas of the downstairs. "Where is my daughter?"

Cal glanced at his watch, saw it was only four-thirty. "She's still in Holly Springs seeing a few patients for a colleague she's helping out." He expressed his regret. "She won't be home until six." Or later. That left them with a lot of time to kill.

"Is she doing this temporarily—I hope?" Margaret said.

Cal nodded stiffly, wishing that his mother-in-law would keep her opinions to herself. "So it would seem."

"May I be frank with you?"

*Actually, I'd prefer you wouldn't.* But since he couldn't

very well tell his mother-in-law to back off, Cal simply waited.

"What in the world is going on here, Cal?" Margaret sat down on the family-room sofa and crossed her trouser-clad legs at the knee. "Is Ashley even looking for suitable employment?"

*"Suitable" meaning anywhere else but here,* Cal thought. "I think you should ask her that," Cal said carefully.

"I have." Margaret looked annoyed. "She's not responding to my emails on the subject and she hasn't returned my phone calls, either."

"I don't know what to tell you," Cal continued in the same polite tone.

"Then let me tell you something." Margaret clasped her hands around one knee and leaned forward urgently. "I am not happy with this situation. You should be encouraging Ashley either to take the job in Maui, at least for a year or two, for the experience. Or you should be pushing her to look for employment worthy of her training and education elsewhere, instead of spending a lot of time and energy on getting married all over again," she finished with a disapproving frown.

Cal went into the kitchen to put a pot of coffee on. "I take it you don't agree with that idea, either?" he asked from across the counter.

Margaret shrugged. "I admit I don't see the point. You and Ashley said your vows to each other once. What has changed in the three years since?"

*Everything. Nothing.* Cal only knew things still weren't right between them. He wanted the chance to start over fresh with Ashley, and this was the surest way to do it. He didn't care if her parents approved of his romantic gesture or not.

Finished, Cal strode back to the family room and sat down opposite Margaret. "First of all, Ashley doesn't know anything about my Valentine's Day present to her. And I am relying on you and Harold to keep the information to yourself. Second, I think it would mean a lot to Ashley if both you and Harold could attend."

"Her father and I are very busy right now. I don't know if it's going to be possible."

Well, then, so be it.

"We did expect better of you, since you gave us your word at the time we gave you our blessing that you would never hold Ashley back career-wise."

*That again.* Cal pushed the words through his teeth. "I've supported her to the best of my ability, Margaret."

"Oh, really." Margaret leaned forward angrily. "Then why is she here now, doing nearly nothing professionally? Why isn't she still pursuing the dream she's had since she was a small child?"

It felt great to be practicing medicine again, Ashley thought, as she greeted her last patient of the day. Great to be busy for at least part of every day all week long… although she had missed seeing Cal; she'd been seeing so much of him recently.

"Hey, Dr. Hart." Polly Pruett smiled. The twenty-three-year-old pregnant bride-to-be was all round, blond softness. Her pixie face glowed with happiness as she patted her burgeoning belly. "The receptionist said you were taking all of Dr. Ramirez's patients this afternoon."

"Yes." The nurse helped Polly lie back on the table while Ashley finished reviewing Polly's chart. Then she began the exam. "Is that okay?"

"Sure." Polly relaxed on the table while Ashley palpated her abdomen.

"How have you been feeling?" Ashley asked, reaching for the gloves.

Polly grinned. "Well, my back hurts. I have to pee all the time so I can't sleep more than a few hours at a time. I'm hungry enough to eat a horse and then some. And I have the gracefulness of an elephant on a parade. But other than that, I'm doing just fine."

Ashley chuckled at the humorous description of life in the ninth month of pregnancy.

"It feels like the baby is dropping, too. Does that mean I'm about to go into labor?" Polly asked worriedly, obviously thinking about the wedding, just two weeks away now.

Ashley switched on the lamp and sat down on the stool, so she could begin the pelvic exam. "A first-time mother can drop four weeks before the due date, and even go two weeks or so after that before she delivers."

Polly frowned. "So it could be six weeks?"

"More like four, max, for you. But nothing looks imminent," Ashley decreed as she finished and ripped off her gloves.

Polly breathed a sigh of relief and pantomimed wiping the perspiration from her brow. "Whew. I'm glad you're going to be at the Wedding Inn when I get married, anyway. That will make me feel better."

Ashley and the nurse both lent a hand and helped Polly sit up. "Well, we aim to please, both at the Inn and here in the office."

Polly made a face. "Now if we can just hold off that snowstorm…"

Ashley looked up from the notations she was making on Polly's chart. "What snowstorm?"

Polly went back to rubbing her belly. "The one in the mountains of Tennessee that is headed our way."

Ashley loved snow—when she didn't have to go anywhere. It was a pain when the roads were bad and you still had to show up for work. "When is it supposed to hit?" she asked, aware she hadn't driven on the wet stuff in almost three years.

"Tomorrow night, or possibly the following morning, depending on how fast the front moves," the nurse said.

Polly nodded. "Didn't you see all the people running in and out of the grocery and hardware stores today?"

Ashley tilted her head to the side. "I noticed a lot of cars. But I didn't think much about it."

"Well, you should," Polly said seriously. "'Cause you could get snowed in for days if we get as much precipitation as they are predicting. So you better make sure you have all the necessities on hand…"

The only necessity for Ashley was Cal, whom she had seen precious little of the last four days. It seemed as if when he wasn't on call, she was. But tonight, they were both due to have dinner together. And she couldn't wait.

Several phone calls and a stop at the med-center maternity ward later—where Ashley diagnosed the patient in question with Braxton-Hicks contractions and sent her home—Ashley was finally en route back to the farm. Unfortunately, Cal's car wasn't the only one in the driveway. Parked next to his was a rental car.

Dinner with Ashley's mother was a cordial if somewhat tense affair. All three of them cooked and then cleaned up together. Then Cal went upstairs to make phone calls to check on his post-op patients while the two women settled down for some private time in front of the fire.

"Obviously, I came all the way out here for a reason," Margaret said in a crisp, businesslike tone.

"To see me?" Ashley quipped.

"I made some phone calls." Margaret reached into the leather carryall that went everywhere with her and pulled out a business card. "Shelley Denova is a headhunter who specializes in getting academic postings for physicians. There is a position coming open at Yale Medical School that hasn't even been advertised yet."

Ashley tensed as her mother applied a pressure to succeed that was all too familiar. The one thing Ashley hadn't missed in Hawaii were the face-to-face confrontations with her folks, and the inquisitions about why Ashley wasn't doing better. It had never seemed to matter what Ashley did. When she had been named salutatorian of her high-school class, they had been disappointed she was not the valedictorian. When she had selected Wake Forest—rather than Harvard—to attend at the undergrad level, they had been upset; they had always envisioned her as "Ivy League" and could not understand why Ashley refused even to apply to the prestigious university. And she didn't even want to think about their reaction when she had decided to go to medical school in Winston-Salem so she could be near Cal, who was doing his five-year surgical residency there. But they had finally gotten their way when they had pushed her to go to Hawaii to finish her fellowship. Obviously, both her parents expected her to continue to put her career ahead of her family. And Ashley wasn't sure she wanted to do that. Especially since doing that for the past two years had brought her nothing but heartache and a loneliness so deep she didn't think she was over it yet. "Yale is in Connecticut, Mother."

Margaret pooh-poohed Ashley's concerns with a wave of her hand. "It's a two-hour plane ride from here to there.

You could work there during the week and see Cal every weekend."

Assuming she got the position; Ashley wasn't sure she would. Not that this was the point, in any case. Ashley regarded her mother in frustration. "That's not the same as living together, Mother."

Her mother couldn't have cared less about the impact such a separation would have on Ashley and Cal's marriage. She looked at Ashley sternly. "You will not be happy practicing medicine here."

Ashley got up to poke at the fire. "You don't know that. I'm not even sure I want to practice medicine full-time!"

Margaret laid a hand across her chest, as if she were about to have heart failure. Her face turned pale. "Don't even joke about that, Ashley!"

Who was joking? Ashley wondered, the hurt and resentment inside her building. If she was going to have a baby she wasn't sure she wanted to work full-time. At least not right away! Not that she could discuss this with anyone just yet, either.

"Now, I want you to pull together your résumé and list of references and call Shelley first thing tomorrow morning. I've written her cell and home numbers down on the back of her card. She's expecting to hear from you. And do not delay. These entry-level positions at prestigious institutions go quickly. You have no time to waste."

Ashley didn't care what her mother thought—this was not a done deal. "And suppose I don't want to apply?" Ashley said angrily, surprised to find her emotions overriding her common sense. Because she, better than anyone, knew you did not talk to Margaret Porter this way. Not unless you wanted a serious dose of blunt talk dished right back.

Margaret covered her eyes with her hand for a long moment. Finally, she drew a deep breath and looked up. "Are you trying to ruin your marriage?"

Ashley slammed the poker back in the fireplace stand so carelessly the whole thing fell over. Embarrassed, she knelt to pick up the wrought-iron fireplace tools. As she stuffed them back in, two more fell out and clattered to the stone surround. "I fail to see how—"

Margaret pointed a lecturing finger at her. "Cal Hart did not fall in love with a slacker, Ashley Porter Hart. You persist along these lines and he is not going to love you."

Bitterness rose in Ashley's throat, choking her. "Are we talking about Cal now?" Ashley countered miserably. "Or you and Daddy, Mother?"

Margaret continued as if Ashley hadn't even spoken. "In successful marriages, the partners grow together." She paused to give Ashley a long reproach-filled look. "In unions where one spouse flourishes and the other does not, boredom and resentment inevitably set in, and the marriage falls apart." Another pause, this one longer and weightier than the last. "Cal is succeeding admirably, Ashley. He's treating pro sports players and college athletes. And you need to stay on track with your career, too."

Cal was just getting off the phone with the medical center when he heard the front door open and close. Then a car started in the drive.

He headed downstairs, reaching the foyer just as a shivering Ashley came back inside. He had only to look at her face to know she was upset. "What happened?" he asked warily.

Ashley shook her head, her eyes moist. She pushed both her hands through her hair. "The usual. She pushed.

And then pushed some more. Only this time I *didn't* just bend to her wishes."

Cal was glad to hear that. He had always felt Margaret and Harold put way too many demands on their only daughter. He wrapped an arm around her shoulders, comforting her as best he could. "I'm sorry. Is she coming back tomorrow?"

"No." Ashley stalked back to the family room. Her hands trembled as she picked up the coffee cups and dessert plates. "She has a nine o'clock meeting at the university tomorrow, so she is taking the six o'clock flight out of Raleigh in the morning."

Noting a fireplace tool had fallen over on its side, Cal righted it and placed it back in the stand. "She could have stayed here overnight."

Ashley did her best to avoid Cal's gaze as she rinsed the dishes and slid them into the dishwasher. "She preferred to be at the hotel at the airport. She felt that would be easier."

Cal saw the business card on the coffee table in the family room. He picked it up. His heart sank as he read the writing on the back of it. "Are you going to call this person?" he said, afraid to know, and more afraid not to.

Ashley shut her eyes and rubbed at her temples as if she had the beginning of a migraine. "I don't know."

Cal thought about the promise he had made, never to stand in the way of Ashley and her dreams. Though it choked him, he forced himself to do the right thing and live up to his word. He drew a deep breath, ensuring his voice was calm, before he replied, "Maybe you should."

Slowly, Ashley opened her eyes. She looked even angrier. More resentful. "Is that what you want?" Ashley asked sharply. "For me to hook up with some high-powered headhunter with connections all over the East Coast so I can get some extremely sought-after job?"

The way she was looking at him then, Cal knew he was damned if he did and damned if he didn't. So he told the truth. "I want you to be happy, Ashley. Right now you don't look happy. So—" he struggled against the selfish need welling up inside him as he closed the distance between them "—if that is what it takes…"

Ashley held up her hands, holding him off. She wheeled away from him and began to pace the length of the two rooms. "I'm just so confused! I'm thirty years old and I feel like half my life is gone and I don't know how to have fun or relax or do anything but work, work, work! And that used to be okay—probably because I was always too busy even to let myself think. But suddenly, it seems like it's not enough anymore, not enough to make me happy, anyway."

"And you should be happy," Cal agreed. He caught her wrist as she passed and anchored her implacably at his side.

Looking more distressed than ever, she flattened her hands against his chest. "But if I don't strive and push forward, harder than ever, I'm going to let everyone else down." Ashley scowled, her frustration with the situation apparent. "My mentor. My mother. My father. Even you." She stomped away from him, her temper igniting into hot flames of emotion that were glorious to behold.

"Hey—" Cal arrowed his thumb at his chest "—don't lump me in with the rest of those clowns. I'm delighted to see you so confused. It makes you as human as the rest of us."

Ashley narrowed her china-blue eyes at him and restlessly tapped one foot. "You'd love me no matter what?" she challenged with a withering look.

Cal nodded emphatically, ignoring the way she had her fists balled and planted on her hips. "I'd love you no matter what."

She tossed her mane of glossy dark hair and snorted in a most unladylike fashion. "Liar."

Cal blinked, sure he couldn't have heard right. "What?"

She stomped closer, her breasts rising and falling with every infuriated breath she took. "Liar," she repeated, not stopping until they were squared off toe-to-toe and nose-to-nose. She angled her chin up at him, her soft lips taking on a defiant curve. "You cannot possibly feel that way!" she told him stormily. She leveled an accusing finger at his chest. "You have to have some opinion of what you want me to do with my life right now, but you won't tell me what it is!"

Cal caught her hand and held it against his chest. "Maybe because which job you take isn't my decision to make!" he shot back, just as irritably.

She regarded him with a hauteur as cold as ice. "So you're just going to let me guess what's going to make you happy?"

Cal frowned, his exasperation beginning to get the better of him once again. Reluctantly, he let her go and watched her step back a pace. "I can't tell you what to do here, Ashley," he told her wearily. He ran a hand across his jaw and realized that although he had shaved that morning, he needed to shave again.

"Why not?" she demanded.

Cal struggled to remain calm as their glances held. "Because if I did, it would make everything bad and selfish that anyone's ever thought about me absolutely true."

# Chapter 8

Ashley stared at Cal, barely able to believe what she was hearing. "Who thinks bad things about you? Cal, you are the most compassionate, wonderful, giving man I have ever met!"

A haunted look appeared in Cal's gray eyes. "Maybe that's who I am now," Cal acknowledged, with a derisive shrug of his broad shoulders. He rubbed a hand across the front of the cashmere sweater he had put on for dinner with her mother. "But it's hard to erase the past."

Ashley took a deep breath to steady herself. He was standing so close to her she could feel the heat emanating from his tall, strong body. "Where is this coming from?" she probed gently.

Cal remained silent, as if he could think of nothing to say that wouldn't make him look even worse in his wife's eyes. She gave him a look that reminded him this was why she was here with him now, why they'd declared a temporary moratorium on sex. So they could start sharing all the stuff they'd been deliberately withholding from each other and really get to know each other, flaws and all.

"It started after my dad died," Cal said finally. He walked over to examine a basil plant on the windowsill that looked to be suffering from lack of care. He plucked off a few brown leaves, added a small amount of water. "At least I think that's when it did."

Ashley watched him throw the leaves into the kitchen trash can. "Keep going."

"You have to understand." Noting the can was nearly full, Cal lifted out the bag and tied it shut. He carried it outside to the cans and put it in. Ashley followed. "It was a very rough time." Cal grabbed a couple of logs for the fireplace while they were out there. Ashley held the door for him as they walked back inside. "We were all so stunned by what had happened," Cal continued as he took the logs over and put them in the basket next to the mantel. "There was no warning." Cal rose, dusted off his hands. "One day my dad left on a business trip. The next day we got a phone call, saying the plane he was on had gone down in the mountains, and there were no survivors."

Ashley could only imagine how terrible that had been.

"My mom, who had always been so strong, was a complete wreck. She had six kids, ranging in age from six to sixteen. The love of her life had just died and she was devastated."

As had been her children, Ashley noted.

"We all went into survival mode." Cal walked back into the kitchen to wash his hands, Ashley at his side. "Mac became the head of the household because he was the oldest son. My mother focused on sorting out my father's affairs, which were a mess, because my dad died without a will." Cal shook his head, remembering. "It took months to get everything straightened out," he related sadly. "And during that time, my mother kept telling us everything was going to be fine, we just had to gather up our courage and go on. And that's when the trouble began."

"Why?"

The brooding look was back in his eyes, stronger than ever.

Cal sighed and rubbed at the tense muscles in the back of his neck. "Because while Mac struggled to help my mom with the financial details, I tried to follow my mother's example of keeping a stiff upper lip and make my four younger siblings toughen up enough to carry on, too." A mixture of regret and self-admonition filled his low tone. "There weren't going to be any tears when I was around," he mocked himself bitterly. "And oh, by the way, since our life was supposedly worry-free financially, I intended to go on the week-long eighth-grade spring break trip to Washington, D.C." Cal sighed, drew in a long, defeated breath. "My mother didn't want me to go. I thought it was because it involved a plane ride from Minneapolis to D.C. and, at that point, she didn't want any of us on planes. But I felt unfairly hemmed in and kept pushing and pushing to do what I wanted."

Ashley felt a soul-deep ache at the pain in Cal's voice. "Tell me more…" she said softly.

Cal shook his head, recalling, his mood as bleak as the overcast winter evening outside. "And all the while I was taking out my own hurt and fear and frustration on my younger sibs." His eyes collided with Ashley's once again. "Until one day, I barely recognized myself," he told her sorrowfully. "And neither did my family.

"And that was when my mother stepped in," Cal continued in a low voice, "I had made poor little six-year-old Joey cry and my mother was furious. She took me aside and demanded to know where my heart was! How had I gotten so selfish? And above all, *why* couldn't I please understand that we just didn't have the money to send me on the eighth-grade trip?"

Ashley's brow furrowed. "You knew that and you still asked?" This didn't sound like the Cal she knew at all. He was selfless to the bone.

Cal turned his glance heavenward, shook his head in mounting remorse. "That was the hell of it—I *didn't* know. In the wake of my dad's death, my mother hadn't bothered to reveal to any of us, save Mac, how severe our financial troubles were. And that made me even more furious—because if I had been given all the information, I would *never* have asked to go on that trip or been such a jerk about it."

Ashley's heart went out to him as she touched his wrist. She looked up at him and commiserated gently, "I can see where you would be hurt and angry, being excluded that way." She certainly would have been!

Cal, however, didn't look as if he felt his behavior was all that justified, despite his lingering frustration with the way his family situation had unraveled back then. "And I was especially mad at Mac," Cal continued ruefully. "I knew my mother had been trying to protect me, but he had no excuse."

So Helen got a pass, as far as Cal was concerned, Ashley realized.

Cal's mouth tightened into a grim line. "But Mac had to know that, at fourteen, I was man enough to handle that information." Resentment clouded his eyes. "Mac said he was bound by the promise he had made to my mother to shield us from worry. But I felt he owed me, too, that he should've done what was right by the family, taken me aside and told me the truth about our family's precarious financial situation."

Ashley saw his point. Deep down, she knew Cal could have handled the news—if he'd been given the opportunity.

"I had a hard time forgiving him for that, though I eventually did it. But I also told him never to cut me out of the loop again."

Only Mac hadn't kept his word, Ashley realized with dismay. Because Helen Hart's secret was not the only one Cal's brother had been forced to keep.

"Anyway," Cal continued soberly, unaware of Ashley's sinking feeling of dread, "the way I was that year made me realize that I could easily be the most selfish SOB around if I let myself. I decided not to let myself."

"I understand not liking who've you become or started to become," Ashley retorted carefully. "I've had my moments, too." She knew all about deeply held regrets—the guilt and second-guessing of events, for she had suffered the same. Not like Cal, in her childhood, but in their marriage.

"But I don't get what all that has to do with me," Ashley continued, after a moment.

"You asked me what I wanted you to do about your job," he reminded her heavily. "You want to know the truth?"

Did she? Reassuring herself that she could handle whatever it was he was about to say, Ashley swallowed around the sudden parched feeling in her throat. "Yes."

He drummed his fingers on the gleaming stainless-steel stovetop. "I'll tell you," he offered in a way that made her heart skip first one beat, then another. "But you're not going to like it."

Ashley flushed under the heat of his regard. She backed up against the counter on rubbery legs, her hands braced on either side of her. She tilted her head at him in silent challenge. "How do you know?"

Cal compressed his lips together ruefully. "Because it's practically Neanderthal it's so damn selfish," he said, eyeing her with a depth of male speculation she found very disturbing. He jammed his hands on his hips and narrowed his eyes. "I don't want you working anywhere that we can't live together in the same house and sleep together every night. I don't want to be second fiddle to your career. And I don't want you being secondary to mine, either." He paused, looking her up and down, from the top of her casually upswept hair to her toes. "I want us—our marriage, our family—to come first. Now and always, even if that means that we both sacrifice some future career success for the sake of our family!"

Doing her best to keep a level head, Ashley folded her arms in front of her. She could feel the blood rushing to her cheeks even as she struggled to get hold of her soaring emotions. "Have you always felt this way—or is it just recently?" she demanded, not sure if she felt aggravated or relieved by his matter-of-fact confession.

Cal leveled his assessing gaze on hers and kept it there. "Always, I am ashamed to say."

Ashley blinked, not sure if she wanted to hug him or slug him as she stammered, "But you never—"

Cal held up a hand. "Because it would have been wrong to hold you back," he interrupted gruffly.

Now he was sounding like her parents. Aware she wouldn't be able to bear it if she ended up being a failure in his eyes, too, she said, "You want to see me succeed. Just like my parents do."

"Yes," Cal admitted, closing the distance between them and taking her into his arms. Holding her against the warmth of his tall, strong body, he gently stroked her cheek. "But I also want you in my life. I want you here with me...too," he told her softly.

Ashley had no doubt he was speaking from his heart. She shook her head, regretting all the time they had spent apart. "I wish you had told me this," she whispered unhappily.

He tightened his hold on her possessively. "Why?"

"Because," Ashley pushed her hands against his chest in escalating frustration, aware she had already endured more disappointment in one lifetime than she had ever expected to endure, "I've wished we could put us first, too! Damn it, Cal, I missed you so much the entire time I was in Hawaii." And had they just been honest with each other, he would have known it!

He grinned victoriously, looking as if he'd had an enormous weight moved from his shoulders. "And here I thought I was the only one who had to force myself to be positive about the separation."

Joy flowed through her in enervating waves, as she realized they had been on the same page after all! Most of the time, anyway. She wreathed her arms about his neck, hitched in a quick, bolstering breath. "But we don't have to be separated anymore." She studied him hopefully. "Do we?"

He looked down at her as if he loved every inch of her. Misunderstandings and all. "Not if I can help it," he promised in a low, gruff voice.

He lowered his head. The next thing Ashley knew they were kissing. Passionately. Tenderly. Hungrily. She curled her fingers into his hair and surged against him, loving the taste and touch and wonder of him. She could feel his arousal, pressing hard against her, as surely as her own blossoming need. And yet, underneath her love for him was her ever-present fear that letting her guard down all the way was risking his discovery of *her* past mistakes. Errors in judgment that a family-oriented man like Cal might find very hard, if not downright impossible, to forgive. And she couldn't bear it if he looked at her with the same disappointment and disillusionment her parents always did.

Trembling, Ashley ended the kiss and pulled away. Their marriage was healing—not dissolving—and she was *not* going to lose Cal, she reassured herself. He was not going to find out about the terrible secret she had kept from the very first days of their marriage; he was not going to discover the lengths she had gone to protect him.

Mistaking the reason for her sudden withdrawal from their steamy embrace, Cal sighed. Apology radiated in his dark-gray eyes.

He obviously wanted to make love as much as she did.

He chuckled cheerfully and tossed her a playful glance that raised her pulse another notch. "We better think of something else for us to do fast, if we don't want to end up doing what we've always ended up doing."

*Making wild, passionate love.* "Well." Ashley thought out loud, her confidence building. "We could try to have fun." She grinned impishly as she thought about the possibilities of the Thursday evening ahead, the joy of just having time to spend with him again. "Some *other* way," she added, hoping for a little inspiration. Because heaven knew all she could think about were the broad shoulders straining against his cashmere sweater, and how it felt to be enveloped in their seductive warmth.

Cal seemed to be struggling with the same feelings, even as his eyes lit with mischief. "And I know just the thing."

"Hide-and-seek!" Ashley regarded Cal in amazement. "You've got to be kidding."

He wasn't.

Ashley threw up her hands. "That's the most ridiculous thing I've ever heard," she declared.

One hand around her waist, he tugged her close and nibbled playfully on her ear. "Afraid you're going to lose?"

"Hardly," Ashley murmured back, trying not to notice how good it felt—how good it always felt—to be in his arms this way.

He lifted his brow. The mischief sparkling in his eyes brought out an answering devilry in her. "Well, you *should* be afraid to lose, sweetheart. You don't know this house half as well as I do."

She tossed her head, already thinking ahead to ways to beat the pants off him. "Even so," she drawled in the most bored tone she could manage, egging him on in the same way he was deliberately baiting her, "it wouldn't be much of a challenge."

He chuckled in anticipation of the competition. "And you always have to be challenged."

Ha! Ashley slapped her hands on her hips and countered indignantly, "Like you don't!"

"True." Cal pulled the kitchen timer out of a drawer and tossed it to her. "Best two out of three."

Her breath hitched in her chest. "And the prize?" Ashley asked.

Cal shrugged and flashed her an impertinent grin. "Whatever the winner wants."

Ashley knew what she wanted—Cal, and their marriage the way it had been at the very first, before their careers had gotten in the way. "Agreed, as long as it doesn't involve seeing me naked," Ashley cautioned.

He had to think about that. But only for a minute. "All right."

She imagined he was thinking of myriad ways to get around that. "I don't trust that grin."

"As well you shouldn't," he told her significantly, the recklessness in him spurring the wildness in her. "I'll step outside the front door. You've got three minutes to hide. And I've got the same amount of time to find you."

"Okay."

Not surprisingly, he won the first round.

She won the second.

The third time they both ended up in the coat closet tucked under the stairs. In just under three minutes, darn it. Which meant... "Okay," Ashley said breathlessly, as he shut them in there together. "You win, bucko. So what do you want?"

"This," Cal said.

One long, hot kiss that went on and on, until her lips were parting under the onslaught, and she was meeting him touch for touch, stroke for stroke. Until she was moaning softly in her throat and clinging to him helplessly. Until she knew—as did he—that old hurts were healing and their marriage really was on the road to recovery.

## Chapter 9

Ashley rushed down the back stairs at seven the next morning, clad in her pink and white flannel robe and slippers. "Cal, have you seen my black dress?"

Cal tore his gaze from her cleavage visible in the V of the shawl collar. No doubt about it, Ashley's body was a hell of a lot more voluptuous than it had been five pounds ago. Not that he'd had opportunity to investigate the changes for himself, as she had refused to let him her see her in any form of undress since they'd reunited.

"Cal!" Ashley said again, even more impatiently this time.

Cal struggled to recall what the question had been. With little result. "Um…"

Ashley came closer, until she was standing right next to him. She smelled of soap and shampoo and the orange blossom perfume she wore. And unless he was wrong, she didn't have much of anything on under that calf-length robe, definitely not a bra.

"It's the kind of stretchy one," Ashley continued jogging his memory deliberately. "I wore it the first night back when we went over to your Mom's to see the family. I can't find it anywhere."

And with good reason, Cal thought, since it was currently with the dressmaker, who was making the dress Ashley would wear when they renewed their wedding vows. Stalling for time, he gave the scrambled eggs another stir. "Did you check the wash?"

Noting breakfast was almost ready, Ashley went to the fridge and brought out the milk, butter and jam. Her arms full, she shut the door with her hip. Watching her lower half in action made him want to groan. He was still aroused from their extended kissing session the evening before. But a promise was a promise, and he had sworn he would demonstrate to her there was a lot more to their relationship than simply sex.

"I didn't put it in the wash." Ashley popped slices of whole grain bread into the four-slice toaster they'd gotten years ago, as a wedding gift.

Cal shrugged, as he cut a grapefruit in half and put the halves on plates. "Well then it probably wouldn't be there."

Scowling, Ashley sat down at the table while he dished up the eggs and sat down opposite her. "I wanted to wear it today."

"Well…" Cal tried to think of a way to get her off the subject, as he pointed to the small TV mounted under one of the cabinets. It was tuned to a morning news show, and the local weather map was on the screen. "You should probably wear slacks anyway. If the snow that they've predicted hits later this afternoon, you're not going to be want to be caught in a dress, anyway."

Not to be dissuaded, Ashley continued, "And I can't find my favorite black bra and black satin panties, either."

Cal had done laundry once since she'd been back. So had she. "Maybe they're with the dress?" he said, struck by how pretty she looked this morning—her golden skin glowing with health, her cheeks flushed a becoming peach.

Ashley added a tiny bit of butter and a generous amount of blackberry jam to her toast. "I can't believe this!"

Neither could Cal. Had he realized she was likely to want her dress and that particular set of undies, he would have picked those items up by now. "They're probably somewhere. You're just not seeing them. Or you put them somewhere and you don't remember," he fibbed.

Leaning back in her chair, Ashley regarded him humorously. "Are you hinting I'm losing my mind?"

"No." But he was going to lose his soon, if he didn't get to make love with her again in the very near future.

Wordlessly, Cal offered her coffee. She declined with a shake of her head and continued to sip her milk.

"I am, however, saying you have had an awful lot on your mind lately, what with helping out Carlotta this week, fielding visits with both our families and trying to figure out where you're going to look for a job."

The laughter left Ashley's china-blue eyes as suddenly as it had appeared. "That at least I know," she told him quietly. "I'm looking for a position right here in central North Carolina and I don't care if it's a high-powered job or something distinctly low-key. I just want to take care of pregnant women and their babies. And that, Cal, is why I wanted my black dress. I wanted to go see the med-center administrator and talk to him about the possibility of me joining the staff at the hospital right here in Holly Springs."

Cal struggled not to let his own selfish needs take control. "That would be terrific," he told her just as seriously. Forcing himself to be as supportive of her professional goals as she deserved, he continued, "But are you sure you don't want to follow up on the lead your mother gave you for an academic posting?"

Years from now, he didn't want her looking back with regret, or blaming him for any dreams not realized. Because that would be just as detrimental to their relationship as his refusing to support her now.

"I'm certain." Ashley leaned across the table to take his hand and squeeze it affectionately. "I may not have had my priorities straight before this, but I do now," she told him, looking deep into his eyes. "And you, Cal, and the—"

"And what?" he said when she stopped in mid-sentence. He studied the stricken expression on her face.

"And our life together," Ashley finished, flushing self-consciously as she squeezed his hand again and smiled, "come first."

Ashley couldn't believe she had almost spilled the beans like that. Part of it was due to the intimacy she was feeling with Cal, since their mutual confessions last night. Knowing he had missed her as much as she had missed him had given her hope that, with a little more time and continued effort, they could make their marriage everything they had once wanted it to be.

And to that end, black dress or no, she had things she wanted to accomplish that morning. Starting with a talk with the hospital administrator in charge of physician recruitment.

Unfortunately, the situation wasn't as positive as Ashley had hoped it would be.

"We're all set with the number of OB's we need right now," Frank Hodges told her. "But I'll talk to the board anyway, see if there isn't something we can do, because we'd love to have someone with your background and training on our staff. In the meantime, I'll make some calls for you, find out which hospitals in the area need an obstetrician," he said. "I'll get back to you on that as well."

"Thank you. I'd appreciate it," Ashley said.

"Bummer," Carlotta said, when Ashley filled her in over lunch in Carlotta's private office. "I was hoping they'd have room for you so I could ask you to join my practice."

That would have been easy. Nice, too, because she and Carlotta worked together so well. "Something will come up," Ashley said confidently. She would see to it. Even if the position she ended up with did not please her parents.

"How are you feeling?" Carlotta asked, as the two of them worked on their turkey sandwiches.

"Pretty good, actually."

"How's the morning sickness?"

Ashley made a seesawing motion with her hand. "Comes and goes. Cherry Life Savers seem to help."

Carlotta grinned, commiserating with a shake of her head. "For me it was lemon-flavored water. If I could take a sip or two of that, I was usually okay."

"How are things on the home front?" Ashley asked. The usually immaculately put-together Carlotta had a jelly stain on her slacks, and instead of the navy flats she should have been wearing with her outfit, she had on black. "Any word on when Nanny Beatrice is coming back?"

"Another ten days. Minimum." Carlotta sighed. A troubled look crossed her face. "Mateo and I are trying our best, but according to the kids, we're just not cutting it. It's almost like she's the parent and we're the stand-ins."

"Surely—"

"No. It's true." Carlotta speared a baby spinach leaf and twirled it around and around on her fork. "And it makes sense, if you think about it." She glanced over at Ashley, sadness reflected in her dark eyes. "Beatrice cared for Juan from the time he was born. Of course she was just a sitter then; he stayed with her while I was in undergrad classes. It wasn't until Elizabetta was born that Beatrice actually moved in with us. And she was a member of the family by the time Lorenzo came along. The simple truth is that our medical practices are so demanding the kids have spent more time with Beatrice than they have with either of us."

Ashley could easily imagine the same thing happening to her and Cal. "Do you regret that?"

"I don't know." Carlotta gazed at the picture of her kids on her desk. "I'm beginning to think I have missed out on more than I ever knew."

Carlotta's words stayed with Ashley the rest of the day, as she saw patients at the office, and even when she stopped at the grocery on the way home along with everyone else in town to stock up on essentials before the snowstorm hit.

The only problem was there was no milk on the shelves. None. When she asked one of the teenage stock clerks if they could bring out more from the back, he just laughed. "We haven't had any since noon and we're not going to get any more until after the snowstorm."

Ashley supposed there were other ways to get the calcium requirement the baby needed. "When exactly is the storm supposed to get here?" Ashley asked. "Have you heard?"

He pointed to the storefront windows. "Lady, it's here now."

Ashley looked. Sure enough, there was snow coming down in big, fat wet flakes. She wished she had paid more attention to the weather report that morning, and probably would have, had she not been looking high and low for her black dress. "How much is predicted?"

"Radio said a little while ago eight, maybe ten inches."

Yeow. Which meant they could get snowed in out at the farm.

Ashley wheeled her basket down the aisles, putting cottage cheese, yogurt, evaporated—and powdered—milk into her cart. The bread was all gone, too, so she picked up biscuits from the freezer section, and cornbread mix, plus several packages of meat, fresh and frozen vegetables, and cereal. The checkout lines were packed, so she ended up standing in line longer than it had taken her to gather her groceries, but finally she was headed out to the lot.

The pavement was slick, so she navigated carefully. As soon as her groceries were in the trunk of the Mustang, Ashley started the car and cleaned the thin layer of snow off the windows. She was shivering by the time she got back into the car. Aware she couldn't get home a moment too soon, Ashley started the drive back to the farm.

The first four blocks went okay. But as she neared the edge of town the roads suddenly got a lot more dicey.

"This isn't the first time I've ever driven in snow,"

Ashley reminded herself, hands gripping the steering wheel. She had grown up, dealing with winter weather. But she hadn't been pregnant then, Ashley thought worriedly. And she didn't like the way this vintage sports car was handling on the slick city streets.

She was about to turn back, stay in town for the night, or at the very least wait for Cal to drive them home in his SUV, when a teenager came barreling around the corner, going way too fast for either his experience or the weather. Ashley had time to gasp, and steer the wheel to the right, to avoid a head-on collision. And then he was spinning past her, continuing on down the street, completely out of control, while the Mustang jumped the curb and headed straight into someone's front yard.

"Ashley? Are you okay?" Mac Hart asked.

Ashley turned to see her brother-in-law coming toward her. He was wearing his Holly Springs sheriff's uniform. His patrol vehicle was parked at the curb.

"I'm fine." Aware this wasn't the first time Cal's older brother had come to her rescue, Ashley climbed out of the Mustang on shaking legs, aware the snow was coming down even harder now. "I was trying to avoid a collision with another car and ended up jumping the curb." A move that while not exactly laudable had been a lot better than the alternative.

"Yeah. One of the neighbors saw it and called it in. I was in the vicinity, so…"

Ashley drew in a quick, jerky breath, glad Mac had only been a minute or two away when it happened. "That teenager—"

"Just totaled his car. He's about two blocks up. Another officer is assisting him. I don't know how the fool didn't get hurt," Mac lamented with a disgruntled frown.

He bent to look into her face. "You sure you're okay?" he asked her quietly.

Ashley had already done a medical assessment, and except for a slightly accelerated pulse, she had come out of the incident unscathed. "Yes. I was only going about fifteen or twenty miles an hour when I hit the grass." She knew she was pale—a look in the rearview mirror had told her that—and shaky. But those were normal reactions to any near accident. "It just scared me to have such a close call." Ashley shuddered, recalling. "I thought he was going to hit me." She'd thought that she would lose her and Cal's baby. She swallowed hard around the growing knot of emotion in her throat. "But he didn't. And except for the bump as I went over the curb I didn't even get knocked around at all." Her safety belt had held her in place. Although now that she thought about it, a shoulder harness would do a much better job of protecting her and the baby...but those hadn't been invented when the '64 Mustang had been made.

Mac gave her a hard, assessing look. "You want me to take you to the hospital?"

Ashley turned her collar up, and moved so her face was no longer directly in the blowing snow, which seemed to be coming down harder and thicker with every second that passed. She saw a few people beginning to gather in yards, a distance away, watching. "No. That would be a fool's errand. I'm serious, Mac. If I thought there was any reason for me to go to the ER, I would." *In a flash.* "But there isn't. It'd be like going to the doctor for a single hiccup." And she wasn't about to do that.

He was still watching her carefully. "If you say so."

"I do."

He clamped an authoritative hand on her shoulder. "I'm taking you home anyway."

Ashley turned and looked at the Mustang. "I can't just leave my car sitting in someone's front yard." She considered herself fortunate she hadn't taken out any of their trees or landscaping. They probably did, too, although they didn't appear to be home....

"I'll get it out for you," Mac continued to propel her in the direction he wanted her to go.

"My groceries—"

"We'll get those," Mac promised her kindly, as gallant as ever. "But first, I'm putting you in the patrol car."

Mac was nothing if not efficient. Fifteen minutes later, Ashley's Mustang was safely parked in a church lot down the street, and they were on the way out to the farm.

"Thanks for doing this," Ashley said, relieved not to be behind the wheel herself at this moment.

"No problem."

"I needed to talk to you anyway."

Mac lifted a brow, but kept his eyes on the road.

Anxiety welled inside Ashley. She turned her eyes to the side of the road. An inch of snow had already fallen, and it was coming down fast. "I never told Cal about what happened that day you took me to the hospital."

Expression grim, Mac adjusted the windshield wipers to a higher speed. He shot her a quick glance. "So he doesn't know you were ever—"

*Pregnant,* Ashley thought. "No." Another chill went through her. She folded her arms in front of her. "And I don't want him to know."

Mac adjusted the heat, so more of it was flowing directly onto Ashley. "Do you think that's wise?"

Good question, and one she had asked herself maybe half a million times. "I probably should have told him at the time, but you know why I didn't." Because she hadn't known how to tell him he had lost what he had never even known he had. "And now it's too late." Ashley's voice caught, tears pressing behind her eyes. "He'd never understand."

When they stopped at the next stop sign, Mac turned and regarded Ashley with concern. "He has a right to know, Ashley."

As Mac continued driving, guilt flooded her heart that she could ever have done something so short-sighted and foolish in the first place. "I would tell him, Mac, if I thought he could forgive me for keeping something like that from him, but—" Ashley's voice trembled and she had to force herself to go on "—I know now that he wouldn't be able to, and I don't want to risk my marriage for something that can never be changed anyway." Because as much as she wanted to undo the past, she just couldn't.

Mac looked as if he still disagreed with her, but he did not argue the point further.

"What's brought this all up?" he asked compassionately.

Ashley took a deep breath. Although she knew she could confide in Mac and trust him to keep whatever she chose to tell him secret, there was no way she was letting him know what Cal still didn't.

Not this time anyway.

"Cal and I are working on our marriage," she said simply. "I don't want anything to interfere with that." Nothing from the present, and certainly nothing from the past.

"I knew it! You're not fine!" Cal rushed into the family room, where Ashley was reclining on the sofa before the fire. He had thrown a coat on over his scrubs. His med-center badge was still clipped to his shirt.

Ashley tried not to make too much of the fact he had

left the hospital before changing into his street clothes, something he never did. She flushed self-consciously, aware she had been "resting" pretty much ever since she got home. Not because it was medically indicated—but because she wanted their baby to know she would do whatever it took to ensure he or she came into the world, healthy, happy and safe. This time there were going to be no regrets, no "what if's" or "if only's." No looking back and wondering…

She put the decorating magazine she'd been reading before falling asleep on the sofa aside. "I gather from that wild look in your eyes that you heard about my mishap with the Mustang?"

Cal grinned wryly in response to her comically ex-aggerated description, but the serious light remained in his eyes. He took off his coat and sank down beside her on the sofa, next to her raised knees. "Mac came by the med center and told me in person." Cal paled slightly as he continued relating, "He didn't want me seeing the Mustang parked there when I was driving home, 'cause he'd figured I would wonder why it was there when you weren't and get all worried. And dammit, Ashley—" Cal's brows knit together in aggravation, as he continued scolding her "—why didn't you *call* me and let me know what happened yourself?"

*Because if I had talked to you on the phone just then I probably would have burst into tears for no good reason other than I love you and don't want to lose you.* And the incident had reminded her that they could lose each other, just that quickly, should luck and wisdom not be on their sides next time.

But she didn't know how to say any of that without sounding…pregnant.

Ashley sighed and ran her hands through her hair. She

had left the blinds open, and outside she could see darkness had fallen. The snow was now three or four inches deep and still coming down.

Cal continued to wait for an explanation.

Ashley gestured helplessly. "Because I knew you were in surgery this afternoon and I was fine. So I figured I would tell you when you got home *which I would have* had your big brother not beaten me to it."

He took the blanket off her lap and visually checked her out, his hands moving over her limbs as if he were conducting a medical exam. He seemed barely able to reassure himself. "You're absolutely sure you're fine?" he insisted.

"Yes," Ashley retorted firmly. She batted his hands away. "Now stop playing doctor, Doctor," Ashley teased, capturing his hands in hers. "And take a breath and calm down."

Cal's eyes grew abruptly moist. "I couldn't bear it if anything happened to you," he told her in a low, hoarse voice.

That quickly, Ashley got choked up, too. She went into Cal's arms and hung on tight. "I don't want anything happening to you, either."

He held her to him fiercely and they clung together like that for several minutes. Eventually, she heard Cal's voice muffled against her hair. "You can't scare me like that again. I mean it, Ashley. Anything happens, you let me know. *Right then.*"

Guilt flashed through her, more potent than a tidal wave. Ashley closed her eyes against the pain in her heart. "I promise," she said thickly. "I won't ever ever hold anything back from you again."

The present, the future, she could fix.

It was the past she couldn't control.

* * *

"It's still snowing." Cal stared out the kitchen windows in amazement. At 11:00 p.m., there was a good six inches on the ground. The trees were coated in white and moonlight reflected off the snow, giving everything a tranquil wintry glow.

"It's been so long since I've seen snow," Ashley murmured, appreciating the beauty of the big fat white flakes still falling from the sky. She shook her head wistfully. "I wish I could go out in it."

Cal came up behind her and wreathed his arms around her waist. He buried his nose in the hair on the top of her head. Their bodies touched in a warm, electric line. "So what's holding you back?"

"We're not kids."

He guided her around to face him and winked at her playfully. "That's not what you said when we were playing hide-and-seek last night."

Ashley laughed softly. "As I recall, that game had a very sexy ending." She still tingled every time she remembered his hot, passionate kisses.

A speculative gleam came into his eyes as he leaned close. "So could this one."

Ashley flushed at the sensual promise in his low tone. "Not in the snow," she protested. It was too cold to stand out there, kissing.

But Cal was not to be dissuaded. "It could start there," he told her affably, already off collecting their cold-weather gear. "But it would end up before the fire."

Ashley let him help her on with her winter coat. Still of a mind for the ultimate in comfort, she said, "Or in the bed upstairs."

Cal stopped suddenly and stared at her. "You really want to make love tonight?"

Why were they still holding back? Hadn't they already proven there was a lot of love—and life—left in their marriage?

"Maybe," Ashley allowed cautiously.

He grinned as he helped her on with her boots.

*Then again...* Ashley bit her lip, unable to decide. She wanted Cal. No question. On the other hand, their no-sex situation definitely had them communicating a lot more, and that had them getting closer than ever. "Or maybe not," Ashley said finally.

Cal shrugged on his own coat, stepped into his boots. "Playing hard to get?"

*Maybe. And maybe I'm just scared that one step in the wrong direction would have us feeling distant and alone again.* Wanting to keep the light mood, she batted her eyelashes at him flirtatiously. "Is it working?" she asked him dryly.

Cal thrust out his chest. Every muscle in his body looked taut, ready for action. He tilted his head slightly to one side. "You know us competitive types, when it comes to challenges..."

Ashley managed not to smile, but could do nothing about the happiness glittering in her eyes. "Hmmmm."

They stepped outside, still inching on their gloves. "You know what this reminds me of?" Cal asked as he took her hand and they trudged through snow piled on the front porch, down the porch steps and in great drifts on the ground.

Ashley savored the feeling of being there with him. "What?"

"The first year we were dating," Cal said as they walked through the stillness of the cold winter night, their breath forming frosty puffs of air. "When you were a freshman at the university and I was in first year in medical school."

"And sometimes the only time we could make our schedules mesh and see each other was late at night," Ashley finished for him.

Cal nodded, remembering. "And we used to walk around campus. And talk. And go to the library and stay up all night, studying. And then go have breakfast."

*I felt so close to you then.* Ashley smiled at him affectionately. "Those were fun times," she said quietly.

He considered her for a moment. "We still have fun times ahead."

Looking into his eyes, she believed him.

"In fact," Cal continued playfully, "we could have a fun time now." He ducked down and came up with a handful of snow. A few running steps backwards, and a ball was arcing her way.

It hit her in the shoulder just as Ashley was reaching down to scoop up a palm full of snow herself. By the time she had it patted into an orb, he'd hit her two more times, once in the thigh, the other ball had ghosted across the top of her head. Grimacing, Ashley threw hers and…missed.

Laughing, Cal looked as if he were a superhero operating in fast-forward. He circled around her and hit her four more times, while Ashley stayed her ground, boot-clad feet firmly planted in the snow.

Cal darted back around to face her. He stopped just short of her, rubbed his gloved hand across his jaw. "You know," he drawled thoughtfully, "you'd come out better if you ran a little instead of just standing there, taking all my hits."

"You think I got a raw deal?" Ashley shook herself from head to toe. To little avail, as there was still snow all over her. Ashley knelt and got another handful of snow, then straightened to her full height.

"Didn't you?" he said.

"Well, let's see." Ashley tranquilly continued shaping her weapon. "Which one of us is all out of breath?"

"Clever." He came toward her to take her in his arms. As he reached her, she rubbed her snowball into the back of his neck. He grimaced as the cold wet stuff went down his shirt, and he looked at her as if he had expected her to do something just like that to him before all was said and done. "You know I'm going to have to punish you for that."

"Now, Cal," Ashley said, laughing at the teasing expression on his face. She put her hands up in front of her. "You wouldn't hurt a lady."

"Maybe not with snow," Cal allowed wickedly. "But I'm not promising anything…about…my lips." He caught her around the waist and tugged her close. The next thing she knew her eyes were closing and his mouth was on hers. His lips were cold and the inside of his mouth was hot. Feeling as though she had come home again, as though she had found her heart again at long last, Ashley melted into the kiss, melted into him.

"Okay, you win. I surrender," she whispered finally, winding her arms about his neck and kissing him back with all the pent-up passion she had inside her.

Cal stroked his hands down her back. "We've got all night. Playtime doesn't have to be over…yet." Cal flashed her a mischievous grin as he tugged on a lock of her hair. "You want another chance? I'll let you have a running start."

Ashley shook her head. Serious now, she kissed his jaw, his cheek, his lips. "I'm not ever running from you again."

\* \* \*

"Ashley, this is ridiculous," Cal murmured from the other side of the locked bedroom door.

"Says the person with the perfect body." She opened the door and motioned him in.

In no hurry—he wanted the night to last forever—Cal followed her inside, drinking in the compelling fragrance of her orange blossom perfume. The master bedroom was softly lit and he took the opportunity to admire the way Ashley filled out her pale-yellow flannel nightshirt. The rounded fullness of her breasts and pouting nipples pressed against the soft cotton, a hint of cleavage visible in the notched collar. His whole body tightened as his gaze dropped lower, and he took in the sexy swell of her hips, the hint of long slender thighs visible beneath the knee-length hem, sexy calves, trim ankles and dainty feet. Honestly, he didn't see what she was so self-conscious about! He smiled in sincere reverence. "You look perfect to me."

Ashley flushed, her gaze drifting over his gray jersey boxers and the arousal clearly visible beneath. "Well, I'm glad you like it." Her glance went to the apex of his thighs before she dashed back to the bed and climbed beneath the covers, which were promptly pulled to her chin.

Abruptly, she looked as nervous as a virgin on her wedding night. "Now turn out the lights," she ordered even more hastily.

As confused as ever, Cal obliged nonetheless and climbed beneath the covers beside her. Maybe this new phobia of hers was something they should talk out, he reasoned. Delaying the moment that he took her in his arms, and losing sight of everything but making her his once again, he reached over and stroked a lock of her dark silky hair. "I don't get it." He let his eyes adjust to the darkness of the bedroom. "You used to really like making love with the lights on."

Ashley sighed and cuddled closer. She turned onto her side, facing him, and ran her palm across the bareness of his chest. "And one day soon I will again."

He felt her hands stroke his shoulders, upper arms, before moving back to the mat of hair on the center of his chest. "Just not right now?"

She leaned down to kiss the U of his collarbone. "I'm feeling a little shy," she continued breathlessly.

Cal could have sworn from the tone of her voice that she was fibbing. He took her hand and pressed it to his lips. Then he kissed the inside of her wrist and forearm. "I was able to help you with that once," he whispered back as her skin heated and she trembled against his lips.

Ashley took his chin in hand and held it still as she brought her mouth to his. She wanted him and let him know it with a sweet, searing kiss. "You don't need to remind me you're the one who helped me lose my virginity."

Deciding she had been in the driver's seat long enough, he turned her onto her back and moved his body over hers. The timing of their encounter and the darkness of the bedroom may have been her call, but in what fashion they actually made love for the first time since she had been back home was going to be his.

"Now that was a fun night." He used his knee to separate hers and slipped between her thighs. Taking both her hands in his, he lifted them up over her head and pinned them there, then moved up, until his arousal fit against her femininity. Her breath caught at the intimate contact. The cotton of their undergarments provided a pleasurable friction.

Still holding her wrists in one hand, he threaded his

other hand beneath the nape of her neck, and angling her head beneath his, he kissed the top of her head, her temple, the sensitive place behind her ear. She shifted beneath him restlessly, moaning as he found his way to her other ear.

"Cal."

"Hmm."

"I want you," she whispered as he lifted the soft veil of her hair and kissed his way down the exposed line of her throat to the U of her collarbone.

"I want you, too," he murmured. Bending his head, he took advantage of the languid ribbon of desire threading through her, kissed her full on the mouth, until a hot flush swept through her entire body and her toes curled against the mattress. Then he kissed her again. And again. And again, knowing no matter how long they were together, he would never get enough of her. Never stop desiring her. Cal had been wanting to make love to Ashley for days now. And his desire was a helluva lot more than just a search for physical release. He wanted to kiss her, touch her and possess her, make her see how right they were together. He wanted her to see how much they were meant to be together, not just for now or next week, but forever. And the best way he knew to do that was by letting their emotions run wild in hot, fevered kisses and caresses, marathon lovemaking sessions and nights spent cuddled in each other's arms.

Whether she wanted to admit it or not, Ashley had been his from the moment they had made love for the first time, years ago, and she always would be, just as he was hers, and hers alone.

A lot of things had driven them apart. Things he still didn't understand. But when he held her in his arms like this, when he kissed her and she kissed him back, he wanted Ashley as he had never wanted any woman. More telling was the fact that he needed her just as desperately. And judging by the way she was clinging to him, she needed him, too.

He was already undoing the buttons on her nightshirt. Tendrils of white heat swept through her as his mouth moved sensually on the hollow between her breasts, then returned with devastating softness to her mouth.

"Tell me you're not too shy for...this," he whispered in a low sexy voice that stirred her senses, as he deepened the kiss and slipped his hand inside to cup the soft curve of her breast.

Ashley arched against him, unable to think of a time, since first meeting Cal, when she hadn't wanted him more than life. He was everything to her, so much more than just her husband...so much more than he ever knew. "You know I'm not," she moaned as his fingertips closed over her nipple, massaging it to a point, then he followed it with his mouth. The pleasure was almost unbearable; everything around her went soft and fuzzy except for the gentle caresses of his lips and teeth and tongue. How was it that he always knew just how to kiss her and touch her? she wondered dizzily, as the familiar feeling of tenderness and excitement swept through her. How was it that he could always make her want to give up everything for him? How was it that he could make her feel so damn good, and so damn vulnerable, all at once? All she knew for sure was that he was so strong and wonderful. He tasted—and felt—so good, so undeniably male, so right.

Cal chuckled softly. "How about this?" he murmured in masculine satisfaction, sliding ever downward and tasting the silky stretch of skin across her ribs.

Ashley's desire to keep a self-protective wall between them faded and she made a soft, yielding sound as he dipped his tongue into her navel. Then he was letting go of her hands, divesting her of her nightshirt. Desire trembled inside her, her tummy feeling weightless, soft. Heat swept through her. Her whole body straining against him, she gave an exultant cry as he slid lower yet, ran his palms across her thighs and found her…there.

The swiftness of her pinnacle caught them both by surprise, as did her wantonness and lack of restraint. The next thing she knew he was slipping off his boxers with the same sense of unbridled urgency. Moving over her once again in the moonlit shadows of their bedroom, he parted her thighs and slid in between. He raised her knees, and entered her—slowly, deliberately—watching her face as he did so. Joy swept through her as their bodies became one and the boundaries that still existed between them dissolved. For the first time in what seemed forever, she felt as if they were really husband and wife. Equal partners. Lovers.

Cal brought her even closer, so her breasts were pressed against the unyielding hardness of his chest. Their mouths mated, just as their bodies did, in one hot, incredible, endless kiss that went on and on…until her breaths were as short and shallow as his, and he was obliging her with ever deepening thrusts that she met with a wild abandonment of her own. Until she was experiencing everything it was possible to feel. Loving him without restraint, and still not able to get enough of him… would never be able to get enough of him.

Just when she thought she could stand it no more, he slipped a hand between their bodies. Her hips rose instinctively to meet him as he touched and rubbed and stroked, and loved her with an intensity that took her breath away. And then there was no more thinking, only feeling. Her heart soared and he took full possession of her. She urged him on, her body tightening implacably around his. He thrust forward, surging completely into her, and then all was lost in the intimate physical passion that defined their marriage.

## Chapter 10

The pain came out of nowhere. One minute Ashley was walking down a street in Charlotte, North Carolina, with her brother-in-law, the next she was doubled over in agony.

"Ashley?" Mac wrapped a strong arm about her waist. "What is it?"

Ashley felt the warm liquid running down her legs, even before she saw the drop of blood hit the sidewalk. "Oh, God, no," she cried. "No…" This couldn't be happening. She couldn't be losing Cal's baby!

"Ashley! Come on, Ashley. Wake up, honey."

With difficulty, Ashley opened her eyes. The lights in their bedroom were on. Cal was bending over her, a concerned look on his face. Her face was damp with tears and, to her horror, she heard herself sobbing out loud.

Cal's hands tightened protectively over her shoulders

as she struggled to get control of herself. "It was just a dream, honey."

"More like a nightmare." Ashley sat up, wiping the tears from her face.

Cal let her go, albeit reluctantly. "You were calling Mac's name."

A cold chill went through her. "What else did I say?"

"Nothing that made any sense. Just 'No. This can't be happening. God, no.' Things like that." Cal paused. "Were you dreaming about your car going off the road this afternoon?"

Ashley shuddered as another chill swept through her, more devastating than the first. She turned her glance away from Cal's and buried her face in her hands. "I must've been. I—I just know I was really scared something awful was about to happen."

She swallowed hard and threw her legs over the side of the bed. One hand went to her abdomen, testing. To her relief there was no pain. She seemed fine. The baby seemed fine. "I think I need to get up and walk around," she said. "Shake it off. Maybe go down to the kitchen and get some warm milk or something."

"Good idea," Cal said. "I'll join you." He got out of bed and went to the closet to get his flannel robe. He was shrugging it on as Ashley disappeared into the bathroom.

To her relief, there was no blood. Nothing to indicate cause for alarm. Which meant, it had only been a dream. Brought on, no doubt, by what had happened earlier... and her guilt.

Mac had been right about one thing, Ashley thought. Keeping secrets from your spouse was a hell of a way to live.

She was going to have to tell Cal what had happened

someday. And she would, just as soon as she felt their marriage was strong enough to handle it.

"I don't know how you're going to feel about this," Cal said. "I know I just bought you that Mustang. But I think we need to trade it in for something with airbags, all-wheel drive and antilock brakes."

Ashley thought about the baby she was carrying, and how devastated she would be if anything happened, especially something that could easily have been prevented by a little common sense on their part. "I think you're right."

"Sentiment is one thing."

"Safety another."

He stirred the milk in the saucepan on the stove. "You want me to put some cocoa in this?"

"Thanks, but the caffeine might keep me awake. If you want some, though—" Ashley knew Cal was no fan of plain warm milk.

"How about a dash of vanilla then and a little bit of sugar?"

"Okay."

He added both to the pan, then poured the steaming milk into two mugs and joined her at the kitchen table. Outside, it was still snowing.

"There's something that's been bothering me. You remember that argument we had right before you accepted the fellowship in Hawaii?"

How could she have forgotten? That had ranked as one of the lowest days of their entire marriage. "The one about me not wanting to have a baby until after I finished my fellowship and settled into a job?"

Cal nodded. "I accused you of reneging on a pretty fundamental part of our marriage."

"It just wasn't the right time."

"I know that now. It was unfair of me even to bring it up. I just want you to know I'm sorry for having said the things I did that day. For the record, I think you'd be a phenomenal mother. But if you decide that isn't what you want, if you can't do it all, I understand—because you are an incredible doctor. And someone with your gift should be practicing medicine."

Ashley's heart began to pound. She regarded him warily. "You're saying it'd be okay if I didn't have a child?"

Cal gestured offhandedly, then stood and went to the cupboards. He rummaged around until he found a box of vanilla shortbread cookies and brought them back to the table. "I'm saying that my rose-colored glasses are off. I've seen other two-physician families trying to juggle everything simultaneously. It's not an easy road." He paused. "So if medicine is all you feel you can realistically handle, then—" he swallowed, making light of the enormous sacrifice Ashley knew he was making "—I'm okay with that, too."

Two and a half years before, fresh from a devastating loss she wasn't at all sure she would be able to bear, never mind go through again, Ashley would have welcomed such a free pass from her husband.

Now, full of hope and joy and fear once again, Ashley's outlook was much different.

But if the same thing happened that had happened before, if she found out she was flawed in some fundamental way, she was going to need Cal to keep thinking this way.

Her feelings in turmoil, her knees shaking beneath the hem of her flannel nightshirt, Ashley stood and went to the kitchen window. She looked outside, at the big white flakes still coming down from the sky. "I can't believe it's still snowing," she murmured.

She heard Cal push back his chair and close the distance between them. Standing behind her, he wrapped his arms around her waist and buried his face in her hair. "I love you," he murmured softly.

Tears filled Ashley's eyes. "I love you, too." She turned so she was facing him. Going up on tiptoe, she pressed her lips to his, the yearning to have nothing standing between them stronger than ever. "So very much..." Then his mouth was on hers in a kiss that was shattering in its possessiveness. He kissed her until desire streamed over her, until she was warm and safe, until she knew as well as he that their making love to each other again was inevitable.

Ashley took Cal's hand in hers. "Upstairs," she murmured.

He looked both disappointed they weren't going to make love then and there—and intrigued to find out what was on her mind.

Bypassing the guest room and the comfort of the master bedroom, she led the way into the master bath. "The stipulation of only-in-the-dark has been lifted?" Cal asked hopefully.

Her actions a lazy counterpoint to his, Ashley shook her head. "Not...exactly." She led him into the shower/ steam room big enough for two, and over to the long marble bench against one wall. Curling a hand around the swell of his bicep, she urged him to sit down in the center of it.

He shifted so he could look up at her, his rock-hard thigh bumping up against her knee. "This is getting interesting," Cal said.

Ashley grinned. She needed something to get her mind

off the nightmare she'd had. A little playtime was just the thing. "Stay right there," she teased, aware just how easy it would be to get used to being with Cal like this and making love with him every night, instead of just every few weeks.

"Believe me. I wouldn't think of moving," Cal drawled.

Ashley sent Cal a coy look—glad to surprise him with something he desired for once—went back into the bedroom and returned with two candles. She set them on the long marble counter beside the sinks. Aware Cal was watching every move she made, his glance moving lazily over her newly voluptuous figure, she paused to light the candles and then turned off the overhead lights. The entire bath was ensconced in a mellow romantic glow. "Nice," Cal murmured, his voice moving over her like a soft warm blanket.

Ignoring the jump in her pulse—it wouldn't do to get too excited too soon—Ashley grabbed a couple of bath sheets and stepped into the enclosed glass shower with him. She turned on the handheld showerhead, adjusted the water streaming out of it to a nice, warm temperature, then temporarily shut off the flow and moved toward him. She set the sprayer down on the bench next to him. "This has to come off." She helped him out of his robe. "And this." She knelt to ease his boxers down his legs.

Cal shook his head in amusement. "How about you?" Looking ready to strip her down, too, he plucked at the hem of her nightshirt.

Trying not to thrill at the possessiveness in his low voice, she disengaged his fingers from the soft cotton flannel. "'Fraid not."

"Ah."

"Trust me. In a few minutes you'll forget all about wanting me naked."

"I don't know that I'd bet on that," Cal told her as she ran the sprayer over his body, wetting down his satiny, hard-muscled flesh.

A sexy smile on her face, Ashley lathered up the sponge with his favorite soap. "Just relax."

"I hate to tell you, Ashley," Cal said, looking all the more mesmerized by what she had planned for them, "but when you're soaping me up where you're currently soaping me up, I'm up not going to be relaxing anytime soon."

"You're right." She held the length of the most male part of him in her hand. Her confidence building, Ashley grinned. "You only seem to be getting more excited."

Cal groaned, this time making no effort to contain his pleasure.

Ashley caressed him daringly. "Maybe I can do something to soothe you."

He made a sound that was part chuckle, part groan. Let his head fall back. "Much more of this and I'm going to be way ahead of us both."

Trying not to think about how his lips felt moving over hers, or how much she wished she could race on ahead of what she had planned and kiss him again, Ashley continued her pattern of lazily soaping and rinsing and flirted back instead, "So I'll catch up."

Cal sighed, his expression one of pure ecstasy as she worked her way across his chest. He leaned closer, bringing with him the tantalizing fragrance of soap and damp masculine flesh. "You're right about that."

Being careful not to get too close lest she lose her focus, Ashley had him lean forward, so she could do his back. "Meantime, I'm in the driver's seat right now," she said as she gently washed his broad shoulders and beautiful back. "So to speak."

Cal smiled at her in a way that could have inspired

a thousand love songs. "Yes," he said softly, "you certainly are."

Although she could tell that if he had his way it wouldn't be for long.

Her pulse racing, Ashley made her way back to the most intimate part of him again. As she lathered up his inner thighs, she could see him begin to throb in much the same way she had earlier. Pleased to have the same effect on him as he'd had on her, Ashley smiled in a way that raised the stakes another notch "Close your eyes," she instructed softly. *I want to drive you wild.*

He shook his head and replied in a voice that sent shivers of awareness ghosting over her, "I think I'd rather watch."

Ashley felt her nipples tighten. And he hadn't even touched her yet. Except with his eyes. She swallowed around the sudden tightening of her throat. Lower still, there was a sudden equally telling dampness between her thighs. "Okay, then." Ashley backed up subtly, putting a tad more space between them. "Watch. Just let me do… what it is I want to do…"

"All right," he said as the air around them grew hot and steamy, and the air between them reverberated with excitement and escalating desire. "You win," he said gruffly, teasing.

When he could bear her torturous seduction no more, he pulled her against him. Mindful of her determination not to let him figure out what she had yet to tell him, Ashley reached beneath her nightshirt. She drew her panties down and off and then knelt astride him, one knee on the long bench on either side of them.

Achingly aware of every hard, muscular inch of him, Ashley dropped her head, lowered her mouth to his and let him lead her where he wanted her to go. She whimpered as he delayed entering her and kissed her with a passion so hot it sizzled.

One hand on her waist, holding her precisely where he yearned to have her, he used the other to stroke, touch, explore. She trembled and he kissed her again, taking her mouth in a caress that was so intimate it had not an ounce of restraint. Her skin grew hot and damp, and her thighs splayed to better accommodate his searching fingertips. Until her breath caught in her throat. "Cal, I can't..."

"I know," he rasped back, leaving a trail of burning kisses across her neck. He cupped her breasts through the fabric of her nightshirt. "I feel the same..."

And then she was whimpering again—this time in frustration, moving down onto him, taking the hot velvety length of him all the way inside her. His hands caught her hips, dictating the slow, sensual rhythm. Commanding everything she had to give, while at the same time giving back everything she had ever wanted, everything she had dreamed...

Again and again, Ashley tempted and teased him, driving them both mad with desire. Withdrawing nearly all the way, then lowering again, closing tight. Until she was able to hear the soft, whimpering sounds in her throat, and the fiercer sounds in the back of his. Until sensations inside her ran riot, thrilling, enticing.

Her spirits soared as he pressed into her as deeply as he could go, making her his, letting her know he was as wild for her as she was for him.

Needing him the way she had never needed him before, wanting to feel connected to him, not just in body, but heart and soul, Ashley continued to kiss Cal back as thoroughly and passionately as he kissed her. Her heart was beating in urgent rhythm to his, and her love for her husband was pouring through her. They took each other to heights and depths they had yet to discover, until they were both lost in the pleasure and in one another. And this time, when they lost control, and surged heedlessly into ecstasy, something changed.

This time, Ashley knew, there was no turning back or away.

No hiding behind the demands of her chosen career.

Or the expectations of her parents, teachers and colleagues.

She had one future. With Cal. And the baby he still knew nothing about.

"Not that you don't already know this, but you and the baby are both fine," Carlotta said the next morning when she and Ashley met at Carlotta's office to compare notes and review patient charts.

Ashley had known that, even before she'd had her friend take a look at her, before they got started on their conferencing. Still a kaleidoscope of emotions twisted through her. She didn't know why she was so nervous about this pregnancy. Was it because of what had happened before? Her guilt over not telling Cal yet? Or just the pregnancy hormones that were making her fiercely protective, and on edge? "That's good to hear," Ashley said finally, as she got off the exam table and adjusted her clothing.

"But," Carlotta continued gently but sternly, as the two women continued on down the hall to Carlotta's private office, "if you were worried you should have gone to the ER yesterday or called me, and I would have come back to the office and examined you."

Ashley knew all that, but it hadn't been necessary. Her mishap with the car had been just that. She'd been more upset about what could have happened, than what actually had.

"So why didn't you at least call me and let me know what had occurred?" Carlotta continued, as she shut the door behind them.

Ashley frowned, knowing she had to be completely honest with someone. She dropped into a seat while Carlotta took the chair behind her desk. "I was with Mac and I didn't want him figuring out I was pregnant," Ashley said.

Carlotta picked up a stack of charts. "Did you think he would tell Cal?"

"No." Ashley turned a ballpoint pen end over end. "Not if I asked him not to do so. Mac can keep a secret." He had certainly done so for her in the past. There had been another reason why she hadn't wanted Mac to find out. Ashley clamped her lips together determinedly. She looked her friend in the eye. "The first man who's going to know about this baby I'm carrying is Cal."

Carlotta's gaze softened compassionately. This, she understood full well. "So tell him," Carlotta advised, one woman to another.

Ashley tensed up again. She got up to pace the small confines of the room and pull two soda cans from the small fridge in the corner. "I can't. Not yet."

"Because of what happened the last time?" Carlotta took a diet cola while Ashley kept the caffeine-free regular soda. Carlotta popped the lid. "Ashley, you know that wasn't your fault!"

Ashley wished she could believe that. She sighed wearily, took a sip of her lemon-and-lime flavored beverage. "I should have taken better care of myself. Realized that twice weekly thirty-six-hour shifts and a pregnancy don't mix."

Carlotta scowled, flat-out disagreeing. "If that baby had been meant to be born, it would have been—no matter what hours you kept or how you rationed your sleep," she lectured. "Your miscarriage was due to the fact that the placenta was abnormal and could not have supported a baby. There's absolutely no indication the same thing will happen this time around. Everything looks normal. And you're only two weeks away from the three-month mark."

"After which time my chances of miscarrying again go down drastically," Ashley recited the information she had been over countless times herself. Information she had no trouble believing when it came to someone else.

"Right."

Struggling with a mixture of fear and relief, she looked Carlotta in the eye. "I'm an obstetrician. I know all this."

"And yet?"

Ashley shook her head, knowing she had to talk to someone. "I'm scared, Carlotta," she said quietly.

Carlotta looked at her with the wisdom of a woman who had been happily married for years. "Cal could be a great help to you right now, Ashley," Carlotta said quietly.

Ashley knew that. And yet… "I don't want him to have to worry the way I'm worrying. It's bad enough I'm going through it." She felt the tears rise to burn the backs of her eyes. "Besides…" She blinked them back in frustration, hating this sign of weakness in herself. She ought to be gutsier when it came to Cal. Heaven knew she didn't have trouble communicating her needs or answering his in bed. It was out of bed, when they were talking about everything else—their relationship, careers, whether or when to have kids—that she struggled. As did he.

"He still doesn't know about the previous pregnancy?"

Ashley shook her head miserably.

"Oh, honey, and I thought my life was a mess."

Ashley wiped away her tears. "Let's talk about your life. How are you and Mateo and the kids doing without Beatrice?"

It was Carlotta's turn to look conflicted. "Well, the good news is the kids are beginning to accept me as Mommy."

Ashley paused, confused. "You've always been Mommy."

"I thought I was Mommy," Carlotta corrected, ruefully. "I think Beatrice was Mommy." Carlotta paused, looking more torn than ever as she ran a finger around the outside of her soda can. "The truth is, I've been missing in action more than I've been around. I was never there to bathe them and feed them and read them stories at night, at least not in an everyday way. Beatrice did all that. So it makes sense they would look to her for the comfort they need, not me. Since she has been gone and Mateo and I were forced to step in, that's begun to change. We realize what we've been missing, and so do they."

"You're saying what? That being a doctor and a mother don't mix?"

"No." Carlotta relaxed slightly. "I'm just saying I think I've been doing a less stellar job on the mommy front than I thought. I'm glad Beatrice has been with us, and I'm very glad that she is coming back in another eight days to be an invaluable presence in all our lives again."

"But?" Ashley discovered her heart was pounding.

Carlotta shook her head. "I'm beginning to realize that with three kids and a husband and a thriving practice, something's gotta give. I just haven't figured out what yet."

"If I were the jealous type, you'd be in trouble about now," Cal told Mac the next day as the two of them climbed out of Mac's SUV, picked up their shovels and headed for the Mustang. It was just where Mac had left it, surrounded by a foot and a half of drifting snow on all sides.

Mac furrowed his brow as if wondering where this conversation was headed.

"Ashley had a nightmare last night and she called out your name," Cal explained as the two of them trudged through the mostly empty church parking lot near the edge of town.

Mac stuck the blade of his shovel in the snow and purposefully began to clear a path. "If I was in her dream, it probably *was* a nightmare," Mac quipped.

Cal chuckled at the joke, before turning serious once again. "I think her nightmare was provoked by the mishap she had with the Mustang yesterday."

The blades of their shovels scraped steadily against the blacktop beneath. "Yeah, she was pretty shaken up for such a minor event," Mac reflected. "Of course I guess any time you lose control of your vehicle, it's frightening," he said as he threw another load of snow onto the lawn. "Particularly for someone who hasn't driven in the snow for several years."

"Except," Cal theorized slowly, "Ashley is normally such a together woman. I mean, nothing fazes her." He watched as their breaths materialized in the cold winter air. "But this did." More so than he would have expected.

"What are you saying?" Mac asked. He paused to wipe the sweat from his brow.

"I'm not sure." Cal had cleared enough to get the trunk open. He extracted the long-handled ice scraper. "I know it sounds ridiculous, but I keep thinking there is something she isn't telling me."

His face expressionless, Mac continued shoveling

while Cal cleared snow off the top of the Mustang. "Have you asked her about it?"

Cal squinted against the glare of the sun bouncing off the snow. Was it his imagination or was his brother now the one acting almost too cool for comfort? "Sort of."

Mac looked at Cal down the bridge of his nose. "What do you mean you 'sort of' asked her?" Mac demanded, whatever else he was thinking hidden behind his aviator-style sunglasses.

Uncomfortable with the close scrutiny, Cal shrugged. "It's not an easy thing to do without coming off like I'm accusing her of something, only I don't know exactly what. I don't think that would be a good way to get our marriage back on track."

Worse than the gnawing suspicion in his gut was the feeling of foolishness accompanying it.

"Speaking of your marriage, how are things going now that Ashley is back on the mainland?"

"Lots better." Cal liked being able to confide in his older brother, knowing that these days anyway, he could trust Mac not to keep him out of the loop on family matters. "Except for her calling-out-your-name-in-her-sleep thing," Cal added wryly.

"Well, there's one way to fix that." Mac flashed a devil-may-care grin.

"Get her to call out mine first?" Cal guessed in a low deadpan tone.

Mac slapped Cal on the shoulder. "Sounds like you've got your work cut out for you, little brother."

## Chapter 11

No doubt about it, Ashley thought several days later as she looked at herself in the mirror. The pants that had been loose when she had purchased them two and a half weeks earlier were not "roomy" any longer. She could still get the zipper up with nary a struggle but, realistically, she wasn't sure how much longer that was going to last. Or even if, ten days from now, when she hit the three-month mark and could finally tell Cal about the baby, they would still fit.

She had gained only another three pounds, according to the scale, but that combined with the five she had gained in the first two months, seemed to have gone straight to her waist and hips.

"What I ought to do is just go to the maternity store and buy some pants that don't look like maternity slacks," Ashley mumbled to herself as she turned this way and that, examining the new pudginess of her torso.

But, fear that if she did that, one of the women in the family would recognize the trousers as pregnancy clothing kept her from doing it. And anyway, there were only ten more days. After that she would no longer have to protect her husband. She could tell Cal he was about to become a daddy and buy herself some clothing more suited for a mommy-to-be.

"What are you doing? And why are you muttering to yourself?" Cal asked from the open doorway. He, too, was getting ready to go to work. He was freshly shaven and his ash-blond hair was damp and scented with shampoo. Shoeless, his shirt open and untucked, he looked so sexy and handsome he took her breath away.

"I'm not doing anything." Ashley swiftly released the hem of her burgundy turtleneck sweater, so it fell back over her hips.

He closed the distance between them in three lazy strides. He lifted his brow. "You were obsessing over your figure again, weren't you?"

Ashley battled a self-conscious flush.

"I wish you'd just relax about it," Cal said, wrapping his arms around her waist. "And let me see you naked again."

Ashley wanted that, too, if only because it would mean she could see him naked. She had always enjoyed the sight of his handsome, well-honed body. Soon, she promised herself, there would be no more secrets between them. No more reason to hold him at arm's length. She turned around, so they were face to face, and tipped her head back. "I've got to start working out first," she stalled.

And she knew what she was going to do, just as soon as she had time—a pregnancy yoga routine.

Tightening his hold on her, he kissed his way down

her neck. "You've got everything you need right down the hall."

He had been very generous when it came to outfitting their new home "gym." Deciding it would be best for both of them if he weren't quite so undressed, she began buttoning his shirt, from the hem, up. "I know." As her fingers brushed his fly, she couldn't help but note his arousal.

Soon, it matched her own. It seemed she couldn't be near him like this without feeling that telltale flutter in her middle, and the tightening of her breasts.

"Yet I haven't seen you on the bike or the treadmill," Cal continued, gently stroking his hands through her hair.

The truth was, Ashley was afraid to get on the fitness machines. Afraid that if she stressed her body in the slightest she would lose their baby. And though, as a physician, she knew intellectually this wasn't true, that moderate exercise was good for her, the mother's heart inside her was busy churning out warnings to "be extra, extra careful" night and day.

"Surprise." She pulled away from him and went to the mirror to finish brushing her hair. She shot him a glance in the reflection. "You've got a very lazy wife."

Cal sauntered over to find a tie on the rack that matched his pale-yellow shirt. "If you're trying to be mysterious," he teased her affably, "it's working."

"That's a nice way to spin it," Ashley joked back. "Mysterious, instead of lazy." While he tied his tie, she twisted the length of her hair and secured it in a clip. "And much as I would love to stay here and discuss my sudden reluctance to exercise, I've got to get a move on. I need to be at the hospital to make rounds by seven, and in the office by eight."

"How come you're going in this morning?" Cal asked,

swiftly hunting down his socks and shoes. "I thought you were only working afternoons."

"Carlotta called while you were in the shower," Ashley said. "Elizabetta has strep throat and Carlotta wants to stay home with her. So I said I would go in for the whole day."

"You want to go in together then?"

Normally, Ashley would prefer taking separate vehicles—she liked being able to come and go as she pleased, and she knew Cal did, too.

"If not," Cal continued affably, "I could drive the Mustang, if you want to take the SUV."

Ashley shook her head. "No, let's go together." There was too much snow still on the ground for him to drive the Mustang. Her concern wasn't only for her and the baby. She wanted Cal safe and sound, too. "The roads are still icy in places, where the snow has been melting during the day and then refreezing overnight. I don't want to take a chance on one of us getting in an accident."

"Okay."

"You're not going to say I'm being silly?"

He studied her a long moment, as if trying to figure out the change that had come over her. She knew what he was thinking—she had never used to worry about such things, and in fact, had poked fun of people who were too safety-conscious.

All that had changed when she became pregnant again, however. Now their family couldn't be safe enough…she couldn't be with him enough.

And though he couldn't quite figure it out, he didn't really seem to mind.

Finally, Cal shook his head. A wistful look came into his eyes, the same one he used to get after one of their commuting rendezvous together whenever he had to say goodbye to her. "Not silly. Beautiful." He put his arm around her waist, guiding her close. "And sexy." His voice dropped another gruff notch. "And bound to make us both late if we don't get our coats and get out of here."

"You're kidding me, right?" Hannah stared at Cal over the hood of the car she was working on. "You can't want me to sell the Mustang for you and Ashley! Now? When you just gave it to her a few weeks ago!"

Cal wasn't surprised by his sister-in-law's response.

Hannah's business, Classic Car Auto Repair, revolved around vintage automobiles. She not only worked on them, she understood the value, and the Mustang Cal had given Ashley was a fine automobile. Hannah knew, because she had not only helped Cal buy the vehicle, she had spent months getting it into top running form and realized full well how sentimental and heartfelt a present it had been.

Cal struggled not to feel remorse at getting rid of the convertible, especially since their reasons for doing so were valid. "It's a great car, and you did a beautiful job restoring it, but we've decided we want something with more state-of-the-art safety features," Cal told Hannah practically. "And we can't really afford to have a twelve-thousand-dollar car we never drive sitting in the barn at the farm, so it's going back on the block."

Understanding lit her eyes. "I'll put the word out. I don't think we'll have any trouble finding a buyer."

Cal nodded, relieved. "Thanks."

Hannah touched Cal's arm. The two of them were more than in-laws, they were good friends and had been even before Hannah had married Cal's sports-announcer brother, Dylan, the previous autumn. "Is everything okay with the two of you? I know how much that Mustang meant in your relationship."

Cal smiled. "It actually was a great gift. Ashley was thrilled when I first gave her the car that we had our very first dates in." And the car, as he had hoped, had marked a turning point in their marriage. So maybe all hadn't been lost, maybe it had served its purpose, and it was time to move on.

Hannah guessed there was more to the story. "But—?"

Cal grimaced. "She lost control of the car in the snow and jumped a curb."

"Dylan and I heard about that—Mac told us. But we understood she wasn't hurt and the car had no damage."

Cal had an idea what Hannah was thinking. They could put snow tires on the vehicle. Or chains on the tires. Or simply not drive it at all in wet winter weather. It didn't snow in their area of North Carolina more than a couple of times a year, if that. During those times, he and Ashley could share his SUV, as they had been the past few days. "That's right."

"But you're getting another vehicle anyway?"

"Tonight, after work." Cal was hoping he and Ashley could find something she liked right away. "We're headed for a dealership in Raleigh that specializes in vehicles with state-of-the-art safety features. The near miss made us both realize we had to be practical as well as romantic. And since there's no way to install air bags in a vintage car like that…we opted to go with something else for her to drive."

Hannah nodded, understanding completely.

"Is everything else okay with you two?" Hannah asked.

Cal paused, not sure how to answer that. On the one hand, he and Ashley had never been happier. They were both living and working in the same place. After several years of guarded exchanges and cautious politeness, they were opening up to each other again. Laughing. Snuggling. Making love—albeit in the dark. For the first time in several years, he felt hopeful they would have the kind of equitable, satisfying marriage they had both always wanted. And yet, there were times, like this morning, when he had the strong sensation that Ashley was still withholding more than she was telling him, and that there were things about her life she would rather he just not know. And for the life of him, Cal couldn't figure out how to get past that.

"Admit it," Ashley said, later that evening after they had parked their two cars side by side in the garage, and emerged to stand between them. She pointed to the shiny fire-engine-red van she had driven home from the lot, while he followed in his SUV. "This wasn't the vehicle you expected me to pick out for myself this evening."

*No kidding,* Cal thought, seeing no reason to fib. "I admit I've always seen you as the sports-car type."

"Instead of a minivan." She turned to survey the buttery-soft cream leather seats and carpeting, seating for seven, a generous cargo area, and a luggage rack on top, then turned back to him. Her lips formed a perplexed pout.

"What don't you like about it?"

*The fact,* Cal thought, *that there is still something you're not telling me.* But not wanting to start a fight by accusing Ashley of he didn't quite know what, Cal merely smiled. "I think it's a perfect family car," he said.

Ashley tensed at the mention of the *F*-word.

"Not that I'm pushing you to have a child right now,"

Cal corrected himself hastily. "I know that the time has to be right for both of us, and—"

Ashley pressed a silencing finger to his lips. The haunted look was back in her china-blue eyes. "Let's not talk about this right now, okay?"

"Then what would you like to talk about?" he asked her softly, unable not to note how gorgeous she looked, even after a long day. In the subdued light of the garage, her classically beautiful features were all the more pronounced. Her dark hair had been blow-dried straight and caught in a clip on the back of her head, but wispy tendrils escaped to frame her face and the nape of her neck.

Ashley shrugged. "Well…"

"Yes?" He could practically see her switching gears. Anything, he figured to get them off the subject of family and children. And when—if ever—they were going to have them.

Ashley swallowed, her expression as distracted as it was uneasy. She turned back to the van that was outfitted with every safety feature currently being made.

Ashley turned back to him and sashayed toward him seductively. "It's obvious to me that you don't think this car is sexy enough." She slipped her hands beneath his coat to caress his chest, in much the same way she had in the past when they'd had problems she didn't want to discuss and preferred to sort out—or maybe just forget altogether—in bed.

This had occasionally irritated Cal in the past…although he never passed up a chance to make love with her.

Making love always made them feel closer—even if their problems remained.

Which was maybe where Ashley was headed with this? The tactic was one she had said she wanted to avoid.

And they had. But maybe she was having second thoughts about this all-or-nothing method of dealing with conflict between them.

Maybe she was trying to guide them onto middle ground.

He couldn't say after the years spent living away from her, and the temporary moratorium on their sex life, that he would mind. Especially when it looked as if she were contemplating initiating a little fun.

"But the car could be sexy." Ashley lowered her hands recklessly.

Cal felt the caressing sweep of her hands down the front of his thighs. Damn, if he wasn't already hard as a rock. "If we were to christen it?"

Ashley glanced back at the vehicle they had just purchased. She paused, bit her lip in a thoughtful way that had him wanting to kiss her and never stop.

"Fortunately," she continued happily, "the passenger seat folds down."

Cal slipped his hands beneath her coat, too. He removed her hands from his body and brought her against him, so her feminine softness curved against his growing arousal. He pressed kisses into her hair, across her forehead, temples. "Sure we won't be too chilly?"

Ashley trembled in his arms and kissed him back—on the lips. "Not if we closed the garage door, got some blankets, and let mutual body heat do the rest."

Cal brought his hands around to cup her buttocks and lift her against him. "Damn if you aren't full of surprises," he murmured, lowering his head once again. They were about to kiss again when they heard the sound of a car moving toward them and found themselves caught in the sweep of yellow headlights.

Too late, Cal realized he should have shut the overhead door as soon as they pulled their vehicles into the garage. Maybe then, they could have pretended not to be home. As it was, they had been caught by the female Hart posse—all three of his sisters-in-law and his sister, Janey.

There were times when family was not welcome. This was one of them.

Not that he would ever be rude. It wasn't their fault that their timing stunk.

"We hate to interrupt," Emma Donovan Hart said as she stepped out from behind the wheel.

Hannah Reid Hart, Lily Madsen Hart, and Janey Hart Lantz soon joined them. "But we were in the area and thought we'd drop by and say hi."

"We also brought some wedding cake for you to taste," Janey said, cradling several white pastry boxes in her arms. "I've been developing some new recipes and I need some more opinions on whether or not to offer them at the shop." Janey paused. Although she knew they had interrupted a romantic moment it did not seem to be deterring her in the least. "You don't mind giving me some fresh perspective, do you?"

"Of course not," Ashley said, shooting Cal a curious look no one else could see. One that said, *What the heck is going on here?*

He had a pretty good idea.

He just couldn't say.

"And maybe some coffee, too?" Lily said, falling into step beside Ashley as Ashley closed the overhead door behind them with a press of a button and led the way into the farmhouse. "If it wouldn't be too much trouble."

"Before we go in, would you mind letting us have a look at your new car?" Hannah said, waylaying Cal, along with Emma.

"I've been thinking about getting something a little safer, too," Emma said.

Cal waved Ashley, Janey and Lily on inside.

As soon as the door shut behind them, he turned. "What the—?"

"The black dress you left with the dressmaker has Lycra in it," Emma said in exasperation. She opened her oversized shoulder bag and got out a small Ziploc bag with Ashley's undies and handed it over to Cal along with Ashley's black dress. "That's what makes the fabric so stretchy." Emma demonstrated before handing the dress over, too.

"So?" Not wanting to get caught with either, Cal opened the back passenger door of his SUV and tossed the clothing onto the seat.

"So we can't get a valid measurement off it." Emma threw up her hands in frustration. "We don't know what her waist size is!"

"What about the underwear?"

Hannah rolled her eyes. "It was bikini, in case you hadn't noticed. It doesn't go all the way up to her waist."

Cal flushed. He hadn't thought about that. "Oh."

"So, at the moment," Emma continued whispering, "all we've got is her bra size, and given the fact she's gained a little weight recently—"

"In all the right places," Hannah sighed enviously.

"Realistically, her bust measurement could be off, too," Emma finished.

"So what do you want me to do?" Cal asked, embarrassed he had goofed this up to such a degree, when the surprise "wedding vow-renewal-ceremony" was only a week and a half away....

Hannah removed a tape measure from her pants pocket. "We want you to take this tape measure and go upstairs and measure the waist and hips and inseam on a pair of pants that you know fits and give it to us. And while you're at it, get us her shoe size, too."

"She only has two pair of pants that she has been wearing since she got back. One of 'em is on her right now. The other is hanging in her closet. But I'm not sure I know exactly how to measure…"

"Can you get me up there without her seeing me then?" Emma asked.

Nodding, he looked at Hannah. "But you have to stay downstairs with Lily and Janey and make sure she doesn't come upstairs."

Hannah smiled, confident as ever. "No problem."

"So why were they really here?" Ashley asked Cal an hour later.

"What do you mean?" Cal asked, ducking his head as he rinsed the coffee cups and plates in the sink. He had never been any good at subterfuge. The fact the fibs were necessary to pull off the surprise anniversary celebration he was planning at the Wedding Inn wasn't making it any easier. He didn't want any secrets between them.

Ashley positioned herself between Cal and the front of the dishwasher. She folded her arms in front of her. "I mean, it's obvious they all wanted to talk to you. And I'd like to know what about. Did the men in the family send them over here?"

Cal frowned and wrapped his arms around her waist. It was time this conversation took another tack. "Why would they do that?" he asked, gently rubbing his hands up and down her spine.

Ashley narrowed her eyes at him as she splayed her hands across his chest. She tilted her head up to better search his face. "You said a few weeks ago the whole family was concerned about us. So was tonight more of the same?"

Cal did not like the feisty look in Ashley's blue eyes. That look always guaranteed trouble. And they'd had enough trouble up to now. "No."

She assessed him obstinately. "Then why did they all show up here and why did Lily and Janey and Hannah do their best to keep me occupied in the kitchen while you-all stayed out in the garage and then went up to the exercise room with Emma?"

"Hey." Cal aimed a thumb at his chest. "I know for a fact that Janey honestly wanted your opinion on those cake samples she brought over."

"And Lily?"

Cal could feel her body melting against his even as her will remained as difficult as ever.

"Why was Lily suddenly so interested in my opinion of various flowers she was thinking of doing for Polly Pruett's wedding?"

Cal shrugged and tried not to think about how much he enjoyed feeling the soft, feminine warmth of her body pressed up against him this way. He smiled, hoping to tease her out of her suspicious mood. "Because she thinks you have good taste?"

Ashley frowned.

"And anyway," Cal continued, kissing the top of her head, "what does it matter why they were here as long as they're gone now and we're once again alone, ready to christen the car we just bought?"

Ashley broke free of his light, protective grasp and whirled away from him. "You're changing the subject," she declared heatedly.

"You bet I am." Cal grabbed her arm and whirled her right back. "I'm tired of talking about my family," he told her. Smiling, he stroked the pad of his thumb across the silken invitation of her lower lip. "When all I want is you."

Her lips parted under the pressure of his touch. He had her backed against the counter, and she leaned back, bracing her hands on either side of her, and putting as much space as possible between the two of them. Which wasn't much, Cal noted. Maybe an inch.

"I'm not going to forget this," she warned.

Deciding they had done far too much talking for one night, he threaded both his hands through her hair. "Then I guess I'll just have to convince you."

The clip was in the way of his fingers. He took it out, and let her hair fall down around her shoulders, like tangled ribbons of dark brown silk.

Ashley caught her breath as he moved his hands through the soft thickness of her hair. "Cal—" It was part admonition, part plea. He chose to obey the latter. Engulfing her with the heat and strength of his body, he lowered his head and delivered a breath-stealing kiss. She moaned, soft and low in her throat. His body responded, heating and surging to life. And he kissed her again, deliberately shattering what little caution she had left. Her lips parted beneath the pressure of his, and he enjoyed the sweet, hot taste of her. He groaned as their tongues twined urgently, and his body took on an urgent pulsing all its own, until there was no doubting how much they wanted and needed each other.

Ashley sighed, trembling and cuddling against him, when they finally broke the kiss. "You are so bad for me sometimes."

He kissed her again, letting her take him where she wanted to go this time, not stopping until the last of the distrust between them had dissolved. "I take it you mean bad in a good way," he teased, as he rubbed his fingers across the tips of her breasts, then slipped his fingers beneath the hem of her sweater and bra, to caress the pearling tips even more intimately.

She shuddered as he traced the weight and shape. "Bad in every way," she teased right back.

"I want to make love to you," he kissed his way down the nape of her neck, pushing the rolled collar of her turtleneck aside.

"I want that, too."

"We could stay in front of the fire."

Ashley shook her head, stubborn as ever. Her hand dropped to his arousal. She enfolded him in her palm with the same tender care he was cupping her breasts. "I want to go back to our original plan and christen the van." He grinned as she used her other hand to unbutton his shirt, and continued her role as aggressor. "You have to start thinking of that van as sexy."

He reached around behind her to unfasten her bra, and fill his hands with her silky warm flesh. "Making love with you in it will do that all right," he promised.

Ashley stepped back, away from him. Knowing, as did he, that if they didn't stop now, they'd never make it out of the kitchen. "You get the blankets and maybe a pillow or two. I'll open up the back and put down the rear seat." She started for the door to the garage.

Cal watched the gentle sway of her hips, and wondered if she knew just how enticing she was, or how much he had enjoyed taming her and making her his. "Just don't start without me," he teased.

Ashley turned and shot him a sultry look that upped his pulse another notch. "Don't you wish."

He grinned.

"Meet you in five," she dictated cheerfully.

"Or sooner," Cal said, his spirits lifting the way they always did when he was about to make love to his wife. Only, when he gathered up the items she had asked for and met her in the garage, Ashley wasn't standing in front of her new van, but rather his SUV. And she looked anything but pleased as she held up her sexy lace undies and black dress and drawled, "I can't wait to hear the explanation for this."

# Chapter 12

"I just bet you can't," Cal said, walking past her and over to the new van. He opened up the back and the sides, and began the process of putting the seat down.

"You knew I was looking for this dress," Ashley stormed, waving it around like a red flag in front of a bull.

"Uh-huh." Cal leaned into the car and spread the quilts out, making a soft cozy bed for them.

"And the undies I usually wear with them," she continued heatedly.

His ash-blond brows drew together as he looked over at her in mock seriousness. "Right."

Ashley stomped over to him, her flat soles connecting loudly on the cement floor. She clasped the missing items in her hands. "So where were they?"

"I could tell you," he said, mischief glimmering in his

eyes. He leaned toward her, his voice low and sexy. "But I'm not going to."

Ashley stiffened, aggravated at the way he'd had her searching high and low for her clothing when he had obviously known right where it was all along! "And you expect me to accept that?"

"I don't see that you have any choice," he said good-naturedly. "Unless you want to hire a private detective." He squinted at her thoughtfully and screwed up the corners of his lips in comical fashion. "Or perhaps grill your clothes on where they've been."

"Har de har har." She watched him plump the pillows, remove his tie, and begin to unbutton his shirt. "And that's it? That's all you're going to tell me?" she demanded in exasperation.

He inclined his head to one side and thought about it some more. "Yep." Somehow, he managed to pry the clothing from her hands and put it back in his SUV. "Now, are we going to have to do this in the dark again or shall there be light?"

A look of distinctly male satisfaction on his face, he took her resisting body in his arms. Ashley stiffened, trying hard not to notice how warm and strong and solid he felt. She tossed her head imperiously. "Who says we're doing it at all?"

Cal chuckled and shifted her closer still. Giving her no chance to argue more, he lowered his head and claimed her mouth with his. Ashley tasted the masculine force that was Cal, felt his mastery in the plundering sweep of his tongue. She still didn't want to give in to him, but his will was stronger than hers. She clutched at his shoulders as he moved his hips against hers and delivered a deep, demanding kiss. With a low moan of surrender, Ashley tilted her head to give him deeper access. His tongue mated with hers, and he delivered another steamy kiss that left her limp with longing and faint with acquiescence and wondering at the magical power he seemed to hold over her heart. They had been a couple for nearly ten years now, married for almost three, and yet every time he took her in his arms, every time he kissed her, her heart pounded and a shiver of unbearable excitement went through her.

"With the lights or without?" he murmured.

"Without."

He helped her into the back of the car, then went back to shut off the overhead light in the garage and returned to her side. He climbed in after her, shutting the car door. Once the dome light went off, there was just enough moonlight coming in from the decorative half-moon windows across the top of the garage door to let them make out each other's shapes. The mood went from slightly cantankerous to highly charged in an instant. The back of the wagon had been a little chilly as she first climbed in. When he joined her, it soon became hot and close. Ashley's heart pounded with anticipation, as they turned onto their sides and tried and failed for several moments to get comfortable.

Ashley began to laugh at the ridiculousness of the situation. And once started, she couldn't seem to stop. He wanted to claim her, and she wanted him to claim her, and at the rate they were going, it was never going to happen; they were never even going to come close to making love in here and christening their new car. They weren't going to be able to lie down, even if they did it at an angle. They were both too tall and the seat wasn't long enough, even folded flat.

"This is absurd," Ashley decided, still laughing. She was ready to call it a wash and head upstairs.

Cal caught her around the waist and brought her back to him before she could beat a hasty retreat. "Not so fast," he told her. Laughter edging his low voice, too, his hands slipped beneath the hem of her sweater, to tenderly caress the bare skin of her ribs. "We haven't tried everything yet."

She sucked in her breath as he reached around behind her to unclasp her bra. Her skin tingled and heated. "Well, almost—"

Cal shifted onto his back, so he was lying flat against the blanket, and guided her on top of him. "You know what they say," he whispered huskily.

"What?"

"Where there's a will, there's a way."

Ashley was about to counter that they'd never get comfortable enough, when his hands claimed her breasts, working the tips into tight, aching buds of arousal.

Suddenly, the situation was seeming much more workable.

Getting the idea of how he wanted this to work, she shifted her body until she was over him, straddling his torso, and then she framed his head with both her hands. His knees were raised, his feet flat on the seat. The back of her hips brushed up against the wall of his rock-hard thighs. Nice, except their heads bumped against the back of the middle seats. Cal cursed and Ashley began to giggle uncontrollably. "Still no good."

"Patience, Ash."

"Cal—"

He brought her head down to his for a slow, leisurely kiss, coaxing response after response from her. "I'm not giving up. Not yet."

He continued to kiss and caress her. She was certainly getting excited.

"Unzip me," he ordered hoarsely.

He caught her hand and guided it to him.

She did as he bid. He was hard and hot and so damn large in her hand.

"Now bring my pants down, just enough. We don't have that much space. Yeah. That's it," he said as she did his bidding. "And yours should go entirely."

A shudder went through her. She wasn't sure she could wait for the time that would take. "Cal—"

"I want you naked, Ashley," he ordered gruffly. "At least from the waist down."

What did it matter? Ashley wondered as her body throbbed and burned with wanting him. He couldn't see her in this shadowy light. Not enough to be able to figure out what was happening with her body, anyway. Wanting to please him as much as she wanted him to pleasure her, Ashley slipped over onto her side. Her fingers trembled as she complied with his wishes. When she would have moved over him once again, he caught her against him and held her so she was still curled up on her side, her head tilted just to the left of his.

He found her mouth at the same time as his hand found her dewy softness. He kissed her and caressed her until the world faded away.

She climaxed with surprising speed. And then he lifted her on top of him once again, caught her waist in his hands, and entered her with one long, slow, incredibly sensual stroke. Ashley felt the heat. Passion. Need. All combined to fuel the fires burning within them, and soaring, they found the release they had been craving.

"You're sore, aren't you?" Cal said the next morning as Ashley struggled to get out of bed.

She nodded ruefully. "Not only where you might expect." Given the heat and ardor with which they'd made love the previous night, she had expected—and was definitely experiencing—the residual tingling in the most feminine part of her that came with being well-loved. "But I'm feeling the effects of our rendezvous last night everywhere else, too," Ashley lamented as she stretched her arms languidly over her head in an effort to work the kinks out. "Arms, legs, heck—" she chuckled and shook her head "—even my derriere hurts!" Which was what they got for never having—um—"exercised" quite that way before.

"Well, if it will make you feel any better, I'm a little stiff this morning, too," Cal said. He swaggered toward her, looking buff and fit, clad in nothing but his boxers. Muscles flexing, he helped her to her feet. "But we can feel good about one thing." He favored her with a sexy smile that did funny things to her insides.

"And what would that be?" Ashley luxuriated in the feeling of his arms around her.

He looked at her gently, protectively. "Our new van not only got christened, it has been established as one very sexy vehicle."

Ashley laughed at the mischievous twinkle in his eyes. "Just tell me we don't have to do it again." She ran her hand across the manly stubble on his jaw.

He caught her thumb between his teeth and caressed it softly with his tongue. "We don't have to do it again. The SUV on the other hand…"

Ashley groaned in mock reluctance. She clapped both hands over her ears as if to shut out what he was saying.

He pried her hands from her head and held them in his as he continued, all confident male "…has a larger cargo hold. Or we could try the front seats."

Ashley groaned louder. What had she started? "How about the bed?" she teased back.

He turned and cast a look behind him. "You mean this old thing with the comfy mattress and plenty of room and nice soft flannel sheets?"

Ashley looked at the king-sized haven with the sleigh bed frame. "Mmm-hmm." She ran her hand over the velvety mat of ash-blond hair on his chest, appreciating the satiny-smooth skin and rippling muscles beneath.

"Well, it sounds nice. But what sounds even nicer, once you get over your newfound shyness, is the master bath." He kissed the nape of her neck, the sensitive area behind her ear. "The master bath is perfect for showering together."

Ashley'd had much the same thought. She curled a hand around the swell of his bicep. "Give me another ten days or so and I promise," she said softly. "We'll explore the master bath."

He teased in a soft low voice that sent thrills coursing over her body, "I'm going to hold you to that, you know."

Ashley loved the playful curl of his mouth, the seductive glint in his eyes. "I know." She rose on tiptoe to give him a sweet kiss to seal the deal.

Cal sighed his regret as the sultry caress came to a halt. "Unfortunately for both of us, I have to get ready for work. Otherwise, I'd be content to hang out here with you all day."

Ashley would've liked to stay and make love with Cal all day long, too. A fact that both pleased and bothered her. She was glad she and Cal were feeling so close, and worried that they were once again letting their desire for each other take precedence over all else. Because if they hadn't made love last night, in the garage and then later, in their bedroom, she was pretty sure she would have found out where her dress and undies had been. Not that this was important. She was sure there was a good explanation for it since Cal was not the type to hide her clothes from her for no good reason.

Although what that reason could have been...

Was he attempting to buy her a new dress?

Had he taken the garments for sizing?

That at least made sense.

Aware he was watching her, and that if he didn't hurry, he would be late for morning rounds at the hospital, she said, "You hit the shower. I'll make breakfast today."

"See you downstairs in ten." He stripped down to his shorts, tossed them in the hamper, and naked, strode for the bath. Ashley grinned at his retreating backside. There wasn't an inch of him that wasn't beautiful, from the width of his powerful shoulders, muscular back and handsome buttocks, to his long, sturdy legs. She had missed seeing him buck-naked, climbing out of her bed. Missed making love with him and being held in his arms all night long. She didn't ever want to go back to the way it had been, prior to her homecoming.

And now that they were close to sharing everything—including the heartbreaking secrets that she had shouldered alone for the past two and a half years, as well as the happier secret she was dealing with now—they wouldn't have to.

All she had to do was work up the nerve to tell Cal the truth. About everything.

"So what is it, Dr. Hart?" Polly Pruett asked anxiously as she scratched at the red bumps appearing on her abdomen.

Ashley explained as she finished examining her patient, "It's called a PUPPP rash. Pruritic urticarial papules and plaques of pregnancy. It sometimes appears during pregnancy and then goes away after you deliver your baby. We can give you some topical medicine to put on it and an antihistamine to stop the itching."

Polly frowned. "Will that make the rash go away entirely?"

"Probably not," Ashley told her sympathetically. "But the meds will make you more comfortable, and the rash is usually limited to the body—it doesn't appear on the face. What I am more concerned about here, Polly, is the fact you've begun to dilate."

Polly looked over at her fiancé. Peter Sheridan was standing against the wall, holding the pregnancy manual Polly carried with her everywhere. "How much?"

Ashley made a notation on Polly's chart. "Two centimeters."

Polly bit her lip. "I could be that way for a couple of weeks, couldn't I?"

"Yes," Ashley told Polly and Peter gently, "but other signs point to you going into labor some time in the next seven days or so."

Polly sat up as quickly as she could on the exam table. She fumbled with the sheet across her waist as she wailed, "But I'm supposed to be married in three days!"

Opposite her, Peter frowned. He looked as unhappy as his fiancée.

Ashley patted Polly's shoulder. "Which is why you might want to think about moving the ceremony up a bit," Ashley suggested.

"I can't do that!" Polly looked as if she might burst into tears. "We have two hundred people coming, and a lot of them from out of town! We have to wait until the weekend."

Peter moved away from the wall. "Polly—"

"Don't even say it." Polly glared at her fiancé, stubborn as ever. "I am having this wedding according to plan."

Peter swallowed and looked at Ashley for help. She wasn't sure what she could do. Polly and Peter's baby was going to be born when he was ready, whether Polly or Peter or the two hundred guests they had invited to their wedding liked it or not. Finally, Ashley said, "My husband and I are both planning to be at the Wedding Inn during the ceremony, so if there are any problems, Cal—who is a doctor, too—will be right there."

Peter breathed a big sigh of relief. Healthy color came back into his face. "Thanks, Dr. Hart," he told Ashley soberly.

"Don't mention it," Ashley said. She turned back to Polly. "In the meantime, I want you to be sure and rest as much possible…"

While Polly got dressed and went out to make her next appointment, Ashley retired to the private office and sank down behind Carlotta's desk. She returned several calls, then smiled as Carlotta breezed in.

"Good news," Carlotta said cheerfully, setting down a stack of medical insurance paperwork she had taken home with her to complete. "Beatrice is back!"

That was good news, Ashley thought, fully aware how much Carlotta's family had yearned to have their nanny with them again. But upon closer inspection, Ashley noted, Carlotta didn't look as if the news were all that good. "So everything is back to normal?" Ashley asked, trying hard not to think about what this might mean to her.

Carlotta nodded, still looking a tad distracted. She ran a hand through her hair. "I know I've imposed enough as it is, but I was wondering if you would consider continuing to help me out through the end of the week, so I could go home at two or so every afternoon and be there when the kids get home from school. It would also give Beatrice a chance to settle back in."

"No problem," Ashley said, glad to continue to be of help. And not just because she owed Carlotta, but because she enjoyed working in the small private practice with her old friend.

But she also knew, as she packed up and left the office for the day, that she hadn't done nearly enough looking for a permanent position for herself.

She could not delay any longer.

She went to the medical center, and caught the hospital administrator as he was getting ready to leave for the day. "Ashley!" Frank Hodges said. "I was going to call you."

"Perhaps we could talk now, then," Ashley said with a brisk, professional smile. Whatever it was, she wanted to get it over with.

He ushered her in and closed the door behind them. He waited until both were seated before he continued reluctantly, "I talked to the board of directors. We're all in agreement we can't take another obstetrician on staff right now—the medical center doesn't have the labor and delivery rooms to support such a move. We could use another gynecologist, though. So if you were willing to give up delivering babies and limit your practice until one of the obstetricians on staff leaves or retires, then we would be able to offer you a spot."

This, she hadn't expected.

Frank rummaged through the scraps of notepaper on his desk. "I've also done some checking with other hospitals in the area. Most are fully staffed with Ob/Gyns at the moment, but Carolina Regional Medical Center has an opening. And they would very much like to talk to you if you're interested in working there." He handed her the name and phone number of the person to call.

Ashley studied the paper, grateful for the lead. And yet... "That's a good hour's drive from here."

Frank nodded soberly. "Right."

Doing her best to contain her disappointment, Ashley got to her feet. "I'm really going to have to think about it. And talk to Cal."

"I suspected that would be the case." Frank stood, shook her hand. "If I can be of further assistance, Ashley," he finished kindly, "please let me know."

Ashley knew there was something wrong the moment she walked in the door. She could tell by the glum, tense expression on Cal's face. She put her things down slowly, shrugged out of her coat. "What's going on?" she asked Cal.

He pointed to the answering machine on the kitchen counter. "There's a message for you."

Okay. Ashley went over to the telephone and pressed Play.

An unfamiliar woman's voice filled the room. "Hello, Ashley. This is Shelley Denova, from Physician Search. We received your résumé and I'm happy to report Yale would very much like to interview you..."

"You told me you weren't applying for that job," Cal said. Once again, he seemed to be watching and weighing everything she did.

"I'm not, and I didn't." Ashley was already picking up the phone. She dialed by memory. Waited several rings.

Her mother's voice came on the line. "Margaret Porter."

Temper soaring, Ashley said in a clipped, brittle tone, "Hello, Mother."

"Ashley!" Margaret sounded delighted to hear from her. *Too bad the feeling wasn't mutual,* Ashley thought.

"I have a bone to pick with you," Ashley said.

Margaret paused. When she spoke again, she sounded confused, "And what might that be?"

Ashley drummed her fingers on the tabletop next to her. "I had a call from Shelley Denova at Physician Search."

"Good news, I hope?" Margaret chirped cheerfully.

Ashley gritted her teeth. She looked over at Cal, ignoring the censuring light in his gray eyes. "I never sent her my résumé."

Another pause, shorter this time. "I had my asistant draw one up and send it over."

Ashley felt the beginnings of a tension headache. She rubbed at her temples. "Why?" she demanded, aware she was very close to losing it with both her mother and her husband. With Margaret, because she had interfered in Ashley's life one time too many. And with Cal, because he had thought the worst of her, when all she had wanted was for him to believe in her, believe in them....

"Because the position was going to be filled before you ever got around to it, that's why!" Margaret scolded tersely. "Honestly, Ashley, what has gotten into you, anyway? You never used to be so lax."

Ashley's temples throbbed. She sat down and dropped her head into her hands. "Listen to me, Mother. I am not applying for that job. And I am not calling Shelley Denova back." She spoke slowly, carefully enunciating every word.

Margaret harrumphed. "It would be very rude if you didn't. You can't afford to burn bridges."

There was only one Ashley wanted to burn at the moment. "Then you better do something about that, hadn't you?" Ashley hung up the phone.

"Whoa," Cal said, looking impressed.

"You have no idea." Ashley was shaking, she was so angry.

He came toward her, hands out. "I'm sorry I jumped to conclusions."

Ashley swept her hands through her hair, encountered a clip, and then just took her hair down. She realized she had a choice here, stay angry with Cal and vent her feelings on him, too. Or let it go. Move on. She found she wanted to do the latter. "It's all right," she told him wearily, forgiveness pouring through her. She shook her head, took a deep bolstering breath. "If the situation had been reversed, and I had come home and heard a message like that on the machine, I am sure I would have wondered what in the heck was going on, too." She tightened her lips together ruefully. As long as they were on the subject, she figured she might as well tell him the rest of it. "Not that I'm exactly flooded with offers right now, in any case."

Cal blinked. "What do you mean?"

He stepped behind her to massage the tense muscles of her shoulders. His fingers were like magic, bringing warmth and welcome relief.

Ashley swallowed, wishing she had better info to relate. "I talked to the hospital administrator in Holly Springs today." Briefly, Ashley explained the situation.

Cal got another chair from the kitchen table and moved it, so they were sitting knee to knee. "Are you going to apply for the job at Carolina Regional?" He looked into her eyes.

Ashley shrugged, her feelings all over the map. Restless, she stood and began to pace the confines of the kitchen, talking anxiously all the while. "If I were to get a job as an Ob/Gyn there, I would have to live within fifteen or twenty minutes of the hospital." She paused to regard Cal practically. "At least during the nights that I was on call. And since you have to do the same here, it would mean we would be apart again, at least four days a week, maybe more."

Cal looked about as enthused as she felt about that prospect. Which, oddly enough, made Ashley feel better.

She didn't want him pushing her away again, telling her they had to toughen up and make these sacrifices for their careers, and put their relationship, their marriage, second at every turn.

"Anyway," Ashley continued softly, beginning to pace again, "I was thinking on the drive home. Maybe the thing to do is take the Gyn position at Holly Springs now, and just wait for an Ob/Gyn slot to open up. It wouldn't be all that long. And we wouldn't have to move or be apart." She paused, searching his face, aware her heart was racing as she tried—without much success—to decipher his non-reaction. "What do you think?"

"I think I'd be happy," Cal said carefully after a moment, looking as if he too were afraid to put his heart all the way out there, lest it get stomped on. He stood and walked to her side. "But," he asked gruffly, "what about you, Ash? What about your needs, wants, desires?"

Ashley swallowed hard and went into his arms. "All I need is you, Cal." She buried her face in his shoulder and hugged him fiercely. But even as she spoke the words, she wasn't quite sure she believed it.

# Chapter 13

"We know you want this to be a big surprise for Ashley, but we're all really nervous about just presenting Ashley with a gown she has never tried on," Janey told Cal during the impromptu family conference at the Wedding Inn.

Emma agreed. "I plan a lot of weddings, Cal. The most important thing to most brides—even those like Ashley who are simply going to be renewing their vows—is their dress. And since you want Ashley to have a new gown, I really think we need her input on which one she wears."

"How are you going to do that without ruining the surprise?" Cal asked.

His mother patted him on the arm. "We've got an excellent plan," Helen reassured him with a smile. "All you have to do is make sure that Ashley arrives at the Wedding Inn on Saturday morning, along with the rest of the Hart women."

"They want me to model wedding dresses for a photographer?" Ashley asked Cal later that evening, as the two of them prepared dinner together.

She had been doing yoga when he came home and was still clad in tights and an oversized T-shirt that kept slipping off one shoulder.

Cal nodded, glad the event he was pitching to Ashley was also completely on the level. He didn't think he could lie to her. Even for a good cause. "A lot of the brides who come to the Wedding Inn—especially the older ones—don't want to try on dozens and dozens of dresses. But it's hard to tell on the hanger what a dress is going to look like on an actual model. So my mother and Emma had this idea that you and Lily and Janey and Hannah could all try on half a dozen dresses on Saturday. Mom has arranged to have a seamstress there to pin the gowns so they will look as though they are perfectly fitted, and a photographer will take pictures of all angles of the dresses. Mom and Emma will compile the photos in an album and then when prospective brides come in—especially busy career women like yourselves—and want to cut to the chase they can flip through the books and pick out the ones they want to try on."

To Cal's relief, Ashley looked amenable to the idea. "They ought to do the same for tuxes." She brought out the makings for a salad while he grilled turkey cutlets on the stove.

Cal flushed, beginning to feel a little guilty at the depth of the deception, despite the necessity of the subterfuge. "They are. My brothers and I have all been roped into doing the same thing on the same day." He went to the fridge to get out the Asian cooking sauce. "So, will you participate?" He poured a little sauce on each cutlet, straight from the bottle, then spread it to the edges with a basting brush. "It will mean a lot to my family if you do."

Ashley had a tendency to feel overwhelmed when surrounded by too many Harts at once. But this sounded like fun. Except for one thing. She hesitated, aware she was going to have to be very careful not to let on to the other women what was going on with her. "Ah…they know I'm just getting back in shape after a period of not working out at all?" she said, thinking of her thickening waist and swelling centerfold breasts.

Cal flashed her an exasperated look. "That's the whole point, Ashley. All of you are gorgeous and accomplished grown women, not anorexic teenagers made up to look like adults."

Well, put that way… "Okay, then," Ashley said, going over to kiss Cal on the cheek. When he took her in his arms, she made it a full kiss on the lips, tender and sweet. She was trembling when they drew apart. She rubbed her thumb across his cheek and looked into his eyes. "I'll be happy to help out." She was pleased to have been asked.

"So what do you think, Ashley?" Helen inquired Saturday morning as she presented Ashley with a huge rack of dresses that several bridal shops had brought over. "If you were getting married today—maybe for the second time—what kind of gown would you choose?"

"Hmm. As much as I liked the scoop-necked gown with the white tulle skirt I wore the first time around, I think if I were getting married now—especially for the second time—I would choose something a lot less Cinderella-ish. I like this one." Ashley pointed to a satin A-line gown, with long sleeves and a fitted alençon lace bodice. "And this one." Ashley fingered a high-necked white lace gown with a straight skirt. "And especially this one." Ashley selected a white silk off-the-shoulder gown with a fitted bodice, basque waist and chapel train. "It's really elegant."

"And it's the type of style that makes your waist look so tiny," the seamstress said.

"Then that's the one for me," Ashley joked, blushing a little as she thought about her ever-expanding waist-line. Another week from now, when everyone knew she was pregnant— especially Cal—it wouldn't be so embarrassing, but right now Ashley knew it just looked as though she was not being very disciplined in her diet and exercise. Which, of course, was all the more reason for notice or comment since Ashley was one of the most disciplined people around.

"Let's try the one you like the most on first," Helen said.

The bodice originally had a lot of give, but when the seamstress had put the pins in, it looked absolutely perfect. As Ashley looked at herself in the three-way mirror, she remembered what it had felt like to be a bride. How full of hope—and happiness—she had been that day. How little she'd known about the heartache and the difficult decisions that lay ahead....

"What are you thinking?" Lily teased, standing still while the photographer snapped photos of her in an ivory tulle dress with a halter bodice.

Ashley forced herself to concentrate on the problems of the past and think about the promise of the future. Her pregnancy was proceeding well. Physically, she felt better every day. Emotionally, more relieved. And as for her relationship with Cal, it seemed at long last to be on the right path again. She could feel the two of them getting closer with every day that passed. And she knew now that it was much more than great sex holding the two of them together. They still had some things to work out, but she was beginning to feel confident that they could deal with anything that came their way now, instead of letting problems drive them apart, as they had in the past.

Janey moved to the mirror, too, studying Ashley's reflection. "Yes. Do tell what you're thinking about that is making you look so happy and content."

Ashley smiled. "How happy I am, actually." *How hopeful about the future.* "I know I've been married almost three years now but I still feel like a new bride in a lot of respects."

"Ahhh," everyone said in unison.

"Maybe it's that extended honeymoon you and Cal have been on lately," Hannah teased as she stood still, so the seamstress could pin the sleeves of the gown she had on.

"I've got to say I've never seen Cal looking happier," Janey added.

"Or more in love," Helen Hart said with a smile.

"So how did it go?" Cal asked when he and Ashley met up for lunch in town, close to the tuxedo shop where the Hart men had been trying on tuxes and getting photographed.

"Great, actually," Ashley reported cheerfully as Cal held the door to the sandwich shop and followed her in. "We had a lot of fun."

They threaded their way to a corner booth. "I'm glad," Cal said, looking pleased. He plucked two plastic-coated menus from behind the salt shakers, gave her one, and kept the other for himself.

"For the first time..." Ashley started awkwardly, not sure how to say the rest without offending.

Cal reached across the table and took her hand in his. He searched her face. "What?"

Shrugging, Ashley cleared her throat. Aware she might sound foolish, she pushed on nevertheless. "I really felt a part of your family this morning, Cal. Like I belonged there with the other Hart women. I don't know." She tightened her fingers in his and looked into his eyes. "It was just so easy today to feel as if I fit in."

"What's this?" Ashley asked when Cal walked into their bedroom carrying a box with a big red ribbon on it.

Unlike Ashley, who was still clad in a tightly belted robe that covered her from throat to ankle, Cal was already partly dressed for the evening ahead in pinstriped gray suit pants and a silver-gray dress shirt that brought out the color of his eyes. He hadn't buttoned the top two buttons of his shirt yet, and the sophisticated red-and-gray-patterned silk tie he planned to wear was draped around his collar.

"Open it and see," Cal advised in a sexy voice that sent thrills coursing over her.

Ashley looked up into his face. He had shaved before his shower, and the sea-and-sun scent of his cologne clung to his handsome jaw. Her fingers trembled slightly as she untied the ribbon on the box. "You have to stop giving me presents," she chided. It made her feel guilty to be lauded this way, when she felt she had done nothing to deserve it.

Cal grinned. "You want me to stop? You're going to have to stop giving me reasons to give you presents," he told her lazily.

Ashley sauntered closer. She loved it when they flirted like this. She put the present on the dresser next to him. "What did I do to deserve this?" Ashley asked softly, for a moment feeling as if she could drown in the depths of his gaze.

Hooking an arm about her waist, Cal pulled her against him and looked down at her tenderly. "That's easy," he told her huskily in reply, curving an arm about her shoulders and bringing her closer still, so she was intimately situated in the hard cradle of his thighs. "You love me—the way I love you."

His softly murmured confession was like a balm to her soul. Ashley's heart fluttered in her chest as she felt his arousal pressing against her, and then his lips were on hers once again, fusing in passion and heat, want and need. He swept the insides of her mouth, languidly at first, then with growing passion until she was lost in the touch and taste and feel of him, lost in the ragged intake of his breath and her own low, shuddering moan. Her arms wreathed his neck, and her body surged into the strong, protective shelter of his. The kiss deepened even more and Ashley sighed. Contentment swept through her entire being. "If we keep this up, we are never going to make it to Polly Pruett's wedding," she scolded ruefully, wishing they could just skip the wedding and stay home—together—in bed. But they couldn't. Not when she had a pregnant patient counting on her.

Cal dropped another kiss on the slope of Ashley's neck, then drew away. "Then we better open that box… hadn't we?"

Brimming with curiosity, Ashley picked the present up again and worked off the lid. Inside, in tissue paper, was a red dress. It had long fitted sleeves, a ballet neck and tea-length circle skirt. "It's the closest one I could find to the black dress that you've been wearing so much."

And it looked comfortable as could be, Ashley thought, longing for the day when she would not have to hide her expanding waistline. "Ah, yes, the one you borrowed without explanation," she said with a smile.

Straightening, Cal began tying his necktie. "I figured if I was going to get you any clothing, I better have some help. Taking something you already loved along with me to the dress shop, seemed like a good idea."

So she had been right about why he had surreptitiously absconded with her clothing. Why then, Ashley wondered, did she still feel as if he weren't quite confiding everything? Pushing her unease away—she was probably projecting her own guilt here—Ashley kept up her half of the teasing. She looked down her nose at him in mock indignation. "Cal. Tell me you didn't show the saleswoman my undies."

Cal grinned, mischief curling the corners of his lips. "Wasn't necessary. But, had she needed more specific measurements, I would have been prepared."

Ashley shook her head, relaxing at their easy banter. "You're a little crazy sometimes."

"Determined." Cal reached behind the knot of his tie to fasten the top two buttons of his shirt. "And yes, I am, when it comes to seeing you have absolutely everything you need."

Ashley watched him draw the knot up to his throat. "You keep this up and you are really going to spoil me," she scolded him affectionately as she straightened the knot, and smoothed the collar on either side of it.

He winked at her. "That's the plan, all right."

Ashley knew if she succumbed to that look, they definitely wouldn't make it to the nuptials. She stepped back a pace, holding the red dress like a stop sign in front of her. "Hang on, while I go put this on."

"You could stay here and do it," Cal suggested hopefully.

Ashley did her best to ignore his devil-may-care attitude and the spike in her pulse. "Yet another attempt to see me naked—or almost?" she taunted.

"Hope springs eternal." He raised his eyebrows in a familiar and charming expression, then looked downward. "As do other things."

Ashley's gaze followed his, as he knew it would. Simultaneously amused and aroused, she flushed at the proof of his desire for her. *Hold that thought for later,* she mused wryly to herself. But in the interest of getting out of there at all that evening, managed only a "Very funny. I'll be right back."

Cal chuckled as she disappeared into the guest bedroom—where all her clothes were located—and locked the door behind her. "You have to get over this newfound shyness of yours sometime," he called after her.

And she would, Ashley thought, as soon as she hit the three-month mark at the end of the following week.

Then, she could—and would—tell Cal everything, Ashley thought, pulling the dress over her head and studying the way she looked in the mirror. And she wouldn't have these damn secrets still wedging distance between them.

She walked out, loving the way the stretchy dress fit. She looked voluptuous, in that fifties-movie star way. "It feels wonderful, Cal."

He eyed her appreciatively. "It looks stunning, too," he told her gruffly. He paused to help her with the clasp of her necklace. "As do you." He shifted her hair aside and kissed the exposed slope of her throat, just behind her ear.

A shiver of desire swept through her.

Cal sighed, regretful. "I suppose we better head to Polly Pruett's wedding."

Because if the two of them stayed there much longer, Ashley knew they were definitely going to make love. She leaned up on tiptoe and kissed him. "Hold that thought for later," she murmured against his lips.

Cal hugged her back. "Will do."

"Are you feeling all right, Polly?" Ashley asked.

Her patient had been rubbing her lower back off and on the entire time she had been in the bridal suite getting ready.

Polly's brows knit together. "I must've slept funny last night because my back has been aching ever since I got up."

Ashley watched as the hairdresser and Polly's mother worked to get the veil attached to the tiara already through Polly's upswept hair. "Any other complaints?"

Polly's eyes sparkled with a mixture of excitement and happiness. She shook her head in exasperation as she adjusted the pearls around her throat. "Relax, Dr. Hart. I'm not in labor."

*Are you sure about that?* Ashley wondered. But not wanting to upset the bride, Ashley merely confirmed, for her own peace of mind, in yet another way, "Then you've had no contractions today at all?"

"Not a one," Polly reported as she moved away from the mirror in a swirl of satin and lace. "Nor has my water broken. Trust me. I am getting through this ceremony and the reception and after that…any time the baby wants to come out and join the world is just fine and dandy with me."

Ashley had to admit Polly's color did look good. "If you're feeling okay, then, I'm going to go out and have a seat with my husband." Ashley leaned forward to give her a hug for luck.

"Sounds good." Polly hugged her back warmly. Then

she caught Ashley's hand, squeezed. "And thanks, Dr. Hart, for being here tonight."

Ashley smiled. "No problem."

"How is she?" Cal asked as Ashley slid into the row and sat down beside him. The soothing music from the string quartet and the soft lighting combined to make a very romantic atmosphere.

Ashley turned her head to the candelabras being lit, on either side of the white latticework wedding arbor, where the couple's vows would be said. Ashley took a deep breath, not sure why she was so nervous, except for the fact that her gut was telling her everything was not as tranquil as it seemed. "She says she's fine."

Cal's brows knit together. "You don't believe her."

"I don't know." Ashley paused and bit her lip. She dropped her voice a confiding notch. She didn't want anyone else to overhear. "Polly could be in the early stages of labor." Ashley shook her head, shrugged. "Then again," Ashley murmured quietly in Cal's ear, "the backache Polly's had all day could be nothing more than the result of all the extra baby weight she is carrying right now." Polly was lugging around an extra thirty pounds—most of which was concentrated in her abdomen. That had to take a toll.

"Well, we're here, no matter what," Cal soothed as he took Ashley's hand in his, "and the hospital is only a fifteen-minute ambulance ride away."

"True."

Cal gave her palm a comforting squeeze. "So just relax and enjoy the event," he advised, leaning over to kiss Ashley's brow lightly.

Ashley knew Cal was right, so she did as he advised—until the bride actually made her entrance on her father's arm. "She's perspiring," Ashley noted to Cal, as Polly lumbered down the aisle as gracefully as an eight-and-a-half month pregnant woman could.

"I've got to admit," Cal whispered back over the music of the string quartet, "it's not looking good."

And it looked worse shortly after Polly's father kissed her cheek and gave her away.

Whatever the minister said was drowned out by Polly's loud gasp and the horrified look on her face.

"What?" Peter Sheridan demanded as parents on either side of the aisle jumped up out of their seats.

"I think—oh my gosh, my water just broke!" Polly wailed.

Everyone looked back at Ashley, who was sitting several rows back on the aisle. Aware Polly's labor was indeed happening, just as Ashley had suspected, Ashley stood and made her way to Polly's side.

"And now I think I feel the baby coming!" Polly screamed.

Okay, that did it. Ashley took Polly's arm. Peter Sheridan took the other. "We've got to get Polly where she can lie down as quickly as possible," Ashley told Peter.

"I can't walk!" Polly cried, gripping her fiancé's hand, hard. "Oh, my...I— Oh, Dr. Hart, it hurts. It hurts so badly!"

Ashley and Cal, who was suddenly right there to assist, helped Polly down to the floor. "Clear the room. Now!" Ashley ordered.

"Oh, dear God—the baby's coming!" Polly cried hysterically as guests stampeded for the exit.

"Call an ambulance, and keep everyone else—except my mother—out of here," Cal told the minister, who quickly rushed to comply.

Ashley had never been more glad to have Cal at her side. She needed his strength and calm in an emergency, now more than ever. "What do you need?" Cal asked Ashley.

Ashley was fighting her way through Polly's sodden organza petticoats. "I've got to see what's going on."

"Scissors?" Cal guessed.

"And sterile cloths," Ashley ordered, distracted. "Whatever you can find to wrap the baby in."

"Is the ambulance going to get here in time?" Polly whimpered, crying in earnest now, while Peter Sheridan crouched beside her, patting her hand helplessly.

Please God, don't let *him* faint, Ashley thought, looking at the groom's increasingly pale color. "Hang in there now, Dad," Ashley told Peter firmly. She looked at him, willing him some of her calm and strength. "We need you to be strong here." She spoke as if underscoring every word.

Peter swallowed hard and nodded in compliance as Ashley finally ripped through the last of the petticoats. Ashley got a look at what was going on. Polly was right, Ashley noted grimly. Ashley could definitely see the baby crowning.

"Do we have time to get to the hospital?" Peter asked as Polly continued whimpering and crying out in pain.

"I don't think so," Ashley said, quickly assessing the best way to proceed. "This little guy seems to be in a hurry."

Polly screamed in terror as another contraction gripped her.

Ashley grabbed Polly's hands and squeezed as Cal rushed back in with a pair of scissors. It wasn't going to be easy, but they had to keep things under control. "Polly. Calm down. Breathe. Just like you learned in Lamaze class. That's it…that's wonderful…no…don't push, honey…not yet…we've got to get you cut out of this dress."

Cal was already cutting through the layers of expensive fabric as swiftly and efficiently as if he—rather than the nurses—did this every day.

"Okay, now. We're ready." The voluminous skirts and petticoats cleared away, Ashley placed a several-inch-thick bed of table linens beneath Polly's hips. "You can push, Polly. Yes, that's it, that's good."

Polly moaned and bore down. Once, twice, three times, until the baby's head popped out. Quickly, Ashley cleared the baby's nose and mouth of mucus.

"One more push, honey—a big one. Yes, yes, keep going…"

Polly complied as Peter cheered her on and their baby slid out the rest of the way. He was a perfect little boy who—going by the scowl on his little face—was none too pleased by the traumatic turn of events. Dark hair, handsome features, about eight pounds. Ashley cradled him, one hand beneath his head, the other under his hips, and picked the new little Pruett-Sheridan collaboration up for his two stunned and elated parents to see. He began fighting almost immediately—little arms and legs flailing—and let out a loud, lusty cry just as the ambulance crew came rushing in.

"Well, that was one wedding we won't soon forget," Cal lamented, several hours after he and Ashley had left the Holly Springs medical center where mother and baby were resting comfortably.

"Nor will anyone else in attendance. But all's well that ends well," Ashley said as she sipped her hot cider. They were home again, relaxing before the fire.

"At least they were able to get married once they were

at the hospital and all the post-delivery stuff was done," Cal said.

Ashley grinned at her husband wryly, happy their own wedding hadn't been that eventful. "Again, not exactly how Peter and Polly planned it."

"But, look at it this way." He toasted her wordlessly. "They'll have a birthday to celebrate along with their anniversary every year."

"True." Ashley stirred her cinnamon stick around in her drink.

Silence fell between them.

Ashley snuggled into the cushions and stared into the licking flames, feeling remarkably content.

"You were incredible tonight, you know," Cal said.

She felt the weight of his head come to rest against hers. Ashley looked down at his hard-muscled thigh, pressed next to hers. She curled her foot and dug her toes into the rug. "You've seen me deliver a baby before."

"But not in those circumstances." Cal lifted his head and she looked over at him. Respect glimmered in his gray eyes. His gaze drifted over her lazily, before returning to her eyes. Then he said what she least expected. "It's going to kill you not to be able to deliver babies while you wait for a slot to open up at the medical center, isn't it?"

Ashley cleared her throat and turned her gaze back to the fire. How did he know what she had been silently lamenting, ever since delivering Polly and Peter's baby? "I'll probably be able to take a call now and then for some of the other Obs in town." She put the best spin on it she could.

And he still wasn't buying it. "That's not the same as seeing your own patients through conception and delivery and postpartum, or delivering a couple of babies a week," Cal disagreed.

No, it wasn't. But maybe the loss of that particular thrill was just the price she was going to have to pay to get everything else she wanted in this life. "I'll get by, Cal," she told him stoically.

Cal frowned. "You just went through four years of college, four years of med school, and three-and-a-half years of fellowship training in maternal-fetal medicine. You shouldn't have to just get by, Ashley. You should be able to be doing exactly what you want at this point in your life."

Or so she had thought. But Ashley had learned the hard way that work satisfaction alone was not enough to make her happy. Not nearly. "I am doing exactly what I want to be doing, Cal." She put her cider aside and slid over onto his lap, so she was seated sideways, her arms wrapped around his neck. She looked deep into his eyes. "And that is be here with you."

Cal threaded his fingers through her hair. "And I'm glad you are," he murmured, wrapping his other arm around her waist, before moving it up and down her spine, "but I also want you to be happy."

Ashley swallowed as she felt the familiar pressure to be everything she could be professionally once again. Not from her parents this time, as was usually the case, but from Cal. She gritted her teeth as she struggled to contain her emotions and attempted to slide off his lap. "We went down this road once before, remember?" she told him tensely. "I ended up in Hawaii, three thousand miles from you."

Cal caught her before she could completely escape and held her in place. His body was as tense as hers. "There has to be a way for you to practice obstetrics now without shortchanging our marriage," Cal repeated stubbornly.

"If there is," Ashley said, suddenly weary to her soul once again, "I have no clue at all what it is."

# Chapter 14

"Let's just drop it," Ashley said as she pried his hands from around her waist and slid off his lap. She bristled as she got to her feet and moved to the fireplace.

Cal remained slouched on the sofa, arms stretched straight out on the cushions on either side of him. "Ignoring our problems won't make them go away."

Ashley flushed beneath his close scrutiny and ran her hand along the roughhewn wood of the mahogany mantel. "Taking my career goals down a notch does not qualify as a problem, Cal." She forced herself to turn and face him once again. There was understanding in his eyes and a strength of purpose that had developed during the two-and-a-half years they had been apart. He wasn't going to let her run this time. Or evade.

Cal countered calmly, "I might agree with you if we hadn't already been down this road."

He was talking about that first summer they were

married, the summer she had lost their baby, Ashley re-called miserably.

He stood and came toward her. "But we *have* been, Ashley. You tried to forget what you wanted to do pro-fessionally when your fellowship program abruptly lost its funding and got cancelled that spring." His calm steady voice penetrated her defenses, like a battering ram against a barricaded door.

"You said, 'No problem, Cal. I'll just forget the lofty goals and go into a regular residency program where I don't have to write a thesis and get the equivalent of a master's degree in medicine.'"

Ashley released a shaky breath—she had said just that.

They stood near enough that she could see the lines of strain on his face and the old hurt in his eyes. And along with that, the determination that their future—and the future of their marriage—would be better.

"So you applied to the other programs in the area and got accepted and were all set to stay here with me." Cal paused, swallowed hard. "And then the fellowship offer came through from Hawaii, out of the blue. Remember?"

Ashley nodded. She hadn't expected it. "The fellow-ship program director here had called around until he found a place that would take me," she recollected. It hadn't been easy. Most fellowship programs had only two or three slots per specialty and carried long wait-ing lists of students, wanting admission. Trying to find a place for a student suddenly displaced midstream had been a nightmare.

"And you decided to take that instead," Cal reminded her, his expression hard, unflagging.

Yes, she had. But not for the reasons Cal thought, Ash-ley knew. Stricken with secret grief and guilt over the loss of their baby, Ashley had wanted only to get away from everything familiar—including Cal—to forget the loss that haunted her.

Cal shook his head, looking equally remorseful as he continued with self-effacing honesty, "Of course, the fact you were so eager to leave was all my fault." He ran both his hands through his hair and left them laced together at the back of his neck. "I shouldn't have been pressuring you to take the unexpected time-out of your education to get pregnant and have a baby. I should have accepted at that point that your medical training had to come first."

Ashley struggled to contain her soaring emotions. She shook her head grimly, not about to let him put this on himself. "You weren't to blame, Cal. We had talked about me having kids during my fellowship before we got married." And agreed they both wanted them, sooner rather than later, just like their friends Carlotta and Mateo Ramirez. Ashley felt her whole body tense. "I just didn't realize how taxing it was going to be on my body working those thirty-six-hour shifts that first year."

"Then you found out how physically and emotionally grueling first-year fellowship is, and you no longer thought it best we try and get pregnant then after all," Cal said.

Because she had miscarried and was afraid to try to carry a baby again, at least during her training years, for fear the same thing would happen. Or worse, she'd find out there was something wrong with her that would keep her from ever carrying his child.

Had their argument only ended there, with her unilateral decision, perhaps it would have been easier to recover. But it hadn't. Cal had told her what was on his mind and in his heart, and the memory of that still stung her unbearably. "And you," Ashley recalled, with no small degree of pain as she looked Cal straight in the eye, "said if we weren't going to have kids then what had been the point of us getting married in the first place."

Cal grimaced at the memory of that awful time. He came toward her, arms outstretched. "I didn't mean it. You know that."

Ashley knew there was a grain of truth to everything that was ever said. She held up a palm to keep him from encompassing her in a hug. She didn't want him to touch her now. "You were right to be angry with me for my reversal in positions, Cal."

Cal dropped his hands, stepped back. "I was selfish."

"The point is," Ashley continued carefully, making certain to broadcast her own culpability in their marital problems, "you never misrepresented your desire to have a large family similar to the one you grew up in." He at least had remained steadfast from the day they had said their vows. Ashley angled a thumb at her sternum. "I was the one who briefly changed my mind."

"You don't feel that way anymore?" Cal questioned, his expression strained as he leaned a shoulder against the mantel, too.

Ashley nodded as feelings of loss and longing, hope and joy, filled her heart. "I want to have a baby with you," she said cautiously.

"I want that, too."

He started toward her. Again, Ashley backed away.

She saw the confusion in his eyes as she continued to keep her distance. "But what would happen if I were infertile or had some problem that wouldn't allow me to carry a baby to term?"

He shrugged his broad shoulders and retorted matter-of-factly, "Then we'd adopt."

"And you'd be okay with that?" Ashley pressed on. She bit her lip nervously. "You wouldn't feel cheated?"

A pulse throbbing in his throat, he continued to probe her face. "Where is this coming from?"

Anxiety swept through her in near-debilitating waves. *Tell him,* Ashley thought. *Tell him now.* But when she opened her mouth, the words wouldn't come. She was too afraid Cal would get that disappointed look in his eyes, the same one her parents had whenever she didn't quite measure up. And she didn't think she could bear it. "I—I don't know," Ashley said finally. And to his considerable frustration, she left it at that.

Cal wasn't sure when he had been so discouraged. All he knew was that Ashley was shutting him out again. And she shouldn't be. The two of them should be closer than ever after delivering Polly Pruett and Peter Sheridan's baby together tonight. And for a short time they had been. Until talk of children had come up and Ashley had closed down once again.

"I'm really tired." Ashley stepped past him and moved around the sofa, toward the adjacent kitchen.

Abruptly, she looked as battle-weary as he felt, Cal thought. And not just in her pretty face. Fatigue was in the set of her shoulders and the weary strides of her long legs. But it was no wonder after the day his wife'd had—spending the morning at the Wedding Inn trying on wedding dresses and being photographed, plus that evening's wedding and the unexpected emergency delivery. Ashley *should* be exhausted.

She sent him an apologetic sideways glance. "I know we had talked about making love earlier, but...would you mind if I just got a glass of milk and went on up to bed?"

Cal was already turning off the lights. "I'll go with you. I'm beat, too."

When they got to their bedroom, Ashley disappeared

into the hall bath to put her pajamas on and get ready for bed. By the time she emerged, face scrubbed and teeth brushed, he was waiting for her in the master bedroom.

But instead of cuddling up to him, as she had been doing the previous nights, she turned onto her side, away from him, and went to sleep. Just the way she had done the first summer of their marriage, when she had first started putting up walls between them and put him—and their marriage—low on the list of priorities of her life.

But Cal knew that time had been different from now. He had been behaving selfishly, devoting himself to his own career, to the point that he neglected her and their marriage terribly. He had not been doing that since Ashley had come back to North Carolina. He had, in fact, been doing everything he could to make her understand just how much he wanted to get their marriage on the right path again and make her happy.

Her moodiness tonight—brought on by the resumption of their discussion about career and family—had merely resurrected old wounds. It was not a predictor of the future, Cal tried to reassure himself.

Ashley rose early. Not wanting to pick up where they had left off the night before, she showered and dressed while Cal was still sleeping. Then she went over to the hospital to check on Polly, Peter and their baby. To her satisfaction, all three were glowing with health and happiness. "So I guess I should call you Mr. and Mrs. Sheridan now?" Ashley teased, admiring the matching wedding rings on the happy couple's left hands.

"Or Mom and Dad." Peter winked as he cradled his sleeping newborn son in his arms.

Ashley paused to admire their newborn, then speaking quietly so as not to disturb the slumbering infant, told them both, "Dr. Ramirez is going to be taking over your care now. I just stopped by to offer congratulations."

"You mean you're not going to be part of her practice anymore?" Polly's face fell.

Ashley shook her head. "My helping out was just a temporary thing." They had explained that to all of Carlotta's patients, when she started.

"But I liked having both of you there!" Polly protested. "It was nice, knowing one of you was always available in case there was a problem or something."

"Where are you going to practice medicine?" Peter asked.

"I haven't decided yet," Ashley said. Cal had been right. She would miss delivering babies. But she would miss him more if she had to go elsewhere to do it.

"We're all hoping she stays at the Holly Springs medical center, but that has yet to be worked out," Carlotta said, walking into the room, chart in hand. She looked at Ashley and the Sheridans. "I guess I missed a very exciting delivery last night," Carlotta said.

"And then some," Peter agreed.

"Have you examined Polly?" Carlotta asked Ashley.

"No. I'm just here on a social call," Ashley said. She started to step out of the room.

"Meet you in the staff lounge?" Carlotta said.

Ashley nodded. She was still down there when Carlotta joined her a few minutes later. "Polly looks great," Carlotta said. "I think we'll be able to send her and the baby both home from the hospital tomorrow."

"Good."

"About your job options..." Carlotta said.

"I've been wanting to talk to you," Ashley said. She had been thinking about it off-and-on since their last conversation on the subject and come up with a few ideas that might—if Carlotta were amenable—offer Ashley the best of both worlds, personal and professional.

"Let's go over to my office then," Carlotta suggested pleasantly, "where we can talk privately."

The two women walked out of the hospital and into the three-story building next door, where many of the doctors' offices were housed.

"I meant what I said about hoping you stay," Carlotta told her soberly as soon as the two women were settled.

Ashley knew Carlotta did. "And I think," Ashley said slowly, hoping her idea might seem as good to Carlotta as it did to Ashley, "I may have figured out a way for that to happen."

Cal smelled something delicious cooking the minute he walked in the door Sunday evening. He had spent the day doing two back-to-back emergency surgeries. The one time he had been able to get away to call Ashley for a minute, she hadn't been home.

She breezed toward him, the angst and fatigue of the evening before forgotten. "You look happy."

Cal took in the loose cloud of dark hair. She was wearing her black slacks and one of his dress shirts— a medium-blue button-down that fell to her thighs and disguised the new voluptuousness of her figure. Excitement sparkled in her blue eyes. "That's because we're celebrating."

He lifted a brow as she wrapped her arms around his neck and kissed him soundly. "I think I've worked out my job situation," Ashley told him, drawing back. "But I wanted to talk to you first before I agreed to anything."

Cal inhaled the orange blossom fragrance of her perfume, felt the softness of her lower body pressed against his. "But you want to agree?" Cal guessed, stroking a hand through her hair. He had a sinking feeling she was going to be commuting to a job again.

Oblivious to his worries, Ashley nodded. She stepped back so they could talk more seriously. "Carlotta and I talked about the fact that we both want to practice obstetrics and gynecology here in Holly Springs, but we also want more satisfying personal lives. So I'm going to join her practice and we're both going to continue to work part-time, just the way we have been. For now, she will work weekday mornings and I'll work weekday afternoons, and we'll alternate our call nights. The money won't be as good—I'll only be making half of what I would be making if I were to work full-time—but I can stay here with you. And then one day, if another full-time staff Ob/Gyn position opens up at the medical center, well, I'll have the option to increase my patient load—within our joint practice—and my income."

"The hospital administration?"

Ashley gave the spaghetti Bolognese sauce simmering gently on the stove another stir. "Carlotta and I talked to Frank Hodges this afternoon and pitched him our idea. I'm happy to report he's one-hundred-percent behind our proposal. They've been losing too many female physicians who can't handle sixty- to eighty-hour work weeks and a family." Ashley paused. "I wasn't sure how you'd feel about it."

Cal blinked. "Are you kidding? I love the idea. As long as you're okay just working part-time." He knew what a go-getter Ashley was. She had always liked to be busy one hundred percent of the time.

For a moment, the veil was back over Ashley's emotions. He felt the familiar distance between them and had the sensation she was withholding every bit as much as she was telling him.

He wanted to talk further, see if he couldn't discover whatever it was that was bothering her, but she was giving him that smile and turning off the burners on the stove. Going up on tiptoe, she fastened her lips to his. As their kiss turned hot, passion took over. And as he swept her up into his arms and carried her up to bed, he figured whatever it was just below the surface could wait. He wanted—needed—to feel close to Ashley. If this was the only way she could let him do that, then so be it.

"Well?" Ashley said the following Friday afternoon, after Carlotta had finished examining her. Another excruciatingly slow week of not being able to tell Cal about the pregnancy had passed. "How am I?"

Carlotta wrote a couple of notes on Ashley's chart. "Weight and blood pressure are fine, the size of the uterus and the height of the fundus are exactly where they should be. Congratulations, kid. You've made it to the beginning of the second trimester." Her smile fading, Carlotta paused. "It must be killing you not to tell Cal."

Ashley nodded, reflecting on the sacrifice she had made in order to protect her husband. "It has been." She adjusted her clothing and hopped down from the table. "But all that is changing this evening."

The two women walked through the deserted office to the private office they were now sharing. "He's going to be upset about your previous miscarriage."

"I know." Finished for the day, Ashley gathered up her things.

"But you *are* going to tell him," Carlotta said, as she did the same.

"Eventually." Ashley shrugged on her winter coat and looped her carryall over her shoulder. "I'm not sure if it will be tonight."

Carlotta gave her a scolding look. "Ashley!"

Ashley held her ground. "If I tell him tonight it will dull the good news."

Carlotta rummaged for her keys then turned off the lights. "The longer you wait, the harder it is going to be."

"I know that." The two locked up and walked out to the parking lot.

Carlotta paused next to Ashley's new van. "Maybe you should tell him about the miscarriage first, and then the pregnancy."

Ashley turned her collar up against the chill February air. "I've been considering that." She turned her gaze to the bleak gray sky.

"But?" Carlotta prodded, when Ashley didn't go on.

Ashley lifted her hands helplessly. "If I tell Cal what happened before, he's going to be worried the way I have been all along. That means he's going to have to grieve the loss of the baby we lost. And although I think he should do that sometime," Ashley set her jaw stubbornly, as the familiar feelings of grief and guilt welled up inside her, "I'm not certain Cal has to do the two things simultaneously."

Cal stopped by the Wedding Inn that evening, en route home from the hospital, to make sure everything was on track for the following evening. To his relief, he found everything was all set. He was on his way back out to his car, when he encountered Mac on his way in.

"Yes," Mac said, before Cal could get a word in edgewise. "I have picked up my tuxedo. And so have all your other brothers. So you can stop worrying. The repeat of your wedding to Ashley is going to go without a hitch."

"I'm counting on it," Cal said.

Mac gave Cal a look that reminded Cal no matter how old the two of them got, Mac was still his big brother, and as such, intended to look out for Cal and the rest of the Hart family. "As long as we've got a moment, how are things going between you and Ashley these days?" Mac asked.

Cal wasn't sure how to answer that. He leaned against the wrought-iron railing that edged the semi-circular steps leading up to the portal of the Wedding Inn. "You heard she accepted a part-time position at the medical center, and is now a partner in a shared Ob/Gyn practice with Carlotta Ramirez."

Mac nodded. He pushed the Stetson that was part of his sheriff's uniform away from his brow. "How's it working out?"

"So far so good," Cal said cautiously.

"And the marriage?"

"Is better than it ever has been."

"And yet…" Mac prodded.

Cal shrugged. Knowing he had to confide in somebody, and that he could trust his older brother to keep a confidence as no one else could, Cal said finally, "She's just so moody these days. One minute she's laughing, the next she's crying. Sometimes I feel closer to her than I've ever felt in my life and then she shuts down, and I feel like she's got secrets and feelings I'll never be let in on, no matter how long I'm with her."

Mac's brow furrowed. "What kind of secrets?" Mac said, pulling his hat down across his brow.

Cal looked at him in frustration. "That's just it. I don't know," he confessed quietly. "And it really bugs me. I'm starting to think I'm a little paranoid. And that's not a good feeling to have where your wife is concerned. Not that you'd know—" Cal couldn't resist ribbing Mac a little "—since you've never been hitched." Except for his engagement, years before, Mac had never even come close to settling down with any one woman. And now, at age thirty-five, Mac was the only one of Helen Hart's brood who was still single.

"Why would I want to do a fool thing like that when I've got my hands full looking after all of you?" Mac jousted right back.

"You're not responsible for anything that goes right or wrong in our lives," Cal said.

Briefly, something akin to guilt flickered in Mac's eyes. And then to Cal's consternation, Mac shut down as surely and completely as Ashley had been doing lately. "Now you're doing it, too," Cal pointed out sagely.

Mac frowned. The barriers went even higher. "What?"

"Cutting me out. Looking guilty."

Mac reached over and brushed a knuckle across Cal's head, the way he had when they were kids. Shaking his head, Mac pushed past and continued up the steps to the Wedding Inn. "You've got too much time on your hands," Mac threw the admonishing words over his shoulder. "Go home to your wife."

Exactly what Cal planned to do. "Remember. It's a Valentine's dinner for the family tomorrow night," Cal shouted up to Mac. "And that's all Ashley knows until she gets here."

Mac waved his acknowledgment and went on into the inn.

The question was, what kind of mood was his wife going to be in? Cal wondered as he drove on out to the farm.

Good, as it turned out. *Exceptionally* good, judging from the dinner cooking on the stove and the red silk robe she was wearing. A table had been set up before the fireplace. It was set with their wedding silver and china. Cal watched Ashley light the candles on the table. Damn, she was beautiful, and unless he was mistaken, she was completely naked under that frilly confection. "Valentine's Day is Sunday," he said, aware Ashley hadn't cooked this many times for him in one week since before they were married.

Ashley turned toward him, her hair falling softly across her shoulders as she moved. "We're celebrating early." She glided toward him in a drift of perfume.

Cal's throat felt parched. As Ashley drew ever closer, his lower half pulsed to life. "So I see."

As Ashley neared him, he noticed the imprint of her nipples pressing against the silk of the robe he ached to untie.

"Because we have something very special to celebrate," Ashley went up on tiptoe and whispered in his ear.

Cal wrapped his arms about her waist, as hers moved to wreathe his neck, and the soft fullness of her breasts pressed against his chest. "We do?"

"Yes." Smiling, Ashley cuddled all the closer. She loosened the knot of his tie, and began to work it free. "You see, there's a reason I've been gaining weight. And feeling peculiar. And craving French fries dipped in chili in the middle of the night."

His heart racing, Cal struggled to take it all in.

And then Ashley was saying the words he had dreamed of hearing for years.

"By August, there were will no longer be two of us, Cal. There will be three."

# Chapter 15

Cal's feelings soared as the impact of what Ashley had just told him sunk in. He wrapped her in a hug, then drew back to look into her face. Tears of happiness glittered in her eyes and fell down her face. But beneath the joy was something else...something uncertain...and full of conflict. Not sure where that emotion was coming from, Cal stepped back slightly to better survey her upturned face. Suddenly, his heart was beating as hard and erratically as hers. "You're sure?"

Ashley swallowed hard and forced another smile. "I've had blood tests, the complete obstetrics workup."

Cal ran a hand down her arm. No doubt about it— she was trembling. And not in a good way. He tried to reassure her with a steadying touch. "And everything's okay?"

Ashley nodded. "Absolutely."

Then what was behind her sudden shift in mood, from

all-out happiness to edgy apprehension? Cal wondered. Was there some medical reason for her uneasiness that she had yet to disclose? And was she trying, even as they stood there, to work up the courage to do so?

"Everything is on track for an August delivery by the stork," Ashley joked.

Cal struggled to search out the possible cause for her anxiety. "August," he repeated, focusing on the facts she had told him thus far. He stopped as her words sank in. "That means you're—?"

"At the very beginning of my second trimester, yes," she confirmed, abruptly looking as if she were hiding something from him again, and worse, feared his reaction to it.

Silence fell between them. The air was thick with tension. Ashley gulped and went back to the table. She lifted a glass of ice water and took a sip. Cal noticed there was a bead of perspiration just above her brow. She really was nervous about this. And not, he thought, because she had feared he wouldn't be happy about the news. No, she had to know that as much as he loved her, he would be over the moon....

He swallowed around the tightness in his throat and stepped nearer. "How long have you known?"

Ashley pulled out a chair at the table, sat down. Looking as if she wanted nothing more than to retreat at that point, she avoided his probing gaze. Probably, Cal thought, because she didn't want him to see the guilt simmering there.

"About three weeks," she said in a low, deferential tone.

Cal shoved a hand through his hair. "And you didn't tell me?"

Ashley blinked rapidly and recovered her composure.

In a voice thick with emotion, she revealed, "I wanted to make sure everything was okay. And, well," she lifted her hand helplessly and drew in another unsteady breath, "things were pretty rocky between us back then. I didn't want us staying together only because of the baby."

Did she really think that little of him? Of them? "You should have told me, Ashley." Cal was angry and hurt at having been left out like that. Worse, he felt like a fool. Now, he knew why she hadn't wanted him to see her naked. Why she had resisted buying more than just a few items of new clothing that fit her better. Why she resisted the heavy-duty exercising that would have helped her get her figure back under normal conditions—because it would have endangered the life of their fetus. And most of all, he knew why she had been so upset when she had briefly lost control of the Mustang he had given her, why she hadn't wanted to drive it again in the ice and snow and why she had agreed to something with every safety option possible....

Abruptly, Ashley looked as unsettled as he felt at the news of her pregnancy and the fact she had chosen not to tell him till now. "I'll never keep anything like that from you again," Ashley promised him sincerely. She looked at him, love—and hope—shining in her eyes.

Cal had a choice. Stay angry and force them both to deal with his feelings, here and now, and ruin what should be one of the happiest nights of his life—or dig deep and find that compassion inside himself his mother had once found severely lacking, and accept Ashley's mistake for what it was and let it go. Although it went against his gut impulse to have this out, here and now—no matter how unpleasant the confrontation—he decided to let it go.

He took Ashley in his arms and kissed her again, pouring all his love for her, all the hopes and dreams he had for her and the baby into the emotion-filled embrace. She was trembling when he lifted his head. They both were.

"So you're happy about this baby?" Ashley whispered, looking more vulnerable and more in love with him than he had ever seen her.

Cal had wanted a family with her forever. And now she was here with him again, and it was really happening. He wasn't going to spoil that. "Happier than I've ever been in my life," he said huskily, curving his hand around her belly and the baby growing inside. And he meant that with all his heart and soul.

Ashley and Cal stayed up late, celebrating, intending to sleep late the next morning since neither of them were on emergency call that weekend. It wasn't to be. At eight-thirty, they heard the doorbell ringing. And ringing. And ringing. Cal groaned and lifted his head from the pillow. His wife was cuddled up beside him, in all her naked pregnant glory. "Are you expecting anyone?" He sure hoped not. He wanted nothing more than to be able to spend the morning noting all the miraculous changes going on in her body right now, and making love to her again and again. But as the doorbell rang yet again, he realized that wouldn't happen until he got rid of whoever was intruding on their Saturday morning.

"I don't know who it could be," Ashley murmured. "Although I can tell you one thing, they're at the top of my *persona non grata* list right now."

Cal agreed. Who came over this time on a Saturday morning without calling first?

"I'll see who it is." Cal tugged on his slacks, grabbed his shirt, and headed downstairs. "And get rid of them. Pronto."

Ashley lay back down. She thought about the night before, and how nervous she had been delivering the news to Cal. With good reason, as it turned out. He had been hurt at first to realize she had kept her pregnancy from him for even a few weeks. She couldn't imagine how he would have reacted if he had known she'd not told him about the earlier pregnancy or subsequent miscarriage in the two-and-a-half years since.

He would have really been furious.

So she had chickened out again.

And though she knew she still had to find a way to tell him—some way, some time—in the near future, it wasn't going to be today. Or tomorrow, which was Valentine's Day and their third wedding anniversary. She wanted to know their marriage was on very solid ground before she risked seeing that disappointment in his eyes.

Downstairs, the front door opened, then closed. Ashley heard Cal welcoming their guests, then more voices. She sat up with a start, jumped out of bed, dressed and joined Cal as quickly as she could. And not a moment too soon, she noted, seeing the uncomfortable look on his face as he puttered about their kitchen, pouring juice, and taking a coffeecake from the freezer and putting it into the oven to warm.

Ashley stood in the portal wishing she'd had time to do more than put on her black slacks and a red sweater and brush her hair. "Mom. Dad."

Both Harold and Margaret stood and gave her cursory hugs. "We're sorry about the early hour, but this was the only time we could get our schedules together to visit with you," Margaret said.

As usual, both dressed in business attire. Not that either were the type to ever putter around in jeans or sweats....

"We were just telling Cal that we can't stay and have

dinner with you this evening." Harold's words seemed rife with hidden meaning as he glanced at Cal.

"That's okay." Ashley smothered a yawn with the back of her hand. "We've got a Hart family thing over at the Wedding Inn to go to this evening anyway. But it's good you're here." Ashley moved to her husband's side. Needing his steadying presence more than ever, she wrapped her arm about his waist and leaned into him affectionately. "Cal and I have some news. We're expecting a baby. Come August, you will be grandparents."

For a second, neither Harold nor Margaret could speak. Then, as Ashley had hoped, her parents both offered her their congratulations and engulfed her and Cal in awkward hugs.

"Well, that's wonderful news, and all the more reason for you to get your career situation straightened out," Margaret said as the four of them sat down together in the family room.

His expression neutral, Cal walked over to start a pot of decaf in the adjacent kitchen. Ashley knew he was giving her room to deal with her parents as she saw fit, without inserting himself into the situation. "I told you— I'm going to be working part-time for the next few years," Ashley explained patiently.

Margaret and Harold exchanged concerned looks. "Ashley, we know you want to be a good mother and you will be, but you can't shortchange the rest of your life," Margaret said.

"You'll never be happy just working part-time," Harold predicted.

Margaret leaned forward urgently. "Furthermore, they haven't filled the position at Yale—"

"No," Ashley said. "I'm not applying and I don't want to hear any more about it."

Margaret frowned. "But——"

Cal walked back in, ready to help her out, if need be.

Ashley held up a hand, letting Cal know with a glance she could handle this. "You have to stop pushing me," she told both her parents.

"But we want you to be happy!" Margaret insisted.

Ashley nodded, affirming she wanted the same thing. "And I will be. But only," she stipulated bluntly, "if I am living my life my way."

Harold regarded Ashley sternly. "We're trying to help you, Ashley."

Ashley knew that, just as she knew her parents loved her, in their own way. Even if they didn't quite know what to do with her. "If you really want to help me," she told them gently, "then let me be me."

"Are you okay?" Cal asked, after Margaret and Harold had left. She certainly looked as if she were doing fine, Cal noted. Although maybe that wasn't a surprise, given the fact that for the first time Ashley had really stood up to Margaret and Harold. She had taken charge of her own life, worried less about what others wanted from her than what she wanted for herself and the two— no make that three now—of them.

Ashley nodded, relief flowing from her in waves. She wrapped her arms around Cal's waist and rested her head against his shoulder. "Promise me that we will never do that to our children," she said quietly.

Cal hugged her close and kissed the top of her head. "I promise."

A contented silence fell between them. Cal stroked his hands through her hair. "They love you."

"That's the sad part." Ashley drew back to look into his face. She splayed her hands across his chest. "I know that. Just as I know I will never live up to this perfect image they have of me. But it's not my problem. It's theirs."

Cal regarded her with a mixture of respect and relief. "So you can deal?"

"With you by my side? I can tackle everything." Ashley smiled.

"Nervous?" Cal asked Ashley as he parked in front of the Wedding Inn, and the two of them got out of their new van.

"Not at all." Ashley tucked her hand in Cal's as they ascended the steps of the palatial, three-story white-brick Wedding Inn. In fact, she was looking forward to this evening with the Harts. Cal wanted to announce the impending birth of their baby to everyone in his family at once. They had decided the Valentine's dinner Helen was giving for the family that evening was the perfect opportunity. "I know your family is going to be happy for us," Ashley continued.

"I think so, too," Cal murmured. Looking every bit as contented and optimistic about their future as she felt, he drew Ashley toward him for a steamy kiss beneath the pillared portico.

No sooner had their lips touched than twelve-year-old Christopher came barreling out the grand entrance, and nearly knocked them down. "Hey! You're not supposed to be kissing yet!" he scolded them cheerfully, then stuck his head back in the front door. "Gramma—they're out here! Kissing!"

"Already?" Janey teased as Cal and Ashley came into the grand hall. Cal's sister looked as though she knew something Ashley didn't. As did Christopher and Helen....

Ashley turned to Cal. "What are they talking about?" she asked.

Cal merely grinned in masculine satisfaction and gave her hand a squeeze. "Let's get everybody together and tell them our news first," Cal said.

"I'll get 'em all down here in no time flat!" Christopher raced through the hall.

Five minutes later all of Cal's family were gathered around him and Ashley. Whatever the secret was, Ashley noted, they all appeared to be in on it, too.

"You wanted to talk to us?" Fletcher drawled.

"Ashley and I have an announcement to make," Cal said in a voice husky with emotion. He brought Ashley in close to his side and held her there tenderly. "We're expanding our family. Ashley is pregnant. The baby should be here in early August."

That quickly, every woman in the family gasped in surprise and teared up. The men, looking no less moved, offered hearty handshakes and congratulations. Christopher turned to his mother, perplexed. "Is this why—?"

Janey clamped a hand over Christopher's mouth before he could finish his sentence. "Not yet," Janey warned.

"Someone care to fill me in?" Ashley prompted dryly. It seemed she was the only one in the room who didn't have a clue what was going on.

Cal turned to Ashley. "You remember when I said I was going to have to get you another present for Valentine's Day?"

Ashley nodded, recalling very well the evening he had gifted her with the Mustang convertible. That evening—and the romantic intention behind it—had marked a turning point in their relationship. "But we already got a van," she protested.

"This is a lot better than a van," a starry-eyed Lily declared.

Again, everyone nodded.

"We're saying our wedding vows again tonight," Cal told her in a voice filled with love. "In honor of our third wedding anniversary."

"I can't believe you all did all this," Ashley said in stunned amazement as the women accompanied her up the sweeping staircase to the bridal dressing suite on the second floor.

Cal and his brothers were headed toward the groom's suite on the other side of the inn.

"Cal's had us busy for weeks!" Janey said, chuckling. "Why do you think I came over asking you to taste cake?"

"And I had you trying on wedding gowns?" Helen added.

"And I had you looking at flower arrangements," Lily said.

Emma nodded. "We thought—correctly, it turned out—your tastes might have changed in the three years since your last wedding, or you just might be in the mood for something different." She took the off-the-shoulder white silk gown with the fitted bodice, basque waist and full gathered skirt off the padded hanger. "We even had this altered for you."

Oh, no… Ashley thought. But unwilling to state they shouldn't have done that when everyone had clearly been trying so hard to please her, she simply smiled. "When is this all supposed to take place?"

"Half an hour. So we have plenty of time to get you ready. Don't worry."

Ashley delayed getting into her dress as long as she

could, letting the stylist Emma had hired fuss with her hair and touch up her makeup, but finally, there was no getting around it; she had to get into the gown.

As she feared, the gown was a lot tighter than it had been when she had tried it on a week before, particularly in the area of her rib cage and breasts. She had to suck her midriff in mightily so it would zip. But as long as she stayed that way—barely breathing—it was a perfect fit.

"You look gorgeous," Emma said.

Janey nodded. "Now for the veil."

More fussing, and flowers were brought in. Then Mateo and Carlotta and a few other close friends of her and Cal arrived.

Before long, the harpist was starting. The women were ducking out, to join the others in the upstairs reception hall that had been readied for the ceremony itself.

"You okay?" Lily asked, as she knelt and arranged the chapel train on Ashley's dress.

*Except I can't breathe.* Ashley nodded, too embarrassed to tell anyone she really shouldn't be wearing that dress....

Lily dashed on ahead, slipping into the room where the ceremony was to be held.

Ashley followed, alone, her bouquet clasped in front of her, for her grand entrance. The pressure on her waist and rib cage and the light-headed feeling got more intense with every step she took.

*Don't be silly. You can do this. It's only a few more minutes...and then the ceremony will be done....*

Determined not to do anything so foolish as pass out halfway to Cal, Ashley drew a deep, quelling breath, and commanded her knees to stop shaking so. Unfortunately, as her lungs filled, Ashley felt her dress begin to rip along her left side seam. Horrified she was about to put on a show for the entire Hart family, the likes of which they had never seen, Ashley gasped at the soft sound of rending fabric and bent over from the waist, both her hands going to her waist.

Once again, it was the exact wrong thing to do.

The additional pressure of binding fabric against her breasts and ribs pushed the air she had just gulped in right back out again. Ashley heard voices coming at her, as if from a great distance away. A rising murmur of familial concern. The next thing Ashley knew, the whole room was swimming, her limbs went limp, and her nose was buried in her bouquet.

For Cal, it was like watching an accident in slow motion.

He'd known something was wrong the moment Ashley stepped into the room. Her cheeks were too pink at first, then too pale, her steps uncertain, wavering. The way she was swaying back and forth, like a sailor on a pitching deck, he would've thought she'd been drinking. Except he knew she hadn't. And wouldn't so long as she was carrying their baby.

But it wasn't until she moaned and bent over from the waist suddenly, clutching her left side, and Mac muttered beside him, "Oh my God! Not again!" that Cal lurched into action.

He dashed down the aisle, toward Ashley, catching her in his arms just as she dropped into a dead faint. Wondering all the while what the hell his brother had meant when he'd said, "Not again!"

Carlotta pushed her way through the family gathered around as Cal gently laid Ashley down on the satin runner in the center of the room. Shades of Polly Pruett's untimely birth flashed through Cal's mind. Except it was way too early for their baby to be born....

"Everyone clear the room," Carlotta ordered, taking charge as Ashley's Ob/Gyn.

Mac was already herding them out, shutting the door.

Ashley moaned and her eyes fluttered open.

"Ashley," Carlotta demanded. "Are you in pain?"

"What?" Ashley struggled to come to all the way. "In pain? Oh God," she prayed out loud. "Not again!"

*What did she mean?* Cal wondered. *Not again!*

*What the hell did Mac know that he didn't?*

"Are you hurting anywhere?" Carlotta persisted, as she looked into Ashley's eyes and checked her pulse.

"No," Ashley shook her head, clearly sure about that much anyway. Ashley blinked again. "What happened?"

"That's what we're trying to find out," Cal told his wife gently.

Ashley put a trembling hand to her temple as she struggled to recall the moment immediately before her collapse. "I don't know. I felt dizzy and then everything sort of went black."

Carlotta palpated Ashley's middle, checking to make sure there was no tenderness. When she found none, Carlotta looked over at Cal. "I think she just fainted," Carlotta told Cal.

Helen knocked and popped her head in. "Cal? I've got some smelling salts if you need them."

Cal went over to get them.

"Is she going to be okay?" Helen asked.

Cal nodded.

Their marriage was another matter.

Cal left Ashley with Carlotta and went to find Mac. "Can I talk to you alone for a minute?"

They stepped into the groom's dressing room and shut the door behind them. "What did you mean when you said, 'Not again'?" Cal demanded. "Have you seen Ashley faint before?"

For once in his life, Mac was at a complete loss for words.

"She's okay, isn't she?" Mac asked eventually.

"What would make you think she wouldn't be?" Cal retorted. And why was his law-and-order older brother looking so guilty? "There's something you aren't telling me, isn't there?"

Mac's jaw tightened. He looked away. Didn't answer. "You should probably talk to Ashley about this," Mac advised.

Cal intended to do just that. He strode back down the hall to the suite where he and Ashley were to renew their vows. He knocked and walked in. Ashley was sitting in one of the chairs, Carlotta next to her, and sipping orange juice. They were talking in low, subdued tones. Tellingly, their conversation stopped abruptly when Cal walked in. They smiled—maybe too brightly and officiously. Both looked as if they were hiding something, just as Mac had. *So now there were three people who knew what he didn't.* His temper rising, Cal looked at Carlotta. "If you don't mind, I'd like a word alone with my wife," he said mildly.

Carlotta patted Ashley's hand—as if in silent support—and stood.

"The ceremony is going to have to be delayed. I've got a problem with the dress." Flushing, Ashley held the glass of juice away from her and showed Cal the left side seam. It was shredded from her breast to waist.

"It's probably best we wait, anyway." Cal looked at Carlotta. "Would you please tell everyone and also make sure that we're not disturbed?"

"No problem." With another telling look at Ashley, Carlotta breezed out.

"Do you still feel light-headed?" Cal pulled up the chair beside her and turned it so they could sit, knee to knee, facing each other.

"No. The smelling salts took care of that." She studied him as closely as he was regarding her.

Cal looked at her mouth—it was damp and soft. He wanted to drag her into his arms and kiss her again, reason be damned. He wanted to take her home and make wild passionate love to her again, and then, when they'd exhausted themselves and run the gamut of their feelings for each other, deal with this mess.

He also knew that it was that same head-in-the-sand, hear-no-evil, see-no-evil reaction that had gotten them to this point.

They had been running from certain truths for years.

They could not continue to do so.

Like it or not they had to deal with each other and these secrets, whatever they might be.

"You look upset," Ashley said.

The understatement of the century if there ever was one. "Shouldn't I be?" Cal replied cordially.

Looking as if she wanted to retreat, she took another long drink and turned her glance to the flower arbor where Cal and the minister had both been standing a few short minutes ago. Ashley swallowed hard. "Because I fainted?"

Cal regarded her warily, his heart working like a trip hammer in his chest. "Because Mac and Carlotta both know something that I don't." He paused, fury rising, as he waited for her to return her glance to his. "Were you ever going to tell me about what happened before?"

Abruptly, she looked exhausted and close to tears. "You know about the miscarriage," she guessed sadly.

Which meant, Cal thought, there had been another baby. One he knew nothing about—until this evening, anyway. His muscles were tight with suppressed anger and resentment. Hurt colored his low tone as he replied, even more softly, "I do now."

Ashley drained her glass, put it aside. Cal noted her hand was shaking.

"Then—?"

Briefly he explained what Mac had said and when. And how he'd refused to answer Cal's questions about his comment.

Ashley released a frustrated breath. The color in her cheeks turned from a pale pink to a dusky rose as she declared miserably, "I never should have put him in that position."

His mood grim, Cal stared at the woman he had been married to for three years. "No argument there," he said sarcastically.

Ashley's lower lip thrust toward him contentiously.

Giving her no chance to defend herself, he stood and moved a slight distance away from her. "And how is it that my brother knows you had a miscarriage and I don't?" he demanded, bracing his legs a little further apart and folding his arms across his chest.

Ashley stood and gripped the back of the chair tightly with one hand. "Because Mac was with me when it happened."

Jealousy ripped through his gut. "Which was?" Cal commanded.

Ashley drew in a quavering breath. "The summer I left for Hawaii. I had planned to tell you I was pregnant when you finished taking your board exams that July, but I miscarried before that."

Pain glimmered in her eyes. She gulped and drew in a second, steadying breath. She was holding on to the chair so tightly her knuckles were white, but to her credit, she did not lower her gaze. "Mac and I were having lunch that day and after we left the restaurant, I got hit with what felt like the worst menstrual cramps I could ever imagine. I doubled over and nearly passed out."

Just as she had a short while before, Cal thought, as she'd come down the aisle toward him.

Which explained his brother's reaction.

"Mac took me to the emergency room. I made him promise not to tell anyone. I said I would tell you."

"Except," Cal pointed out bitterly, aware he had never been as angry with her as he was at that second, "you never did."

"Because," Ashley explained, her voice rising emotionally, "the time was never right."

"Oh, I think you could have found the time, if you had wanted to."

She grimaced; she'd deserved that. "You're probably right."

"So why didn't you?" Cal's exasperation mounted until he felt as if he were going to explode.

Ashley threw up her hands and began to pace, ripped gown and all. "Because I didn't want you to hurt the way I was hurting, Cal."

Except he had hurt, Cal recalled miserably. More than he ever would have had she only possessed the courage to tell him what he'd had every right to know. Then and now. He studied her silently, then summed it all up in a low, disparaging voice meant to inflict as much hurt in her as she already had in him. "So, instead you just let me think your unhappiness that summer was about losing your fellowship and deciding to take on a less prestigious residency, and about my desire to use your unexpected sabbatical to have a baby, when you—all of a sudden—weren't quite ready?" What a mess. He scoffed at her in contempt as he concluded his recitation of the chain of events that had nearly destroyed their marriage. "And then, just to make sure we were both as absolutely miserable as we could be, you decided to pursue a fellowship after all and headed for Hawaii?"

Now, she was angry. "You told me to go!" she reminded him.

Cal couldn't believe she was defending her actions. He glared at her, not sure if he wanted to kiss her or shake some sense into her. "I was trying to be supportive!" He had wanted her to be happy. And he'd thought—falsely, he now realized—that her being in the fellowship program had been key.

"And I was trying to spare you!"

"All right," Cal said with as much indifference as he could feign. He hated the mixture of self-doubt and regret her actions had engendered in him. "Let's say I buy all that." But he wasn't sure he did. To him, it sounded like feeble excuses. "Why haven't you told me about the baby you lost during all this time?"

"Because things were already strained enough between us without adding that to the list," she whispered softly.

"So in other words, you were never going to tell me," Cal concluded roughly.

Ashley shook her head disparagingly. "I guess I sort of thought that ship had passed. That if I did tell you, and you found out how long I had kept it from you, you wouldn't be able to forgive me."

Cal couldn't deny he was really angry and hurt, anymore than he could deny they still had a wedding to go through this evening, and a whole family still on the other side of the closed double doors, waiting. He turned away from her wearily, "I'll go get the women and see what can be done about your dress."

"Wait a minute." Ashley rushed after him and grabbed his arm. "You're not really planning to continue with the ceremony this evening...are you?"

Cal turned and regarded Ashley stoically, his sense of duty kicking in. "My family is all here," he reminded her with a weariness that came from his soul. "The room is ready. The dinner, the cake..."

She cut him off with an arch look, stomping closer. "And you and I are in the middle of the biggest fight we've ever had in our life!"

"What does that have to do with renewing our wedding vows?" Cal asked.

*What did it have to do with their wedding vows?* Ashley wondered silently, upset. Just damn near everything!

She looked at her husband, the sadness welling up inside her almost more than she could bear.

She had never wanted either of them to feel the way they did right now. She had never wanted to be in a position where she had to worry constantly she would make a misstep or not live up to his considerable expectations, and feel his crushing disappointment in her. She wanted to be free to be who she was, to know she could make mistakes and still be wanted and loved. She wanted to know that forgiveness was always an option, that their love and their marriage and damn it—the family they were now creating—were strong enough to weather any difficulty thrown their way.

But Cal obviously didn't feel the same way. "Look,"

he said, coming toward her, the aggravation he felt still plain on his face. "You know I'm disappointed in you. And—for the record, Ashley," he continued sternly, "I have every right to be. But that doesn't change what has to be done."

Ashley stiffened. She held her head high as she forced herself to admit, "You're correct about that, all right."

"Where are you going?" When she didn't answer and just kept walking, he moved to block her way. "You can't run out on us again."

He was talking as if she had a choice. Tears gathered in her eyes. "I can't stay and spend the rest of my life having you look at me like that, either," Ashley told him sorrowfully. Her voice caught; it took everything she had to force herself to go on. "I'm not going to be the thing you most regret, Cal." She paused, shook her head. "I spent my entire life never living up to the expectations of my parents and feeling bad about myself. I can't be with someone who can't accept anything less than perfection! Because I have news for you, Cal," she whispered softly, looking deep into his eyes. "I am not perfect and never will be—and neither will our child!"

"Ashley," Cal warned, looking all the more betrayed, "if you walk out on me again, it's over."

"Don't you get it, Cal?" Ashley said evenly. She swallowed hard around the gathering knot of emotion in her throat. "It's already over. It has been for years."

# Chapter 16

"So this is it, hmm?" Helen Hart asked Ashley the next morning, shortly after arriving at the farm.

Ashley ushered Helen past the two suitcases, packed and ready to go, in the foyer. Fighting the wave of sadness moving through her, she shrugged her shoulders listlessly, then turned to face her mother-in-law. "It has to be. Cal isn't going to forgive me." Ashley paused, the ache rising in her throat. She blinked back tears. "I guess I knew it all along, which is why I couldn't bring myself to tell him," she confessed in a low, defeated voice.

Helen wrapped a comforting arm around Ashley's shoulders, in that instant giving Ashley all the understanding and compassion Ashley had wanted from Cal. "You were protecting yourself," Helen soothed.

"And Cal." Ashley hugged Helen back, then led the way back to the family room, where they could sit down. "Unfortunately," Ashley reached for a tissue as the tears began to flow, "all I ended up doing was driving him away."

Helen waited for Ashley to wipe her eyes. "Losing a baby is one of the hardest things a woman goes through, I know." Helen caught Ashley's look. "I was pregnant seven times. Six of those times I delivered healthy babies, but once, between Mac's birth and Cal's," Helen's voice caught, "I wasn't as lucky."

Ashley regarded Helen steadily. "Cal never said anything about that to me."

Helen's eyes filled with suppressed sorrow. "He doesn't know, nor do any of his siblings."

And yet, Ashley thought, you're telling me. "Why haven't you told them?" She twisted the damp tissue in her hands.

Helen lifted her palms in a helpless manner. "Because it hurt too much to talk about, even to Cal's father."

"But he knew that you lost a child?" Ashley ascertained quickly.

"Oh, yes." Helen nodded sagely. "He was there when it happened and he took me to the hospital for the care I needed. But I wouldn't discuss what had happened with him after I was released. I knew he was grieving as much as I was, but I was barely hanging on as it was. I just didn't think I could cope with his sadness, too."

Ashley understood that. She hadn't wanted to deal with anyone else's pity for what she had been through, not her Ob/Gyn's at the time, nor Mac's. And especially not Cal's.

"So I pretended everything was fine, when it clearly wasn't—"

Ashley knew what that was like, too.

"—and six months later, I was pregnant again and we were full of hope and nine months after that we were lucky enough to have Cal. And then of course four more children after that."

"And everything worked out all right in the end." Ashley took comfort in knowing Helen had gone on to have a large, healthy brood, despite her miscarriage.

"To a degree," Helen stipulated cautiously. "I still have my fair share of regrets about how much time Cal's father and I wasted. My husband was the love of my life and I was the love of his, but we squandered too much time quarreling over petty things because we thought we had all the time in the world to set things to right. But we didn't. My point is this, Ashley." Helen gave Ashley a long sober look. "None of us can ever know what the future holds for us. All any of us have is the here and now."

Helen was making it sound easy when it wasn't. "Marriage is tough," Ashley said.

"You're right about that," Helen agreed readily enough. "But that should not prevent you from looking at the big picture and thinking about what really matters."

Ashley knew what really mattered to her—Cal and this baby they were going to have. But that didn't mean she wasn't afraid to fail again. She was.

"A lot has happened," Ashley told Helen wearily, aware even as she spoke that she was getting the unconditional love and understanding from Helen that she had always wanted from her own parents. Cal's mother knew that Ashley was flawed, that she made mistakes, but Helen didn't care. Helen loved her and wanted her to remain part of the family, anyway, Ashley realized, her spirits lifting.

"And a lot is going to happen in the future, too," Helen concurred sagely. "Some of which you'll be prepared for, some of which you won't."

Ashley guessed what Helen was going to say. "But it will be easier for us if we're together."

Helen nodded. She reached over and patted Ashley's hand. "It's not too late. There's still time for you and Cal to get your priorities straight and make your marriage as strong as it should've been all along."

Cal was still stretched out on Mac's living-room sofa when Janey, Lily, Emma and Hannah marched in. All four wives were followed by their husbands and Mac. It looked like an intervention, and then some. The only family missing—save his mother, wife and unborn child— were his nephew Christopher, and Lily and Fletcher's yellow Labrador retriever, Spartacus. And he figured the latter two had been barred on grounds they were too young to hear any of what was about to be said.

Cal used his forearm to shield his eyes from the mid-morning sun. "Go. Away."

"We warned you if you didn't get this right we were bringing the Hart women in," Mac said.

Cal muttered a string of swear words not meant for delicate ears. "I don't need your advice. Any of it," Cal said. Furious, he sat up and swung his legs over the edge of the brown leather sofa.

"We beg to differ," Janey stated coolly. She folded her arms in front of her, still looking as if she wanted to wring his neck.

"Where the devil did you get off walking out on Ashley last night?" Fletcher demanded, slapping his cowboy hat against his thigh.

"You should have stayed and married her!" Lily agreed.

"I'm already married to her," Cal snapped.

"From the gist of your behavior toward her, your vows need some refreshing," Dylan scolded.

"If you will recall, that was the original intention," Cal volleyed right back.

Joe shrugged. "The road to hell is paved with good intentions."

Cal glared at the entire group. "Hell is about where I am right now, all right," he muttered, raking his hands through his hair.

Hannah smiled at him sympathetically. "Tell her you're sorry," she advised.

Cal blinked. "Me?"

"Yes, you!" Dylan replied.

Cal aimed a thumb at the center of his chest. "I'm not the one who kept a secret for nearly three years!"

"Right," Janey acknowledged sarcastically. "You're the husband she didn't feel secure enough to confide in."

Cal slouched back on the sofa. "Hit me where it counts, why don't you?"

"She loves you," Lily said.

"Yeah, well, she has a funny way of showing it." Cal thrust his jaw out pugnaciously. "The minute the going gets a little tough, she gets going."

The women exchanged deeply frustrated looks. "She's not leaving town," Emma said finally.

Yeah? That was news to him. "She went home to pack," Cal bit out. "And she said she would be out of the farmhouse completely by later today. What do you call that?"

Loud feminine sighs echoed all around. They were followed by a few choice, muttered words from the Hart men. "Ashley felt you should live at the farmhouse because you put the work into it," Lily explained. "She is planning to move in with us, since Fletcher and I have the house with the most room."

"I wouldn't advise letting that happen," Fletcher said, giving Cal a warning look.

It seemed as if everyone in the family had turned against him, Cal thought. Which was ludicrous, since he wasn't the one at fault here! He stood, bristling with anger. "I've given that woman everything I could possibly give her. I was even willing to support her taking a job away from me again if that's what it took to allow her to fulfill her dream of delivering babies."

Janey interjected gently, "No one is disputing you're the master of the grand, romantic gesture. Telling your wife to take a two-and-a-half-year fellowship three thousand miles away. Locating and giving her the '64 Mustang you two had your very first date in. Making plans to renew your wedding vows on your third anniversary. Those are all wonderful actions, Cal. But relationships aren't made in isolated, dramatic moments—they're built in the small everyday things. Just being there for her, day in and day out, with a heart full of love and unconditional acceptance would have been enough to make her happy."

"Would it?" Cal wasn't sure. Maybe he had never been what Ashley needed.

"Yes, if you had given her what she most wanted," Emma said softly.

Cal sank down on the sofa once again and buried his face in his hands. "And what is that?" he demanded in frustration.

Janey's husband, Thad, explained in simple coach-like fashion, "The permission to be human, to make mistakes."

"To know," Lily added, "no matter what, that you'll be there for her."

"Her soft place to fall," Emma added gently.

Cal scowled and peered up at them through his spread fingers. "This is beginning to sound like an episode of Dr. Phil."

Hannah grinned, all tomboy mischief. "Would you *like* to be on his TV show?" she asked.

Cal swore like a longshoreman, knowing if anyone could arrange it, Hannah, the inveterate dealmaker, could. "No," he said stonily.

Mac stepped forward, the male patriarch of the Hart family once again. "Then we suggest you take a hard look at yourself and do whatever it is you need to do to set things to rights with Ashley," Mac advised.

Cal spent the rest of the morning defending his actions to himself. But by the time he had gone for a run, come back, had breakfast, showered and shaved, he could no longer deny the truth.

And neither, he decided, could Ashley.

So, swallowing his pride, he slapped on some cologne, and headed back out to the farmhouse he had purchased with such high hopes.

And found, to his stunned amazement, that it looked like a convention of Harts, too. Each and every sibling had a car parked in his drive. His mother's car was parked next to Ashley's van.

Grimacing, Cal slammed out of his SUV and stalked up to the porch. Damn it all, wasn't it enough his entire family except his mother had read him the riot act? Did they have to barge in and inflict their views on Ashley, too?

Temper flaring, he let himself inside and found to his stunned amazement that the two large empty rooms at the front of the house had been transformed. White folding chairs were arranged in a semi-circle around a trellis decorated with red roses, perfect for Valentine's Day. On the other side of the foyer a buffet reception was being set up by his four sisters-in-law. They were dressed as they had been the evening before, in their Valentine's Day finery. "About time you got here," Janey drawled.

His mother came through the hall, carrying several bottles of fine champagne and another of sparkling cider. "If you're looking for who I think, she's upstairs," Helen said.

Mac strode through the hall. He glanced at his watch, reporting, "The musicians will be here shortly."

Dylan followed. "Ditto the minister."

Cal thought about commenting, then decided enough time had been wasted, enough mistakes made. It was time to set things right, permanently this time. He took the stairs two at a time and continued on down the hall into the master bedroom. Ashley was seated on the bed, wearing the dress she'd had on the evening before, when she'd fainted. It had been expertly repaired and appeared to give her plenty of breathing room this time. If possible, she looked even more gorgeous than she had the evening before. She was sipping a small glass of orange juice as he walked in. She raised it in silent toast. "Just in case."

"Not planning on fainting on me again this afternoon?" Cal asked.

"I am about to marry someone." She drained her glass and set it aside.

"And that someone better be me," he told her gruffly.

"Is that a proposal?" Her voice suddenly sounded as rusty as his.

He nodded. "If you'll still have me."

"Oh, I'll have you all right." Ashley drew him down to sit beside her on the bed.

They sat there quietly, hands linked as surely as their hearts.

"I'm so sorry," they said abruptly in unison.

More silence. And a few tears this time, too.

"I should have told you," Ashley whispered.

Cal tightened his grip on her hand, knowing he never wanted to let her go. "I should have understood why you didn't," he countered thickly.

More tears, his and hers. "I was scared I'd lose you," Ashley confided. Turning, she went all the way into his arms.

Cal lifted her over onto his lap and wrapped his arms around her. "Believe me, I know a little bit about that."

Ashley rested her head on his shoulder, her low voice muffled against his jacket as she clung to him tightly. "I don't want to lose you, Cal."

He tucked a hand beneath her chin and lifted her face to his. "I don't want to lose you, either."

Ashley smiled and kissed his lips. "Then what do you say we go downstairs and make it official..." she whispered tenderly "...the second time around?"

"To love and to cherish...in joy and in sorrow...from this day forward..."

"And now that Ashley and Cal have reconfirmed their original wedding vows, Ashley and Cal have something to promise each other," the minister said.

Ashley took Cal's hand in hers. "I, Ashley, promise to tell you everything, the good, the bad, the exciting and the mundane. I pledge to have faith in you and faith in us. The only steadfast rule being that we love and understand each other more with each and every day."

Knowing those vows would be easy to keep now that they finally knew what was important in this life, Cal lifted their clasped hands and kissed the back of Ashley's wrist. He looked deep into her eyes and spoke with all the love in his heart. "I, Cal, commit myself to you and to this marriage with all my heart and soul. I promise always to remember that it's not whether we make mistakes, but *when* we make them, that we forgive each other, learn and grow from them, that is important…because loving each other and standing by each other in good times and tough times…is what marriage is all about."

The minister beamed. "Cal and Ashley. Having affirmed your love for the second time, I now pronounce you husband and wife. Cal, you may kiss your bride."

And Cal obliged.

\* \* \* \* \*